THR3E

by

CONRAD JONES

The DI Braddick Series
Brick
Shadows
Guilty
Deliver us from Evil

Detective Alec Ramsay Series
The Child Taker
Criminally Insane
Slow Burn
Frozen Betrayal
Desolate Sands
Concrete Evidence
Thr3e

Soft Target Series
Soft Target
Soft Target II 'Tank'
Soft Target III 'Jerusalem'
The Rage Within
Blister
Unleashed

The Anglesey Murders
Unholy Island
A Visit from the Devil
Nearly Dead
A Child for the Devil
Dark Angel

Copyright © 2019 rewrite Conrad Jones
All rights reserved.
ISBN:
ISBN-13:

CHAPTER 1

It was without doubt the biggest bonfire that Toni had ever seen but her excitement turned to fear when the flames reached the Guy Fawkes, engulfed its legs, and the dummy began to scream. She remembered being transfixed as the flames devoured the thrashing effigy, silencing the mesmerised crowd. Its arms flailed wildly, the rubber mask blackened and blistered as the screams reached a stomach churning crescendo. Suddenly there was nothing but the sound of the fire, wood spitting and cracking and the roar of the flames. The inferno engulfed the figure until its shape was no longer distinguishable as human. Red hot embers floated skyward like a swarm of orange fireflies and tendrils of smoke crept among the crowd, searching for their eyes, making them sting and water. The sickly-sweet smell of burning human flesh drifted with it. Long seconds ticked by and then the crowd reacted as one and all hell broke loose.

Toni's mother dragged her backwards, away from the bonfire but she couldn't look away. She watched the organisers frantically trying to extinguish the flames, but it was an impossible task. The fire had a grip, and nothing could halt its progress. One man ran as close as he could and launched the contents of a fire bucket towards the raging conflagration, but the heat was so intense that none of the sand reached the base of the fire. Although she was terrified, it confused her. The bonfire had been nearly five metres high. Tons of wood was ablaze, white hot at the base. How on earth did the man think he was going to extinguish the inferno with a bucket of sand? The man was shouting for help as he ran back with his empty bucket, desperate for someone to help but no one else neared the bonfire, the heat too intense. He repeatedly turned in a circle as if doing some manic rain-dance, his mouth open and pleading but nobody could help.

Three uniformed police officers had dragged the man away to a safe distance as they summoned backup on their radios. Eventually the fleeing crowd had closed in and blocked her view and she had held on tightly to her mother's hand as they made their way across the wet grass towards where she had parked the car. Mud squelched beneath her pink wellington boots. People were pushing and shoving to escape the scene giving no thought to the safety of others around them. She saw several people bowled over and trampled; the air turned blue with expletives as the worst side of human nature came to the fore. It was every man for themselves and screw everyone else. Panic begot panic and chaos reigned. Children were crying, confused, and frightened. Mothers shrieked as their infants were separated from them and fathers turned on each other aggressively trying to protect their offspring. The wet grass was like an ice-rink and obstacles lurked invisible in the darkness. Some around her fell and staggered to their feet quickly while others stumbled and failed to rise, swallowed by the tide of frightened spectators.

Toni was mesmerised as the crowd flowed away from the horror. As they ran, it dissipated, and the sounds became clearer and less confused. She overheard one parent telling his children that it had been a joke and the firework display had been cancelled because of the rain. Another explained that it was probably a tramp who, had crawled into the unlit bonfire to sleep. Toni didn't believe either. Voices were raised and angry, cursing and swearing as the frightened crowd ran to their vehicles. She lost her footing a few times, but her mother held her firm, pulling her up to her feet. The crowd thinned as they reached the perimeter of the park and a cold wind cut through her clothes. As they'd approached the Ford, the heavens opened, and they were drenched before they eventually climbed in. Toni could still remember how the sirens had screamed towards them; their blue flashing lights blurred by the deluge on the windscreen. She had felt cold and wet and more than a little frightened by the incident. Her mother fastened her into her seat, and she had talked to her all the way home, her voice comforting but she fielded any questions about what they'd witnessed. The heater had soon warmed the vehicle and her eyes became heavy.

When they arrived home, her mother made her a hot milky drink and tucked her in bed. She read Rapunzel to her twice in an attempt to take her mind off what they'd seen but her sleep had been troubled by nightmares. She had dreamed that a burning figure reached out to her, begging for her to help, calling her name over and over but she couldn't move her limbs to help. The figure's skin blistered and peeled and then melted like candle wax dripping from the skull in rivulets of wax and blood. Her visions were terrifying, and she woke with a cry several times covered in cold sweat. Her mother had soothed her with a damp flannel and held her hand until sleep eventually embraced her, but she found no peace there. She had tossed and turned in a fitful slumber that was filled with ghouls and burning figures that thrashed and danced through her tortured dreams.

It was two days later that they found out that the man, who had burnt alive, was her father. Her life disintegrated around her as her mother went through a breakdown and her aunt was drafted in to help out domestically. Her aunt was the only person who called her Antonia, which she hated. A month to the day that her father died, her mother left home for work and never came back. Toni had felt abandoned. She couldn't describe the hopelessness that she felt inside. One moment her parents were there and the next, they were gone. She truly understood the meaning of being alone and those feelings of desolation and emptiness had been her constant companions ever since.

CHAPTER 2

Twenty Years Later

Antonia Barrat had a bad feeling about the night ahead. Her source had told her to be at the derelict tobacco mill on Jamaica Street at least an hour before midnight. Once part of Victorian Liverpool's thriving port, the area had become a rat-run for crack houses and prostitution. She shivered as she looked up at the tall building silhouetted against the yellowish light pollution from the city beyond. An L-shaped pulley jib protruded from the top storey, five floors above. It was once used to lower bales of tobacco onto horse drawn carts but in the darkness of the night it looked like a hangman's gallows. All the doors and windows at the front had been shuttered with perforated sheets of steel but her informer had identified an entrance, which could be opened with a strong tug. Finding the door had been a mission in itself. Tall weeds and brambles covered the rubble strewn ground making progress slow, painful, and noisy. Thistles pierced her jeans and scratched her legs and nettles prickled her hands. They dared not use torches on approach and she had scratched her shin and twisted her ankle before they'd reached the entrance. The metal hoarding screeched loudly as they pulled it open enough for them to climb through. The noise seemed to echo from the ancient walls for minutes rather than seconds. They had hoped for a silent entry, but it was far from that. Her heart was thumping against her ribs and she felt light-headed and weak at the knees at the thought of entering the decaying structure.

As she climbed into the towering warehouse, her resolve became significantly weaker than it had been during the planning stage. Inside, the building was a maze of cluttered corridors and rotten staircases. Tendrils of rope dangled from the floors above like the tentacles of some giant hidden sea-monster. Thick curtains of spiders' webs hung across the doorframes and passageways, daring any intruders to delve deeper into the building. The ground floor had a thousand hiding places and they scurried about looking for the perfect one. They walked through the main chamber and approached a wide arched doorway. A huge granite keystone supported the arch. Through the arch was a set of stone steps, which led down to the cellar space. Toni shone the torch around as she descended slowly. She had taken only a few of the steps down before she caught the reflection of the light shimmering on the mossy walls. The steps disappeared into deep dark water. The cellar area appeared to be completely flooded. Their torches illuminated a cavernous water filled void with a vaulted ceiling, which seemed to reach on forever. Milky coloured stalactites were growing from the joints between the huge stone blocks that formed the ceiling. The water appeared as black as oil and in her mind's eye, bottomless. The lights sent rats the size of cats scurrying along ledges for safety. Thick dust covered the steps at their edges, undisturbed for decades but the centre steps were marked with multiple sets of boot prints. Someone had been down the steps recently. She ducked to get a better view, but she couldn't see where the cellar ended and there was no sign of human life down there. They looked at each other, silently discounted the cellar, and climbed back into the warehouse.

As they searched, it became clear that the stairs to the upper floors were not usable. The steps were cracked and broken and too many were missing completely. There were gaping holes too wide to bridge. Toni was sure that there was no access to the upper floors and there were no exits or windows at the rear of the building. In short, it was a death trap.

'I don't like this, Mike,' Toni whispered. They hadn't known each other for long but she was thankful that he had agreed to come along.

'Good, I'm glad it's not just me,' her companion muttered. His London accent grated on her. 'I was beginning to think I was losing my nerve.' He smiled weakly. 'We knew this would be dangerous, Toni.'

'I think we've bitten off more than we can chew,' she whispered. Her bottom lip trembled as she spoke. 'I prefer to be much further away and let the camera do the work. If this goes wrong, we've got no exit.'

'Why do you think they picked this place for a meeting?' Mike ran a gloved hand through his short dark hair. Age had streaked it grey above the ears. He had told her that he was forty, but she thought that he was ten years older, at least. 'I think they've used this place before.' He waved his torch at a collapsed staircase to their right. 'There's one way in and one way out.' He pointed to where they'd entered. 'If their men don't walk out of that door alive, they'll grab anyone that leaves before they even get onto the pavement.' He paused. 'And then God knows what they would do.'

'That's reassuring,' Toni whispered sarcastically. 'We could leave now and hope we hear about a meeting somewhere else,' she said with uncertainty. Her voice trembled with fear. She had been torn between taking what she knew to the police and investigating further herself. Now she wished that she had chosen the first option.

'It's too late. We could be seen leaving. If they think we're nosing around their business, we'd end up in a deep hole in the forest.' Mike warned. 'It's definitely too late for that,' he grinned coldly in the darkness. The torchlight cast deep shadows beneath his eyes. 'They don't know we're here, so we have an advantage. We've checked around the building and we know we're the first here. We can duck behind there, sit tight and sweat it out,' he added, pointing to a rotten staircase. 'You've been waiting for this break for weeks, years even.'

'I really need a wee,' she grimaced. She didn't know him very well; in fact she didn't know his second name but he was right. She had come too far to stop now. They both had their own reasons for being there. She crossed her Hunter wellington boots and squeezed her thighs together. The material of her black denim jeans rustled in the silence. The urge to pee waned slightly.

'Shush!' The sound of metal grating against metal sliced through the darkness. They turned off their torches and froze to the spot. Toni could feel her blood pumping through her ears, her senses ultra-aware. The inky blackness seemed to press in, suffocating her. She held her breath and listened intently. The old building creaked and groaned with every gust of wind that buffeted it. Each sound threatened danger approaching from all directions. The blackness that surrounded her seemed to have darker patches within. Deeper shadows neared and then drifted away as her eyes adjusted and her mind played tricks.

Drip, drip, drip, she heard from the flooded cellar behind them, a dull thud from the floor above and the creaking of rope swinging in the breeze came from behind them. Every sound seemed deafening in the darkness. She pulled the hood of her black parka over her long dark hair to hide her face. A heavy door slammed closed and footsteps echoed off the crumbling brick walls. They looked at each other and crouched behind the broken steps of a rotten staircase, which gifted them a hiding place and a clear view of parts of the warehouse, broken in places by the huge cast iron columns that supported the upper floors. Toni squeezed her eyes closed and held her breath. She was so frightened that she thought she might wet herself.

CHAPTER 3

The Past

Toni was eight years old when her father was murdered; a mere child. She could remember the debilitating pain of his loss as if it was yesterday. There were times when she cried so hard that she couldn't breathe, when salty tears mingled with saliva and dribbled from her chin. She could remember her eyes stinging and the dreadful fear that the grief would never subside, that the ache would never leave. The hollow sense of loss was crippling and there didn't seem to be an end to it. It was a black cloud surrounding her, all-encompassing, crushing her spirit, and sucking the energy from her. She could barely function.

Her father had treated her like a princess. 'Daddy's princess,' he used to say into her ear whenever he picked her up and spun her around until she felt dizzy. His bristles would prickle her face and tickle her neck and she would laugh until she thought she would wee. She idolised him. He was her hero and when her mother had sat down and explained that he wasn't coming home again, she cried so much that she couldn't catch her breath. The pain was suffocating.

He used to go away for weeks at a time, but she always knew that he would come back with an armful of presents and a huge smile on his face. She had gone with him a few times, mostly on his shorter runs, sitting high up in the lorry cab with her feet up on the dashboard eating all the things that her mother said were bad for her. Once, he took her abroad on a long run. She could remember seeing fields and forests covered in deep snow, like the pictures on Christmas cards, as if it was yesterday. They ate with her father's workmates and one of them gave her a cuddly stuffed reindeer called Rudolph. She kept Rudolph all through her life; he still had a place on the chair in her bedroom. Her father worked hard, and she missed him terribly when he was away. The days that he had to leave for work were horrible and she pined for him from the moment that he left, until the second he walked back through the door. This time he wasn't coming back, and she felt like her heart would explode into a million pieces. Of course, her mother didn't tell her that they'd witnessed his death, that would be too cruel for a child to take but over the following weeks, she heard snippets of whispered conversations. Little by little the picture formed. The adults tried to hide it from her but the more she listened the more she learned.

'A terrible accident?'

'Could he have been drunk and staggered into the park by mistake?'

'Can you think of anyone who may have had a grudge against your husband, Mrs Barrat?'

'Did he owe anybody any money?'

'How long had he been driving onto the continent?'

'How many times had he driven abroad?'

'How much is the mortgage payment on your house?'

'Do you own your cars or are they on HP?'

'Your television and furniture look to be very expensive, Mrs Barrat…'

'We think your husband was murdered, Mrs Barrat…'

Toni hadn't understood at first. Why would the detectives ask such horrible questions and say such evil things? Everyone that knew her father loved him. He was a nice man, a good man, a good father, and a good husband. The questions went on for weeks and their small family rallied around to support them, for a while anyway. When the police began questioning the wider family, most of them drifted away. Toni began to see suspicion in their eyes and hear doubt in their voices. The police came and went as if they lived there, stroking her hair and patting her on the head like she was a needy pet. At the time, she thought that her mother wanted them there to protect them, to make them feel safe but looking back, she wasn't so sure.

Friends and family called day and night to ask her mother about her father's death; each visit was like scratching the scab from a wound and prompted a new wave of tears and sobbing. Each time she recounted the story it brought a new flood, more wailing, more anguish, more whispering, and a little more information. Toni listened to both their facts and their speculation and she learned a little more every day. Her mother tried her best to be strong around her, but she was shattered by the loss. She was a rock through the daylight hours but at night when all the doors were closed and everyone had gone home, her agony bubbled to the surface and her desperate sobbing was excruciating to listen to. Hearing her mother's anguish through the bedroom wall was almost as unbearable as losing her father. Toni remembered her eyes, usually so brown and happy, were red and swollen with a distant look in them. She lay awake night after night and listened to her sobbing in the dark hours feeling helpless, unable to take the pain away. She would creep into her mother's bed and snuggle next to her, her cheek resting on a tear-soaked pillow. The scent of her father's aftershave still lingered on the cotton. Their suffering shared lessened the pain a little and they had each other, for a short while at least.

CHAPTER 4

The Warehouse – 00:05

Toni held her breath as three figures appeared from her left. Her heart sank when she saw their masks. They scanned the dark corners of the warehouse with powerful torches. Her heart threatened to burst from her chest as the beams flickered towards their hiding place. It was impossible to see their faces, but she could hear them muttering in a guttural language. She listened intently to catch a word that would help her identify their ethnicity. None of them were local. Her blood ran cold and her throat felt so dry that she could barely swallow. The information that she had been given was vague but related to local criminals. She was not expecting foreigners in balaclavas. This looked like big trouble with a huge capital 'T'. Toni was confused, angry, and frightened. Her source had sent her into something that she had not been expecting. This looked shady at least and downright dangerous at best and she wanted nothing to do with it. She could hardly stand up and ask if she could leave; whatever was about to happen, would happen regardless. Mike nudged her with his elbow. It took all her effort to tear her eyes from the men and look down at what he was pointing to. He pushed a notebook into her hand, and she strained to read the word on the small page. 'Russian?' She nodded in the darkness. Maybe. Her source had been way off the mark.

She heard them moving towards the cellar entrance to her right. One of them walked down the half a dozen wide stone steps to the water. His heavy boots clomped; each footstep echoed through the building. She heard splashing noises. Then she heard something else. A dull humming sound, distant and rhythmical drifted to her. As it grew louder, she realised that it was the low purr of an engine. She frowned in the gloom as she imagined it to be an outboard motor. What had they missed? The cellar was flooded, yes but a boat? Her view of the men was blocked by a thick support column. She craned her neck, desperate to get a better look. Mike gripped her elbow. She could hardly see his face, but she sensed the warning. 'Keep still'. The engine was coming closer, quiet but steady. The sound of water lapping at the walls below them grew louder. Something was happening below them, but she couldn't see a thing. The urge to stand up and get a better view was overwhelming. She had to see. The engine chugged for a moment longer and then the noise died to nearly a stop. The sound of something thudding reached them. Rubber against stone?

'How many got through?' A gruff voice drifted to them. The accent confirmed Mike's note. She was convinced that they were Russians.

'Only twelve,' an English voice replied. He was from the south, maybe London, maybe closer to the coast. She couldn't decide for sure. 'We lost three on the way. The balloons burst inside them.'

'Ivor won't be happy,' the first voice growled. 'He's expecting fifteen.'

'I've got the surgeon removing any recoverable parcels, but it'll take a few days.' The southerner ignored his moaning. 'This isn't a SAGA cruise, you know, shit happens. It is what it is.'

'And the zombie?'

'All three kilos as agreed, in the case.'

'He wants to be sure it will make ten kilos when it's cut,' the voice asked.

'Tell him that the manufacturer said that it's tried and tested. Three kilos of this stuff cuts up to ten or fifteen if you want it to. Once it's compressed into tablets, you'll sell them for thirty quid each all day long. This stuff is rocket fuel; there's a reason why they call it zombie. Ivor knows the score.'

'You had better hope that he does.'

'You let me worry about Ivor,' the Londoner replied chirpily. 'It's swings and roundabouts. We'll make up the amount we lost in the three girls on the next delivery. Now stop fucking around and get them out of my rib. I need to catch the next tide.'

Rib? she thought. Toni envisaged an inflatable dinghy with a rigid bottom, the boat of choice for drug smugglers and people traffickers. She had heard them called Zodiacs. Splashing and shuffling noises drifted up from below.

'Get out!' A sharp slap was followed by a whimper and the sound of women sobbing. She couldn't believe what she was listening to; drugs that she had never heard of being handed over by the kilo and women being traded like animals. This was way out of her league. She could feel cold perspiration covering her skin, the sweat of the terrified. The sound of multiple pairs of feet splashing in the water echoed through the mill as the women climbed the stone steps. She could hear hushed voices growling orders, each word coated in venom.

She felt Mike nudge her arm gently. He held her digital camera in his hand. She had used it before to record undercover observations. It had an infra-red mode, which allowed her to film in the dark. Toni shook her head. It was a great piece of kit, but it couldn't film through iron and stone. He put his finger against his lips and then pointed to the column. She grabbed at his sleeve to stop him, but he was gone, moving like a cat in the darkness. Toni felt her hands beginning to shake with fear.

She wanted to shout after him. 'Don't risk it!' echoed around her mind. 'You bloody fool!'

Her stomach was tied in knots and she closed her eyes to calm her nerves. When she opened them, Mike was out of sight too.

'Move them to the van quickly,' a voice called.

Toni heard the boat's engine purring again. There was a splash and then the engine grew louder before fading away. The men came back into the main body of the warehouse. This time, they herded twelve smaller shapes between them. They were all dark skinned, some much darker than the others. She could make out afro hair, hunched shoulders, bruised arms and legs, some with jeans and trainers others with bare bloody feet. They moved as one huddled together without a sound, lambs to the slaughter; any protest or fight already beaten out of them. Toni could smell their despair. She wasn't sure what she thought was going to happen at the mill, but she hadn't expected an exchange as significant as this. It was way beyond what she had wanted to witness. Had she suspected that this was going to happen, she would have gone to the police immediately, but that option was no longer on the table.

The men bundled the women past her hiding place towards the entrance in silence. She still couldn't see the men's faces, bar the odd flash of skin. White, Mediterranean, Black? She had no idea but what the hell did she expect? They were breaking so many laws that she couldn't count them, so they were hardly likely to show themselves.

The sound of the metal hoarding being pulled open bounced off the crumbling walls and she held her breath and waited for it to slam closed to signal their departure. She felt a gust of wind from the river blowing through the open door and then the sound of wood splitting snapped through the building. The loud crack was deafening in the darkness. It was followed by a muffled cry and a dull thump as something heavy hit the dusty floor.

'What was that?' One of the men hissed.

'There's someone else in here!'

'Get them in the van,' an angry voice snapped. 'You come with me!'

She heard heavy boots running towards her. Torchlight reflected from the walls, searching and scanning the nooks and crannies. She could hear them breathing and smell their sweat as they ran by. They reached the cellar entrance and paused. A low moan came out of the darkness to her right. Was it Mike? Her breath caught in her lungs. She was frozen with terror. A beam of light flickered between the wooden steps above her. She ducked and squeezed her eyes closed, her hands covered her face and she curled up, her knees against her chest. The sound of their breathing was close, and she waited for the touch of rough hands to grab at her. She heard the moan again.

'There!'

She heard the men running away from her, but she still couldn't look. Her body wouldn't listen to her brain. She was unable to move an inch.

'Who are you?' A voice growled. She heard a slap and then a cry of pain.

'I'm no one,' Mike's voice crackled. 'I was sleeping in here.'

She heard shuffling and the sound of a body being dragged.

'Search him.' More shuffling. A groan of pain.

'I've broken my leg,' Mike pleaded. 'I was sleeping up there and fell, please. I'm just a homeless drunk. I didn't see you,' he babbled. 'I didn't see anything.'

'Really?' The voice sounded sarcastic. 'You sleep with a digital camera stuffed in your boots?' Toni listened and slowly uncurled. She peered from her filthy hiding place and watched as one of the men flicked through the last few images that the camera had captured. The light illuminated his eyes and lips. He was white. Toni could see his mouth twist to a sneer. 'This fucker was filming us!'

'Are you police?' A powerful kick to his face followed the question.

'No,' Mike gurgled through broken teeth. He spat blood onto the floor. 'I'm no one. I was just here. Take the camera.'

'If he was police, he wouldn't be alone and we'd be in handcuffs by now,' the foreign man said shaking his head. 'Grab him. He's coming with us. Ivor can decide what happens to him.'

'Please!' Mike groaned. Toni felt tears welling in her eyes as the man pressed a Taser to the back of his neck. She heard the electricity crackle and saw the blinding blue light as fifty thousand volts silenced Mike's protests. Her vision blurred as she watched them drag him away. The metal door screeched once more. She was so frightened that she waited forty minutes before she thought about moving. The urge to pee was excruciating and she squatted and sobbed as the smell of her own urine drifted to her. When she was done, she tiptoed from the warehouse and then sprinted the half a mile to her car with tears running down her face. She was breathless as she opened the boot, took out her handbag, and grabbed her mobile. Toni dialled 999 but she had no idea what she was going to tell them when they answered.

CHAPTER 5

Toni was cold, tired, and afraid. The waiting room at the police station was basic and smelled of stale sweat, mingled with disinfectant. Six hours had ticked by slowly since she made the 999 call and she had recounted her story to many different faces thus far and made a formal statement. The Drug Squad, River Police, and detectives from other syndicates had all spoken to her since then. Uniformed officers had responded to her call first but when they realised the urgency of the situation, they were quickly backed up by detectives and an Armed Response Unit. She was unclear at first if they believed her or not, but eventually they'd taken her word for it and searched the mill. She felt panicked at first, desperate to help Mike but as the hours ticked by, numbness had crept in. The police were talking at her, not to her.

They had been kind and sympathetic at first but once they'd established her identity, their attitude towards her changed dramatically. The detective constable, who was dealing with her couldn't get out of the room quick enough, mumbling something about 'making her DI's week'. On the way out, she had slammed the door closed behind her and over an hour had gone by since. They had taken her mobile 'for her own safety' and she began to wonder if she was going to be placed under arrest, although she couldn't imagine what the charges would be if they did. Despite her innocence, Toni felt terribly guilty. She tensed when she heard the door handle rattling.

'I'm sorry for the delay, Miss Barrat,' an attractive female with short dark hair and elfin features said, as she breezed into the room. Her grey suit and open necked white blouse gave her a look of professionalism. A man the size of a house followed her though the door. His close-cropped greying hair and leather jacket gave him the appearance of a bouncer. 'I'm Detective Inspector Annie Jones and this is Detective Sergeant Jim Stirling.' He nodded silently in greeting as he closed the door. There was no warmth in his expression. His eyes looked her up and down discreetly before he looked away. She could feel him scrutinising her. 'We're from the city's Major Investigation Team.'

'At last.' Toni sighed with relief. They had sent the big guns to see her. At least she knew that they were taking her seriously. Toni appreciated the cut of the DI's suit as she sat down opposite her although her shoes looked to be on the cheap side. 'Have you found Mike?'

'Not yet. I need you to explain what happened last night.' The detective frowned and shook her head as she spoke. 'We're a little bemused by what exactly went on.'

'For God's sake!' Toni sighed. She rolled her eyes and stared at the ceiling, her jaw hanging open. Tiredness was fraying her temper. 'I've made a formal statement,' she said with a deep intake of breath. She looked at her watch impatiently and tutted. 'I've been over this a hundred times.' She looked from one detective to the other with her eyes wide open in question. 'Don't you speak to each other?'

The detectives were unruffled as they exchanged glances. 'Yes. We've spoken to all the officers that you have but I'm still unclear because you're not telling us everything.'

'I have told you everything in my statement.'

'I've read it several times, but we need to hear it from you, Miss Barrat,' the DI said curtly. She smoothed her skirt with her palms. Toni noticed something strange about her eyes. 'I know it's frustrating for you and a little annoying, but I need you to work with us here.'

'I'm sorry. I'm just so worried about Mike,' Toni said with a sigh. 'It's been a long night and I'm tired. Have you found them? Is there any sign of Mike?'

'All we found at the mill were footprints,' the DI shrugged, 'which goes someway to corroborating your story. It must have been traumatic for you.'

'Yes, it was,' Toni said. She relaxed a little. The detective had calmness in her voice, which put her at ease. 'It was frightening to say the least. I should have done something to stop them.' Toni bit her lip to stop herself from crying. 'I was so bloody terrified that I just froze to the spot. I should have done something.'

'If you had,' Stirling leaned in as he spoke, his voice gruff but reassuring, 'You wouldn't be here now and we wouldn't know that two people were missing until it was too late. There was nothing that you could have done.'

'It all happened so quickly. The whole thing feels like a bad dream.'

'I'm sure it does.' Annie sympathised. 'What I don't understand is why you were there?'

There was a change in the detective's tone. Toni hesitated before she answered. 'I had a tip from one of my sources. We were there to observe what was happening.'

'You had a tip?'

'Yes.'

'About what exactly and who gave you this information?'

'I can't tell you that,' Toni said in a shaky voice. 'But it wasn't what I expected. If I had known what was going to happen then I would have come straight to you.'

'What did you think was going to happen in an abandoned mill after midnight?' Annie asked calmly. She looked at Toni and waited patiently for an answer, but none came. Toni shrugged and shuffled uncomfortably in her chair. 'I'm not trying to give you a hard time but I'm curious why two seemingly intelligent journalists would put themselves in a situation like that?'

'Obviously, we didn't expect it to be so dangerous,' Toni said meekly. Guilt flooded through her mind. She was finding it hard not to break down. The muscles in her thighs were twitching with nervous energy. 'There's always an element of danger in what we do. We know that it's part of the job.'

'Oh, come on be honest,' the DI sighed. 'I don't think that your friend realised how dangerous the situation was, do you?' Toni didn't answer. She couldn't think of anything to say. 'Didn't it cross your mind that your lives were in danger?'

'Of course not,' Toni said deflated. 'I never would have gone there if I had thought for one minute that that would happen.'

'So, your informer gave you specific information that something was going down, but it was non-life threatening?' Annie asked sarcastically. 'Without knowing the whole story there isn't much to work with. Did you think that the story was so good that it outweighed the risk?'

'Of course not.'

'Why go there then?'

'I told you'—Toni sighed—'I had a tip and we acted on it. If I'd thought we could be in danger, then I wouldn't have gone. We were working on a story, that's all.'

'Why all the secrecy when we're trying to work out who could have taken your colleague?' Annie shrugged. 'We know what you write about. You need to give us something to work with here. Was it related to anything that you've covered before?'

'I keep repeating myself. I had a tip that something was going to happen at the mill.' Toni looked away as she spoke. She felt the big detective staring at her, scrutinising everything she said, and analysing her body language. 'I didn't know exactly what was going to happen. That's the truth.' Toni felt caged. Her guilt was painful and being pressurised by the police wasn't helping. The woman inside wanted to tell them everything but the professional inside knew that she couldn't.

'I can't see a journalist of your reputation sneaking around in the dead of night because an informer thinks that something might happen?'

'That's the way it happened. I got a call. We went to the mill and it all went tits up.'

'But who did you think you were going to be observing?'

'I had no idea.'

'You must have thought that there was an element of safety there, like a policeman for instance?' Stirling asked. There was an edge in his voice. Toni felt her stomach knotting. She wanted to curl up and cry. They weren't actually saying that she was responsible for Mike's abduction, but the intent was obvious.

'Did you go there looking for another story about bent coppers?' Annie Jones smiled thinly. 'Not that it matters to us,' Annie said nudging Stirling with her elbow. He shook his head in agreement. 'We just need to know.'

'I knew that would come up!' Toni rolled her eyes. 'It had nothing to do with that.'

'I think you thought it would be a nice safe payoff,' Stirling said. 'Take a few pictures of some money changing hands and you've got another front-page expose about police corruption, but you stumbled into something much worse?'

'I know what you lot think of me, but it has nothing to do with this,' Toni said defensively. She looked the DI in the eyes. 'I do my job just like you do. I expose the truth, nothing more and nothing less.'

'Debatable,' Stirling grunted. Toni looked at him and figured that at least two cattle had donated their hides to make his jacket. 'Most of the accusations in your book were proved to be questionable at best and downright untrue in most cases.'

'I don't know where you get that from, Sergeant. When was anything disproved?' Toni frowned and blushed with anger. She could see the distaste in his eyes. 'That's news to me that anything was disproved.'

'I don't care about your book, Miss Barrat, and neither does Sergeant Stirling.' Annie glared at him. 'Does he, Sergeant?'

Stirling made to say something but changed his mind. He shook his head and smiled coldly. 'It has no bearing on this investigation, guv.'

'Good. Can we get back to my question?' The DI shot Stirling a warning glance. 'Your profession doesn't concern me at this stage but the reason that you went to that mill will give us a starting point.' She paused. 'Let's start again, shall we?' Annie half smiled. 'What were you doing at that mill?'

'I was following up on a lead. I didn't expect things to go so far and I certainly didn't ask for what happened.'

'We're not sure exactly what did happen. That's why we're here to try and work it out.'

Toni held her palms towards the ceiling and blew air from her cheeks. 'Where do I begin?'

'At the point where you received information that a crime was going to take place at that mill would be good,' Annie said calmly.

Toni shook her head. 'Let's not go there, shall we?' she said thin lipped. 'My sources are confidential and that's that.' She looked both detectives in the eye trying her best to be assertive.

Annie sat back in her chair. She couldn't see any point in pursuing further for now. Antonia Barrat wasn't going to crack. 'Okay, just run me through what happened.'

Toni relaxed inwardly as the focus shifted. 'We were observing events at the mill when three men walked into the warehouse. They went to the cellar, which is flooded. I heard an engine and a brief exchange of words, which involved them talking about three kilos of 'zombie' and that they had twelve women.' She paused to correct herself. 'The Londoner said that they had lost three because the balloons had burst. I presumed he meant that they were drug mules and three women had died.' She looked at the DI for a response before carrying on. 'Then a group of women were herded out of the door. They were all black. It was horrific.' Her voice broke for a second and she took a deep breath to compose herself. 'All I could think about was the news coverage from Italy and Greece, all those poor Syrians drowning in the Med, desperate to get to Europe.' She wiped a tear away. 'And the shambles at Calais, it breaks my heart. They are so desperate to get here aren't they?' The detectives nodded in agreement. 'They would swallow anything to get passage here, wouldn't they?' Toni took a deep breath before carrying on. 'Mike tried to find a better vantage point. I tried to stop him but I daren't make a sound. They were only yards away.' Her voice cracked with emotion again. 'He was gone in a second. I think he tried to hide on some stairs, but they gave way and he fell.'

'You heard him fall?'

'Yes,' Toni flinched visibly as she recalled the memory. 'I heard wood splintering, then a thud. The next thing they were stood over him. They found his camera, used a Taser on him and then dragged him out.'

'You can't describe the men?'

'It was too dark.' Toni frowned. 'I heard them. One of them sounded Russian. The man in the rib was a Londoner.'

'And the girls?'

'They didn't speak, all black.'

'What is Mike's full name?' Annie said reading part of her statement.

'I don't know for sure,' Toni said embarrassed.

'Don't know or won't say?'

'I genuinely don't know,' Toni stressed. 'Don't you think that I would tell you?'

'I'm not sure that you would.' The DI raised her eyebrows in surprise. 'So, you went to witness a crime taking place in a derelict mill in a particularly rundown area of the city with a man called 'Mike', but you don't know his second name or what you were going to witness?'

'I don't know his real second name. He uses Mike James when he's introduced but I did a little digging and it's an alias. He's an investigative reporter,' Toni tried to explain. 'He posts his articles online as 'Mikroscope'. He has a volume of credible work. Sometimes we need to keep our identity secret and I had to respect that.'

'You must have researched him in detail,' Stirling said, his eyebrows raised.

'Of course, that's how I knew James was a false identity,' Toni said impatiently. 'I ran checks on several of his articles. The IP addresses were all over the place, Paris, Riga, Istanbul, Marrakesh. He writes some provocative stuff, never worried about naming names. He had covered his track well. He was a ghost.'

'Okay, maybe we can look into that in a bit more detail' —Stirling shrugged— 'How did he get there?'

'By car I presume.'

'Where is his car?' He tilted his head as he spoke. 'We can trace who he is through his vehicle.'

'I don't know where he parked.'

'You arranged to travel independently and meet at the mill?'

Toni nodded her head. 'We do that unless both journalists are from the same stable. It makes it difficult to follow us that way.'

'I really wouldn't be so sure of that,' Annie said.

'Why not?'

'Because the first rule of surveillance is not to be seen doing it.'

Toni blushed again. She was under no illusions as to how naive she sounded. 'We arranged to travel separately and meet at the mill.' She felt the need to defend their actions. 'We have done this type of surveillance before, Sergeant,' she protested.

'I think you have relied more on luck than judgement so far.'

Toni ignored the dig and continued. 'We agreed to use my camera and to leave our mobile phones in our vehicles so that they couldn't scan them,' she added proudly.

'Scan them?' Annie said to Stirling. He nodded as if he was impressed.

'Yes,' Toni regained some composure. 'They can scan buildings for electronic devices you know?'

'They can?'

'Yes,' Toni quipped. 'And you know that they can. Trying to belittle me isn't going to help to find Mike.'

'Yes, we do know that.' Stirling paused to think. 'Do you have his mobile number?'

'Yes, but I'm sure it's a burner phone,' Toni bit her bottom lip nervously. 'I have an email address too.'

'We'll need them both,' the DI said. She leaned forward and touched Toni's wrist. 'Your friend Mike is missing and in grave danger and we need to know who he is but we're struggling. Unless we get lucky with CCTV then we're stuffed. You do understand that, don't you?'

'Of course, I do,' Toni said quietly. A sharp pang of guilt shot through her.

'Why did he agree to go with you?'

'We were working on similar stories.' Toni stretched the truth. 'And I don't like the dark. I wanted some company.'

The DI frowned. 'I'm curious. What did he expect to gain from going?'

Toni looked at her wellingtons and thought about her next words carefully. 'We met online on an information sharing website. I had posted an article about the Met's HTT,' she paused to explain. 'He was very interested because he was familiar with the area and some of the detectives involved. He had written about their HTT too.' Toni stopped and looked at the detectives. 'You know that HTT is their Human Trafficking Team.'

'We know what it is,' Stirling grinned sarcastically. 'Pretend that we know what we're doing for a moment and carry on.' Toni blushed again. The big sergeant looked like he had been hit in the nose with a shovel, but he had intelligence in his eyes. She hadn't meant to insult either detective it was just that her nerves were getting the better of her.

'Sorry'—Toni half smiled—'I didn't mean to imply…'

'That we're thick?' Stirling grunted.

'Yes. I'm very sorry.'

He smiled and Toni relaxed a little. 'It's important that you tell us everything. That's all that matters.'

Toni swallowed hard and steepled her fingers. She wasn't sure where to begin, or how much she could tell them without crossing the line. Mike had been adamant that he was being tailed, hence his caution. 'He said that he had worked on some trafficking cases down south and that he was positive that the gangs in London had links with Liverpool. You know, because of the port. They sometimes use containers on cargo ships for smuggling.' The detectives exchanged glances again. The DI rolled her eyes skyward and puffed out her cheeks. 'Sorry, I'm stating the obvious again. I'm nervous. He had a southern accent. I don't know if he lives down south, but he was certainly from there.'

'It isn't much to go on.' Stirling said flatly. 'Can you think of anything that could help us to identify him?'

'What about the blood on the floor?' Toni said excitedly. 'They kicked him.' She looked from one to the other. 'He spat blood onto the floor.'

'There's blood on the floor of the mill?' Stirling said taking his mobile from his leather jacket. He looked like he was going to make a call. Toni nodded enthusiastically.

'Yes.' Toni nodded again.

'We should be testing that, shouldn't we?' he said to the DI with a quizzical expression on his face.

'You think so?' The DI frowned. She turned towards Toni and shrugged. 'We didn't think of that.'

Toni realised what was going on. 'You're taking the piss.'

'Our forensic team are working on it,' the DI said flatly. 'But it's way too early to get any results from it. Do you remember what my sergeant said about pretending that we know what we're doing?'

'Yes, and I know that you know what you're doing. And so do I,' Toni insisted.

'We wouldn't be sitting here now if you had done your homework.'

'We didn't realise that there would be no exits at the back until we got in there. They must have sealed them up or something. And if we had known that they would use the fact that the cellar was flooded, then we would have picked a better hiding place and none of this would have happened.' She tried to sound composed but failed miserably. 'I know how this appears, but I am not stupid.'

'At this moment in time, Miss Barrat, that's debatable.' the DI smiled coldly.

'I beg your pardon?' Toni said offended. She flushed red and felt her temper fraying. 'Are you suggesting that I am stupid, Inspector?'

'The windows and exits at the rear of the mill were not sealed,' the DI sat forward as she spoke. 'There were no windows or doors. It was a security design used at most big ports. The mill owners of the day had them built that way to stop pilfering.' She raised her eyebrows to emphasise her point. 'The only windows and entrances were on the front elevation of the warehouse so that tobacco couldn't be thrown out of the rear of the building to friends and family below. Tobacco was very valuable commodity back then.' Annie paused to let the information sink in. 'And your 'flooded cellar' is not a cellar.' Toni looked at her Wellington boots and cringed inside. How could she have been so stupid? If the detectives doubted her intelligence, then who could blame them? 'It is actually an artery of the canal system, which links directly to the port. The mills were built above them. That's how their goods arrived.'

'On barges, through the flooded cellar,' Stirling cocked his head as he spoke. 'Which isn't a cellar and isn't flooded…'

'Now, I know that you're not a stupid woman, but on this occasion, you didn't do any research at all, did you?' The DI eyed Toni with a knowing look, 'Any journalist worth her salt could have discovered what I've just told you about the mill on the Internet in five minutes, which tells me that you received your 'tip' shortly before you went to the mill, leaving you no time to prepare.'

Toni shuffled uncomfortably in her chair. She folded her arms and nodded slowly. 'Yes, you're right. I shouldn't have rushed in,' Toni said with a sigh. 'It is my fault that we went there. Sorry.' She blew air from her lips. 'If I'm coming over as a bit of an arse it's because I feel sick with guilt; I apologise but I'm really trying to help.'

'We need you to trust in the fact that we know what we're doing. We don't have much to work on at the moment, Miss Barrat,' Stirling said calmly. 'There's no CCTV in that area, not much evidence at the scene, no body, no signs that a crime took place and we don't know the identity of the man that was kidnapped, except that you called him Mike.' He sat back and Toni imagined that his chair would be under immense stress. 'You can see where we are at, can't you?'

'Yes, square one.'

'We're not even on square one,' Annie said shaking her head.

Toni racked her brains. She felt like an amateur. 'God, I feel so bloody useless,' she said. 'The men mentioned a name'—she paused—'in fact, they mentioned it twice.'

'Go on,' the DI said.

'I heard them say that they would let 'Ivor' decide what to do with Mike.'

'Ivor?'

'Yes.'

'That's it?'

'It's Russian,' Toni added. As soon as she had said it, she wished that she hadn't. She knew that it was a useless piece of trivia. 'I think.'

'It could be.' Stirling nodded. 'It could be Welsh too. Remember 'Ivor the Engine' from the children's programme?' Toni shook her head. 'Before your time,' he added with a smile. 'It is similar to John or Dave or Mike. There are versions of it worldwide, but it's something, thank you.'

'It doesn't help us much right now but if we catch someone, then who knows?' Annie agreed.

'You must be able to do something for heaven's sake?' Toni said quietly. She ran her fingers through her hair. As the facts ran through her mind, she couldn't see anything else beyond what the big detective had said. They didn't have anything but her unsubstantiated story. 'Surely,' she said desperately. A tear broke free from her eye and rolled down her cheek. 'There must be something you can do to find him?' Her voice tailed off to a whisper.

'You can do something to help us find him,' the DI said folding her arms. 'We need the name of your source.'

'I can't give you that.' Toni shook her head. Part of her wanted to scream the name of her source but she couldn't. Her ethics defined her. She had worked hard in a competitive field and although she wasn't popular with the police, the Crown Prosecution, or the Probation Service, she had their respect. If she gave away her source, no one would speak to her again. Discretion and integrity were her promises to any would-be whistle-blower. Without them she would be finished. 'It would cost me my reputation.'

'Not telling us could cost Mike his life,' Stirling countered. There was no malice in his voice. He could see Toni was shaken. 'I'm not trying to frighten you, Toni.' He paused. 'Do you mind if I call you Toni?' She shook her head. 'I'm just stating the facts.'

'I can't reveal my source,' she bit her lip. 'And I'm not sure it would help if I did.' She tried to convince herself as well as the detectives. 'We didn't think that we were going to witness that. We had no idea.' She seemed to drift for a second. 'Have you ever heard of this drug 'zombie'?' She looked at Stirling quizzically.

'Never,' he answered with a shake of the head. 'But there's a new drug on the streets every day especially with legal highs. We'll look into it though and I'm sure the Drug Squad detectives who you spoke to are already on it.'

'It is crazy.' Toni sighed. 'I can't believe it happened.'

'What did you think was going to happen?' Annie probed again.

Toni raised her eyebrows and shook her head. 'I can't say but it wasn't anything like what happened.'

'You're hanging your colleague out to dry.'

'You can't make me feel any guiltier than I already do.'

'Like it or not,' the DI continued. 'Your colleague was taken by a very professional gang. From what you have told us, they were in and out of the deal in ten minutes?' Toni thought about it and nodded. 'Let me ask you this. Why do you think they took him rather than killing him right there where he fell?'

'They found the camera,' Toni blushed again. Not for the first time she wondered about the pictures he had taken before he had fallen. 'And obviously he was a witness.'

'Yes, he was, but what had he actually seen?'

'I've told you.' Toni sighed.

'You're missing the point,' Annie stressed. 'What had he actually seen?' Toni looked confused. 'Nothing!'

'What are you saying?'

'You said that all the men were masked.'

'Yes.'

'So, what could he have seen that could have put them away?'

'Nothing I suppose.'

'Exactly.' The DI crossed her legs and smoothed her skirt again. She shook her head almost imperceptibly and stared into Toni's eyes. Toni realised that her left eye was damaged. The ghost of a jagged scar ran down her cheek, well disguised by her make-up. 'You told me that they found his camera and realised that he had filmed some of the exchange,' the DI shrugged as she spoke. 'These people are extremely protective of their organisations and now they know that they have a leak. They took him to ask him how he knew that they would be there, why he was filming them and who else knew that he was there. They will apply pressure to discover how he knew about their handover and I mean the most extreme pressure.'

'Oh, my God,' Toni cringed inside. Her eyes widened as the reality of the situation struck home. 'Do you think they'll torture him?'

'Undoubtedly, they will. These traffickers are ruthless, and it doesn't matter how tough this guy is, he will tell them what they want to know eventually,' Stirling said solemnly. 'The chances are that he's already told them about you and who your source is,' Stirling added as he looked at his watch. 'Assuming that he knew anything about you or your source?'

Toni looked at the big detective, her top lip quivered as she answered. 'He didn't know anything about the source.' Her answer implied that he knew who Antonia Barrat was.

'How well did he know you?' Stirling asked.

'Not very well.'

'Assuming that he did his research, he would know where you work and where you live?'

Toni shook her head and thought about it. Okay, she was freelance, but he would know who her main customers were. She suddenly felt vulnerable; vulnerable and afraid. Like she had when her father died, and her mother vanished; sick and empty inside and numb to the core. She stared at her trembling fingers. Her nail varnish needed repainting. New varnish wouldn't stop her fingers shaking. She couldn't think of anything that would. 'He could have found out that much, yes.'

'But not where the information came from?'

'No. I didn't share it with him. I don't disclose my sources to anyone.'

'In which case,' the DI sat forward and clasped her hands together, 'we have to assume that they will be coming to ask you who told you about the mill. They have a leak and they will want it plugged very quickly.' Annie shrugged. 'So, you can either tell us where it came from, or you can wait for them to come knocking on your door.'

Toni felt like she had been kicked in the stomach. She craved corruption and scandal, sought it out on a daily basis but she didn't want this. Her sources had been a mine of information for years, but they were on the periphery of an extremely dangerous section of society. Their world was way too dangerous for her to survive in. She didn't want to go down that road, not now, not ever but the men who took Mike had her camera and that could be a huge problem. 'I can't divulge my source,' she said tight lipped. 'That is final.' She looked at her watch again. 'I really need to go.'

'Have you got a deadline to meet?' Stirling asked bluntly. 'I hope you're not thinking about writing this up, Toni.' She shook her head. She had thought about it but only briefly. What could she write without evidence? She had witnessed something dreadful but to rush an article would be wrong. 'You would be seriously endangering your friend's safety if you do.'

Toni seemed shell-shocked. Her face appeared blank and emotionless. She checked her watch again. 'I need to get home.'

The DI checked her watch too. 'You have children?' Toni nodded silently. She did have children, but they weren't the issue right now. She didn't like people knowing about her private life. She did her utmost to protect them from the world. Losing her father and mother at such a young age had taken a toll on her. She knew that she was damaged by the experience, but she had been determined that her loss wouldn't ruin her life. Damaged but not broken; that was her motto. She didn't talk to anyone about her home life and she intended to keep it that way. 'You need to get home and get them ready for school?'

Toni looked at the DI and blinked. She ignored her question. Let her think whatever she liked. Toni was done. 'Are we done here?'

'You do realise that you're in grave danger, don't you?' Annie asked her, her voice calm, yet firm. Toni nodded her head and stood up. 'Think about your family, Toni.'

'My family have nothing to do with this,' Toni said putting her bag over her shoulder. 'I would like my mobile phone back please and then I'm going home.'

Detective Inspector Annie Jones looked at Stirling and then pointed to the door. 'Give Miss Barrat her property and show her out, please.' She shook her head and stood up, handing over her business card. 'We'll have a marked car follow you home and sit outside your house for a few hours.' She sighed resignedly. 'Make sure that you keep in touch, Toni, and if you see or hear anything suspicious, call me directly.' Antonia's eyes seemed to glaze over as if she wasn't listening anymore. Her mind had switched off. It was a common defence mechanism that Annie had seen many times. The adrenalin was wearing off and shock was taking a hold. Whatever had happened in the mill had stunned her. She was a thick-skinned journalist, turned author and documentary maker, who had uncovered a corrupt ring of police officers that reached from new uniformed officers on the beat, up to a senior Area Commander. She had been threatened many times during the investigation, but she didn't back down. Annie had a grudging respect for her. She also knew that the fallout from writing a book and filming a documentary about corrupt police officers would pale in comparison to what would happen if an organised trafficking syndicate set their sights on her. Annie was convinced that it wasn't a case of if but when.

****

At the same time a few miles away across Liverpool Bay, the rib floated silently into a rickety boathouse on the North Wales coast near Flint. For decades it had been used by a local fisherman, now long dead. His nets and lobster pots were still stacked up in the corners, a rank smell of decayed fish and mould drifted from them. The planks were warped and splintered, and part of the roof had collapsed a few years before, but it served its purpose. The boathouse was one of many hideaways. They moved the rib from one remote location to another every four days, regardless of whether it had seen action or not. The smell of the sea mingled with the dank odour of rotting wood. The water beneath the wooden berth was shallow and it lapped gently against the pilings. On a calm night, the sound was soothing. Tonight, it emphasised his solitude.

      He looked skyward and caught a glimpse of the moon from behind the dark clouds, but it was just a fleeting glance. Spots of rain began to fall, a few at first and then it quickened with each passing moment before becoming a perpetual downpour. He pulled the collar of his bubble jacket tightly closed and fastened the zip to the top, but it didn't stop raindrops from trickling down his neck. The urge to smoke a cigarette was overwhelming but he couldn't risk being seen from the water. Compromising the abandoned boathouse would anger his employers. He would wait until they came for him. The mudflats behind the boathouse were impassable on foot, shifting pools of quicksand made the walk to shore lethal. They would pick him up in a larger boat when there were no other vessels in the area. As he tied the rib to a rusty mooring ring, he heard the sound of a diesel engine approaching from the east. It was too dark to distinguish what type of vessel was approaching but he was confident that it was them. If it wasn't, then they would sail on by towards their destination. He waited for the noise of the engine to draw closer and then checked the mooring rope was fastened tightly. The wake from the boat began lapping at the mudflats and gentle waves made the rib rock slightly. A gull called out in the darkness, disturbed by the approaching boat. It was an eerie sound, out of place when the sun went down. The gull sounded the alarm that danger was approaching.

He stood at the bow of the rib and waited for the vessel to come into sight. It rocked slightly from side to side. The rain had become more persistent and he was beginning to feel the cold in his hands and feet. The silhouette of a boat loomed against the light pollution from the dwellings on the far coast. A powerful spotlight illuminated and shone directly at the rib, blinding him momentarily.

'Turn the light away from me!' He hissed, protecting his eyes with his hand. 'What is your problem?'

'Did you have your mask on at the mill?' a voice from the boat shouted. The dazzling light burned into his eyes making him squint.

'Mask?' They always wore masks. They had to. It was rule number one. 'Of course, I did, why?'

'There was someone at the handover snapping pictures.' The voice replied.

'You're fucking kidding me,' he said. The rib rolled gently on the swell. 'Was it the police?'

'We're not sure yet.'

'Well, how do you know then?'

'Where is it?'

'Where is what?'

'Your mask.' He hesitated. Just for a moment but it was a moment too long; too noticeable.

'I tossed it in the river.'

He momentarily registered the pain in the palm of his hand as a nine-millimetre bullet ripped through the flesh and bones, before it slammed into his forehead, liquefied his brains, and then blew the back of his skull off.

CHAPTER 6

The greasy spoon cafe was packed with the usual faces. Shopkeepers, office workers, and local builders were sitting eating breakfasts from plates the size of bin lids. Condensation misted the windows and the irresistible aroma of bacon pervaded from every molecule of the building.

'Morning, Margaret,' Kayla said chirpily as she stepped through the door. Her smile lit up the room. A bell dinged as she closed the door behind her. The cafe buzzed with the sound of chatter and the air was warm and moist. She could understand why it was so popular with people on their way to work. Kayla had used it daily since she had opened her shop next door.

'The usual?' Margaret said, waving a spatula dripping in grease. Her thin lips formed a nicotine stained smile and deep wrinkles ran from the corners of her eyes to her hairline, like the lines on a protractor. Her face was a warning to anyone who smoked twenty a day for twenty years; this is what you'll look like. 'It's ready and waiting for you.' Margaret tapped her nose with her index finger. 'Hey, that bloke from the bakery called in again,' she said with a sly wink. 'He was asking about you again.'

'Can't say that I blame him,' one of the builders, Charlie, said loudly. 'He probably wants to show you his donuts, Kayla.' His friends laughed raucously.

'Or his sticky iced fingers,' another added.

'He could be a secret master-baker,' Margaret joined in.

'Will you lot pack it in.' Kayla laughed. 'The poor man might be just lonely. I'm sure someone will go out with him… eventually.'

'Not you though, Kayla.' Charlie winked.

'Not me, no.'

'Wouldn't you like to go out with a real man, Kayla?' Charlie said biting into a burnt sausage.

'Why, do you know any?' Kayla countered. Charlie blushed and smiled.

'That was cruel.'

'I tend to go for men who can eat their breakfast without dribbling egg yolk down their front.' Charlie stopped smiling and looked down. His chequered shirt was clean. 'Made you look,' Kayla said as she paid for her food. 'Thanks, Margaret. Can you do me a chicken mayo for dinnertime?'

'Will do, love. I'll drop it in later, Kayla.'

Kayla Yates walked out of the cafe and immediately missed the moist warmth and the comforting aromas. She took a few steps to the front of the shop next door as a cold breeze bit at her fingers. She balanced her coffee and bacon sandwich in her right hand while her left clicked the remote which activated the metal roller shutters that protected her business. The motor whirred and the shutters rattled open loudly. Yates's Gold Emporium. Every time she saw the sign, she felt a rush of pride. She had built it up from a stall on a Sunday market, buying and selling gold and silver jewellery, squirrelling the profits away each week. She branched out onto eBay to supplement her income. After five years of spending Sundays standing in a field, rain or sun, wind or snow, light summery mornings or pitch-black November dawns, she had enough money and stock to put down a deposit on a high street premises and open it with a respectable selection of goods. Lord knows there were enough of them at the time. The nation's high streets had degraded to a parade of pound shops, charity shops, bookmakers, and money lenders. When she had first opened her doors, she was the happiest person in the city. Kayla Yates, business owner, entrepreneur, and independent woman. By lunchtime that day her friends and family had left the shop and instead of a rush of excited customers, the cold harsh reality of running a fledgling business crept through the door. A few curious browsers and the local window cleaner touting for business were the only people that entered the building for the remainder of the day. Kayla was a survivor and she adapted quickly. Four years on, she was making more money than she had ever imagined, although it wasn't all legitimate.

The rollers fell silent and she used her key to open the door, using her shoulder to close it behind her. She typed the alarm code into the keypad and flicked on the lights. The smell of bacon was making her mouth water and she slipped her sandwich from its brown paper bag and took a bite.

'As long as Margaret keeps frying bacon next door, I'll never be able to keep to my diet and I'll never be a veggie,' she said to herself, as she took a long sip of her coffee. 'We're open for business, don't all rush in at once,' she muttered as she took the 'closed' sign from the door. 'Don't fall over each other in the crush. There's plenty for everyone.'

A light drizzle was beginning to fall, which would dissuade some potential browsers from venturing out. In the early days, that would have bothered her but now her business didn't rely on footfall passing the door. The Internet provided her with a much less fickle customer base and her pawnbroker service drew people to her like a magnet whatever the weather. Government austerity following the recession had forced people to sell their valuables. Computers, mobile phones, watches, rings, chains and bracelets were currency and she snapped up whatever came through the door and resold it at a handsome profit on her website.

Kayla gulped her coffee and checked her window display. She had an impressive stock of designer watches. Rolex, Tag, Armani, and Gucci, some new, some pawned, some fakes, and some stolen. They glistened in the window behind reinforced plate glass. Her display was impressive. It made passers-by stop and stare, although most could only dream of owning one. There were gaps on the stand where the most expensive pieces stood. They were stored in her safe. She removed them every night before closing up and put them on display again every morning. It was a monotonous routine but despite her shutters, the insurance company insisted on it. She took another bite of her sandwich and walked through her empire, catching her reflection in one of the mirrors that covered the walls behind the counter. She liked her new highlights, blond over chestnut, reaching to her shoulder. Her denim shirt was washed to pale blue in contrast with her black jeans. It set off her grey eyes. She was fast approaching thirty-five, but she turned the heads of men half her age, nonetheless. The landline began to ring, and she cursed as she swallowed a mouthful of bacon before answering.

'Yates's,' she said putting the phone beneath her ear. She took a quick sip of her coffee to wash down her breakfast. 'How can I help you?'

'Great telephone voice, Kayla.' The voice joked. She recognised it but couldn't put a name to it. 'It's Jason.'

'Hello, Jason,' Kayla said. She still didn't have a clue who he was. 'What can I do for you?'

'It's more what I can do for you.'

'I see,' Kayla remained polite, but she stuck two fingers up at the phone. She remained quiet, already bored of the conversation.

'How's business?'

'Busy thanks,' she said checking her whitened teeth in the mirror for scraps of meat.

'Do you remember that Rolex that I brought in last week?'

'Oh, yes,' Kayla clicked who it was. Jason was a regular, so she was polite, but she didn't like him. He was too cocksure, too forward, and too unhygienic to like. 'What can I do for you?'

'I've got a couple more Rolex watches, one Oyster, and a Submariner. What can you give me for them?'

'Have you got receipts?'

'No.' He sniggered.

'Have you got the boxes and certificates?'

'No.' He chuckled sarcastically. 'I heard that you can supply certificates.'

'You heard wrong,' she lied. His comment had wiped two hundred off the deal instantly just for his cheek. 'Bring them in and I'll take a look at them and see what I can do.'

'Nice one, thanks. I'll be there before twelve.'

'See you then, bye.' She hung up and smiled in the mirror again. A pair of high-end Rolex watches with new counterfeit paperwork and boxes would net her a few grand. It was a good start to the day. Kayla finished her coffee and headed for the secure room at the rear of the shop. She heard the front door open and turned around and was surprised to see Antonia Barrat walking in. Her face was ashen, dark circles beneath her eyes, and she had obviously been crying. The expression on her face told her that something very bad had happened.

CHAPTER 7

Half of the fourth floor of the fortress-like police headquarters, Canning Place was occupied by the Drug Squad. Built on the banks of the Mersey in a time when civil unrest was a consideration, it was designed with its defence uppermost in mind. The exterior walls were impossible to scale and the narrow windows at each corner made it easily defendable, like a medieval castle. The Major Investigation Team occupied the other half of the fourth floor. Annie stepped out of the lift, followed by Stirling, and headed for her office. She was troubled by Toni Barrat and her unwillingness to cooperate, but her hands were tied. Until it became legal to shake information from a witness, there was nothing she could do. Persuasion was a powerful tool when used to appeal to common sense, but on this occasion common sense had not prevailed.

'Annie,' a voice called from behind her. She turned to see her opposite DI from the Drug Squad, Miranda Snow, beckoning her. They had climbed the ranks together and had become friendly, although sometimes their squads' jurisdiction caused friction between them. They hadn't had an argument that couldn't be settled over Italian food and a bottle of merlot. 'I was coming to find you.'

'Glad I have saved you a job.'

'I might have saved you one.' Miranda smiled. She was tall but painfully slim and her black trouser suit seemed to hang from her frame as if it belonged to an elder sibling. Her curly black hair was scraped from her face into a tight bun at the back of her head. 'You'll want to see this. I know you will,' she grinned. Her dark brown eyes sparkled with mischief. 'How did it go with Barrat?'

'As expected'—Annie sighed—'She can't give up her source as it would ruin her reputation.'

'She has a reputation to ruin?' Miranda said sarcastically.

'That's what I thought,' Stirling grunted.

'I have the feeling that the disrespect is mutual,' Miranda joked. 'Did she have anything useful to give us?'

'She was certain that they used a rib, so we've got the Port Authorities checking the canal links and shoreline CCTV. They're adamant that all waterway access to the buildings in that area were sealed off in the seventies but it wouldn't take much to cut through the grills and they would be in and out unseen. Once the rib reached the river, it could vanish in no time.'

'Are you thinking a bigger vessel in the port or anchored in the mouth of the estuary?' Miranda asked.

'It could just as easily have gone upriver or across the estuary to North Wales,' Stirling said. 'There are plenty of places to launch a rib. It's all speculation unless we get lucky with the Port Authorities or the traffic cameras. Failing that we have zilch.'

'I may be able to help you there.' Miranda winked.

The three detectives headed into the Drug Squad section, where a number of screens were being studied by a dozen detectives. They were greeted with silent nods and half smiles. She pointed to the largest screen. 'As you know, there are no CCTV cameras around Jamaica Street, so we asked the guys at traffic to look for vans entering the main arterial roads around the dock roads along Parliament Street. We got lucky.' She pointed to the grainy image of a black Volkswagen pulling out from a side street. 'Twenty minutes past twelve, which fits in with our timeline, yes?'

Annie felt a rush of adrenalin. She always felt it when a lead popped up. 'What did the plates tell us?'

'It was stolen from the Wirral two weeks ago,' one of the detectives answered without turning around. He followed a line on the map with his pen. 'We can follow it down the dock road as far as Aigburth, but we lose it here near the airport at Speke. Apparently, Vice has been focusing on a number of properties in this area for months, one in particular, and we're guessing that they're connected to what happened last night.'

'So, they're still in the city,' Annie raised her eyebrows and looked at Stirling. He shrugged and nodded. She smiled at Miranda. 'Good work. What has Vice said about it?'

'They have been watching an address in that area for the last three months. They know it's owned by an Eastern European gang and they're putting money on it being the destination for the women before they split them up and sell them on.'

'We don't have long,' Annie said. 'They won't keep them there for long.'

'Superintendent Franklin from Vice has jumped on it.' Miranda rolled her eyes. 'He's with the ACC now getting authorisation for Forced Entry Teams, Armed Response Units and he has a helicopter on alert. We're welcome to tag along but Vice are running the show. We're bystanders on this one unless they find the drugs.'

'What do you know about this 'zombie' drug,' Stirling asked. 'I've never heard of it.'

Miranda looked at her DS, a man Stirling knew as Sykes. He turned and pointed to one of the screens. The image of a cargo ship appeared and came into focus. 'We think it began coming in from Amsterdam about six months ago,' Sykes explained. Stirling couldn't help but think that he looked like Mike Tyson in spectacles. 'Zombie is a form of Ketamine Hydroxide, which we all know and love as the horse anaesthetic of choice on the streets. It is usually called 'Special K'.' Stirling frowned as he listened. 'K is related to Phencyclidine or PCP as we know it, but Ketamine is less than ten percent as potent as pure PCP,' he paused to make sure they were following him. 'Zombie is both drugs mixed together in powder form. In its purest state, it is lethal, so they cut it and press it into tablets.' He shrugged. 'Its effects gave it its name. Zombie is the most powerful hallucinogenic we've ever encountered.'

'And because it is so potent…' Miranda smiled.

'Everyone wants it,' Stirling finished off her sentence.

'Correct,' Sykes said removing his glasses. 'Users are paying thirty pounds for one tablet. It has devalued anything else out there. I could buy an ecstasy tablet for less than two quid now.'

'I bet the ecstasy dealers are pleased,' Annie grimaced.

'Matrix is telling us that things on the streets are not good. Tensions are rising and people are looking for those responsible for bringing it in.' Miranda shook her head. Matrix was the undercover arm of her department and their information was priceless. 'The thing is, no one is sure who is bringing it in. Everyone wants a piece of the action and to sell it, but they don't know who is importing it. Market instability leads to trouble. This is the first definite lead on the importers that we've had.' She shrugged. 'That's why I'm so miffed that Vice is leading the raid.'

'I suppose if they've been staking the place out for months, it's their call,' Annie argued. She didn't care who put the handcuffs on them. She just wanted them banged up behind steel and concrete. Annie was in a very small and unfashionable club, who believed that the force was more effective when its departments worked in tandem. Some detectives were more interested in personal glory than justice. 'It sounds to me that they have the biggest investment in manpower at the moment. It's their ball for now.'

'You're right.' Miranda nodded with a frown. 'But aren't you just a little bit pissed off?'

Annie shrugged. 'A little.' She mulled over what had been said. Something bothered her. 'You said that Vice think the property is owned by Eastern European money?'

'Yes,' Miranda answered. 'Why?'

'Just something Barrat said earlier about Russian accents.'

'It is an easy mistake to make unless you're familiar with the language.'

'I suppose so.' Annie looked at Stirling. 'Can you find out when Vice are moving on the address. I want to be there when they knock the doors off.' Her mobile rang. She answered it and her face darkened as she listened. 'Okay thanks. Stay on her.'

'Problem?' Miranda asked. She was distracted by her own mobile ringing.

'I'm not sure.' Annie frowned. 'Antonia Barrat didn't go home. She stopped off at a pawnbroker's shop near Kensington.'

'I doubt she's selling her family jewels,' Stirling grunted. 'Do you think she's gone to see her source?'

'That's exactly what I'm thinking. Run a check on the owners of the business.' Annie felt the hairs on her neck tingle. Something didn't add up. 'We might need to pay them a visit.' She waited for Miranda to finish her call.

'That was Vice.' Miranda sighed. She shook her head, a worried expression on her face. 'The house that Vice were watching...' she paused, '...they think it's on fire!'

'They think it is?' Annie frowned. 'It either is or it isn't.'

'Apparently, the entire terrace is going up.' Miranda looked at Annie, her face deadpan. 'Could be a coincidence.'

'And I could be Mrs Clooney, but I'm not. Let's go and take a look.'

CHAPTER 8

The North-West Air Operations Group consists of four helicopters that cover five police forces, Merseyside, North Wales, Greater Manchester, Lancashire, and Cheshire. Annie could see that one of the choppers had taken position over the area between Sefton Park and the river. Thick black smoke spiralled skywards towards it from a row of three storey Victorian townhouses. Crowds were gathering at the cordons at each end of the street where uniformed officers struggled against the wind to hang yellow tape from the lampposts. Three fire engines poured water into the front of the burning buildings; the resulting towers of steam mingled with the smoke as they climbed skyward. Firemen clad in yellow and using respirators entered one of the buildings and the time ticked painfully slowly by as Annie waited for them to reappear. All eyes were fixated on the doorway, from which billowed thick black smoke. When they eventually did appear, they carried the naked body of a male between them. Paramedics rushed forward but Annie had seen enough corpses to know that he was beyond medical help. A prayer would be more apt.

'Shall we get a closer look?' Miranda said quietly. They watched as the body was placed onto a stretcher and carried towards a row of waiting ambulances. 'Are you seeing this?' Miranda hissed as they approached. 'Do you think this is your missing reporter?'

'No chance.' Annie shook her head. The man was cuffed, his hands behind his back. She could see where the zip ties had cut deeply into the flesh. Black scabs had formed around the wounds, which told her that they were old. His face was swollen and bruised black and blue. The upper eyelids were deep purple. His fingers and toes were nothing but blackened stumps. 'He's been interrogated for a long time,' Annie observed. 'See the tattoos on his shoulders,' Annie pointed to the images of epaulettes that were inked onto the man. 'They're a sign of authority in the Russian mob.' His chest and back were covered in multiple tattoos, but they were faded with age and she couldn't see them in detail. Each image had its own meaning while the man lived but they meant nothing anymore. 'If Vice are right about the property being owned by an Eastern European gang, this man was very much a rival.'

Stirling loomed into view and gestured with his head. Annie and Miranda followed him until they were out of earshot. 'The fire crew told me that the place is empty,' he leaned towards them as he spoke. 'They cleared out in a rush. No sign of any girls and no sign of any drugs on the upper floors. They're in the cellar now. Our dead friend there was left tied to a chair next to the front door. They wanted us to find him.'

'I thought Vice had the bloody place under surveillance,' Miranda shook her head. She folded her arms and studied the burning buildings.

'Not for twenty-four hours a day.' Stirling shrugged. 'No one signs off on twenty-four-hour surveillance anymore. They had eyes on the place until eleven last night. They don't know where the fire started yet. It could have been further down the terrace, but I doubt it.'

'I can take a good guess. They had plenty of time to pack up and leave.' Annie added. As she spoke, there was a commotion between the entry teams. They listened as the comms buzzed excitedly. Three females had been found in the basement. They watched in silent anticipation as a second suited entry team rushed into the smoke-filled house followed quickly by a third. Paramedics stood stoically as close to the conflagration as they could, stretchers and oxygen at the ready.

'DI Snow?' A uniformed officer approached them.

'That's me,' Miranda said with a frown.

'I've got a message from DS Williams from Vice. He's at the back of the buildings searching a garage and some outhouses. He said that you need to see what they've found.' He paused. 'Excuse me for asking,' he said to Stirling, 'aren't you from MIT?'

'That's right.'

'I think you might want to come too,' the constable said grimly. 'If you follow me, there's an alleyway at the far end that will take us around the back.'

Stirling looked at Annie. 'You go,' she ordered. 'I want to see who they bring out. I'll follow you around in a minute.' Stirling nodded and the group moved off quickly in the direction of the alleyway. Annie focused her attention back on the burning house. The recovery teams had been gone for an uncomfortable length of time. She checked her watch. Forty seconds at least had gone. Fifty ticked by and then sixty. The silence outside was palpable. All she could hear were the engines of the fire tenders and the hissing of water turning to steam. Seventy seconds went by silently, then eighty, and then ninety.

There was an ear-splitting explosion as the windows of the house next door exploded outwards, showering the emergency responders in a maelstrom of splintered glass. Annie ducked instinctively as huge plumes of orange flames were propelled skyward.

'Gas main!' a fireman shouted. A second smaller explosion rocked the buildings. 'Get the hoses on that house!'

'I thought all the services had been cut?' A fire officer called over.

'They're working on it, Sir.' The officer shook his head and began to rant into the comms. Whoever was on the other end of the tirade was receiving the sharp end of his tongue, but the message was loud and clear. 'Turn the fucking gas off!'

Raised voices signalled that the first team was coming out. They stumbled through the doorway; the limp body of a female hung from their shoulders. Annie could tell from the way her knees were bent and her toes dragged along the floor that she was unconscious, or worse. Paramedics ran forward and helped them to carry her. They were a safe distance from the blaze before they put her gently onto a stretcher. As she approached, Annie could see deep welts around her wrists. The wounds were fresh, the blood still flowing. She was white European, which created more questions than answers.

'The bastards chained them to a radiator in the cellar,' one of the firemen said as he removed his mask. 'What kind of people would chain them up before torching the place?'

'Bad ones,' Annie grimaced and patted him on the back. 'The other two?'

'They're in a bad way, guv.' He shook his head, his eyes filled with tears. 'Smoke inhalation. We had to cut the chains to get them free. It took too long. Two of them are still breathing but only just.' As he spoke, the other teams appeared from the darkness within the burning house. The women that they brought from their smoke-filled prison were almost identical to the first, blond, white, and nearly dead. Annie watched as paramedics applied an oxygen mask to one and began mouth to mouth on the second. They looked like mannequins at a first aid conference, lifeless, and as still as the first woman. The medics worked hard and then others took turns to resuscitate them. There was nothing that a detective could do to help them, no matter how good they were.

She backed away and headed through the throng of responders towards the alleyway. It was difficult to spot, hidden between two hedgerows. The hedges were overgrown and conspired with the trees to hide the gap between the houses. The paving stones were uneven and strewn with broken glass and fast food wrappers. There were discarded syringes and empty beer cans dotted about and the alleyway smelled of urine. As she reached the rear access road, she spotted a group of detectives and uniformed officers milling about to her left. A single fire fighter sprayed tons of water onto the slate roofs from a hydraulic platform. At that point, it was succeeding in keeping the flames from reaching the rear elevations.

The road was narrow and covered in asphalt. It was wide enough to drive a large vehicle through and the garages were big enough to park a van inside. She noticed several black tyre marks scorched onto the road. Someone had left the rear of the house in a hurry and the vehicle had been carrying a heavy load. The walls at the back of the houses were high. Each house had a garage that faced the access road and an outhouse in the backyard. When she reached the back gate, Stirling waved her into the yard. His expression spoke volumes. She had seen it before many times, and it indicated that nothing good had happened.

'You need to see this, guv,' he growled as she neared. He ducked under the doorframe into the garage. The smell of human excrement filled her senses. Against the far wall, four plastic buckets stood in a line. She could see garden netting draped over each bucket. As she approached, the smell intensified. The buckets held human waste that had been passed through the netting. 'It looks like they were trying to recover the drugs from the mules when they had to leave in a hurry.' Annie nodded her agreement. 'One of them must have excreted her parcels before they left.' Annie knew what was coming but she didn't want to hear it. She waited for Stirling to complete his sentence. 'There's a black female in the outhouse. She's malnourished, dirty, and her throat has been cut ear to ear.' They walked out of the garage and into the brick outhouse. Annie knew that it would have been the toilet when the houses were originally built in the 1800s. Outside toilets seemed prehistoric when she thought about it but in those days, they were a huge step up from a bucket beneath the bed. Only the upper classes had a toilet at all. She scanned the narrow yard, but it didn't reveal much. The borders were overgrown and strewn with fast food wrappers and black bin bags were piled up near the back door. When she looked into the outhouse, the brutality of the traffickers was clear for all to see.

The body of a young black female lay sprawled on the stone floor. She was on her back, hands tied together. Her eyes were open wide, and her mouth was twisted into a silent cry for help. The gash to her throat was so deep that Annie could see her spine glistening. A congealing pool of blood had spread beneath her and its coppery smell lingered in the dank air. A fly fed greedily from it. Annie thought of the journey that the girl would have endured; thousands of miles crossing deserts, mountains, and seas to wind up with her throat slashed in a dark damp toilet block, a long way from her family.

'So, they weren't trafficked for sex,' Annie muttered. 'They're mules and once they've shed their cargo, they're of no value.'

'It certainly looks that way,' Miranda said from the doorway. 'The poor girl wasn't out of her teens.' As she spoke, DS Williams from Vice approached.

'This is a first-class fuck up!' he moaned. The other detectives just looked at each other.

'How did they manage this without being busted already?' Miranda asked. Williams blushed. 'I thought you had the place under surveillance.'

'Who told you that?' Williams asked defensively.

'Your Governor.'

'He doesn't know his arse from his elbow sometimes.' Williams lowered his voice and leaned in closer. 'We have been running an opp on Number 2, which is at the bottom of the terrace.'

'What?' Stirling grunted.

'We were watching Number 2. There were punters coming and going from there all hours of the day and night. They must have been living here and working down the road. This place wasn't even on our radar until the fire boys kicked the front door in. Watch this space, because Franklin is going to be getting a massive kick up the arse.' Williams winked and walked away to answer his mobile.

'How can an opp not have connected the two buildings?' Miranda asked incredulously. 'I'm just glad that Vice was running it.'

'Every cloud,' Annie agreed. 'The three women in the cellar are touch and go. They're white Europeans. They chained them to a radiator before they torched the place.' Annie sighed. 'They obviously didn't want to leave any witnesses behind.'

'Why not take them?' Stirling mused. 'Just to be sure.'

'Maybe they didn't have room to take them?'

'Makes sense,' Miranda agreed.

'They cut their losses here and made sure that they couldn't talk and that the drugs were safe,' Stirling added.

'We have to assume that they cleared out because the handover at the mill was compromised,' Annie said. 'We have eleven girls full of cocaine and a missing reporter and the clock is ticking for them.'

Stirling nodded; his hands deep inside the pockets of his leather. 'Do you think our missing man 'Mike' coughed to being accompanied at the mill?'

'Looking at the state of the other victims,' she nodded, 'there's no doubt in my mind,' Annie felt a cold chill touch her and she shuddered. 'I can't help but think that this is already running away from us and we're still in the dark.' She took out her phone and dialled. 'One thing is for sure… this is way beyond a Vice stakeout now. I'm calling the Area Commander's office. We're all on this one now.'

'Do you want me to take a crack at the pawnbroker's shop on the way back to the station?' Stirling asked as he watched the mutilated body being dive-bombed by flies. 'I'm curious as to why Barrat didn't go straight home. If her source is there, then I might be able to convince them to talk.' Annie nodded and then turned to talk to the Area Commander's secretary. As Stirling walked towards the alleyway, he took one last look at the smouldering houses and the helicopter above. Whoever they were looking for had a talent for being one step ahead of the law and they didn't mind causing carnage in order to destroy evidence. They were also very adept at murder in order to clean-up loose ends and that worried him immensely.

CHAPTER 9

Jason Greene pulled up across the street from Kayla's Emporium and took a good look around before turning the engine off. He had said that he would be there before lunchtime and he didn't want to appear to be too keen, even though he was desperate for the cash. He liked Kayla but he was wary of her. Kayla Yates was a good-looking woman but when it came to business, she was a shark and she could sense blood in the water from a mile away. If he turned up too early, her offer for the watches would be lower, much lower. She would know that he needed the money quickly and react accordingly and that would cost him dearly. For the last few years, he had sold merchandise to her a couple of times a month and each time, he felt that he had undersold his goods but she was discreet and she always paid with cash. No questions asked and no proof of purchase required. He knew that the police and insurance companies had fulltime dedicated staff that trawled the Internet searching for stolen goods. Online sites like eBay were no longer an option for professional handlers. Kayla was the safer option to fence goods even if the price was lower.

Jason looked up and down the road and then opened the car door; the temperature dropped immediately. A breeze blew in from the river and carried rain with it. It was the type of drizzle that made him miserable. It was the type of drizzle that his games teacher at school didn't deem wet enough to cancel the lesson despite all the kids looking like drowned rats within ten minutes, dithering and shivering with their hands shoved in their shorts seeking warmth. He pushed the sickening thoughts of school away as he closed the door and jogged across the road to the shop, pausing as a green bus roared past splashing his Adidas trainers with dirty water. A new pair shot straight to the top of his shopping list.

As he entered the emporium, the door alarm beeped alerting the shopkeeper that they had a customer. Pleased to be out of the rain, he closed the door and glanced at the display of watches in the window. A glass panel allowed customers inside the shop to see the window display. It was an impressive collection, although there were a few empty stands where the high-end stuff usually sat. He wondered if maybe Kayla was running low on her Rolex stock, which was good news for him. He stored that information for later, but he wasn't getting carried away with himself. It was more likely that she had been distracted from the business of setting up and overlooked putting out her expensive watches. She was too wily to run out of the most desirable brands. It just wouldn't happen. He took a few steps inside, expecting to see her pretty face smiling at him from behind one of the counters but they were both unattended.

The odour of her perfume lingered in the air beneath the unmistakeable smell of bacon, but she wasn't there. As he hadn't eaten, he wasn't sure which odour was the most attractive.

Certain that she would be in the secure office at the back, Jason browsed at the mobile phone cabinet, which was a veritable treasure trove of communication devices. It held a wide selection of makes and models, most of them boxed, and less than a year old. Several of them were more recent than his. His eyes lingered on a smart watch with built-in GPS. Talking to friends via a device on your wrist, which could tell you where you were in the world, was one of his childhood fantasies, although it didn't really matter what other people thought about you when you are six. As an adult, talking into his watch in a city centre bar could be seen as being a knobhead. He thought about the blokes who walked around with a Bluetooth earpiece fixed to the side of their heads day and night, funny how they never seemed to get a call from anyone. The word 'knob' sprung back into his mind again. Smart watches may have arrived, but he decided that he wasn't cut out for one just yet. They were for the young and the crew of the Starship Enterprise. The more conventional devices were the way forward. A new mobile phone went to number two on his shopping list just below the new pair of Adidas.

There was still no sign of Kayla. The minutes ticked by and he wondered where she was. He coughed loudly as he moved across the shop to look at the display of cameras, keeping one eye on the door at the rear. There was no response, so he coughed louder still. He knew that she could see the entire shop floor through the reflective glass. She was probably on the toilet or talking on the telephone negotiating another purchase. She was expecting him, and she knew who he was and why he was there, so there was no rush. In fact, she was probably making him sweat on purpose to gain the upper hand before the bartering began. Maybe he was overthinking her business acumen. Would she purposely make him wait just to throw him off balance? Five minutes turned into ten and he was beginning to think that she was taking liberties with his time when he heard a muffled cry from the office. It was female and it was stifled.

His blood froze in his veins. He had never been brave. His early years had made him a victim, bullied at home and at school. He had developed a sixth sense for knowing when danger was coming his way. Avoiding the bullies at school had become an art form, navigating the alleyways and entries so as not to be seen, learning the times and the places where the predators would be had enabled him to avoid many a kicking. Even now as an adult if he sensed violence approaching, he bolted for the exit. The voices of self-preservation in his head whispered, 'get out'.

'Kayla,' he called but it came out as a croak. He cleared his throat and called louder, 'Kayla, are you okay?'

Silence answered.

'Kayla!'

Silence.

'Kayla, it is Jason Greene.' Nothing for a second and then he heard a muffled shriek and a thud. A deep dull thud followed by empty nothingness again. He could hear a buzzing noise in his ears and his throat was painfully dry. Jason backed towards the door. A brave man may have run to the office to see if he could help the damsel in distress, but he wasn't a knight in shining armour. He was a coward and that was fine by him. Cowards lived while heroes died. Didn't nearly all heroes have to die to gain that coveted title? They could keep it. Breathing was far more important.

'Kayla!' he shouted as loud as he could, but she didn't answer. 'Kayla!' He called again and then sensing that something was amiss, he ran for the door and opened it. He paused for a moment as his conscience pricked him. There could only be a few reasons that she wasn't answering; one was that she was being robbed or she was dead or dying. He could have checked on her but if he interrupted a holdup, he may get shot. If she was dying from a heart attack or similar, he didn't know how to give CPR so he would be of no use to her. He couldn't telephone for an ambulance without attracting attention. Ambulance men usually called the police if there were suspicious circumstances. The knowledge that he was carrying two stolen Rolex watches burned into his mind, but he couldn't leave her. 'Kayla! I am going to phone the police!' He slammed the door behind him and looked up and down the street. There was no one around. The rain was keeping people indoors. He jogged across the road back to his car and took out his mobile. Coward or not, he dialled 999.

CHAPTER 10

Raitis Girts wiped the moisture from his palms onto his jeans. Perspiration trickled down his shaven scalp across his protruding forehead and into his eyes. Rivulets of sweat ran over the three rolls of flesh at the back of his head and soaked his shirt before it trickled down his thick tattooed neck. It wasn't particularly warm; in fact, it was cool outside the van; it was the precarious nature of his business that made him sweat. Pedestrians scurried along the pavements with their coats fastened tightly but the temperature inside the Volkswagen was uncomfortable to say the least. The atmosphere in the cab was tense. Condensation on the windows made it difficult to see without having the heater on full blast, which in turn made the terrible stink worse. The stench coming from the women in the back was unbearable. He could smell their vile breath, the weeks of sweat and grime in their hair and on their skin but worst of all was the disgusting odour of excrement. His colleagues had plied them with laxatives at the house, boxes full of them. It was what they always did when a shipment of mules arrived.

They had followed the usual procedure. How could they know that they would get a frantic call to move the women and move them quickly? They couldn't reverse the effects of the laxatives once they were ingested so they'd thrown a couple of plastic buckets into the back with the women. The drugs were beginning to take effect and conditions were becoming dire. The buckets had reached overflowing within an hour of leaving. They could have brought bleach, toilet rolls, and bin bags but they simply hadn't had the time. The only compensation for Raitis as the driver, was that he didn't have to stay in the back of the van to sift through the buckets of shit for balloons full of cocaine. For that he was truly grateful.

They had to leave the city without driving on the motorway networks where, number plate recognition cameras would pick them up quickly. He stuck to the back roads until they reached the river. As they crossed the Runcorn Bridge, he indicated left and steered the Volkswagen along a slip road that headed into an industrial area, which hugged the banks of the Mersey for miles. It was once the heart of the petrochemical industry but in the last decade the area had become a mishmash of fertiliser factories, engineering workshops, auto-body shops, and engine breakers. It was a warren of lanes, access roads, and disused warehouses. Their predicament was dire. They needed to dump the Volkswagen. Despite swapping the plates that morning, it was hot. Everything to do with the handover at the mill was hot. When the call had come to move the women, he wasn't given a destination to drive to. He was ordered to drive until told otherwise, which was risky with a van full of mules, not to mention three kilos of zombie. Possession of drugs with intent to supply and human trafficking carried heavy jail terms, which were all part of the job, but that didn't make it any easier on the nerves. If they were caught, they would be convicted and deported. Being sent back to the Latvian authorities was a death sentence.

When the call came that a switch had been arranged, he had punched the air in relief. They were to swap the Volkswagen for a white Mercedes Sprinter van at a breaker's yard near the Mersey. He felt the pressure lift immediately. The Mercedes Sprinters were built with a sealed bulkhead between the driver and the cargo bay. He would be free of the stench and the police wouldn't be looking for that type of vehicle, two reasons to be cheerful. All they had to do was get to the yard, swap vehicles and they could drive around for days if necessary camouflaged by the million other white vans on the roads.

Raitis slowed as the road narrowed and he took the right fork that he hoped would lead to the unit that he was looking for. He was desperate to open the window but he daren't. Every now and again he heard a shriek of anguish from the back. They were certainly loud enough to be heard from the pavement or a passing vehicle with the windows down. He had to keep going and suffer for the cause. The mules were suffering from stomach cramps and the shortage of buckets was making tempers fray. He could hear his colleagues barking orders at them, especially Oleg. If the women protested, they were encouraged not to by a hard slap, kick, or punch. He could hear Oleg shouting and then the thud of a fist or a boot against flesh followed by the sickening sound of them whimpering. Raitis had worked with some violent men, but Oleg was evil.

A few minutes on and the road became a dirt track pitted with deep potholes, which made the journey even more uncomfortable. There were fewer buildings on either side now and the ones that he could see were rundown or completely derelict. Between the broken-down structures, green fields spread out left and right for at least a mile. The river was on one side and the high railway viaduct was on the other. Beyond them he could make out sprawling housing estates. There was no sign of the garage that he was looking for. He checked the GPS on his phone. His battery was running low, sapped by using the route finder. He was about to give up looking when he spotted another track to the left. It traced a wide arc across one of the fields and at the end of it he could see a collection of buildings that surrounded a huge barn. The sign fixed above the barn doors was too far away for him to read but he figured that this was the place. They were about as isolated as one could be in the suburbs. He checked his mirrors, took a good look around to make sure that they were away from prying ears and eyes and opened his window. The air was the sweetest that he could remember tasting despite the tang of fertiliser that tainted it. Compared to the air in the van, it was the purest of the pure.

Raitis couldn't get the van out of first gear as they trundled along the track. His two colleagues in the rear were cursing him, the track, the women, their boss, and life in general. Under different circumstances, their profanity would have made him laugh but there was nothing funny about their situation. When they were told to chain the women to the radiator in the cellar, he had thought that they would be sent back to pick them up later on. He felt sick to the core when Oleg set the building alight. The three women that they left behind were Latvian, like him. He felt sorry for them. They had been tricked into becoming prostitutes by Ivor Markevica and his cohorts. Faced with the choice of taking a legitimate job earning two hundred Euros a month or less in Latvia, or travelling to the UK and potentially earning ten times that amount, it was easy to lure young women away with the promise of highly paid jobs. Once they were in transit, they were easy to capture and easy to control. If they didn't do as they were told, their families in Latvia were slaughtered one by one until they capitulated. The traffickers were ruthless and brutal.

Raitis had become friendly with the three women and he had nearly intervened when the house was torched. Letting them burn knocked him sick. He had watched how brutally Oleg had dispatched the black girl once she had passed the drugs through her system. He had slit her throat in the blink of an eye, cleaned her blood from the blade with her hair and put the knife back into its sheath before she had stopped twitching. Oleg was an animal, permanently angry with the world. He was an ex-mercenary with a bitter hatred of the Russians. Many Latvians resented their country's occupation by the Soviets, but Oleg's hatred was on a different level. Raitis wanted to help the Latvian women, but he feared Oleg. Had he tried to intervene; he would be lying in the outhouse next to her with his throat cut. To stop Oleg, he would have to kill him, but he was too far up the food chain for that to happen. Raitis had allowed himself to get too close to the women, but he wouldn't make that mistake again. He couldn't set out on a one-man crusade to stop the trafficking of women. They were contraband, nothing more.

The van lurched violently to the left as the front wheel dropped into a pothole, it bounced out, and then lurched again as the back wheel followed suit. It prompted a chorus of cries from the back of the van including several questioning his ability to drive. The world record for the number of times the word 'fuck' can be used in one sentence was shattered. He ignored the abuse, eager to swap vehicles as quickly as possible. The sign above the converted barn was clear now, Fletcher Bros. This was the right place. He pushed the van as fast as he could. As they neared the garage, a man wearing blue overalls and boots opened the barn doors to reveal two vehicle bays. He had heavy boots and a beanie hat pulled down over his head to just above his eyebrows. Raitis could see a white Mercedes van in the left-hand bay. The man waved him towards the empty bay on the right.

Inside the barn was a modern workshop fitted with hydraulic ramps, and deep inspection pits. The walls were covered with steel spanners and wrenches of every shape and size and power tools were fixed to organised racks. It was a professional setup and Raitis was impressed. He had taken an apprentice mechanic job when he first left school, before the opportunity of earning a hundred times more as muscle arose. The garage that he had worked in was almost prehistoric in comparison. He nosed the van in as far as he could, and the mechanic closed the door behind him. It was a huge relief. He turned off the engine, opened the driver's door, and jumped out. The sound of the van's rear doors opening told him that his colleagues were as desperate to get out of the stench as he was. He could hear Oleg cursing at the top of his voice but then he suddenly went quiet.

Raitis walked towards the back of the van and stopped in his tracks when he was faced by two men holding pump action shotguns. His colleagues were already stood with their hands above their heads.

'Put your hands up and get on your knees.'

'What the fuck is this?' Oleg snarled.

'Do it now,' the mechanic who had opened the doors ordered. His accent was British, probably local, and that spelled trouble. Raitis noticed that his hands were spotlessly clean. Neither of the men looked grimy enough to be one of the Fletcher Bros. 'I won't repeat myself and I really don't care if you live through this. I don't have to kill you, but I will if needs be.' Raitis did as he was told, followed closely by the other two. They knelt and put their hands behind their heads. 'Good, now where is the zombie?'

Raitis looked at his colleagues. They didn't have much choice but to tell them. He kept quiet and left it to Oleg to speak. 'It's in a briefcase on the front seat.'

One of the men gestured with his head and a third man that he hadn't noticed went to check for the drugs. 'Do you know who those drugs belong to?' Oleg sneered. 'You're already dead men.'

'I've got the case. Cuff them to the van.' The mechanic ignored Oleg as if he hadn't spoken. He was ice cool.

'What about these lot in here?' One of the men looked into the back of the van. The black women were huddled together as far away from the back doors as they could against the front seats. They were mesmerised by what was happening. He shook his head in disbelief at the smell and covered his nose with his sleeve. 'They must be carrying something inside them, there's shit everywhere in the back of the van.'

'Untie them and leave them. They look like they need a break.'

'You had better get used to the smell of shit,' Oleg snarled, 'because you're up to your necks in it. You have no idea who you're fucking with.'

'If you speak again, I'll blow your head off,' the mechanic said calmly. 'Do you understand me?'

Oleg nodded and spat on the floor. Raitis was cuffed to Oleg by one hand and then attached to the tow bar by the other. The metal bit painfully into his flesh. Oleg's other hand was cuffed to the van, making it impossible for him to stand up.

'There are balloons full of gear in this bucket.' One of the men said as he untied the mules. 'Could be heroin or cocaine; it would be a shame to leave it behind?'

'We'll take it and see what the boss wants to do; could be a decent bonus in it for us. As long as we have zombie, nothing else matters but hurry up!' It was obvious to Raitis that the mechanic was a pro. He wouldn't think twice about eliminating them if they caused problems.

'Okay, keep your hair on.' The last but one girl was cut free. 'That's it, ladies, you're free to explore. You'll find all the restaurants and bars in the city centre, just a half an hour ride on a number 79 bus. Keep hold of any balloons that come out of your bottom and you'll be very wealthy women,' he wittered to himself as he freed the last girl. The women rubbed their wrists and cowered in the van, wide eyed and confused, frightened, hungry, and tired. 'They haven't got a clue what's happening, have they?'

'Let's move,' the mechanic shouted. The three men jogged to the Mercedes and climbed in. Exhaust fumes drifted into the bays as it pulled forward. When the van was clear of the barn, one of them jumped out and slammed the doors closed. Raitis heard keys and the sound of the locks being fastened. 'See you, boys. Enjoy the rest of your day!'

'Fuck you!' Oleg shouted after them. It was a futile gesture. They had been stung good and proper. 'We need to get out of these fucking cuffs,' he moaned. Spittle flew from his lips as he spoke. His face was purple with anger. 'I will find them and skin them alive. We need to get out of here!' He was panicking. What had happened wasn't necessarily their fault, but Raitis knew how things went down when an operation went wrong. The shit rolled downhill. They had been in charge of the zombie when it went missing, therefore they were responsible, and Oleg knew it too. 'Ivor will bury us alive.'

'Don't panic,' Raitis said calmly. 'This was not our fault. We have been stitched up. There was nothing that we could have done.'

'You can explain that to Ivor for me,' Oleg scoffed. He looked around the garage in a panic. Sweat trickled down his forehead. 'Look at all those tools on the wall. We can use them to get out of here and then follow those bastards.'

'They're long gone by now.' Raitis said shaking his head. 'What we need to know is who is the rat. If we find the rat, we find the drugs, and Ivor will be happy on both fronts.'

'You can turn into Sherlock Holmes if you want to but right now, we need those bolt cutters.' Oleg pulled hard as he spoke hurting Raitis's wrists.

'Take it easy, Oleg.'

'Hey you!' Oleg shouted to the women in the van. They were untied but still cowered in the van. 'Get out of there!' Oleg's face was red with anger and frustration; the veins at his temple pulsed visibly. 'Get out of the van!' he shouted.

'Don't shout at them,' Raitis said. Oleg turned and glared at him. 'You will panic them. Talk to them calmly.'

'Fuck off, you pussy,' Oleg snapped. 'Hey! Move it quickly!' he shouted again. 'Get out of the van. I need you to pass me those bolt cutters.' The women stirred and one of them reached for the door handle. 'Yes, that's it. Pull the fucking handle and get out. Move it!'

'Calm down,' Raitis said shaking his arm and looking him square in the eyes. 'We need to stay calm or we're not going to get out of this without being locked up for a very long time. Are you listening to me?'

'What?' Oleg's eyes seemed to focus. 'What are you bitching about now? I am trying to get us out of this.'

'Listen to me,' he explained calmly. 'I think that they're going to tip off the police as soon as they're a few miles away,' Raitis said. 'They know the women have drugs inside them. Why do you think that they left the women behind?'

'Why would they do that?' Oleg frowned. 'There's no way they would phone the police.'

'Why didn't they kill us, Oleg?'

'What?'

'They didn't kill us because they know that we won't be around to bother them. Think about it for a minute.'

'It doesn't make any difference. We need to get out of here, so unless you have a better idea, shut up!' Oleg turned back to the women. He pointed to the door. 'Get out of the fucking van!'

'It is obvious that we need to get out of here, now calm down and stop shouting at them. We need them to stay calm.' The women were chattering to each other. They seemed to be settling down. It had dawned on them that their captors were now handcuffed to the van and couldn't reach them.

'Get out of the van!' Oleg was losing control. His face was a mask of anger. The women looked at him with contempt.

'Calm down,' Raitis said again. As he did, he noticed one of the women opening the side door of the van. They were still wary of Oleg but as they moved towards the door nervously, they seemed convinced that he couldn't do anything to hurt them. They climbed out and huddled closely, taking comfort from each other. They were talking to each other at a hundred miles an hour which seemed normal, but they were staring and pointing at Oleg with blank dead eyes, which wasn't normal. Raitis could feel the hatred radiating from them.

'Hey,' Oleg ranted. He pointed to the wall as best as he could with his cuffed hand. 'Pass me those bolt cutters.' The women looked at him blankly. 'There you stupid bitch!'

'Oleg, shut up and stay very calm,' Raitis sensed a shift in their mood. The fear was dissipating and now there was hatred in their eyes. 'We do not want to freak them out.'

'What are you talking about?' Oleg sneered. 'Will you stop bitching!' He pointed to the wall where the tools were displayed. 'Get them for me,' he shouted at the group of women repeatedly. 'There. Pass me those bolt cutters!' he bellowed at the top of his voice. The sinews in his neck stood out like wires ready to snap. The women continued to stare at him angrily but none of them moved. There was an expression of defiance on some of their faces and it was an expression that was spreading. 'Listen to me! Pass me those cutters and do it now!'

One of them followed his gaze and looked over her shoulder at the tools. Raitis was amazed as she walked over to the wall where the cutters were hung on a rack. He couldn't believe that she was doing what he had told her to do. It looked like she was going to help her captures to break free. *Fear has a strange effect on people*, Raitis thought. He watched as she stood with her back to them for a while studying the tools.

'Good!' Oleg nodded. He laughed like a lunatic. 'They're right in front of you, you stupid bitch! Pick them up, hurry up!'

She ignored him and turned to the others, speaking in a language that Raitis couldn't understand. The others walked closer to her and chattered looking over their shoulder every now and then. Raitis was baffled until she picked up a long handled lump hammer and stared at Oleg. The others each picked a tool, some heavy, some sharp. They had hatred in their eyes as they approached. Then Raitis knew exactly what they were going to do.

CHAPTER 11

Jason Greene was reporting what he thought was a robbery in progress at the pawnbroker's shop when the door opened, and two men walked out. They were bruisers, heavy leather jackets and grade one haircuts. He reckoned that they were too old to be serving military although they had the look of those that had. One of them locked the door with a key and Jason noticed a tattoo between his thumb and forefinger. It was a spade with a three at the centre. They looked up and down the street furtively before heading past the cafe and across the road. Jason raised his mobile and snapped off some pictures. As he did, one of them looked directly at him. His heart stopped beating in his chest as their eyes locked. Time seemed to slow down; it almost stopped completely. There was anger in the man's eyes and if looks alone could kill, Jason would be dead. It was obvious that he didn't want his face on camera; not one bit. The man stopped and turned to walk towards him, but his accomplice pulled him back. At first, Jason couldn't understand why but then he heard the faint sound of a siren. The men began to run away but one of them took out his mobile and snapped a picture of Jason and his Range Rover. His pulse was still racing when a black Ford screeched to a halt outside the emporium. A man the size of an oak tree climbed out and ran to the shop door. He rattled the handle and pushed his shoulder against it, but it wouldn't budge.

Jason took the Rolex watches from his pocket and stashed them under his seat and then he opened the door. He had to help Kayla if he could. 'They locked the door behind them,' Jason shouted across the road. 'I saw them leaving.'

'Did you call the police?' Stirling asked.

'Yes.'

Stirling turned around and waved him over. 'You saw someone locking the door?'

'Yes,' Jason jogged to him. He pointed in the direction that they'd run. 'They ran that way; two big guys with cropped hair.'

'How do you know that they don't work here?'

'I know the owner, Kayla. We were going to do some business. She told me to meet her here this morning but when I got here, the door was open, but the shop was empty. I hung around for a bit, but she didn't come out of the back then I heard a noise in the office and called the police. They're on the way.'

'They're already here,' Stirling grunted. He took a step back and then launched himself at the door. His shoulder connected with the frame, but it barely moved. It was reinforced to jewellery store industry standard and it was going nowhere. As big as he was, he needed some assistance.

'I've got a heavy bar in the boot,' Jason offered.

'Go and get it.' Stirling nodded. He pressed his face against the glass and looked inside. Nothing looked out of place, which was odd if a robbery had occurred. A marked police interceptor arrived on the scene and the uniformed officers climbed out. It was closely followed by a second. 'DS Stirling, MIT.' He flashed his ID.

'What can we do to help, Sarge?'

'Call an ambulance for a start.'

'Yes, Sarge.'

'Have you got a big red key in your boot?' Stirling asked, referring to the heavy battering ram that the force used to break entry.

'No, sorry, we're on traffic detail but we were closest, so we responded.'

'I've got the paramedics on the line. What are the injuries?'

'I don't know yet,' Stirling said as Jason returned with a metre-long piece of iron. He took the metal from him and looked at it. 'What is your name?'

'Jason Greene.'

'Okay, Jason, I won't ask what this is doing in your vehicle,' he said with a wry smile as he took the bar from him. Jason Greene blushed. Stirling aimed the bar at the crack between the door and the frame below the lock, ramming it in as deep as he could. It bit into the frame and he forced it one way and then the other, feeling the frame crack. He drove it deeper as the gap widened and then forced it hard to the left, but it wouldn't budge.

'Do you want a hand, Sarge?'

'Yes, lean on this with me. Ready, one, two, three!' They leaned on the bar with all their body weight. A gap appeared at the bottom and they jammed the bar further into it, wrenching it hard, and fast. Stirling slammed his shoulder hard against the door and it splintered and cracked before it flew open. 'We're in!'

Stirling headed straight for the office door. He twisted the handle and it opened. The office was roomy and bright despite having no windows. A slim computer monitor sat on a tidy desk and a stack of well organised shelves were fastened to the back wall. To his left, there was a tall Cannon safe and a stack of cardboard boxes marked with the shop's logo. A single chair lay upturned on the floor and a small pool of blood no bigger than a saucer stained the carpet. Apart from that, nothing looked out of place and there was no sign of Kayla Yates. Stirling called back to one of the uniformed officers.

'Bring Jason in here.' The officer stepped outside and returned with him in tow. 'Did you actually see Kayla in here today?'

'No, I didn't see her. I spoke to her on the telephone.' Jason was confused. 'Isn't she in there?'

'No.'

'But I heard her cry out.'

'You're sure?'

'Positive,' Jason lied. He was almost sure that he had heard her but not certain. He couldn't be positive what he had heard. 'I called the shop just after nine. I spoke to her and she told me to come in. The door was open. She must be in there.'

'You're sure that she didn't leave with the men that you saw locking the door?'

Jason fumbled in his pocket and took out his phone. He scrolled to the pictures he'd taken. 'Here, look.'

Stirling looked at the pictures. 'We'll need those photographs,' he said waving a uniformed officer over. 'We need these pictures sent to MIT immediately.'

'Yes, Sarge.'

'You can send them to me before you go,' Stirling said as he looked at the pictures. Sure enough, there was no sign of anyone on the pictures but two men.

'What is your number?' Jason asked. Stirling handed him a business card and Jason sent the photographs. The big detective looked angry and confused. 'Have this picture distributed to traffic too,' he said to one of the uniforms. 'They must be in the area somewhere.'

'Yes, Sarge.'

'Can you follow me, constable?' He gestured to the second uniformed officer to follow him and they went back to the office. 'There's a small toilet there with no windows. I need you to walk the office with me. Check every inch of floor, ceiling, and walls as you go.'

'Sarge.'

They walked around the room in opposite directions, but it was empty.

'Once more but this time double-check.' Stirling sighed. He stamped his right foot every few feet, searching for an access hatch to a cellar but the entire floor was concrete. The uniformed officer knocked the walls with his baton but there was no other way out of the office. 'She can't vanish into thin air.'

Stirling looked around again and his eyes focused on the Cannon safe. It was tall and wide. The uniformed officer raised his eyebrows and puffed out his cheeks. 'It's definitely possible,' he said reading Stirling's thoughts. 'But if she's in there, she's in trouble.'

Stirling approached the safe and tried the handle. It didn't budge. It was just below chest height tall and a metre wide. 'If she is in there, we've got minutes to get the thing open.' He pressed his ear to the cold metal door. It was six inches of composite; not a sound came from within. He picked up the iron bar and thumped the end against the door and then listened again. He couldn't hear anything but the blood racing through his ears. Stirling looked around again as his mind computed the options. There simply was nowhere else that she could be. 'Get on the comms and get me any safe experts that we have on our books, locksmiths, or welders, whatever it takes to get that door open. We need them now. If they can't get here in half an hour, tell them not to bother.'

'I'm on it, guv.'

Stirling took out his mobile and punched the speed dial for the DI. It rang three times before she answered.

'I'm on the other line; I've got the Chief on hold. What have you got?' Annie said. He could tell that she was driving and trying to do a dozen things at the same time.

'I'm at the pawnbrokers but when I arrived, there was a robbery in progress called in.' Stirling paused for a moment.

'Bloody hell!' Annie said surprised. 'Have you spoken to the owner?'

'No. That's why I'm calling. The owner is a woman called Kayla Yates, but she isn't able to talk right now.'

'Is she hurt?'

'I think so. A witness saw two men leaving the shop and locking the door. I've gained access but there's no sign of her.' Annie remained silent. Obviously as baffled as he was. 'There are signs of a struggle and there's no other way in or out. I think she's been rammed inside the safe, guv.'

'Is it a robbery or is it something to do with our case?'

'There are no signs of a robbery, guv.'

'Jesus,' Annie's voice was just audible. 'What are you doing about it?'

'I've put out a call for safe experts, locksmiths, and welders. All that I can do now is to wait.'

'Is there a computer there?'

'Yes.'

'Google the make and model of the safe. If anyone knows how to get into it, it will be on the net.'

'Will do,' Stirling said moving behind the desk. He hadn't thought of that but then that's why she was his DI. 'We need to pick up Antonia Barrat and find out why she went to see Kayla Yates, guv. She needs to be in protective custody whether she wants it or not.

'I'll have her brought in,' Annie agreed. 'Call me as soon as you have news.'

'Will do.'

Annie switched calls with a sick feeling in her guts. 'I'm sorry to keep you, Sir,' Annie apologised. 'It would seem that someone else wants the name of Barrat's source.' She pulled her car off the main road towards the parking compound at the back of Canning Place. The rain became more intense and the tourists visiting the Albert Docks were scurrying for cover in plastic raincoats every colour of the rainbow. The Liverpool eye turned slowly, unaffected by the weather. 'When she left the station this morning, she went straight to a pawnbroker's shop in Kensington. It appears that the owner has been assaulted and locked inside her safe.' The gates opened and she steered her vehicle into an empty parking bay. The Chief's silence was an indication of his concern. 'DS Stirling is at the scene. He's pulling out all the stops to get her out.'

'Her?'

'Yes, Sir,' Annie said. 'The owner is female.'

'Marvellous!' The Chief muttered sarcastically. 'Do we know what Barrat was expecting to witness at that mill?'

'No.'

'Is she looking for another police corruption headline?' There was bitterness in his tone; bitterness and concern.

'She wouldn't divulge any information about her source or what she was investigating.'

'No, I bet she wouldn't. She was quick enough to call us when she was in danger, wasn't she?' Annie didn't justify his statement with an answer. 'How many dead at the fire?'

'One of the trafficked women and one of the women found in the basement didn't make it. The other two are touch and go. We won't know if they're going to pull through for a couple of days.'

'And the woman in the safe,' he added with a snort. 'How likely is it that we get her out alive?'

'I don't think it's very likely.'

'Nor do I. This case is running away from us, Inspector.'

'We have a briefing scheduled in three hours, Sir. Will you be able to attend?'

'No, I'm heading to a meeting in London this afternoon. Superintendent Ramsay is flying back from Malta tomorrow morning. I need you to take the helm for now until we appoint a Senior Investigating Officer.'

'Yes, Sir.'

'For God's sake, get this bloody mess under control before then!'

'Will do, Sir,' Annie said calmly. She didn't feel calm. The Chief hadn't asked enough questions to know the full details of the case or to be able to offer any useful advice. Reading between the lines, he was more concerned about how the events would be written up in press. A kidnapped journalist, people trafficking, a woman beaten, and locked in her safe; she could write the headlines herself. Her focus was on the victims; her superior's priority was the public's perception of the Merseyside division and that rankled.

CHAPTER 12

Paul Fletcher had to get his brother Pete to a hospital quickly but he daren't move until he knew that they'd gone. He listened intently to what was going on. After what seemed like an age, he heard the Mercedes engine fire up and he heard it pulling out of the service bay. The sounds of the garage doors being slammed closed and locked drifted to him and then there was an angry male voice shouting and swearing. His accent was foreign. Paul was confused when the anger in the voice was replaced by fear. He listened to the screams coming from the service bay and they'd made the hairs on his forearms bristle. He had heard the term 'bloodcurdling' many times but never really understood its true definition until that moment. The fear in the wailing was audible. He could actually hear terror and anguish in their cries, and it made his blood run cold. He could make out two or maybe three men and God knows how many women. There were many female voices shouting in several languages that he had never heard before. Whatever was going on in their garage, it wasn't what had been arranged and it didn't sound like it would end well. He couldn't envisage what was going on, but it was bad. The female voices were angry, of that there was no doubt. At first, the men were shouting words, mostly 'no' but their voices were soon replaced by screaming. Their fear was contagious, and Paul was beginning to panic. What if they came for him next?

They were helpless. He had to do something. His brother still hadn't regained consciousness and the colour had drained from his face; he looked grey. When he heard the diesel engine leaving, he figured it was the men with the guns that had left, and he began to grind his bindings against the edge of a metal shelf. Five minutes later, he was free. He untied Pete and rolled him onto his side and then placed a bundle of clean cloths under his head to make him more comfortable.

Paul turned the closet handle and pushed. It was open, having said that, he couldn't remember ever having a key for it. He opened it an inch and peered through it. The corridor was clear. He tiptoed along the corridor until he reached the door that led into the service bays. It was partially open. The shouting had reached fever pitch, but the screaming had subsided somewhat. He held his breath as he looked around the doorframe to see what was going on. When he did, he immediately wished that he hadn't. He saw black women, flashes of silver and splashes of claret. The scent of blood floated on the air. Paul closed the door quietly and locked it before slamming a deadbolt home and then he walked quickly to the outside door. Through the window, he could see that the service bay doors had been shut and padlocked from the outside. Whoever the women were, they were locked in but there were plenty of tools in there that could be used to break out. If they set their minds to escaping, then it would take minutes. He couldn't waste time. They were distracted by their bloodlust. It appeared to be too late for the men that they were beating. There was nothing that he could do against that many armed women. The men were a bloody mess and the screaming had all but ceased.

The Fletcher brothers had made a bad decision to make some quick money. Business had been slow, and their cash flow was unpredictable. They had some big accounts but the bigger the company, the slower they were at paying. They had needed a cash injection into the business, but he wanted nothing to do with whatever was going on in their garage. If they ended up facing criminal charges, so be it. He needed help and his brother needed an ambulance. As he walked into his office, he took a deep breath before picking up the telephone and dialling 999. When the call was picked up, he paused before saying, 'Police and ambulance please. You'd better send a lot of them.'

CHAPTER 13

Stirling googled 'Cannon Executive Safe' and the product link appeared. He cut the link and pasted it into the browser with 'How to open' as a prefix. The screen filled with methods to drill and open the lock but no two looked the same. There were several animations and three YouTube links. As he paged down, a news report from San Diego caught his eye. He clicked on it and read the headlines. A young girl aged seven, who had been taken to a new office block by her father, had climbed into a safe and the door had slammed behind her. He read on and then shouted for the uniformed officer.

'Any joy with an expert?'

'Nothing, Sarge. They're putting calls out but nothing yet.'

'I need you to go into the cafe next door and ask if there are any builders in there or if they know any local builders that use heavy duty drills.'

'Sarge?'

'A little girl was trapped in the same model of safe and no one had the combination,' Stirling said pointing to the screen, 'and they feared that she would suffocate. Her father, who was a fitter on site, managed to drill several holes through the door so that his daughter could breathe. It was three hours before the safe was opened and there was no doubt that his quick thinking saved her life. We need to try the same.'

'Yes, Sarge. I'm on it.'

Stirling read on through the specifications and gleaned as much information as he could. His eyes kept drifting to the safe. He wanted to put his fist through it and drag her out.

'Sarge,' the uniformed officer interrupted his thoughts. 'This is Charlie Boyle. He owns a local building firm. He was just on his dinner break.'

'Hello, Charlie, I'm sorry to interrupt your lunch,' Stirling offered his hand. The stocky builder reciprocated. His thick sandy coloured hair was coated with dust. 'I know this may seem odd, but I need some holes drilled through that safe and I need it done in the next ten minutes.'

Charlie looked at the safe, a confused expression on his face. He rapped on the door with his knuckles and sucked air between his teeth as if he was pricing an extension and upping the price by a thousand pounds. His hands were dry and caked in cement. He rubbed the grey stubble on his chin and shook his head. 'I'm not sure it can be drilled.'

'It can definitely be drilled,' Stirling said firmly. He turned the computer monitor towards him and pointed to the screen. 'If you look here, this safe was drilled with both titanium and diamond tipped bits. It took a while to break through, but they managed it.' The uniformed officer looked surprised. Charlie shook his head in disbelief. 'I've read it and it's genuine. A man in San Diego drilled holes in the same model of safe and saved his daughter from suffocating.' He allowed them a few seconds to read what was on the screen. 'Have you got the drills capable of doing it?'

'Yes.'

'And titanium drill bits?'

'Yes.' Charlie looked confused again. 'That little girl was suffocating you said?' He narrowed his eyes as he spoke. 'Are you telling me that someone is in that safe?' Stirling nodded slowly. 'Jesus Christ!' His eyes widened. 'Is it Kayla?'

'I think so.' Stirling nodded. The builders jaw dropped open. He looked like he had been punched in the stomach. 'Do you know her?'

'I see her in the cafe every morning,' Charlie stuttered. 'She's one in a million.'

'She really needs your help. She needs it right now.' Stirling could see he was shocked, but they needed to move quickly. 'We don't have much time, Charlie.'

'Give me two minutes,' Charlie looked wounded. He stared at the blood on the floor and dialled on his mobile. 'It's me. Listen. I need the Bosch drills and the titanium bits. If we have any diamond tips, bring them too.' He had an afterthought. 'We'll need some kind of coolant to keep the bits keen. Get Kenny to go to the supermarket and tell him to buy as many six-pint cartons of milk as he can carry. I'm in Kayla's shop next door to the cafe. Bring everything we have and make it snappy. She's in trouble.' He put the mobile away and knelt in front of the safe. His face had darkened to a mask of concern. 'How long has she been in there?'

'I don't know for certain but it's less than half an hour.' Stirling gestured to the computer. 'I've Googled that make and model. The specifications are here. It means nothing to me, but it might help you to know where to drill.'

Charlie studied the spec and pulled a tape measure from his belt. 'According to this spec, there are reinforced plates around the lock mechanism so if we drill above and below, we have a chance.' He moved the tape again. 'It says the top half of this safe is comprised of lockable storage, a sort of safe within the safe and metal shelving.' Charlie looked at Stirling and frowned. 'That means that the only space for a large bulky item is in the bottom third. I'm not sure that you could force a human into that space without…' He didn't finish his sentence.

Stirling understood what he was saying. He didn't comment as he couldn't think of anything positive to say. It was a relief when two of Charlie's employees arrived with four hard storage cases and a carton of milk.

'This is Noodle,' Charlie introduced his workmates, 'And this is Greggs.' Stirling acknowledged them with a nod and a half smile. Shaking hands wasn't an option as they were fully loaded with kit.

'Margaret donated the milk so that we can get started,' Noodle said enthusiastically. 'Kenny has gone to get some more from the supermarket although fuck knows what he'll come back with. He thinks it's a wind up.' He stopped talking when he saw the safe; an anxious look crossed his face. 'Is she really in there?'

Nobody answered his question. Charlie gestured to the safe door. 'I'll start eight inches above the lock, Noodle, you start eight below. We'll use the titanium bits for now and see how we get on. Greggs, I want you to use the diamond bits and go for the side.'

'Got it.'

They opened the cases and assembled the business end of the drills with chuck keys, while slotting the power packs into the handles. Charlie placed the bit against the cold metal and squeezed the trigger. The first drill kicked into life, a second drill just a minute later. Greggs aimed the diamond bit against the middle of the side wall and the drill began to whirl noisily. Stirling felt his stomach tighten into a knot when after two minutes the drills had barely scratched the surface.

CHAPTER 14

Toni closed her eyes and let the hot water soothe the stiffness from her muscles but they still ached and no matter how many times she soaped her skin she couldn't seem to wash away the filth. She could still smell the odour of the women at the mill and it wouldn't go away; neither would the questions in her mind. Where had the women come from, and what nightmares had they suffered to make them desperate enough to leave their homes and their families behind and travel thousands of miles without ever knowing their destination? What horrors had they endured from the traffickers along the way and where had they been taken to now? What would happen to them, would they live or die, and would death be the kinder option? Was Mike being tortured for information that he didn't have? Her head was spinning with a myriad of scenarios, none of which were good.

She tilted her head backwards and let the spray hit her face; it ran through her hair and down her back, its warm caress took the stress away for a moment and let her linger in a world where there were no problems. She wanted to stay there a while longer, but reality summoned her back into the real world. When she opened her eyes, the questions returned with a vengeance. The entire episode had been a nightmare. One that she couldn't come to terms with. It wasn't something that she could shake off and put to bed, in fact she had a niggling feeling that it was going to haunt her for a long time to come. There didn't seem to be an outcome that could offer any closure, no satisfactory endings, or questions answered but then that was the story of her life.

She had thought briefly about talking to her partner about exactly what had happened, but it was difficult to explain the anxiety and fear that she had experienced. How can you convey your mental turmoil to someone who wasn't there and hadn't experienced the fear? She didn't think that it could be done. There were so many PTSD sufferers nowadays, mostly soldiers. She had interviewed several of them for an article but hadn't really appreciated their plight. They suffered alone because they couldn't convey their pain to their loved ones. How could they? You had to see what they'd seen to begin to understand what they were feeling. As much as she loved her partner, she hadn't been able to find the words to explain how she was feeling. The trafficked women and the feeling of helplessness had triggered the memories of losing her parents. She shared their sense of hopelessness and their desperation. She had been there and felt it, bought the T-shirt, worn it, washed, and ironed it. 'Hopeless' was a lonely place to be. They were surrounded by others and yet alone, just as she had been after her mother's disappearance. Her feelings of guilt couldn't be shared with anyone else. Her deep sense of anxiety for the women was hers alone and she would have to come to terms with it and cope, or it would consume her. She knew the human condition was a fragile one, but she had never appreciated just how fragile until now.

She turned off the water and instantly wished that she hadn't. As the air touched her skin it chilled her, and goose pimples covered her from head to toe. She reached out for her towel and wrapped it around her shoulders; its thick pile quickly absorbed the moisture from her skin and warmed her. She stepped out of the shower. The black floor tiles were heated, an expensive addition to her home following the success of her book. She had had the bathroom extended into an extension at the rear of the house. It was an L-shaped wet room with a walk-in shower that could fit a small saloon car inside it. The water jets sprayed from all angles, washing and massaging simultaneously. At the other end of the room was a floor to ceiling mirror with a make-up area built around it. She checked the marble shelf where she had set her stuff down while she showered and saw the screen on her phone flashing. Her mobile had been constantly ringing since she left the station, but she wasn't ready to talk to anyone yet, especially her editor, who had been ringing nonstop since eight o'clock. There was no doubt in her mind that she would have heard the bones of her story already and she would guess that there were photographs. Toni could hardly wait to log on to her Dropbox account. The pictures that Mike had taken would have uploaded instantaneously. Part of her wanted to see them but the other part was terrified of what they would show. It was the frightened part of her that had stopped her from accessing them so far.

It wouldn't stop her editor, Julia Fox from wanting to see them. Julia Fox had a number of sources within the civilian employees at police headquarters and she had no qualms about using them, but she seldom checked how credible their information was. Julia would print the phonebook if she thought it would sell newspapers. She paid well and they would be queuing up to tell her about one of her freelance reporters being a witness to trafficking, a drug handover, and a kidnapping. That was journalistic gold dust. She would have to speak to her at some point because if she didn't, Julia Fox would print her own version of events. The screen stopped flashing as the answering machine kicked in.

Outside at the rear of her property, a man named Letva Lapsa crouched in the shadows and watched the house. His muscular frame was hidden by the black clothing that he wore. The bathroom lights had gone on twenty minutes ago, but he hadn't moved an inch since then. Patience was the difference between success and failure, life and death. She would be drying herself off soon, naked, and vulnerable. Then he would move. Until then he could rehearse what was to come in his mind. He had trained for operations like today for years mastering tracking, watching, waiting, questioning, and the disposal of a target. Time had dragged since she had left the police station but now time had run out for her. Finally, they knew who she was and where she lived. His fingers touched the hilt of his knife and he slid it silently from its sheath. The movement was barely a whisper on the gentle breeze. The blade was blackened steel to stop it reflecting light, razor sharp one side with a double serrated edge the other. It was a thing of violent beauty designed for one thing only, the destruction of tissue; the blade was honed to slice and to cut and the saw edge was expertly engineered to rip flesh and splinter bone.

The knife felt reassuringly heavy as he checked his watch and slid it silently back into the sheath. He checked the backpack and then he was ready. Instinct told him it was time. He moved silently; his weight expertly distributed between each boot to lessen any sound. Hugging the shadows at the edge of the wall, he moved with stealth and purpose and he was at the back door in under a minute. He knew it was alarmed. There were contacts fitted to the door and motion sensors covered the entire ground floor. She was cautious and professional but then so was he. If anyone entered the ground floor of the house by force, the alarm would sound. The box on the exterior was wireless and powered by the mains and supported by a built-in backup battery. Cutting the mains electricity wouldn't stop it from ringing. Knocking it off the wall wouldn't stop the internal box from ringing either and that was loud enough to alert nearby residents. Breaking into the ground floor wasn't an option.

Without pausing, he reached for the fishing twine, which he had hidden behind the drainpipe earlier that morning when she first arrived home. One tug was enough to free up the rope, which it was tied to and it uncoiled and fell from the roof with a dull thud. He listened intently.

Nothing.

Pulling the rope with his left hand, he checked that it was still securely fastened to the chimney stack and once he was happy, he put his right boot against the wall and climbed. His powerful upper body took his weight making it look as if he was walking up the wall. He was quiet and swift, and his powerful limbs pulled him to the top of the drainpipe in under a minute. He climbed onto the flat roof of the extension that Toni had had built a year before and squatted low. He could see condensation on the inside of the bathroom window and the silhouette of a female moved towards the bedroom. If his mission had been simply to silence her then she would have been dead already. She needed to answer some questions. He would enjoy the asking but she certainly wouldn't. He kept low as he crept towards the house. He was across the extension roof in seconds. There was a Velux window on the main structure, which allowed light into the converted loft. That was his way in. Clearing up as he went was essential. He cut the rope from the chimney and let it fall into the back yard before sliding the blade beneath the beading which held the double-glazed unit in the frame. The glass unit slid out silently and he twisted the locking handle inside and opened the window before putting the glass unit back into place and tapping the beading around the glass. Rebuilding the window took half a minute at best.

Lowering himself quietly into the loft, he pulled the window closed and locked it. Even close inspection from the inside wouldn't belie his entry point. He moved like a liquid across the attic to the access hatch and crouched next to it. It slid open easily, without making any noise. He listened to the sounds from the house beneath him. There was a marked police car at the front of the house, but they couldn't see the rear of the structure. Letva knew that they wouldn't be armed, which gave him a huge advantage. They thought that they could offer her protection, but they couldn't. Not from the people that he worked for.

Toni padded across the tiles into her bedroom and flicked through her iPod. She had surround-sound fitted all through the house as part of the renovations. The screen showed 'Little Lion Man', Mumford and Sons. It was an ode to anyone with regrets and she often played it when her soul was unsettled. She pressed play and looked into the mirror. Her figure was pleasing on the eye, lean but not thin, firm but not muscular, and her regular sessions on a sunbed kept her skin tanned. She hummed along as Mumford became more agitated.

'It was not your fault but mine. It was your heart on the line. I really fucked it up this time, didn't I my dear, didn't I my dear?'

That was how she felt. She had fucked up. Her ambition and greed had blinded her to the point where she hadn't researched the mill before walking into it blindly. She was so desperate for the story that she didn't consider the consequences properly. A dull thud outside made her look towards the window and the landline began to ring. She was tempted to answer it just in case it wasn't Julia Fox but there was no way of knowing so she ignored it. As she wrapped a small towel around her long hair, she heard a loud knock on the front door. She wasn't expecting anyone to visit and she never had cold callers. Her driveway was gated, the garden walled, and secured. The fingers of fear touched her spine; the goose pimples returned in an instant. Her breath quickened and she could feel her heart pounding in her chest. She had hardly had time to imagine who it was when another knock echoed up the stairs, louder this time. She grabbed her dressing gown and struggled into it when she heard a shuffling sound outside on the extension roof. She turned Mumford down a touch and listened again.

Looking out of the bedroom window she could see the familiar stripes of a marked police interceptor on the road at the front of the house. Its presence allowed her to relax a little. Her breathing slowed slightly, to almost normal. A uniformed officer stood at the gate talking to a man in an ill-fitting suit. They were looking at the house as they spoke. Another loud knock reverberated through her home. She turned and caught sight of a shadow moving on the roof of the extension but when she tried to focus on it, there was nothing there. One second it had been there and the next it was gone. Her mouth went dry and there were alarm bells ringing in her head. She edged closer to the rear window and peeped around the edge of a navy-blue velvet curtain. Raindrops streaked the glass as they raced downwards to the sill. Her eyes scanned the flat roof, left to right.

Nothing.

Bang, bang, bang on the front door. The noise made her jump. She drew the curtains closed and moved back from the window, hand shaking with fear although she didn't know why. Bang, bang, bang, louder this time.

'Miss Barrat!' A voice called through her letter box. 'It's the police. We need to talk to you immediately.' She was fixed to the spot for a moment, but another sharp knock snapped her into action. 'Miss Barrat!' Bang, bang, bang. 'Can you open the door please!'

'I'm coming,' she called. She was flustered. Flustered, confused, and frightened. She checked her appearance in the mirror, slipped her feet into her slippers and headed along the hallway to the stairs. Stainless steel frames held black and white pictures of her family. They lined the walls from the top of the staircase to the bottom. She held the walnut banister as she descended. Her legs felt shaky and her knees were weak. The letter box was open, fingers poked through and eyes watched her. She felt scared in her own home for the first time in her life. 'Who are you again?'

'Detective Constable Maxwell,' the voice said. 'Detective Inspector Annie Jones sent me. I need to talk to you urgently, Miss Barrat. Open the door please.'

Toni hesitated at the bottom of the stairs. She pulled her dressing gown tightly closed and opened the door. Detective Maxwell and his colleague eyed her suspiciously. His black skin glistened with rain. He straightened his tie and stepped in without waiting to be asked, flashing his ID as he did so.

'This is DC Lucas,' Maxwell introduced the other detective. 'We need to take you into protective custody, Miss Barrat,' he said abruptly.

'I don't have time to sit in a police station all day,' Toni said defensively. Not being in control was fraying her nerves. 'I told the DI this morning that I can't divulge who my source is and my position hasn't changed.'

'There have been some major developments since then.' Maxwell looked at the photographs on the wall and frowned. He looked bemused. 'Can you tell us what you were doing at Yates's Emporium this morning?'

'That's none of your business.' Toni distractedly rubbed her hair with the towel, trying hard to be aloof.

'Did you leave the police station and go straight to see your informant?'

'What?' Toni asked incredulously.

'Did you go direct to see your source at the pawnbrokers?'

'Don't be ridiculous!'

'Maybe you were angry with them or you wanted to warn them about what had happened?'

'Now you are being ridiculous.'

'Why is that so ridiculous?' Maxwell shrugged.

'Because it is!'

Maxwell tucked his hands inside his pockets and shook his head. He had a quizzical look on his face. 'Someone thinks that you went there to see your informant.'

'What the hell are you talking about?'

'Someone went to see her after you did.'

'Who did?' Toni felt sick inside.

'We don't know.' He shrugged. 'Why did you go there?'

'To see Kayla!'

'Kayla Yates?'

'Yes.'

'Is she your informant?'

'No, of course not!'

'How do you know Kayla?'

'We live together. She's my partner for God's sake!'

CHAPTER 15

Annie leaned against the van to put on her stab vest. Miranda Snow stood smoking a cigarette and kicked at the wheel, impatient and irritated. The wind blew in off the river and brought the smell of rotting fish with it. They were downwind of fertiliser factories that bulldozed mountains of waste fish into their concoctions every day. They were great for growing plants but not so good for the local residents that lived within the range of the prevailing winds. Annie could see why they'd picked that unit for a vehicle exchange. The Fletcher Bros garage was a reasonably big operation and considering that it was within the city limits, it was fairly remote. The skyline was dominated by the suspension bridge. Its huge green girders seemed to glimmer against the grey clouds. Her attention was drawn by the area helicopter swooping overhead. It wasn't often that she was beneath it twice in one day. Her feet had hardly touched the ground since the first report about Antonia Barrat. The case was snowballing out of control and the brass still hadn't appointed a Senior Investigating Officer. She was hoping that whatever was left behind at Fletcher Bros would give them something concrete to work on. Armed units had entered the premises and so far, all was quiet.

'Clear!' The armed unit's senior officer signalled that it was safe to enter the garage. 'We need paramedics in here quickly!'

Annie and Miranda walked towards the building, heading for what she assumed was the customer reception area. It had been manufactured from a conservatory and bolted onto the front of the converted barn. The difference between the old and new was stark. The glass roof allowed the light in and gave it an airy feeling. Three of the walls were glass; the wall behind the counter was solid and decorated with certificates and photographs of custom-built supercars. Two beaten up red leather settees provided seating. Annie spotted a large calendar that depicted a blond 'mechanic' wearing fishnet stockings, thigh length boots and not much else. Annie didn't believe that she was a mechanic at all. She did have a spanner in one hand, although why she was licking it was beyond Annie.

'Why do I feel that I've been transported back to the 80s?' Annie mumbled.

'I am way too young to remember them,' Miranda said from behind her.

'You keep telling yourself that.' Annie grinned sourly. The reception desk ran wall to wall, waist high with an access hatch that was raised. Annie stepped through the hatch and then through a doorway that led to the main office.

'This is Paul Fletcher.' The senior armed officer said as they walked in. Inspector Norris gestured to a man in oily overalls who was handcuffed and sat on a chair. Fletcher's curly brown hair was receding, and he wore a full goatee beard and thick moustache. He had his head bowed, looking at his steel toecap boots. 'He made the 999 call.'

'What happened?' Annie asked.

'I am not a hundred per cent sure what happened. We were tied up and shoved into a cupboard. We didn't expect any of this,' Paul Fletcher said forlornly.

'Who put you in the cupboard?'

'Three men walked in with shotguns. We had no choice.'

'What did you expect to happen?' Miranda asked.

'We agreed to swap a van for a customer, no questions asked.' He shrugged. 'They paid us upfront to dismantle a Volkswagen van and we sold them a second-hand Mercedes. That was it.' He looked at Annie as he spoke, and she could see from the look in his eyes that he was masking the truth. 'The Merc has gone so I'm assuming they left here in it.'

'I want the registration of that vehicle,' Miranda snapped.

'The paperwork is on the desk there. They're copies; they took the originals.'

Miranda picked up the registration document and handed it to a uniformed officer. 'Have this called in immediately. The occupants are armed and dangerous.' The officer nodded and stepped outside to use his radio. 'When was this 'sale' arranged?' Miranda asked sarcastically.

'This morning.' Fletcher blushed. 'It was a rush job.'

'You didn't think that it was suspicious?'

'I didn't think it was going to be 'this' illegal,' he stuttered. 'They stitched us up completely. I didn't expect this…'

'I bet you didn't,' Annie murmured. It wasn't the first time that day that she had heard that. She didn't think that the Fletcher brothers were involved with the traffickers. Paul Fletcher certainly wasn't. He wasn't the type, but it didn't detract from the fact that they were aiding drug dealers. Whether they were aware of it or not was irrelevant. Ignorance was no defence from the law. 'Who is "they"?' Annie asked.

'I didn't ask. The money was too good to turn down.'

'How were you approached?'

'By telephone,' he stammered. 'It was via an existing customer. We were wary of the deal in the first place. It was too good to be true and we couldn't see what harm it would do but when they turned up with guns…' He shrugged. 'My brother Peter tried to talk our way out of it and got his skull cracked for his troubles. By then it was too bloody late.'

'Where was the caller from?'

'What?'

'What accent did the caller have?'

'I didn't speak to them. My brother did,' he looked confused. 'Why would that matter?'

Annie ignored the question. 'The men that hit your brother and tied you up, were they foreign?'

Fletcher shook his head as he thought back. 'They had local accents.' He frowned as he thought of something else. 'The men in the garage were foreign. That is a definite. I heard them shouting, Polish or Russian or something like that.'

'Okay, Mr Fletcher,' Annie said with a sigh. 'We'll need to sit down with you and talk in detail about who this existing customer is.' Fletcher nodded and returned his stare to his boots. 'Do the CCTV cameras work?'

'Yes, but they took the disks.'

'How do you know that?'

'I saw them when they were tying us up.'

She gestured to a uniformed officer. 'Get him to Canning Place.'

'The paramedics are with his brother,' Norris gestured to a hallway that ran from the office to the service bays. 'He's had a nasty blow to the head, but he seems to be responding.'

'We'll need to send someone with him to casualty,' Annie ordered.

'I'd rather it was an armed escort,' Miranda insisted.

'Agreed,' Norris said, 'I'll have two of my men with him in the ambulance.'

'Excellent.' Annie nodded. She was anxious to get into the service bays. 'Let's see what we're dealing with.'

'I hope you have a strong stomach,' Norris said. He gestured to the hallway and Annie followed him. Armed officers stood on each doorway making sure that the scene remained secure until the DI was ready. 'Between their bowel movements and straightening things out with their captors, our female guests have made quite a mess.' He tried to make light of the situation, but his expression belied the dark humour in his words. It was a coping mechanism for many in the force. They walked down a dark corridor; the walls scuffed with oily handprints. A door on her right led into the converted barn. The roof was arched and high, clear Perspex sheets allowed daylight inside. 'Under normal circumstances, it would be prudent to handcuff their hands behind their backs but in light of their stomach problems I am not so sure that it is helping the situation.'

Annie stepped inside and immediately recoiled. The stench was revolting. Miranda took a small pot of vapour rub from her coat pocket, smeared a dab beneath her nostrils and then handed it to Annie as she looked around. The eleven Africans were lined up against a long workbench that ran the length of the wall, hands cuffed in front of them. Their heads were bowed, eyes darting left and right full of fear and trepidation. Blood spatter stained their dark skin. She could smell them. It was the thick cloying smell of the unwashed. It mingled with another more familiar aroma. Death. The Volkswagen was the same make and model that they'd seen on the CCTV. The side loading door was open; as were the doors at the rear. Three bodies hung from the bumper and tow bar like the bloody carcasses of slaughtered game. A puddle of blood, the circumference of a paddling pool had spread around them. Green clad paramedics exchanged shakes of the head as they checked the men for signs of life.

'These two are dead. This one has a pulse,' one of them said in a monotone voice. There was no excitement in his tone and as Annie looked at his injuries, she could see why. He looked towards Annie. 'It's faint but it's there.

'Any ID?'

'Nothing. Can we get him set free of the van, Inspector?'

Annie nodded although her facial expression showed that she didn't hold out much hope for the injured man, pulse or not. His head was swollen out of all proportion, the face unrecognisable as human. She looked at Norris and he signalled to two of his men.

'Make sure he has a two-man escort. He's not to be left alone at any point.'

'I want all three fingerprinted ASAP,' Annie added.

'We need to move him now,' the paramedic shrugged. 'Or he has no chance at all.'

'Move him. We'll have him printed in the ambulance.' Annie offered. 'It's the best I can do.'

'You're all heart.'

Annie ignored the jibe. Her sympathy for traffickers and the like was non-existent. If the man lived, he wouldn't talk. If he died, he wouldn't talk so she simply didn't care. He had had no compassion for his victims when he was healthy, and she had none for him now that he was broken.

'Who chained them to the van?' Miranda asked cryptically.

'I don't know,' Annie said with a shake of her head. 'Is this a double-cross by their own people or were they hit by a rival mob?'

'They left the mules behind,' Miranda mused. 'They left the men alive too. This was not the Russians.'

'They don't leave anyone behind to tell the tale.'

'Exactly.'

Miranda circled the Volkswagen and searched the driver's cab. Annie studied the bodies of the men. She knew that Miranda was desperate to find the zombie. Stopping a delivery of this new narcotic would be a huge coup for the Drug Squad but it would also stop the collateral damage caused when a shipment of such a powerful substance hit the streets. It would be her teams of detectives that would be left cleaning up the mess after all. Preventing it from being distributed at all was the ideal scenario but Annie had the feeling that others wanted the shipment even more.

'There's no sign of the zombie,' she cursed. 'We can take our pick for murder weapons though,' Miranda said as she noticed a number of bloodstained tools scattered across the floor. Annie walked to the back of the van and looked inside. The smell of excrement became stronger. Miranda pointed to one of the buckets inside. 'There are parcels in here. I'm guessing there is cocaine in them so why leave them behind?'

'Maybe they have passed them since being here. Whoever hit them knew exactly what they wanted,' Annie said, glancing at the women. 'Do any of you speak English?' One of the women nodded. She had shoddy trainers and jeans that looked like they hadn't been washed for seven years or more. 'What is your name?'

'Una,' the woman replied. Her eyes were full of fear.

'Where are you from, Una?'

'The Congo.'

'Where did you meet these men?' Annie pointed to the back of the van.

'Calais,' Una said. 'They tell us if we swallow their drugs, we can be taken to England. They beat us and rape us and they kill my friend.'

'I know they did.' Annie nodded. 'They can't hurt you anymore. We will take care of you now.' Annie smiled and turned back to Miranda. 'I think that a rival crew targeted the vehicle switch,' she pointed to the butchered men, 'they cuffed them, took the zombie and scarpered, leaving them restrained, but alive.' She gestured to the mules. 'They realised that their captors were incapacitated and took advantage of the situation. Beat them to death.'

'Karma is a bitch.'

'It is indeed,' Annie agreed. 'We know Barrat witnessed a handover this morning, which was compromised by a leak and now this. This tells me that the leak is high up in the organisation.'

'I agree. I think they told their bosses that the mill was compromised. They have a witness. Their bosses shit themselves and tell them to move the cargo from Aigburth in a hurry. They arranged a plan 'B' in a hurry and tried to lose the Volkswagen. With the vans swapped, they were going to take the mules to a safe location, but someone knew exactly where and when the switch was going to be.' Miranda frowned. 'This gang has an informant in the hierarchy, and they are going to be desperate to find out who it is.'

'Which leads us back to Antonia Barrat,' Annie agreed. 'If I was running that operation, I would make it my number one priority to question her and I wouldn't stop until we had.'

'You're having her brought in though, right?'

'Yes.' Annie nodded. Her lips thinned. 'But we can't protect her forever.'

Miranda shook her head. 'How do you want to do this?'

'Your team is going to be busy here, so I'll arrange taking prints from them,' Annie pointed to the bodies, 'and see what pops up on the system. I'll have the interview with Fletcher organised and follow up on whoever set this vehicle switch up.' She paused. 'You take the paperwork from here and chase up the Mercedes that they left in. As for the mules and the cocaine, you're the Drug Squad detective so you're welcome to them.'

Miranda nodded and half smiled. 'I'll get some interpreters down to the hospital and the station when we process the mules. They may be able to tell us something more about who brought them here.' Her mobile rang and she waved at Annie and walked away leaving her to have one more look around the van. Annie avoided looking at the bodies again. There was nothing to be gained from that. She needed to escape the vile mixture of odours although she knew that she would be able to smell them long after she had showered. It would cling to her nostrils for days.

CHAPTER 16

Jim Stirling felt like his eardrums would explode as the three drills whined incessantly against the metal. Their progress was painfully slow, and the air was filled with the smell of scorched metal and boiled milk. There was a pile of blunted drill bits growing ever higher in the middle of the room and he was seriously concerned that they would blunt them all before they could penetrate the safe. The diamond tipped bits were doing the most damage and the side wall appeared to be weaker than the door, but they were still a long way from penetrating it. His mobile rang and he reluctantly left the office to take the call. Kayla's Emporium was busier than it had ever been, unfortunately everyone was in uniform and they weren't buying.

'DS Stirling,' he answered.

'Sarge, its Max,' Maxwell used his nickname. 'Listen, I am with Antonia Barrat at her house.'

'Good. Is she okay?'

'Yes.'

'Don't take any messing about from her. She's in danger.'

'That's not why I'm calling, Sarge.'

'What's up?'

'Antonia Barrat and Kayla Yates are in a relationship.'

'What?'

'They're partners, Sarge.'

'What?' Stirling frowned. 'In the pawnbroker business?'

'No, Sarge. They're partners, as in they live together.'

'Why didn't you say that in the first place?' Stirling mumbled a little embarrassed. 'That explains why she came straight here this morning.'

'It does. It never crossed my mind.'

'Nor mine.'

'She wants to know what's happened to Kayla.'

'What does she know so far?'

'Nothing. I said there had been an incident at the shop involving Kayla and now she's panicking. She's ringing her mobile constantly.' Maxwell lowered his voice. 'She's demanding to be allowed to drive to the shop.'

'Don't let her go anywhere alone.'

'I've told her we can't take her there yet but she's kicking off. Unless we physically restrain her, I can't see how I can stop her?'

'Jesus.' Stirling sighed. He shook his head and then a thought occurred to him. 'Ask her if she knows the combination to the safe.'

'The safe?'

'Just ask her.'

'I'll have to go back into the house. Give me a minute.'

'Hurry up, Max. This is urgent.'

Stirling heard him muttering and the sound of his footsteps. Then a door opened, and he could hear a woman's voice. She was angry and upset. He heard Max ask her about the safe combination followed by Antonia launching a string of expletives which he couldn't make out, but it ended with 'You fucking idiot'.

'Did you hear that?' Max moaned.

'Put her on the phone.' He heard shuffling and more swearing from her.

'Who is this?'

'DS Stirling, Toni. We met this morning.'

'Where is Kayla?'

'She is at her shop.'

'The phone is engaged and she's not answering her mobile.'

'She can't answer it right now.'

'Is she hurt?'

'I think so.'

'You think so?' she snapped. 'What does that mean?'

'Exactly what I said,' Stirling remained calm. 'I think that she is hurt. Do you know the safe combination?'

'Is this some kind of joke?'

'It is no joke, Toni.' The irony of asking the author of a book about police corruption the combination of her safe wasn't lost on Stirling. 'Kayla is in dire trouble. I need the combination to her safe.'

'Are you mad?' she hissed. 'Why would you need to open the safe? I demand to know what is going on.'

'While you're arguing with me, Kayla is dying!' She was stunned into silence. 'Now do you know the combination or not?' the big detective snapped. She remained silent. Stirling could almost hear the cogs in her brain winding. She was running through every possible scenario as to why the police would need the safe combination. 'You need to trust me. I'm trying to save Kayla's life. Do you know the combination?'

'Yes.'

'Then give it to me before it is too late.'

She paused unable to see why he was so insistent. 'I don't understand why you would need to open the safe.'

'It is best that you don't for now. I need that number and I need it now.' His tone became more urgent almost pleading.

'Have you got a pen?'

'Yes,' Stirling scrambled in his jacket pocket for a pen. 'Go on.'

'Zero, five, one, four, two, eight, two, six, five.'

'Thank you, now I need you to go with Detective Maxwell and do everything that he says,' Stirling said quickly. He hung up and ran to the office. The incessant whine of the drills grew louder. 'I've got the combination, Charlie,' he shouted to the builder. The three men stepped back while Stirling bent to enter the combination. His index finger was shaking as he punched the numbers into the lock.

Zero, five, one, four, two, eight, two, six, five. As the last digit was entered, the mechanism whirred and clicked, and the door opened.

CHAPTER 17

The Past

Antonia Barrat remembered the night that her mother didn't come home as if it had happened a few days ago. Her memories of painful times had such clarity. Coming so soon after watching her father burn to death, it was a crushing blow. After the funeral, her mother had tried to return to her job as an accountant, part time. She did a half day here and there at first not wanting to leave Antonia for too long. It was her intention to build up to a three-day week, but she never had the chance. One Thursday afternoon, she kissed Antonia on the cheek and left home for the office to meet with an important client. She never turned up and when she was late coming home, Antonia panicked. She had spent that first night nervously biting her nails and looking out of the curtains much to the annoyance of her aunt, who was equally as concerned but tried hard not to show it.

'Come away from the window, Antonia. The neighbours will think we're spying.'

'Have your bath, Antonia. I'm sure she'll be back by the time you're ready to get out.'

'Drink your milk and eat your biscuit while we wait. I'm positive that she won't be long.'

'Come on to bed, Antonia, I'll read you a story until she comes home.'

'Now you sleep tight and don't have bad dreams. When you wake up, Mummy will be home, you'll see.'

Antonia didn't sleep tightly, and she did have bad dreams and when she woke up her mother wasn't home. She never came home. The police were at a loss. They explored every possible avenue but as the days turned into weeks and weeks became months, they scaled down their search. Her mobile phone and bank accounts had shown no activity since the day that she disappeared; apart from her salary being paid in. They never actually said that they thought that she was dead, but Antonia knew that they were thinking as much. First, her father was murdered, and then her mother vanished and there was no tangible explanation why. Not that an explanation would have mattered back then; all that mattered was that they were gone, and Antonia was heartbroken.

Her aunt had done her best to look after her under the circumstances; she had recently had her own tragedy when her husband had drowned. She did her best to keep her positive, but no amount of promises or reassurances could have comforted her. She was a child robbed of her parents. Her world had disintegrated in the space of a few months. She had been loved, truly loved. She had felt loved every second of the day and only when that love was cruelly snatched away did, she realise how all-encompassing her parents' love had been. They had protected her, wrapped her in a blanket of unconditional love as parents do and when the blanket was ripped from her, the world had become a frozen desolation. The emptiness that she felt was infinite. Her heart had become a void; a black hole. Nothing could console her grief, stop her tears, or mend her broken heart. She was simply shattered. Her loneliness was debilitating. At night she begged and pleaded to God and to Jesus and to all the saints to bring back her mother and father, but they didn't listen. They were gone and she wanted to be with them even if that meant dying. She didn't want to live without them.

As the years went by, she stopped begging God to make things right. He wasn't listening and if he was, he didn't care. She stopped waiting for her mother to appear and her tears became less frequent. Not because the pain eased but because she had nothing left. The emptiness inside remained and she spent her early years searching for something to replace the love that she had lost. She found it hard to make friends. Relationship after relationship failed and the void could never be filled. She fell in love in her early twenties, married quickly and had two beautiful children but her insecurities drove him away and he left in the third year of their marriage. His abandonment of their home only reinforced her belief that everyone that she loved left eventually. She loved her children, Charlotte and William and shared custody with her ex-husband. He worked from home and had them Monday to Friday, when Antonia picked them up from school. She had them every weekend and every school holiday but when she took them back to their father her world became empty once more.

In a crowd, she was still a lonely woman. At work, she had few friends and found it difficult to fit in at social events. She tried and failed to feel the warmth from another's embrace. In the arms of a lover, she remained ice at her core. She could go through the motions, smile at the right moment and laugh politely at the right time but nothing truly satisfied; nothing filled the endless void inside her. Toni had never questioned her sexuality until life led her down a road where she met her soul mate. Nothing had made her complete, until she met Kayla Yates.

CHAPTER 18

Antonia ran up the stairs taking them two at a time. Anger and frustration bubbled away beneath the surface, driving her to the edge of insanity. Why did that big oaf demand the safe combination? What the hell could they possibly need that for? It was the not knowing. Kayla was in trouble, life threatening trouble but they wouldn't tell her what was wrong. How does that work? Here she was again with a loved one in peril and she knew nothing about it until it was too late for her to do anything about it; helpless and hopeless.

Again.

The not knowing was excruciating. She was verging on becoming hysterical. Antonia Barrat was not a weak woman. Life had hardened her. In the workplace she was as sharp as a blade. Where some struggled under the pressure of deadlines, Toni flourished. Life's trivial issues bounced off her as if she was titanium but beneath the bulletproof exterior was a frightened little girl. She couldn't lose anyone else. Tears streamed down her cheeks and she could hardly suck any air into her lungs. Kayla was in mortal danger and there was nothing that she could do about it. Helplessness and hopelessness, her old companions returned.

Again.

Kayla could die. The detective had told her as much, but he wouldn't expand. How dare he decide that she couldn't be made aware of the situation? How dare he? If there was a chance that she could lose her then she had every right to know. She couldn't lose Kayla, not after everything that she had endured. Her heart had been broken so many times that she wouldn't survive another loss. Not this time around and not Kayla. Surely the world couldn't be that cruel; surely not.

Her legs pumped furiously, driving her up the stairs. As she neared the top of the stairs, she heard a woman screaming, 'No! No! No!' over and over. The voice was muffled as if submerged under water, but it was also strangely familiar. She felt a draft on her damp skin. A breeze that could only have come from outside, but it didn't register in her brain as unusual. Nor did she question its source. She kept running towards her bedroom desperately trying to force oxygen into her bloodstream. The woman's screams were deafening and reaching a piercing level. The word 'no' had become a long and drawn out wail of pain and agony. She tripped over her own feet and fell heavily onto her front. She jarred her arms and cracked her chin against the floor, clacking her teeth together hard. The screaming stopped abruptly, and she suddenly realised that it had been her own anguished cries that she had heard. She remained still and tried to get a grip on her emotions. That frightened girl was a woman now.

She couldn't allow her emotions to regress; she had to regain control of herself despite feeling that she might implode.

Detective Maxwell followed Antonia up the stairs. Her reaction to hearing that her partner was in trouble was to be expected, if not a little dramatic. His job was to get her to Canning Place in one piece and he intended to do that. She had flown up the stairs like a banshee and he was a few steps behind her when she fell. She fell hard. The crack to her chin had thrown her head backwards painfully. She lay still for a few seconds. That worried Maxwell but at least she had stopped screaming. He knelt next to her and felt for the pulse in her neck. It was strong. She murmured and groaned and turned onto her back rubbing at her jaw with her hands.

'Ow,' she moaned. Her eyes opened and cleared slowly. They were red and watery. 'What did I do?'

'You tripped.' Maxwell pulled her to her feet and let her steady herself. 'Are you okay?'

'I think so,' she said a little embarrassed.

'Are you sure?'

'Yes.'

'You need to get dressed and throw a few essentials into a bag, toothbrush, deodorant and a change of clothes will do for now. We can come back at a later date for you and pick up anything that you need.'

'Kayla?' Antonia fought back a sob. 'What has happened to her?'

'The sergeant will let us know how she is as soon as he knows anything solid, okay?' Maxwell squeezed her elbow. 'He didn't tell you anything because he doesn't want to speculate until he's certain. You understand that?' Antonia nodded. 'Get yourself packed and dressed and we'll take you to wherever she is.'

'Promise?'

'Once we know for sure where she is, yes.' Maxwell nodded. He didn't know why he had made that promise. Maybe he couldn't stand to see a woman so upset. His wife always told him that he was too soft to be a detective. She said that one day he would listen to a criminal's sob stories and let them go with just a telling off. She wasn't far off the mark hence he was still a DC after five years. 'Hurry up. We need to get a move on.' Antonia headed for her bedroom without a sound. She felt sickened inside. Her angst was gut wrenching. She was frightened and she could feel her stomach starting to cramp.

Above their heads, in the loft, Letva listened to their exchange and cursed under his breath. They were taking her into protective custody. He lifted the hatch a fraction and peered through the gap. The black detective was wide at the shoulders and just as wide at the hip. He looked soft around the middle, but he was young, and he was heavy, and he wouldn't go down without a struggle. Letva didn't know where his partner was but he knew that he would have one and that he wouldn't be far away; two detectives inside and two uniformed officers outside. The odds were against him. He needed to talk to the Barrat woman, at length. He needed time alone with her to find out what they needed to know. His employer wanted everything done discreetly. Killing police officers wouldn't go down well although hurting a few never caused a problem. He sighed and decided that trying to take her now would be foolish, but he could send her the message. It would be a message that she wouldn't forget. He reached for the rucksack and opened it. Emptying the contents, he proceeded with plan B.

CHAPTER 19

The safe door clicked open an inch. Stirling reached for it and gripped the edge with his fingertips. He pulled it wide open and looked inside with his breath stuck in his chest. The broken twisted body of Kayla Yates was indeed in the safe.

'Paramedics!' Stirling bellowed. They were on standby in the shop area and were next to him in an instant. Kayla was crammed into the lower section of the safe. Her heels were beneath her buttocks, her feet splayed at an odd angle. A throaty gasp came from one of the paramedics. Stirling couldn't see her face. Her head had been forced between her knees and twisted away from them; her arms were behind her back, twisted and pointing in unnatural positions. She looked like a rag doll crammed into a toy box. The urge to drag her out was overwhelming but he knew that he could do more harm than good if he did. He had no idea if she was alive or not. His instinct told him that she was not. The cramped space, limited air and the obvious severe damage to her limbs indicated that she had suffered an agonisingly slow and painful death, finally suffocating.

A paramedic tried to find a pulse, but her body was at an awkward angle.

'We need to slide her out and keep her in that position,' another paramedic said. 'You take her head and her knees, and I'll take her feet and hips. Be careful with her neck.' His colleague looked pale, but he agreed. They had both seen too many ruined bodies to be squeamish. 'Sergeant, I need you to grab her belt and lift her when we're ready.' Stirling nodded. They knelt and reached for Kayla, each grabbing their given part. Stirling gripped her leather belt and felt the warmth of her flesh beneath his knuckles. He was almost certain that he had felt her twitch. It could have been his imagination, maybe wishful thinking but he felt hope rushing through his veins. 'On three, one, two, three!'

They pulled and nothing happened. Kayla remained stuck for a second.

'Again, harder this time. On three, one, two, three!'

After another tug her body slid from the safe, limp, and floppy at the joints. The paramedic felt for the pulse in her wrist. His face showed no reaction as he moved his fingers to her neck to try again. He nodded his head and gestured to the oxygen tank. 'She's alive.' He looked at Stirling. 'Just. We need to get her in ASAP.' He turned to his colleagues. 'Cut the zip ties from her wrists.' Stirling stood up and stepped back. The oxygen mask was put over her nose and mouth. Her eyes were swollen closed and a deep purple colour near the bridge of the nose. Her eyelids flickered and she sucked in a deep breath. It was the best thing that Stirling had heard all day. 'Let's get a line into her. I need fluids and a spinal board. We can't lay her flat. It will cause her less pain if we move her as she is.' Her arms were twisted against the natural bend of the elbow, the joints dislocated and swollen. Stirling felt sick as he noticed the lumps at her shoulders which were also dislocated; the ball joints prised from their sockets. He couldn't tell if they'd broken her to put her into the safe or if it had been part of an interrogation. It didn't matter for now. Tendons and ligaments would mend, and bones could be set. The mental trauma may linger but her flesh would heal eventually. The surgeons could fix her; that was their job. His was to catch the bastards who had done this to her.

CHAPTER 20

Maxwell checked the spare bedrooms and the bathroom to make sure that they left the house secure. The windows were fitted with decent quality locks and she had a good alarm system. Once he had checked them, he was wandering from room to room passing the time until his charge was ready to leave. He looked at the roof of a large extension. One of the spare bedrooms gave him a good view of it. It was ideal for would-be burglars to use as access to the upper floor windows or to climb onto the roof. He glanced across the slates and noticed that skylights had been fitted to allow light into the attic. They were a weak point, but the property had intruder alarm sensors fitted throughout the house. He made a mental note to ask Antonia if they were fitted in the loft too. If they weren't, they needed to be. Max checked his watch. She was taking a long time in her bedroom and he was becoming irritated. They were protecting a vulnerable witness from what was potentially an international drug cartel. Organisations like that didn't take any prisoners and he had nothing more lethal than a pen on his person. The longer they delayed, the more likely an incident would happen. He went to her bedroom and put his ear against the door.

'Are you okay in there?'

Silence.

He knocked again, louder this time. 'Antonia, are you okay?'

Silence.

'Antonia!'

Silence. He twisted the handle, but it was locked from the inside. Irritation was fast being replaced by fear. He was about to knock again when the door was snatched open.

'I'm all right,' her voice made him jump. She looked nervous and poked her head around the door, hiding her body from view. He noticed that her lip was quivering. 'Have you heard anything about Kayla yet?'

'Not yet.' Max checked his mobile just in case; the screen was blank. He peered around the door. She was still dressed in her robe. 'Are you planning on getting dressed any time soon because we really need to be going?'

'I'm sorry.' She blushed. 'My stomach. It always decides to play up when I become anxious.' She shrugged and tried a smile. 'I will be downstairs as quick as I can. I promise. Waiting outside my bedroom is a little unnecessary and you're making me more nervous if I'm honest, so please...' She gestured to the stairs with her head. 'Wait down there.'

Max frowned and shook his head. He looked at his wristwatch as if that would speed things up. 'Leave the door unlocked,' he warned.

'Oh really!' Toni sighed. She was more embarrassed than angered by the request. 'Is that really necessary?'

'If you pass out or have an accident, I need to get to you. I'm here to protect you so please don't make my job any more difficult than it already is.' He tilted his head and raised his eyebrows as if speaking to a naughty child. She rolled her eyes to the ceiling and nodded. 'Good. And be as fast as you can.' She nodded again and pushed the door too but not closed. 'Once you're packed, we need to go in a hurry,' he said to the door. He sighed and reluctantly turned towards the stairs. It wasn't ideal but fear affected victims differently. If she was going to have a case of the squirts, then he would rather it happened in her bathroom than on his backseat.

Letva watched the black policeman amble down the stairs. He exchanged a few words with his partner in the hallway and then they stepped outside the front door. He had detected the scent of cigarettes earlier, but it was not pervading from inside her house. It had been carried in by the detectives when the front door opened. The smell clung to their clothes and their skin. He could sense their concern. They were nervous and he could smell their fear. They were taking the opportunity to smoke while they waited for her to get dressed. He slid the hatch open and sat on the edge of the frame, dangling his legs over. Taking his weight with his hands, he lowered himself down silently. All the time he was ultra-aware of the surroundings. Barrat had walked through her bedroom into her bathroom. He heard her footsteps and he heard the slight creaking sound as she sat on the toilet seat. He tiptoed to her door, pushed it open slightly, and then moved to her bed where the thing that he was looking for had been left. Picking it up, he slipped back into the hallway as silent as a ghost. The second bedroom was to his left. He crept inside and placed it on the dressing table, leaving the message next to it. It took less than ten seconds. He moved back onto the landing. Pulling the door closed, he jumped for the hatch, grabbed the lip, and pulled himself back into the attic in one fluid movement. He pushed the lid over the hatch but made sure that it was askew; not too obvious, just enough.

Toni waited until the stomach cramps had eased. She was desperate to get to Kayla's shop, desperate to see her, desperate to hear what had happened and desperate to hold her tightly in her arms. Nothing would stop her from getting to her, nothing except her nervous constitution. Times of severe stress led to her body emptying the contents of her intestinal tract in the space of minutes. The worst of it was gone. She opened the medicine cabinet and took two Imodium tablets. Needing to sit on the toilet every five minutes was the last thing that she could handle at the moment. She looked at her face in the mirror and decided to take another two just in case. Better to be safe than sorry.

Once she knew that it was safe to move from the toilet, she padded into her bedroom, dropping the robe in a heap. She grabbed a pair of faded jeans from a drawer, stepped into her underwear and then slipped into the denim before pulling on a jumper. It took her seconds to tie up her hair into a ponytail and slip on a pair of black Uggs. She took a quick look in the mirror, horrified by the bags beneath her eyes, she dabbed some concealer beneath them and then grabbed for her handbag.

It was gone. She frowned and swore beneath her breath. Had she left it in the bathroom? She jogged into the bathroom and checked. There was no sign of it. Had the detective taken it in a bid to hurry things up? If he had, she would bend his ear. That was for sure. It held her keys, her phone, her make-up, and her purse. You do not interfere with such essential kit, policeman or not.

'Detective,' Toni shouted. Her bedroom door was ajar. 'Have you moved my handbag?'

There was no reply. She walked briskly to the top of the stairs. The two detectives were stood outside just beyond the front door. She could see them from the knees down. 'Detective Maxwell,' she called.

'Yes,' he answered walking towards the house. He pushed the door as he stepped inside. 'Are you ready yet?'

'Have you moved my handbag?'

'No,' Max said flatly. 'Why would I move your bag?'

'Are you sure?'

'Positive.'

'Well someone has.' Toni put her hands on her hips. She was red with embarrassment and anger. All she wanted to do was go to Kayla. 'They must have. It was on the bed.'

'Is your mobile in the bag?' Maxwell frowned. He had his 'I'm talking to a child' face on again.

'Yes.'

'Then I'll ring it and we'll see where your bag is,' he said patiently. He scrolled through his numbers until he found hers. He pressed dial and they listened. Her mobile began to ring. 'It's up there somewhere.'

Toni could hear her ringtone, but it was muffled. She frowned and listened intently. It sounded like it was coming from the spare bedroom. She couldn't remember going in there never mind taking her bag. She sighed angrily and opened the door. Sure enough, there was her bag on the dressing table. It was odd. She hardly ever went in there. At first glance, the room was still and looked normal. Toni walked towards her bag and the ringing became louder. She was confused as to how it had come to be there and there was something else out of place, something that didn't belong there. Her brain didn't register what it was because it was a random shape; random and yet somehow familiar. She squinted as she tried to make sense of what she was looking at.

'Have you found it?'

Toni heard him but she didn't answer his question. She stopped in her tracks and stared at the dressing table. Her handbag had been placed in the middle; its reflection caught her eye in the wide mirror behind it. She couldn't compute what was she was looking at. It was next to her bag but it didn't belong there in her bedroom, in her house; in fact, it didn't belong anywhere this side of nightmares.

'Antonia!' Max called. Curiosity filled his voice. 'Have you found your bag?'

She opened her mouth to speak but no sound came out. The object was roughly triangular but the edges were softer, sort of blurred. Focusing on it was difficult as it was transparent and so were the contents. She could see through it and see its reflection behind it and so it bamboozled her brain. Suddenly it began to make sense. It was a clear polythene bag filled with a clear liquid; maybe water. The bag was tied at the top making it narrower and giving it a triangular shape. It was vaguely familiar as it reminded her of fairgrounds when she was a child, where you could win a goldfish in a bag of water. She always felt sorry for the fish, confined to such a small space. This bag was similar except she couldn't see a goldfish. Something was floating in the liquid; two orb shaped objects. Toni focused on the nearest. The back of the orb was ragged, pink tendrils floated behind it.

'Antonia?' Max shouted louder, concern now in his tone. She could hear him on the stairs. As his concern grew, he reverted to a more formal address. 'Will you answer me please, Miss Barrat!'

As she watched transfixed, the orbs rotated slowly to reveal blue circles with black centres; an iris and a pupil on each. Toni realised that she was staring into the dead eyes of Mike James. Lots of people have blue eyes and yet she instinctively knew that they belonged to Mike. She put her hand to her mouth and stepped backwards away from the dressing table. There was an oblong piece of paper pinned to her handbag. The words on the note were scrawled in red lipstick; simple and direct but effective, nonetheless.

DELETE THE PHOTOGRAPHS

Her knees buckled and she stumbled onto all fours. She felt bile rising in her throat and she vomited. Her stomach contents, acid yellow goo splattered onto her beige carpet. She couldn't turn her gaze from the bag. She wretched again and for the second time that day, she heard herself screaming.

CHAPTER 21

Maxwell and the other officers scoured the house, batons drawn, and poised to strike at the intruder. Whoever had broken into the property was both skilled and fearless. That worried him. He was embarrassed that someone had managed to get so close to his primary. His embarrassment was trumped by his fear.

'I need photographs of both the handbag and the clear bag and the note and then make sure that they reach forensics ASAP for printing,' Maxwell ordered the uniformed officers nervously. They were all under no illusions how dangerous their situation was. Training took control as they followed a well learned procedure. 'When the CSIs arrive, have them check the loft first. The hatch is offset. That is how the cheeky bastard got in.' His mobile buzzed and he gestured towards the stairs with his head. Toni followed him nervously, frightened to leave his side. She had managed to gain control of herself momentarily. 'Sarge,' he said as he answered it. 'There's been an attempt to get to Toni.'

'What?' Stirling growled. 'Is she okay?'

'Yes, Sarge,' Max said deflated. He threw Toni a disparaging glance. 'Someone broke in here and left Antonia a message.'

'What?' Disbelief tinged his voice. 'While you were there?'

'Yes, Sarge. I think they came in through the loft,' Max explained as they reached the front door. He visually checked around the garden and then pushed Toni towards the car. She clung to his arm tightly. 'They left a plastic bag with eyeballs floating in it.'

'Human?'

'I think so. Blue ones. And a note saying, 'delete the photographs' was pinned to her handbag.'

'Delete the photographs?'

'That's what it says.'

'What photographs?'

'I don't know, Sarge.' Max bundled Toni into the back of their Audi and signalled to the driver to keep an eye on her. 'I need to get Toni out of here in a hurry.' He closed the car door and walked away so that he could talk without worrying her. 'They could be in the house. We can't search it all safely without help. I've called for armed backup to escort her in but if they've got the balls to break in while we're outside then she's exposed wherever she is, until we get her to the station.'

'Agreed,' Stirling grunted. The more he learned about the way this crew operated, the more concerned he became. Their response to any threat thus far had been both rapid and destructive. They were not afraid of striking the fear of God into anyone that encroached on their business. Antonia Barrat and Mike James, if that was his name, had walked into a wasps' nest and given it a good hard kick and now the wasps were riled and determined to attack anyone within range. 'These bastards are not messing around. They must have followed Toni from the station to the pawnbrokers and assumed that Kayla Yates was her source. Kayla was 'questioned', if you know what I mean.'

'I understand.'

'They were disturbed so they rammed her inside the safe.'

'I see,' Max tried not to let his disgust reach his face. He turned his back so that Toni couldn't see his expression. 'Will she live?'

'I wouldn't bet on it, to be honest.'

'Look, Toni is pretty shook up at the moment, but she's going to ask me what happened. How much do I tell her?'

'Tell her whatever you need to, to get her to the station. Under no circumstances do you take her to the hospital, okay,' Stirling ordered. 'She'll be a sitting duck in a building that size. There's no way that we can protect her there. Once we know Kayla's prognosis, we can look at it again. I'll meet you back at the station and we can discuss these photographs with Miss Barrat.' He paused and swallowed his rising anger. 'She is withholding information from us and I'm beginning to get a little pissed off with her.'

'Just a little?'

'Don't wind me up.' Stirling warned. 'I'll see you there. Do not move without the armed unit.' The call clicked off.

'Yes, Sarge,' Max agreed with the disconnected line. He turned to Toni and grimaced. Her eyes were full of shock and anticipation. He walked back to the vehicle and opened the door. 'Kayla is stable but she's not out of the woods yet.'

'Oh God!' Toni bit her bottom lip and looked out of the window. She felt as if her guts were being squished in a giant vice. 'What happened to her?'

'We're not certain but we know that they locked her inside her safe.'

'The safe?'

'Yes.'

'That's why he wanted the code?' Toni's voice was a whisper. Her face greyed. She frowned as her brain computed the terror that she must have felt being forced into such a limited space and how frightened Kayla must have been when they closed the door. 'Can I see her?'

'Soon.'

Toni knew that meant 'no' but she was too shaken to argue. She didn't think that the day could possibly get any worse.

CHAPTER 22

The Major Investigation Team had set up the incident room in their section of Canning Place. Although a Senior Investigating Officer hadn't been appointed yet, it was assumed that MIT would be at the helm. Annie had been handed the reins until a decision was made. Her section was buzzing and detectives from the other departments that were involved were milling about, waiting for the briefing to begin. She heard the lift arrive and was pleased to see Stirling's huge frame appear. He caught her eye and headed in her direction. Her team was dispersed and disorganised and that made her uneasy. She needed to know who was doing what and when. She wasn't a control freak outside of work, but she did need to be in charge of any investigation; completely in charge. If she didn't know what was going on, how the hell could she steer an investigation in the right direction? Some of her detectives didn't like her scrutiny but they mistook it as a lack of trust in their ability. She wasn't analysing their performance, she was evaluating every piece of evidence and slotting them together in her mind. The detectives that appreciated that fact flourished under her and those that didn't floundered.

'Ten minutes, everyone!' Annie called across the office. 'Check your messages, make any last calls and fill up your coffee cups. We'll get started at three o'clock.' She stepped back into her office and waited for Stirling to step inside before closing the door. She leaned her back against it and took a deep breath. 'I could do with starting today all over again.'

'It has not been the best, guv.' Stirling slumped into a leather swivel chair that looked as if it might buckle beneath him. 'We need to get a grip of this lot before they do any more damage. Did you get anything at the garage?'

'It's early days yet.' Annie shrugged. 'Two dead bodies and a third with his head bashed in, a busload of mules, who are now murder suspects and two brothers, who are so stupid that I'm surprised they know one end of a spanner from another. The drugs were long gone.'

'They're being set up at every turn,' Stirling said. 'The handover at the mill was leaked this morning and then when they try to recover their security and move the drugs, they're hit again. They have a leak at the top of the tree.'

'Absolutely right.' Annie frowned, 'And Antonia Barrat has a bloody good idea where the information is coming from.'

'Did Maxwell call you?'

'Yes.' Annie nodded. 'How many crooks do you know that have the skill and the balls to break into a house while there are police cars outside and detectives inside?'

'Not many.' Stirling wagged his finger. 'I don't think it's a matter of 'balls'. I think it's fear.'

'I'm listening.'

'Whoever is in control doesn't accept failure. His operation has been compromised and he has sent out his minions with a brief to rescue the situation and not to return unless they're successful. They're prepared to do whatever it takes because the repercussions are more frightening than being arrested.'

Annie nodded as she mulled it over. Stirling was right. The sad truth was that a few years in a UK jail would hardly strike fear into the heart of a career criminal from Eastern Europe. When all things were balanced, the rewards of crime were far too enticing. 'Sadly, you're right. How long will Max be?'

'Not long,' Stirling looked at his watch. 'He was waiting for an armed escort.'

'Do we know what photographs they're talking about?'

'No but Barrat does. She's taking the piss out of us and she'll get someone killed if she doesn't come clean.' Stirling's face darkened. His jaw tightened as he spoke. 'Kayla Yates is a mess, guv.' He shook his head as he recalled her injuries. 'They broke her like she was a Barbie doll; her joints were ripped out of their sockets. I wish Barrat had seen the state of her when we pulled her out of that safe. She wouldn't be as keen to mess us about if she had.'

'Any CCTV from the shop?'

'There are images of them entering the shop. Brazen as you like, guv,' he scoffed. 'One of them shut the door and locked the Yale lock and the other grabbed her by the hair and dragged her into the rear office. They stopped the cameras from there and took the discs, but this morning's footage is on the hard drive.' He shrugged. 'They made sure that we couldn't see their faces but a regular customer, Jason Greene photographed them leaving the shop. He was waiting in the shop to see Kayla and became suspicious when she didn't come out of her office. We have their faces on his photos.'

'How did he get in if they locked the door?'

'Apparently, it's a security feature,' Stirling explained. 'If the Yale lock is activated from the inside without a code being entered into the alarm, the system assumes that the shop is being robbed and it opens the lock after three minutes.'

'That is clever.'

'It saved her life. If Jason Greene hadn't disturbed them, she would be dead. No doubt about it.'

'They really want to know who their leak is, don't they?' Annie looked out of the window as she spoke. To her left, the huge Ferris wheel, 'The Liverpool Eye' rotated slowly and to her right a humungous cruise ship was moored at the pier head. Tourists streamed from the liner into the Albert Docks. The river was the city's lifeline; it had brought trade and wealth to Liverpool for centuries. Unfortunately, not all the cargo that it brought was good. Some people made their fortunes and others suffered and died. Life in the big city went on regardless. 'Let's bring everyone up to speed and find these animals.'

CHAPTER 23

Detective Constable Maxwell waved at the Armed Response Unit, who rode in a BMW X5. The driver and another officer were in the front seats while two officers in body armour, armed with Heckler and Koch MP5 Carbines, sat either side of Antonia Barrat in the back. Maxwell was in the passenger seat of a Vauxhall Omega and the plan was for the Omega to clear the way through the traffic using their blues and twos if necessary. The marked traffic interceptor that had been stationed outside the house would follow up the rear. The driver of the X5 flashed his lights to signal that he was ready. The blue light on the roof began to turn and illuminated for a second before it became still once more.

Max clicked his seat belt home and the Omega pulled forward towards the gates. The gates whirred into motion and began to open. The Omega slowed to a stop as they drew level with the pavement so that the driver could check for traffic both ways. The driver nudged forward slowly and then slammed on the brakes throwing Max towards the windscreen violently. The seat belt dug into his chest and shoulder painfully.

'What the hell are you doing?' Max snapped at the driver.

'He stepped out of nowhere!'

A well-built male in black clothing blocked their path. His hands were empty, hanging at his sides. Max looked up and stared into the eyes of Letva Lapsa. His eyes were steely grey and fixed on the X5 behind them. He stood impassively like a statue. The driver sounded the horn, but he didn't flinch. There was no response at all. Max looked in the mirror and saw that the armed officers were poised to deploy. He couldn't decide if the man was alarmed like a rabbit in the headlights or blocking their way purposely.

'Sir?' The comms crackled.

'Do not deploy unless you see a weapon.' Max said into the comms. He opened his door and climbed half out, keeping his body behind the door and windshield. 'Move!' Max ordered flatly. Letva looked at him and cocked his head slightly as if deciding what to do. Max felt his breath stuck in his throat. His lips went dry. He was surrounded by armed officers and yet he felt frightened. Surely it was just his nerves. He could just be a passing stranger. There was something sinister about the man but having him bundled away by officers with machineguns was overkill and would require a lot of explaining to his superiors. There was a mountain of paperwork attached to every time a weapon was drawn. 'Step to the side, Sir,' Max pointed at the pavement with his finger.

Letva nodded almost imperceptibly. His eyes were dead like those of a shark; the grey a startling contrast against his dark hair and stubble. He seemed to be considering something. The driver honked the horn again, making Max jump. Letva switched his gaze to the driver, the piercing stare threatening to turn him to stone. He took another glance at the X5 and then stepped to the side allowing them to move. Letva nodded to Max as the convoy inched forward and then he turned and walked away. As the X5 drew level with him he caught Toni's eye. A thin smile touched his lips. It sent a shiver down her spine. The convoy pulled onto the road and accelerated away. Toni wanted to leave without looking back but she felt compelled to turn around. When she did, the man with the grey eyes had vanished.

CHAPTER 24

The briefing was underway when Stirling felt his phone vibrating. He checked the screen and opened an unread text message. The forensic laboratory had messaged that the first batch of results were in. He logged into the terminal that he was sitting at and pulled up the information. He scanned the results while Annie summarised the case so far and each department shared their results.

'You have all got summary sheets from the case book to take away and information files have been sent to your computers.' She looked around to make sure everyone was happy and had a copy of the sheets. The MIT was fifty-three detectives strong and they were working with representatives from Drug Squad, Matrix, Vice, and the various port authorities, which swelled the numbers to over seventy. 'I want to start at first base,' Annie continued. 'Antonia Barrat received a tipoff from an as yet unknown source that something dodgy was going down at one of the derelict mills on Jamaica Street. We don't know what she was expecting to witness but she obviously got more than she bargained for.' Disparaging comments were whispered among the audience. Annie held up her hand to quieten the room. 'I know how most of you feel about the woman but if we're honest about it, all she's done is exposed a load of bent coppers in a very public manner.' Silence descended. 'I'll accept that there was some collateral damage from her documentary and that our force came out of it with egg on its chin but if the dirty coppers hadn't been there…' She let the sentence hang. 'We will deal with her in exactly the same way that we'd deal with anyone else. She will receive our best efforts and she won't feel any prejudice towards her from anyone in this room, understand?' She met the eyes of as many of the gathering as she could to reinforce her point. 'On the other hand, she doesn't get any special treatment either. If she messes us about and hinders our investigation then believe me, I'll jump on her from a great height.' Annie turned to Sykes from the Drug Squad. 'Can you fill us in on what you have so far please?'

Sykes stood up and took off his glasses. Removing them turned the room into a sea of blurred faces. It was easier for him that way. 'About six months ago we began to hear rumours of a new drug that was beginning to seep across Europe. I'm sure that you have all read the updates. For those that haven't, zombie is a hybrid drug manufactured by mixing PCP with ketamine.' He wiped his glasses on his tie. 'In its pure powdered form, it's lethal. Dealers are cutting it and then pressing it into tablet form so that it can be ingested slowly. If the buyers crush the stuff and try to snort it, smoke it, or inject it then they've the trip of their life before they die. Twenty-two deaths in Amsterdam this year alone have been attributed to zombie.' He paused to allow the information to hit home. 'Our Matrix officers are telling us that the word is spreading about it rapidly. Everyone wants to try it, but it's only available from certain dealers and we don't know who they are yet.'

'Where is the stuff coming from originally?' A blurred face asked from the back of the room.

'We don't know the source, but we know it's coming in via Amsterdam. The Dutch police have had two officers disappear while trying to infiltrate the zombie distribution network. They're missing presumed dead. Whoever is shipping the zombie is keeping their security tight.' He put his glasses back on and the world came into focus. 'We didn't know anything about this shipment until Antonia Barrat contacted us. Our usual leaks and sources are clueless about this network. Three kilos of uncut zombie are out there somewhere, which could possibly make between ten to fifteen kilos for pressing.' He looked around. 'The average tablet weighs three hundred milligrams. We could have forty thousand tablets, minimum, on our streets.'

'We've talked to dealers who have heard rumours of punters paying thirty quid a tablet,' a Matrix officer added. Permanently undercover, his tracksuit and baseball cap made him distinctive among this particular crowd. 'Any new drug is at a premium when it's introduced. Whoever shipped this product in is set to make or lose millions. I'm assuming that the original traffickers dropped the ball at the vehicle switch. Another gang from the city hit them?'

'That's what I think.' Annie nodded. 'I'm not sure that they dropped the ball, more like someone stole it from them.' She thought for a few seconds. 'How many outfits in the city could pull this off and distribute this drug without being wiped out by whoever brought it in?'

The Matrix officer took off his baseball cap and rolled it in his hands. 'We don't know who is dealing this on the streets, but somebody does,' he paused. 'Let's assume that the name of a dealer popped up and then they traced the drugs back up the food chain to the importers. Once they knew who was bringing it in, all they would need to do is find a source within the organisation.'

'Okay, that makes sense. I'm listening.'

'There are plenty of outfits capable of taking the drugs from the Fletcher Bros garage. Three men with shotguns, right?'

'Right.'

'Anyone could send three men with Mossberg shotguns in a van but only one or two could cut it, press it into tablets and then have the muscle to distribute it with impunity.'

'Fletcher was adamant that the gunmen were local.'

The Matrix officer shook his head. He looked towards Sykes who took the lead. 'If they were local then they're working for someone else. The local gangs keep their heads down nowadays. If they don't then they vanish. Between the Turks, Russians, and Albanian outfits there isn't much breathing room.' He shrugged. 'Why don't I take my team and follow up on the customer that approached the Fletchers about the vans and see if we know them or their connections?'

Annie nodded and smiled. She glanced at Miranda for the go ahead. Sykes was a key part of her squad and she didn't want to stand on her toes. Miranda nodded that it was fine. 'Do that, thank you,' Annie said. 'His name and contact details are in the notes. Rick Grainger.'

'We'll go and speak to him once we're done here.'

'Okay thanks, Jim Stirling will come with you. Let me know if you have any joy,' Annie said. Stirling nodded at Sykes, who returned the gesture. She moved on quickly. 'Where are we with the van that they used at the mill?'

'Nothing so far, guv,' one of her detectives answered. 'We're waiting on CCTV from the tunnel police, but they may have crossed the river over the Runcorn Bridge so we're checking footage there too. It may have been garaged as soon as it was stolen.'

'Okay.' Annie looked towards the river policemen. 'Can you bring us up to date?'

'The Coast Guard found a burnt-out Zodiac an hour ago just off the North Wales coast,' a sergeant from the waterborne force reported. His uniform was similar to his colleagues on land but with different insignia. The Port of Liverpool Police were essentially a small force unto themselves. 'We're having the wreck recovered but there's not much left. First reports indicate charred human remains aboard.'

'Thanks,' Annie said turning towards the detectives from The Vice Squad. 'Are you any closer to knowing who owns the property in Aigburth?'

'No, guv,' a balding detective in a crumpled suit replied with a shake of the head. 'The limited company that owns the deeds is a subsidiary of a shell company registered in the Cayman Islands. It's a dead end.'

'What about the directors of the limited company?'

'Three Latvian men are listed as the directors and company secretary. We have never been able to contact them. There's no trace of them being in the country since the company's conception four years ago.'

'What about the women that were in the cellar?'

'One of them has recovered enough to talk but she's not saying anything.'

'Do we know where they're from?'

'Nothing, guv. No form of identity on them. If I had to guess, I would say that they're Latvian.'

'Guv,' Stirling interrupted. 'This might shine a little light on things.'

'Go on.'

'The fingerprints taken from the three men at the garage were run through the system and we have two hits. One of the dead men is Oleg Markevica. He's got a record as long as my arm, drugs, prostitution, and firearms. There are two outstanding warrants with the Met, one for grievous bodily harm and one for possession of drugs with intent to supply.'

'Latvian by any chance?'

'Yes.' Stirling nodded. A murmur spread through the room. 'The second set belongs to Raitis Girts. He's wanted for murder in the Czech Republic. He's Latvian too.'

'Tell me he's in the Royal Hospital and not the mortuary.'

'He's in the Royal.'

'Guv,' the Vice detective said sheepishly. Annie looked at him and nodded that he should continue. 'One of the directors of that property is Oleg Markevica.'

'The facial recognition checks on the two heavies at the pawnbroker's shop have come back trumps too,' Stirling added. His mouth was twisted into a scowl. Annie had a rough idea what he was thinking. It would involve throttling him. 'One of the men,' he sent the image to one of the screens as he spoke, 'Andris Markevica, forty-five-year-old Latvian from Riga. INTERPOL have him listed on trafficking and firearms charges in Lithuania, Estonia, and the Czech Republic. He's been linked to the murder of a family in Latvia,' Stirling paused. 'Mother, father, and two children.' There was a dark silence in the room.

'The same surname, Markevica,' Annie broke the gloom, 'can't be a coincidence?'

'You don't like coincidences.'

'You're right, I don't. Okay, so we have a connection.' Annie put her hands together. 'Let's run with Raitis Girts as he is the only one still breathing. I want his records as far back as when he was just a twinkle in his father's eye. See what INTERPOL have on the other names too. If he is wanted for murder in the Czech Republic, then they will have a list of known associates.'

'We've got close contacts in Prague,' the Vice detective added. 'I'll run with that straight away, guv and then get onto INTERPOL.' Annie nodded and he headed out of the section with purpose. 'We'll find out who the Markevicas and Girts work for.'

'Barrat told us that she overheard them mention the name 'Ivor' several times. They mentioned him in the context that he was the boss,' Annie said. 'Given that this appears to be a family affair, let's search for an Ivor Markevica or Ivor Girts and see what comes up.'

'I'm running both names as you speak,' Stirling replied with a half grin. 'Using my initiative, guv.' His remark prompted a few chuckles from around the room.

'Good, that's what we need.' Annie heard the lift arriving on their floor. The doors slid open and from the corner of her eye, she caught the figure of Kathy Brooks stepping out of it. Her auburn hair was tied into a ponytail and she had left her whites in the mortuary. She sidled over to where Stirling was sitting and handed him some reports. The urge to take a look at what she had found put her off her stride for a moment. 'Is there anything from the mules?' Annie asked Miranda. She shook her head with a thin smile.

'They're simultaneously being processed and passing balloons full of cocaine. It's messy.' A wave of subdued laughter rippled through the room. It wasn't funny, no one thought it was funny, but they laughed anyway. 'I think it will be a few days before we'll have anything productive from them. We've completed preliminary tests on the coke and it's Peruvian. Not that that will help much; most of it is nowadays.'

'Seems you have a lot of questions with no answers?' Kathy Brooks interrupted. Annie nodded and hoped that she had something to help them move the investigation forward. 'We processed the blood from the floor of the mill, and it has come back with a match.' She handed Annie a file and a memory stick. 'Mike James was born Michael Peter Jameson in London. He joined the Met in 1990 at the age of eighteen. Up until last year, he was a sergeant on secondment in the Met's Human Trafficking Team. Apparently, he had a breakdown following an investigation into a refrigeration truck that contained sixty-five bodies.'

'Wasn't that in Calais?' Stirling asked.

'That's right.' Kathy nodded. 'The Met offered him a compromise agreement and managed his resignation on medical grounds.'

'They paid him off,' Annie added.

'Basically, yes.'

'But he seems to have maintained an unhealthy interest in the traffickers,' Annie added. 'I want to know who his relatives are, friends on and off the force, previous employment, any disciplinary issues, the state of his finances, his romantic involvements and exactly who he has investigated in the last twelve months.'

'We're on that, guv.'

'His personnel file is on that stick. I need to get back to it. You lot keep sending me exhibits to process.' Kathy gestured to the lift, rolled her eyes, and walked away with a wave of her hand.

'Okay, let's sort out the basics and then we can get on with the nitty-gritty.' She turned to her font of knowledge; a detective fondly known as Google. 'Google will supervise all exhibits and the indexing of all information received from the various teams. If you do not fill out the evidence logbook properly, he has my permission to be very annoyed and give you a kick up the arse. I want any and all names that come up dealt with thoroughly. We trace them, interview them, and eliminate them and I mean every single name got it?' Her question was met with enthusiastic nods. 'No slipups on this one,' she warned. 'I need all your initial reports with him by close of play today, understood?'

'Guv.' A mass reply came from the detectives.

'All the medical reports and witness statements need to be with him by lunchtime tomorrow at the latest.' That request was met with a groan. 'Good.' Annie smiled. 'Once we have solid identification, we need bank account details, ATM cards, mobile phones, and the works. Enough talk. You all know what is expected. Let's get on with it. I don't want any heroics. If a lead gives you a name or an address, it's to come back to the team for risk assessment and we'll action plan everything. Our targets are professional killers, remember that at all times. Anything out of the ordinary, talk to me directly.'

CHAPTER 25

Ivor Markevica was having a conversation on his mobile while he looked out of his hotel window at Wenceslas Square, Prague. Built from the 1300s onwards, the buildings were a mixture of Romanesque, Baroque, and Gothic styles. The streets were teeming with tourists and the square was one of the most photographed parts of Prague. He was amused by how photography had evolved. The emergence of the selfie had changed things forever and the selfie-stick was a genius invention, annoying but genius. He smiled as he watched dozens of tourists posing in front of the historic buildings holding their sticks aloft. The city had him hooked from the moment he had arrived. Walking through Prague, it was easy to transport himself back six hundred years. Tourism fuelled the city's economy. The ornately carved statues that covered the stone bridges over the River Vltava were magnets for millions of visitors but when the sun went down, the city took on a different personality as sightseeing gave way to the sex industry.

Ivor had made millions from its dark side. Trafficking women and drugs had made him more money than a man could spend in ten lifetimes. It was not an industry in which the weak could survive. Only the smartest, hardest, cruellest, and the most ultra-violent had any longevity in the trade. Ivor fit all those requirements and then some. He stood tall and even though his mid-fifties were behind him; he was heavily built. Hours of pumping iron every day for decades had added slabs of muscle to his upper body. His arms and chest were covered in ink and his greying hair was cropped close to his scalp. He had a disarming smile that had led many a foe into a false sense of security. Behind the tailored suits and charming smile was a narcissistic beast.

'Exactly what the fuck is going on?' Ivor asked calmly. He was renowned for his icy calmness. It was a trait not many had. One minute he could be talking perfectly normally to one of his employees and the next he could empty a magazine of nine-millimetre bullets into their face. There was no warning. The forests of the Vidzeme Uplands were littered with the bodies of both his friends and his enemies. He was an ice-cold killing machine with the IQ of a Mensa member.

'I am trying to find out exactly what has happened, Ivor,' Letva replied. 'It is complicated.' He kept his answer as vague as possible because he didn't know the truth yet. 'One of our men is an informer.'

'Who?'

'I don't know yet.' Letva sighed. 'The shipment was compromised at the handover at the mill and they found a journalist hiding in the building with a camera.'

'A journalist?' Ivor said surprised. 'A Russian, a Turk, a fucking Estonian I could believe, but a journalist?'

'Yes, I thought the same when they told me. I was expecting them to say the Karpovs had an insider or something,' Letva said thoughtfully. 'He couldn't have been there by accident. He had information. There's no other explanation.'

'Why would somebody tip off a journalist?'

'It's beyond me. The building was ideal for the delivery. We have used it many times with no problems.'

'Which one?'

'The old mill on Jamaica St.'

'I know it. Not even the tramps use that area.'

'Exactly. There was no chance of accidental contamination. The journalist was there because he knew what was going to happen. He had taken photographs, so they took him to find out how he knew about the handover.'

'They questioned him?'

'Of course.'

'What did he know?'

'He didn't know where the information came from. If he did, he didn't tell. Oleg questioned him personally. There's no way anyone holds out.'

'He likes that shit.'

'He does,' Letva agreed. 'When Oleg told me, what had happened at the mill, I guessed that he wasn't alone, so I sent one of our men back to check the mill over. When he got there, the police were there. They were swarming all over the place. He noticed a woman talking to them. She was upset so he guessed that she had been there too. He followed her to the police station, and I had two men waiting for her when she left to go home. Her name is Antonia Barrat. She's a freelance journalist and documentary maker.'

'Is she going to be a problem?'

'Yes. She wrote a book exposing corruption in the police force. It has given her a lot of kudos within her industry. She could attract attention to us.'

'I don't like the sound of this, Letva. What did they see?'

'We don't know exactly what they saw. Oleg told me that Jake wasn't wearing his mask at the handover. There were pictures of him on the camera and I am concerned that the pictures were uploaded immediately.'

'He wasn't wearing a mask?'

'No.'

'And someone has uploaded pictures of him?'

'Yes. I've already taken care of him.'

'That is a shame. He was useful with his boats.'

'I'll replace him, but that isn't an issue for now'

'He was known to the police. If they get their hands on those photographs, they would be led straight to him. I would not trust him not to make a deal to save his own skin. He knew too much about our operation.'

'He's not a problem to us now.'

'You're sure that these photographs could be a problem for us?'

'The model of camera that he had has the facility to upload to social media immediately; this one is linked to an information storage site. My concern is that the site is for sharing information and others may be able to access them.'

'Do you mean other journalists?'

'Yes. He may have been the only one with access to the photographs, but it is better that we act as if there are others that can access them. We should take the appropriate actions, yes?'

Ivor thought about the different connotations and smoothed his tie with a tattooed hand. It was better to play on the side of caution. 'Yes. Deal with them.'

'Once I have spoken to the Barrat woman, I will know one way or the other. I went to her house, but the police beat me to her.'

'Letva,' Ivor lowered his voice to a cautionary tone. 'This is not Latvia nor is it Kosovo or Afghanistan. You are in one of the United Kingdom's biggest cities. You are not in a war zone. I cannot afford to have a trail of dead bodies across the UK. You understand me, don't you?'

'Of course.' Letva replied calmly. He wasn't sure what Ivor knew.

'We cannot have the police focusing on us. It would be very bad for business,' Ivor paused, 'very bad indeed. I cannot have any adverse attention coming our way. It must be tidy, understand?'

'Have you spoken to your brother, Andris?'

'Not yet. He isn't answering his mobile. That's why I called you.' Ivor could sense that Letva wanted to tell him more and that he wasn't going to like it.

'Look, Ivor, things haven't been tidy at all. In fact, it's a total shitstorm.' Ivor remained silent and listened. 'I'm afraid that there are some casualties already,' Letva decided now was the time to tell Ivor how bad things were. Ivor remained silent still and it was unnerving. Letva could sense his anger simmering. 'Two of our men followed the Barrat woman from the police station to a pawnbroker's shop in Kensington. They thought that maybe it was her source. When she left, they went in and questioned the owner, a woman called Kayla Yates. They went way too far.'

'Do we know her?'

'No.'

'Was she her source?'

'I don't think so. The woman is in hospital and the police are all over it. There were a dozen police cars outside that shop.'

'For God's sake.' Ivor sighed. 'Which clumsy bastard did this?'

'Your brother, Andris.'

There was a long pause as Ivor thought things through. Letva could feel the tension on the line. 'Andris did this to a woman in a shop in broad daylight?'

'Yes. They didn't ask for permission from me, Ivor. They took it upon themselves to rush in. I know Andris is your brother but he's too impulsive. He has made a complete mess of this.'

'Is the woman going to die?'

'My contact at the hospital says that she is in a bad way. She is in surgery. It's touch and go.'

'What the fuck were they thinking?'

'I don't know but they were interrupted by a customer who came into the shop.'

'Interrupted?' Ivor sounded confused. 'How can they have been interrupted?'

'The door wasn't locked. They assured me that they had locked the front door, but someone walked in, and they had to leave in a hurry. They were photographed by a witness leaving the building.'

'More photographs? Come on, Letva,' Ivor sounded mischievous. 'You're joking with me now, right?'

'No.'

Silence.

Letva decided to get it all out on the table. 'Look, I am trying to clear up this situation here. Once I realised that the handover had been compromised, I had to convince them to relocate the mules and the drugs and arrange for the vehicle to be switched. Andris and Oleg were bickering like children. It was like talking to a brick wall.' Letva stood his ground. 'Your cousin Oleg was in charge of the house in Aigburth and he left a disaster behind. Andris couldn't control him.'

Silence.

Letva waited for a response but none came. 'Are you still there?'

'Yes.'

'Did you know that he had taken one of the Karpovs to the house?'

'No.' Ivor said quietly. He cleared his throat. 'What happened?'

'He did this off his own back, Ivor. Andris and I did not know what he had done.'

'And?'

'He fucked up.' Letva passed the blame expertly. 'He put the whores in the cellar, left Karpov's body in the hallway and set fire to the building.' Letva didn't know that Oleg had slaughtered one of the mules too. 'The police will be climbing up our backside and there isn't much that I can do about that. It is too late.'

'This is a catastrophe.' There was a long pause. Letva remained quiet. 'I need Oleg sent back here immediately,' Ivor said flatly. 'He has caused enough damage.'

'Oleg is dead, Ivor.'

Silence.

'Something went wrong at the vehicle switch. It was compromised too,' Letva said flatly, no emotion in his voice.

'Compromised how?'

'From what I can gather, they were hijacked at the switch. Oleg and the others were tied up by whoever hit them and beaten to death. We lost another man with him. Raitis is still alive but he's critical.'

Ivor leaned against the window; the glass felt cool on his forehead. He didn't need to work again. There was enough money coming in for him to sit on a beach for the rest of his life, but the money would be no good to him if he was rotting in a Czech prison. He could see his anonymity unravelling. 'Two of our men are dead and their bodies were left where they can be printed and identified?'

'Yes.'

'So, when I said that I can't afford to have a trail of bodies across the UK, I was wasting my breath?'

'Basically, yes. The damage was already done. What do you want me to do?'

'You need to silence this journalist and the witness at the pawnbroker's shop and anybody else that could be of any concern,' Ivor spoke very slowly to reinforce his point. 'We need to regain control of this shambles, but it has to be done professionally. I do not want any more bodies on the streets, Letva. Am I making myself clear?'

'I have not left any bodies on the streets, Ivor,' Letva replied sternly. 'In all the time that I have worked for you, have I ever left any evidence behind?'

'Point taken,' Ivor conceded. Letva was the ultimate pro. He would take down a target and make them disappear. Even Ivor didn't know where half of his victims ended up. 'Make these people vanish before the police start making progress. They will already have names and they will quickly make the connection to our European operations. They will link Oleg and Raitis to Prague.'

'Oleg made this mess. Andris and I will clean it up.'

'Good.'

'You haven't mentioned the drugs,' Letva said nervously.

'What about my drugs?' Ivor didn't seem perturbed that his cousin and another employee had been killed and his question sounded like an afterthought.

'They were stolen from the switch.'

'By who?'

'I am working on that, Ivor. I do not know yet.'

'I don't like losing my goods.'

'I will have them returned.'

'You need to.' Ivor sighed. He looked at the tattoo between his finger and thumb, the number 3 on the ace of spades. Its significance was never more relevant than now. 'Someone needs to pay for this mess. We have an informer in our midst. Who was the rat?'

'I can't be sure yet. I need to speak with the Barrat woman to be certain.'

'How soon can you do that?'

'The police have her in protection.'

'Discretion, Letva. Don't leave any more leads for the police to follow. Are you sure that you can get to her?'

'Absolutely. There are always opportunities.'

'Good but be careful. Who do you think is the informer?'

'I think it was Raitis,' Letva lied. The truth was that he didn't know. One of the three men that went to the handover was an informer, of that he was certain, but he didn't know who. Two of them were dead so it was in his best interest to hand his boss a head on a plate. 'I had my doubts about him but now I am almost certain.'

'What makes you think that?'

'Andris told all three of them where the pick-up was to be, but he said that only Raitis knew where the van switch was to happen,' he elaborated his lie. 'If he lives, I can set a trap for him and hope that he walks straight into it.'

'Can you get to him in hospital?'

'Of course. If he lives.'

'I sincerely hope that he does, Letva. I want to know who has betrayed us.'

'I will find them and the men that took them.'

Ivor had faith that Letva meant what he said but he wasn't as convinced that he could deliver. 'I need to speak to my brother. Where is he?'

'He is cleaning up his mess.'

'The witness at the pawnbroker shop?'

'Yes.'

'Find him, Letva and make sure that it is done tidily,' Ivor warned. 'When you are done, tell him to phone me. I am tired of wiping his arse.'

'I will be in touch.' Letva hung up.

'Did you hear all that?' Ivor stepped away from the window and looked at his wife, Marika. She was sitting on a dark red leather captain's chair. Her dark brown eyes looked at him intently. She crossed her long legs, her beige leather trousers creaked as the material rubbed against the chair. She swigged from a bottle of Budvar and smiled.

'I heard it.' She flicked her long brown hair from her shoulder. 'What do you think?'

'I think he's a fucking liar. What about you?'

'I never liked the man. There's something not right about him.' She stood and joined him at the window. 'What makes you so sure that he is lying to you?'

'Raitis called me when they left the mill. I knew that the shipment had been compromised and that they would lose my drugs, so I had it taken from them. He told me where they were switching vans and I sent the team to take the zombie and make sure it remained safe. I didn't count on the mules turning on Oleg and the others.'

'You knew the rest of what he said, already?'

'Most of it yes. Andris is my little brother so he's telling me what Letva is up to, but he isn't being completely honest about his own fuck ups.' Ivor took the bottle of beer from her hand as he spoke. 'He is impetuous and sometime a little stupid, but he is loyal to me. I need to make sure that the zombie gets to the tablet press and I need to settle things down before they fuck things up completely. We need to make a trip to the UK.' He drank greedily from the bottle and then handed it back to her. She finished it in a few gulps. 'Sometimes if you want something done it's better to do it yourself.'

CHAPTER 26

Andris followed the Range Rover until it pulled into a pub car park. He waited for the driver to climb out of the vehicle to confirm that it was Jason Greene. In hindsight, he should have taken a few seconds outside of the pawnbroker's shop to take the mobile phone from him and to break his neck, but the sound of sirens approaching had startled him. He knew that the police would have copies of the images already but without a witness's corroboration that they came from their device, they would be of no use in a court of law. They couldn't prove when a photograph had been taken without the device and the photographer. A good barrister could throw enough doubt at a jury that they would never convict. Andris needed to remove both the device and the owner from the equation. He watched Jason walk across the car park and enter the pub through the rear entrance. The Range Rover was parked away from the other vehicles beneath some trees. Greene looked shifty and nervous, looking over his shoulder constantly. Andris considered that he might be aware that he was being followed but he dismissed the idea quickly. Whatever Greene was worried about, it was something else other than what had happened that morning. Andris wanted to see what was going on inside. He climbed out of the Ford that he was driving and walked towards the pub.

Inside, Jason went to the bar and ordered a pint of lager. Most of the tables were full of a mixture of suits having a drink after work and elderly men playing dominos. A bandit beeped noisily as a man in a white tracksuit fed it with his dole money. Jason paid for the beer with his last fiver and slipped the change into his jeans. His beer was cold and had a bite. He felt like drinking ten more, but he didn't have any cash. His deal with Kayla hadn't come to fruition and he hadn't thought about what he would do if it didn't come off. A flurry of bills had landed and depleted his dwindling funds. He had relied on her too much and put all his eggs in one basket. He had tried to contact some of his old buyers, but their response had been less than cordial. The Rolex watches were his only collateral and he needed to convert them into cash as quickly as possible.

'All right, Jason,' a familiar voice came from behind him. He turned and looked at two men in their forties. One of them he knew as a local dealer and small-time crook Rick Grainger, the other was a stranger to him. They were sharply dressed in the latest brands, jeans, T-shirts, and trainers. Both men wore designer beards and had wrap-around tattooed sleeves on their arms. There was an air of menace about them. 'We'll have two lagers, Jason my mate. It's your round, isn't it?'

Jason blushed. He felt his pockets for effect. 'I haven't brought any cash with me, sorry.'

'He hasn't brought any cash,' Rick nudged his companion. Jason could tell from his pupils that he was on cocaine. They sniggered like a couple of schoolboys. 'They take debit cards behind the bar, don't you, mate?' The barman nodded that they did. 'See, they take cards, which makes it your round. Now get the fucking beers in!'

Jason shifted nervously from one foot to another. His face reddened more. 'I lost my cards. I'm waiting on new ones.'

Rick sneered and shook his head. He stepped up to the bar and ordered two pints, paying with a twenty-pound note. Handing one of the drinks to his friend, he gestured to an empty table. They walked over and sat down. Rick took a long swig from his beer. As he swallowed, he pointed to Jason's jeans. 'Show me your wallet, Jason.'

'What?' Jason asked nervously.

'Are you deaf?'

'No.'

'Then show me your wallet.' Rick shrugged and put his glass down. He glared at Jason.

'What is your problem, Rick?'

'I'll tell you what my problem is. I think you're lying to me and I don't deal with liars.'

'Lying about what?'

'Losing your cards.'

'What is wrong with that?' Jason asked. He feigned being offended. The memories of being bullied at school came flooding back. There were a hundred Ricks at school, and they all seemed to zero in on him. 'I've offered you some quality merchandise and you come in here throwing your weight around. I really don't need this.'

Rick frowned and looked at his companion. His companion glowered at Jason. Jason had the same sick feeling in his stomach that he used to have when the bullies cornered him. 'Have I offended you?' Rick asked politely.

Jason took a sip of beer and swallowed. He could feel his hand shaking as he put his glass down. 'Not really. I just don't see the need for the attitude.'

'Attitude?'

'You know what I mean.'

'No, I don't.' Rick leaned over the table threateningly. 'Explain it to me. How have I got an attitude?'

Jason felt his face blushing again. He was withering beneath their stares. 'I think you're being unnecessarily aggressive. I realise that you're letting me know that you're not going to be mugged off in a deal and I appreciate that. Do you want to see the gear or not?'

Rick sat back and relaxed a little. He sipped from his pint and looked around. The other drinkers were too busy chatting and playing their games to be interested in what they were talking about. 'I still think that you're lying to me. When was the last time you called me with gear to sell?' He shrugged. 'Two years ago, maybe three?'

'Why does that matter?'

'I would have thought that it was obvious.'

'Not to me, no.'

'Let me explain.' Rick raised his forefinger like a teacher in front of a class. 'You don't call me to offer me gear for two years, then out of the blue you need to see me urgently. You have the deal of the century for me.' Rick smiled like a snake. 'How many people did you call before me, Jason?' Jason blushed again and felt like standing up and running for the door. 'How many people told you to fuck off before you thought about calling me?' Jason looked at the floor. His confidence was crushed. 'The way that I see it is this.' He sat forward and stared hard at Jason. 'You have been selling your gear to that slag in Kensington. For some reason, she has bummed you off and you're up the wall without a ladder, so you call all your old buyers until someone bites.' He cocked his head to one side. 'How am I doing so far?' Jason shuffled on his stool and shrugged. Rick was spot on. 'Then you turn up here without a pot to piss in, not enough money to buy us a pint and come up with a load of old bollocks about losing your bank cards. Now tell me if I'm wrong but if you expected me to believe that then I think you're a bit of a cheeky bastard, don't you?'

Jason looked around. The pub was filling up, but he still felt completely alone. He sighed and took a drink from his pint. 'Do you want to see the watches or not?'

'Do I want to see a couple of snide watches from a nobody like you?' Rick finished his pint and slid the glass across the table. 'Have you got the boxes and certificates?'

'No.'

'Fuck off, Jason.' Jason looked shocked. 'Get out of here now before I lose my temper. Do you think that anyone will believe that they're genuine?'

'They are.'

'Don't waste any more of my time.'

'Look, I'll take less than I wanted. I'm in a bit of fix at the moment.' Rick's companion threw the contents of his glass into Jason's face. The liquid splattered down his front. Jason tried to wipe the beer from his eyes. The pub fell silent and all eyes were on them.

114

'Rick told you to fuck off, so why are you still here?'

Jason held up his hands and stood up. 'Okay, I'm going.' He turned on his heels and walked towards the door, soaked and mortally embarrassed. He wasn't sure what to do next. He had broken into his last fiver. There was no diesel in his vehicle, and he had no cigarettes. He opened the door and broke into a jog in case they decided to follow him, give him a good kicking and take the watches for free. Tears of embarrassment stung his eyes and ran down his cheeks. The fresh air soothed his shattered nerves and he couldn't get away quickly enough. He felt sick to the pit of his stomach. Sick and pissed off that he wasn't hard enough to stick up for himself. He hated bullies. They always seemed to zone in on him as if he had a target on his forehead. They always had and unless he turned into a ninja overnight, they always would. As he opened the door of the Range Rover, his eyes filled with tears, anger and resentment fuelled his despair. Just when he thought that life couldn't get much worse, a heavy blow to the back of his head sent lights flashing through his brain. His knees buckled and he felt himself being dragged along the ground as another blow switched his lights out.

CHAPTER 27

Antonia Barrat groaned internally as they drove through the gates of Canning Place. It was a daunting thought that once they had her inside that soulless building she couldn't leave until they said so. The smell of male sweat inside the BMW had become more intense with every mile; her escorts were burning adrenalin, their minds in a heightened state of readiness. She could literally smell their angst in the air. As they neared the rear entrance the convoy slowed to a halt and she could feel the tension dissipate as the gates closed behind them. The officers charged with keeping her safe seemed to relax immediately. When the doors opened and the sea air blew in from the river, she took in several deep breaths. She was helped from the vehicle and guided towards the lift that would take them into the dark heart of the headquarters. Detective Maxwell had spoken to her several times on the way, but she hadn't heard a word that he had said. His lips were moving but the sound wasn't being processed by her brain. She felt the lift moving upwards, registered the doors opening, and she instinctively stepped out into a wide office space. The sound of telephones ringing struck her first, then the buzz of a hundred conversations happening simultaneously. The noise seemed to be weirdly amplified by her mind. Toni knew that it was fear, shock, and stress that had warped reality. She followed Maxwell through the organised chaos, his eyes full of both concern and contempt. He didn't like her, none of them did. She could sense it as they looked at her. It didn't matter. She didn't care. All she wanted was to see Kayla. She needed to hold her, smell her hair, and feel the warmth that spread between them when they embraced. Kayla always whispered, 'I love you, Toni, and I'll never leave you'. She needed to hear that. Nothing else mattered now. Her mind took her away from the frightening reality of the situation that she was in.

    Toni had drifted through her teens in a daze. Her aunt tried hard to make life as normal as she could but normal didn't happen. They moved three times before she was sixteen; each time involved moving schools and losing a set of friends. It was difficult to slot into school when her peers had been associated with each other from primary school onwards. Emotional bonds, strong friendships, and dislikes were already well established. Being the strange face in the playground wasn't easy. Curiosity drove some to befriend her, asking where she was from and why she had left her old school, most looked upon her as an intruder. She was the weird girl with no parents. Her teachers were always supportive and sympathetic to her plight but moving so frequently severed any bonds that she made.

She never wanted for anything. Her aunt made sure that she always had nice clothes to wear, new shoes, designer coats in the winter; money wasn't an issue. She was given a decent amount of pocket money every month to buy the latest albums, make-up, and the odd milkshake and burger in town on a Saturday. Her aunt loved her. She could never deny that, but she wasn't her parents. The burning sense of loss never left her, not for a moment. There was always something missing. At seventeen, Toni was at college listening to her English teacher rattling on about literary classics inspired by World War One when her headmistress called her from the class. There was a policewoman there, who explained that her aunt had been killed in a road accident. That left her truly alone. Toni didn't have a breakdown; she didn't collapse or become hysterical. It was as if she had been expecting it to happen. Everyone that she loved left eventually.

CHAPTER 28

Toni was mesmerised by the sequence of recent events that had all started with a phone call the previous night. If she had missed it, none of the knock-on events would have happened. Kayla would be safe in her shop counting her money and polishing her gold and Toni would be at home by now, cooking a meal for them, uncorking a bottle of Shiraz to allow it to breathe. They would have talked about their holiday plans and what they wanted to see the most. Kayla yearned to see Cambodia and the Far East, while Toni fancied Mexico. They had talked about it every night for a week but in a short period of time, their lives had changed dramatically. Everything had gone wrong because of one, thirty second phone call.

'Do you want a cup of tea or coffee?' Toni heard the voice, but it didn't register that the question was aimed at her. She was sitting on a swivel chair although she had no recollection of how she had arrived there. Annie Jones leaned towards her and waved her hand in front of her eyes. 'Toni!' She clicked her fingers loudly. Maxwell closed the office door and the volume level went down a few decibels. 'Are you okay?'

'Clearly not, Inspector,' Toni said adjusting her weight in the chair. 'I'm not feeling myself.'

'You have had a nasty shock.'

'That's the understatement of the week if ever I heard one.' Toni frowned as reality returned to her. 'How is Kayla?' She made to stand up. 'When can I see Kayla?'

Annie put her hands gently on her shoulders. 'She is in surgery. They won't let you see her until they have finished. As soon the doctors are happy, we'll take you to see her.'

'What is wrong with her?'

'I'm not a hundred per cent certain yet,' Annie lied. 'My detectives are at the hospital. They will call me as soon as there is any news. Do you want some tea? It will help with the shock.'

'Yes please.'

'White?'

'White with one sugar please.'

Annie gestured to Maxwell and he went to order their drinks. When he closed the door, she turned back to Toni. 'Things have become a little out of hand, haven't they?'

'You could say that.'

'The message that they left at your house.' Annie watched her every move. 'What photographs do they want you to delete?'

Toni reddened and looked at Annie sheepishly. The image of the eyeballs floating in a bag returned. 'Mike must have taken some pictures at the mill. My camera automatically uploads to my Dropbox account. They obviously know that the camera uploads and they're assuming that I have them.'

'Do you have them?'

'I haven't looked yet but if he took them, they'll be in my account.'

'Can you access them from my laptop?'

'Yes.'

'Do it.' Annie turned her laptop to face her. 'Let's see what it is that they're worried about.'

Toni typed the site's name into the search bar and then clicked on the link. After entering her email and password, her account appeared on the screen. There were seven unopened files in the 'pictures' box. 'They're here,' Toni said over her shoulder. 'Shall I open them?'

'Yes.' Annie nodded 'And save them onto this please,' she added as she handed a memory stick to Toni. Toni opened the files and they looked at the images. All seven showed the mules disembarking from the rib and they'd clearly captured the face of the man who sailed it. Annie silently contemplated the mystery of the burnt remains off the coast of North Wales. His employers were taking no chances. He hadn't worn a mask and because of that they'd turned him into cinders. 'These are very useful. Does anyone else have access to these files?'

'Only my editor at *The Post*.'

'And does she know anything about what has happened?'

'I haven't spoken to her but that doesn't mean that she doesn't know. There are plenty of people in this building who are willing to talk to her for the right price.'

'I don't suppose you want to corroborate that with some names, do you?'

'I don't know them. She keeps her informants a secret too.' Toni half smiled. 'She hasn't opened the files yet. They were unread but if she thinks to check the Dropbox, she'll find them. Shall I delete them?' Annie nodded to the affirmative. Toni clicked *delete* without hesitation. She could retrieve them from the recently deleted box later. 'I guess that solves one problem, doesn't it?'

'It's far from over, Toni and people are dying,' Annie warned her. 'These people won't stop until they have answers and you have the answers.'

'You're making it sound as if it's my fault.'

'I make no apologies if that is how it sounds.' Annie shrugged. 'We're looking for members of a Latvian crime syndicate. They're wanted here, in the Czech Republic, and their own country for drugs, people trafficking and murder. They in turn are looking for the leak in their organisation and they're prepared to kill for it. We can only assume that Mike Jameson is dead. Lord only knows what he went through before he died. Kayla was beaten and stuffed into her safe.' Annie paused as Maxwell returned with a tray of drinks. She waited patiently as he placed the cups on the desk. 'This syndicate has some particularly dangerous men working for them. You can see that can't you?'

'Yes.' Toni took a sip of tea with a shaking hand.

'They won't stop until they find the leak and they'll leave no hiding places unchecked until they find you. They want to know who it is, and we can't help to protect you or Kayla unless you help yourself. We need to know who told you about the mill.'

Toni took a deep breath and blew the air through puffed cheeks. She couldn't hold out any longer. There was nothing to gain and much to lose. 'There is no way that you can tell anyone that I gave you this information. I will not testify to it in court, understand?'

'I understand.'

'I have a number of informers on the payroll. Some are more useful than others. This particular source was one of my less useful informers. His information was always vague and usually incorrect,' she stopped to wet her lips. 'To be honest, he was a bloody nuisance, always asking for stupid amounts of money for crappy titbits of information. I got the distinct impression that everything he sold me was second hand or overheard. I can give you his name, but I have no idea where he would have heard it from in the first place.'

'We'll deal with that,' Annie replied irritably. 'What is his name?'

'He is called Rick.' Toni began. 'He's a small-time crook with a huge ego. If he did half of what he tells me that he does, then he wouldn't need my money. He seems to be a wannabe gangster rather than an affiliate. Do you know what I mean?'

'I meet his type every day, Toni.' Annie nodded. 'What is his full name?'

'His second name is Grainger. Richard Grainger but everyone calls him Rick.'

'Rick Grainger,' Annie said. His name rang a bell. He was the man that called the Fletcher Bros garage to arrange the vehicle switch. She checked her delegation sheet. Jim Stirling and Sykes from DS had gone to arrest the same man, Rick Grainger. That couldn't be a coincidence.

CHAPTER 29

Rick Grainger was a worried man. He was a small-time dealer who snorted more of his stock than he sold, which left him with severe cash flow issues. In his world, cash was the root of all evil, not drugs. Cocaine had been his poison since his teenage years. He loved the highs and despised the lows that followed. The highs became increasingly harder to hit and the lows became deeper, darker, and full of paranoia and depression. That wouldn't be a problem if he had had enough cash to maintain the highs on a permanent basis. He could make a few grand a week selling his stock, but he needed double that amount to pay his bills and fund his habit. He often bought stolen goods to sell on, but it still didn't put a dent in his outgoings. His suppliers had identified his failing years ago and they utilised his weaknesses. They manipulated him to their own advantage. Rick did work for them and many others to make up the shortfall in his earnings, exchanging his services for drugs and money.

As the years went by, his tasks had become increasingly more dangerous. At first, he was asked to move a kilo here and there, picking up money and delivering it wherever he was told to. He became a familiar face about town, a link between people who would normally be deadly rivals. Doing business with the opposition was a necessary evil on occasions and could be made more bearable if an intermediary was employed. Rick was the intermediary of choice. Most of the city's organised gangs knew him or knew of him. He was useful and he was easy to manipulate because he was always in need of money or cocaine or both. In the early days, he enjoyed being a face around town. His friends were in awe of him when well-known gangsters said hello and chatted to him in pubs and clubs. He had minor celebrity status in the underworld and his minions were easily impressed by it. The flipside was that it caused jealousy and resentment and when push came to shove, no one really trusted him completely because they could never be sure who he was actually working for at any one time. He was a pawn in a dangerous game. The result was that he remained in the lower echelon of the drug world, living from one day to the next, always chasing the next ounce of sniff and wondering how he was going to pay the mortgage. He watched his associates grow richer and richer while he waited for that one opportunity that would change his life and elevate him to being a player. Life had passed him by. His associates asked him to do increasingly risky jobs. Jobs that no one else would consider doing for a pittance. The law of averages meant that it was only a matter of time before he got caught.

When he saw a black man with a look of Mike Tyson walking up his path with another man who was built like an oak tree, he knew that they were detectives. This time he had bitten off far more than he could chew. They knocked on the door in a manner that indicated that if he didn't open it, they would come through it. Rick sighed and swore loudly. He debated running out of the back door but swiftly ruled it out. None of his associates would thank him for bringing the police to their door. There was simply nowhere to run to. He swallowed hard and opened the door.

'Richard Grainger?' Stirling said, thrusting his ID into his face. 'DS Stirling and DS Sykes, we're part of the Major Investigation Team.'

'What do you want?' Rick asked as he stepped back. He nervously stroked his manicured beard with his tattooed left hand.

'We need to talk to you about an incident that took place at the Fletchers' garage.' Stirling pushed the door open and stepped inside, forcing Rick backwards. 'Can we come in?' His stare communicated that the answer was yes.

'Help yourself, why don't you,' Rick protested. He turned and walked into his living room. 'Do I need to call my solicitor?'

'Have you got a solicitor?' Sykes asked sarcastically.

'Yes.'

'Who has a solicitor these days?' Stirling turned to Sykes. 'Do you have a solicitor?'

'Only when I'm getting divorced.'

'Fair point. Mind you you're not a drug dealing scumbag,' Stirling looked back at Rick with a frown. 'I don't know the answer. Do you think you need your solicitor?'

'You two are comical, aren't you? What do you want?' Rick snapped. He looked from one detective to the other. They looked like they could be front-row forwards for Big Bastard United. 'I'm in a rush so make it quick.'

'You're not going anywhere. Sit down,' Sykes pointed to an armchair. Behind his glasses his expression had become more Tyson-like than before. Rick figured that Sykes could knock him through the wall with a left jab, so he sat down without any argument. Sykes looked around the room. It had the trappings of money and poor taste spotted around it. A large screen plasma television was mounted to the wall and an expensive long leather corner suite was draped in fake animal furs. Zebra, leopard, and tiger adorned the suite. 'You do a bit of big game hunting in your spare time, do you?'

'Fuck you.' Rick smiled sourly. He sounded less rattled than he felt. 'What do you want?'

'You're familiar with Paul and Peter Fletcher?' Stirling intervened. 'They run a garage unit near Runcorn Bridge.'

'Yes, I know them. They service and MOT my cars.' Rick knew that there was no point in lying at this stage. They would have checked all the paperwork at the garage before they knocked on his door.

'Cars plural?'

'I buy and sell. They service a couple of cars a month for me.' The fact that most of them were insurance scams and chopped and welded stolen vehicles wasn't to be divulged right now. He sold them for his associates for a small split of the profits. He had never seen half of the vehicles that he 'owned' briefly. 'What is the problem, has one of my MOTs run out? I would have thought that you better things to do.'

'Funny,' Sykes said without smiling.

'Do you think he's funny?' Sykes asked Stirling.

'About as funny as a burst haemorrhoid.'

'How are they by the way,' Sykes asked politely.

'On the mend.' Stirling shrugged. 'Good days and bad.'

'Are you two for real?' Rick interrupted.

Sykes raised his index finger, 'Oh yes, I was saying. Paul Fletcher has informed us that you brokered a deal with them that involved them dismantling a Volkswagen van.'

'He's mistaken.' Rick's eyes indicated that he was lying.

'I don't think that he was.'

'I don't know what you're talking about.'

'What time was it he made a statement?'

'About two hours ago,' Stirling said staring at Rick. 'You made the call and set up the switch. We know that you did.'

'I set up a lot of deals with the Fletchers. I can't remember.'

'Really?' Sykes had a crooked grin. 'There was an incident involving the Volkswagen van that resulted in the seizure of a large amount of class A drugs, people trafficking and the death of two men, probably three by the end of today.'

'And anyone involved in the deal is implicated. Murder, trafficking, distribution of class A's…'

'What?' Rick went pale. 'I think you've been on class A's, mate.' He had a stab at bravado but failed miserably. The two detectives towered above him; their stares seemed to penetrate inside his skull searching for lies. 'Isn't one of you supposed to be the good cop?'

'He is consistently funny, isn't he?' Sykes said to Stirling.

'Hilarious. I'm in danger of wetting my pants here.'

'They'll love you in jail.'

'I'm not going to jail because I haven't done anything wrong.'

'Paul Fletcher says that you have. He's very pissed off with you, isn't he?' Sykes said shaking his head.

'Very pissed off,' Stirling agreed. 'His brother Pete is even more pissed off. He is in hospital with a fractured skull. I think they'll want to have a word with you when he's better.'

'I haven't done anything wrong.'

'So, you didn't ring the garage this morning and ask them to clear their workload for the day, dismantle a Volkswagen, and sell a Mercedes Sprinter?' Stirling asked gruffly. 'Because Paul Fletcher has made a statement saying that that's exactly what you did.'

'Hold on a minute!' Rick stood up and held out his hands. His face blushed red. Stirling noticed a tremor in his fingers. It was obvious that Fletcher had spilled the beans and tracing that a call had been made between them wouldn't take long if it hadn't been done already. 'I didn't know anything about a Mercedes van, and I didn't know anything about a Volkswagen. I made a phone call for a customer and nothing else.'

Stirling shook his head and walked to the rear of the house. He looked out of the window. The back garden was quite large but overgrown. A child's tricycle was abandoned in the long grass, its paint blistered and rusting. 'Have you got kids Rick?'

'A daughter.'

'How old is she?'

'She'll be seven this December.'

'Seven,' Stirling eyed the tricycle again. It had been there a long time, neglected and unused. 'You haven't seen her for a while have you?'

'Her mother won't let her come here, the bitch.' Rick moaned. 'I have to go to a contact centre for supervised visits.'

'Why is that?'

'What the fuck has it got to do with you?' Rick protested. The questions about his daughter had put him on the back foot but then Stirling knew that it would.

'I don't like you. I don't like what you do but I'm concerned for you.' Stirling shrugged. 'We're investigating a very serious series of events including murder.' He paused for effect. Rick looked like he was about to vomit. 'The courts are very strict nowadays and you can be guilty by association. It looks to me that you're involved in our case, doesn't it?' Stirling asked Sykes.

'Definitely,' Sykes agreed. 'In a case like this, everyone linked to it is looking at hard time and the rats will begin to turn on each other. The ones that turn first are the ones that don't do as much time.'

'So, if you want to see your daughter without any bars between you before her twenty-first birthday, then you had better not lie to me again.' Stirling handed him a copy of a vehicle registration certificate. Rick read it and sat down heavily in his chair. His hands were visibly shaking. 'Now do you want to tell us your side of the story before we arrest you?'

'Once lawyers get involved it will be out of our hands, Rick,' Sykes added. 'We won't be able to help you once that happens.'

'You say that you didn't know anything about the vans, Rick but according to this you sold the Mercedes to the Fletcher brothers a couple of months back.' Stirling watched the expression on Rick's face as he spoke. 'Paul Fletcher told us that it had a busted head gasket. They fixed it up ready to be sold on but there were no takers until you brokered the deal with a gang of very nasty drug dealers that is. It was your van.'

Rick put his head in his hands and closed his eyes tightly, but the problem didn't disappear. 'I never actually owned this van,' he said with a wobble in his voice. 'I just buy and sell vehicles on. People use my name and I get a percentage, honestly!'

'Honestly?' Stirling spoke to Sykes again. 'Honestly is an unusual word for a bloke like him to use, isn't it?'

'Very unusual.' Sykes nodded. He took his glasses off and pointed them at Rick. 'I bet you couldn't spell the word never mind understand its meaning.'

'Fuck you,' Rick snapped. 'I'm not saying anything else. You had better arrest me and take me in. I want a lawyer.'

'Turn around and put your hands behind your back.' Stirling nodded slowly and shrugged. 'Have it your way. You're under arrest for conspiracy to supply. You do not have to say anything, but it may harm your defence if you do not mention something that you later rely on in court. Anything you do say may be given in evidence, understand?' Rick nodded. 'Of course, you do. You've been here a few times before, Rick but never for something this heavy. If I was in your shoes, I'd have a serious think on the way to the station because the next few sentences that pass from your lips could determine how old you are the next time you get to hold your daughter.' Sykes took him by the arm and pulled him towards the door. Rick didn't put up much of a struggle. He reckoned that Sykes would rip his arm off and beat him to death with the sticky end if he misbehaved. Stirling took a quick glance around the room and then followed on. He made sure that the door was locked and then headed down the path.

Sykes paused at the edge of the pavement. Their Volvo was parked across the road. It was a busy street lined with terraced houses and the odd row of shops and there was a big pub on the corner to his right. To his left was a pedestrian crossing. There was a bus lane nearest to him and then two lanes of traffic to navigate to reach their car. He decided to wait for Stirling.

He couldn't see a gap in the traffic, and he would need an extra pair of hands to open the vehicle and put Rick into the back. A double-decker bus crammed with commuters crawled by on the opposite side of the road. A number of the passengers held their phones to the glass, filming the man in handcuffs. Others looked on; their faces impassive. Sykes was distracted by them. The public's ghoulish fascination with uploading images of other humans suffering in some shape or form rankled with him. He was distracted by the curious expressions on their faces and didn't hear the Range Rover approaching. He didn't hear it accelerate. He turned his head only when he heard it mount the kerb by which time, it was too late. Rick screamed and Sykes's voice blended with his, both cut short and silenced in an instant. Stirling stood frozen to the spot and watched helplessly as the four-wheel drive behemoth mowed them down on the pavement and then sped off into the traffic.

CHAPTER 30

Julia Fox had been an editor on the Daily Post and Liverpool Echo for five years and she was still not thirty. She left university with a first-class degree and climbed the promotional ladder quickly, trampling her opposition along the way. Although it was a regional rag, it was the ideal job to cut her teeth before a more permanent move to one of the nationals in London. Julia was as sharp as a razor and cruel with it. She was being groomed for greater things but in the meantime, she intended to manipulate and squeeze her journalists for every ounce of news that she could. Antonia Barrat was one of her freelancers; one of the better ones. Julia knew that she had been involved in an incident that dwarfed anything that they'd covered for months but she couldn't speak to her. She knew that Toni had been taken back to Canning Place but not why. Whatever had happened, it was dramatic, and drama sells newspapers. She had received snippets of information but not enough to make a coherent article. It was too early to run with what she had. She needed corroboration before she could go to press.

It had been a long arduous day that had produced a number of mediocre half-page stories and the usual mundane crap about how long the city's football managers would last. With both teams knocked out of the cup competitions and staring at mid-table finishes, all that mattered was which of the two would finish higher than the other. She didn't give a toss either way, but the city was football mad and they had to balance their coverage so that one team didn't have more exposure than their bitter rivals. Julia had decided to brighten her day by taking a group of her finest journalists to a new restaurant for cocktails. Panoramic 34, situated on the 34th floor of the West Tower had views across the estuary to the Welsh mountains to the west and the tall buildings of Manchester city centre to the east. She had used the place a few times to reward employees or impress contacts. Night or day, the view was impressive.

As the cocktails flowed, her team was beginning to loosen up. She took her Samsung out and checked her messages. One email jumped out at her. It was a Dropbox notification. It informed her that several files had been deleted from an image sharing folder, which wasn't unusual but the name of the person that had deleted them was. They had been deleted by Antonia Barrat. Julia accessed the account and opened the folder. She could feel her breath shortening. Adrenalin pumped into her veins. There was only one reason why Toni would delete images while she was in police protection and that was because she had been told to. Julia clicked on the recently deleted folder and opened the seven images. Her head went into a spin. The national news was focused on Syrian refugees drowning in the Mediterranean. Every day brought a new story of the human tragedy that was unfolding as millions tried to migrate and here she was looking at digital images of drug dealers unloading African women from a dinghy.

'Finish your drinks,' Julia clapped her hands together. Her employees fell silent, the smiles falling from their faces. 'Antonia Barrat has uploaded some diamond images.' She held up her phone. 'The women in these photographs are being held somewhere. You two, get yourselves to the Royal and find out if any of them have been treated there and better still, any of them admitted. The rest of you, I want the river police, the border guys and all of your contacts on the force spoken to tonight. Get me some substance to back up these pictures.' Her team exchanged glances, some excited and some confused. 'What are you waiting for?' Julia grinned wildly. 'This is the biggest scoop that we've had this year. Get gone!' Despite not speaking to Antonia Barrat, Julia would make sure that the images were on the front pages of the morning nationals.

CHAPTER 31

Stirling checked the injured men and clicked into autopilot. He made a mental note of the registration plate, called for ambulances, and backup and then communicated the vehicle's details to the traffic division. They put an instant 'be on the lookout' alert against it and informed him who the registered owner was, and that the vehicle wasn't listed as stolen. The name of the owner, Jason Greene was bizarrely familiar but now was not the time to debate the connections in his head. He kept at the back of his mind the fact that a colleague was down. There were some essential processes that needed to be put into motion. As he did so, he knelt and felt for a pulse. There wasn't one. Richard Grainger was dead; his broken and twisted body was buckled above the waist. He had been given no chance against a ton of metal moving at speed. His face was frozen; a mask of fear. Anger boiled to the surface as he approached his colleague. Dalton Sykes was face up; his head tilted at an abnormal angle to his body. Dark red blood ran from his right ear. His glasses were shattered, eyes wide open, glassy, lifeless, and staring. A different sequence of events, a moment's hesitation or one step in a different direction and he could have been lying next to Sykes, broken and bleeding and dead.

Members of the public approached and offered help. He showed them his ID and explained that there was nothing that could be done unless they'd seen the driver. None of them had. It had happened too quickly. A uniformed patrol arrived first on the scene. Their grim expressions showed that the responders were aware that an officer had been killed in the line of duty. They took plastic sheets from their vehicle and covered the bodies. Two ambulances arrived in quick succession and a number of traffic cops and community support officers arrived.

'I want every mobile phone off that bus,' Stirling ordered a uniformed officer. The bus driver had pulled in on the opposite side to offer help, not realising that he had also handed over thirty witnesses to the police. 'If any of them have filmed what happened, get them to Bluetooth the videos to your phones and get them sent to me at the MIT.'

Stirling knew that at least one of them would show them who was driving the Range Rover. He also knew that it wasn't a random hit and run. They very rarely happen on the pavement. He was convinced that the Latvians had silenced Richard Grainger and murdered a Detective Sergeant in the process. Stirling walked back to the ambulances and watched as the two men were loaded aboard. His mobile buzzed. The screen showed that it was the DI calling.

'What happened?' Annie asked. 'Are you hurt?'

'No, I'm fine, guv.'

'Sykes?'

'He's dead. He didn't stand a chance. The bastard came out of nowhere, mounted the pavement, and mowed them both down.'

'Grainger?'

'Dead, guv.' He sighed. 'I got the plate. It is registered to a Jason Greene.'

'The witness from the pawnbrokers?'

'Traffic sent me his licence photograph. It is him.'

'Was he driving?'

'I couldn't see. It happened too quickly but I'm sure that we'll have video footage of the driver. There was a busload of people filming the arrest. Some of them must have captured him.'

'While you were arresting Grainger, Toni Barrat gave me his name as her informer.'

'Jesus,' Stirling growled. 'He's not going to tell us anything now. I suppose it makes sense that it was him. He made the call to arrange the vehicle exchange, or so Fletcher would have us believe.'

'Exactly. Makes me ask why Jason Greene would want to kill him,' Annie said exactly what Stirling was thinking. 'I've got their records, both are low level criminals on the periphery, dealing, handling stolen goods but nothing major. It is not beyond the realms of possibility that they knew each other.'

'He wouldn't have done this, guv. He just wasn't the type,' Stirling said. 'He took photographs of Andris Markevica leaving the pawnbrokers. If Markevica knew that he had photographed him, it's not too much of a stretch to assume that he would go after him. We need to look for Jason Greene, but my guess is that he is already dead.'

'Markevica takes Greene out and then uses his vehicle to make sure that Grainger didn't talk to us.' Annie knew their scenario was solid. 'Miranda will be devastated; they worked together for years. How are you doing?'

'It's all a bit surreal, guv.' Stirling sighed. 'One minute he was next to me the next he's gone. A couple of seconds either way and…'

'You can't think like that. There's no way that we could have seen that coming and even if we had, what could we have done?' Annie said. 'We've dealt with ruthless bastards before and we'll have to again, but we're not psychic.'

'These bastards play by different rules, guv.' His voice sounded flat and emotionless. Annie knew that what he had seen would knock him sideways. Watching a fellow officer die in front of his eyes could only highlight how fragile his own mortality was. Stirling was a brute, hard as nails and difficult to rattle but he was still just a man beneath. His wife and daughter were his life and seeing death up close made him appreciate that fact. It accentuated the fragility of life. 'I need to call home; you know how it is, guv. I need to make sure that they're all right.'

'Do that,' Annie said. She felt a little bit sad that she had no one to call but her career was her spouse. 'I'll need a quick drink when we're done today.'

'Me too, guv. I'll finish up here and then come back to the station. See you later.'

CHAPTER 32

23:00

Gary Powell was the man who posed as the mechanic. He orchestrated the theft of the zombie from the Fletcher Bros premises and the job had gone well. Gary ran through the day's events in his mind. He opened his fridge and reached for a can of Stella. He closed the door and leaned against it as he opened his beer and drank thirstily from it. The disguise of overalls and work boots had been exchanged for faded jeans and Reebok trainers. His greying blond hair was still damp from the shower. He emptied the tin in three visits and then crushed the can and tossed it into the bin. Gary opened the door and grabbed another Stella. He needed to drink to slow down his mind. It had been racing on full throttle for over twelve hours. Closing the fridge, he turned and leaned against it and thought about what had happened. He stared at the briefcase and holdall that were on his dining table; one full of cocaine, the other full of zombie. It had taken him half an hour or so to sort the bags out; it had been a crazy day. Working for Ivor in any capacity made him edgy but he paid well; too well to turn him down. Lifting the drugs had been simplicity itself. The Latvian gang were not expecting anything untoward to happen. They had caught them off guard and the heist had gone as smoothly as it could.

Once they'd ditched the Mercedes, they switched vehicles twice and drove around for an hour before he was happy that were not being followed. He dropped off his associates at different locations and then went to one of his properties. There, he showered and then left the house via an internal garage door. He walked through the back garden to the rear gate where he removed the weather shield from an innocuously parked motorbike. He climbed on and rode ten miles across the city to a long stay car park where he parked the bike and switched to a black Vauxhall Corsa. Nobody could possibly have followed him without being seen and he arrived home without incident. It was a well-practised method of neutralising any counter-surveillance. The shipment was intact, and he was safe but despite being at home he still couldn't relax.

Home was a two-bedroom detached on a new housing estate near the city centre. He had three other houses but this one was where he felt most at home. It was close to where he sometimes worked on the doors of the city's busiest clubs. He moved jobs as often as possible, never wanting to be identified with a single employer or venue. It paid the mortgages on the various properties that he owned. Since leaving the Marines three years earlier, he had worked in close personal protection in both Iraq and Afghanistan. The money was phenomenal, but he limited himself to one tour a year. Recently he had found that doing the odd job for Ivor could be worth more than his legitimate incomes combined.

They had met the year before when Ivor, his wife Marika and brother Andris were enjoying a night out in the city. They were ordering champagne from the bar of the VIP lounge in one of the more exclusive venues, when Andris became involved in an altercation with a local man. Within minutes, the argument had escalated and Andris was on his back looking at the sharp end of a broken bottle. Ivor was impressed when Gary disarmed the man, locked his fingers painfully against his wrist in a manner that made it simple to escort him to the fire exit without any further fuss. Most of the customers were oblivious to the fact there had been an altercation. Ivor had thanked him, and they chatted for a while. The offer of occasional work was made, and Gary agreed to think about it.

Guarding a briefcase in Liverpool was far less dangerous than transporting a high-level politician through the extremist filled streets of Baghdad, plus the climate was less severe. Sweating buckets inside combats and body armour with sand in every crevice of his body was no fun. It didn't take long for Ivor to offer him some highly paid work and once Gary realised that in comparison to working in the Near East, it was easy money, he was keen to take more. Now he was standing in his kitchen staring at a shipment of drugs waiting for a Latvian drug lord to call to arrange to pick up his merchandise. Things had become a little surreal. Part of him felt that he had slipped from hero to zero, crossed the line from light to dark. It was easy money, but he felt both guilty and vulnerable, nonetheless. He put it down to a fear of the unknown. This was unfamiliar territory. His mobile rang and he checked the screen. Unknown caller.

'Hello,' he answered abruptly.

'Is my merchandise safe?' Ivor asked forgoing any greeting.

'Yes. I'm looking at it.'

'What happened at the garage?'

'Nothing much.' Gary felt his skin tingle. There was an edge to Ivor's voice. 'We took the drugs, left everyone alive, just like you asked.'

'You haven't listened to the news today?'

'No, I've been busy working for you.' Gary sighed. Ivor had a knack of beating around the bush. He tried to draw information from people by asking vague questions or telling half-truths. 'What's the problem?'

'Two of my men are dead, the other is critical in hospital. That is the problem. You fucked this up.'

'What?' Gary asked incredulously. 'We didn't kill them!'

'You freed the mules. They killed them.'

'Shit.' Gary sighed. He ran his hand through his hair nervously. 'I thought that they would break out and run for it to be honest. I didn't see that coming.'

'No, you didn't, did you?'

'I followed your instructions to the letter,' Gary countered. 'Which means neither of us is psychic.' The line remained silent for a few seconds.

'Hmm, in hindsight I don't suppose that you can be blamed for that,' Ivor said calmly. Internally, he was fuming but he needed all his assets onside. 'As long as my shipment is safe, we can overlook any mistakes for now. I will be landing in the UK tomorrow morning.'

'Where are you flying to?'

'It is better for me that no one knows that,' Ivor chuckled. It would only take one phone call from a disgruntled rival or employee to INTERPOL and they would cover every flight into every UK airport. 'No offence.'

'None taken.'

'Good,' Ivor agreed. 'I will call and arrange the time for the pickup. Where is my merchandise?'

'It is better for me that no one knows that,' Gary said with a hint of sarcasm. 'No offence.'

Ivor paused. The silence was brooding. 'None taken. I'll call you tomorrow when I've landed.'

'You do that,' Gary said hanging up. He tipped up the Stella and emptied the tin in two gulps. It would take several more of them to calm him enough that he could sleep.

Ivor put the phone down and looked out of the hotel window at the Albert Docks; the River Mersey looked like inky black silk and the street lights reflected on it were bright yellow gems, twinkling at him from the darkness. The huge Liverpool Eye turned majestically, illuminated against the night sky. The bars and restaurants below them were buzzing. He caught a glimpse of Marika's naked body in the mirror. She was as beautiful now as the day he had first seen her gyrating around a pole in Prague. Once she was ready, they would go and eat something. Liverpool was a lively city and they could do as they pleased. Life was good apart from the mess that his people had made. The UK was too small and too civilised to attract attention to his illegal activities. His brother and his associates had acted irresponsibly and completely against his wishes. They thought that he was still in Prague and that was his intention. Things had become complicated. There were too many loose ends that needed to be dealt with. He checked the GPS on his laptop and the satellite image zoomed down to map distance above the city. An arrow flashed red near the city centre. Ivor zoomed in closer. The briefcase full of zombie was located on a new housing estate less than five miles away.

CHAPTER 33

'It scares the crap out of me that three kilos of zombie are out there somewhere,' Miranda Snow said shaking her head. Her eyes were bloodshot from tiredness and tears, although they'd been stemmed for now. A public display of grief wouldn't be appreciated by anyone. There would be a time and a place for that. She kept her voice down as the tables around them were full of late-night drinkers, albeit most of them were on the force. The Navigation was the nearest pub to Canning Place and if an investigation dragged on, it was frequented by police officers of all ranks and departments that called in to unwind on their way home. It was one of the few pubs in the city where the shoplifters didn't go to show their wares. 'We don't know if the outfit that lifted it know what it is that they've stolen. What if they think it's coke? Can you imagine what would happen if it fell into the wrong hands?'

'It doesn't bear thinking about,' Annie said finishing her red wine. 'Here he is,' she said as she spotted Stirling walking through the door. She waved her empty glass and pointed to Miranda. Stirling rolled his eyes to the ceiling and headed for the bar. They had all worked over eighteen hours but sleep wouldn't come easily. Despite arranging to be in early the next day, they all needed a drink. 'I'm hoping that he's got some good news.'

'We're due some,' Miranda emptied her glass. She looked agitated and disinterested. Her eyes kept darting around the bar. Stirling arrived at the table and delivered another round; two large glasses of Merlot and a pint of cider. He put them down on the table and sat opposite Annie and next to Miranda.

'Thanks, Jim. What's the latest?'

'Andris Markevica killed Dalton Sykes,' he said turning to Miranda. Her attention was brought back to the table. She sat bolt upright in her chair. 'From the cameras on the bus, we got three clear images of him driving the Range Rover.'

'Have we found the vehicle?'

'Yes.' He nodded and slurped his cider. 'Burnt out a few miles away from the scene. CSI are there now but don't hold your breath, it's toast.'

'What about Jason Greene?' Annie asked.

'No sign of him at home and no sign of him in the vehicle.' Stirling waved at a colleague across the bar. 'INTERPOL sent over a file on Andris Markevica and his associates. I've sent it onto your email addresses and shared it with the team.'

'Come on,' Annie prompted him. 'Don't drag it out.'

'Andris Markevica is a psycho. He's linked to dozens of gangland murders in and around Riga. The thing is that the Latvian police are prone to lose evidence and witnesses seldom reach the courthouse. After years of watching him walk away from charges, they encouraged him to leave the country for a few years.'

'Encouraged him?' Annie frowned.

'He was an embarrassment to the system.'

'You had better leave Riga or…'

'If you read between the lines, it makes sense.'

'Sounds like we got the short straw,' Annie said. 'It sounds like he thinks that he's untouchable, which goes some of the way to explain how anyone would have the balls to break into Toni's house and terrify her while we had officers outside. That still hasn't sunk in. We have stumbled across a snake pit.' Annie rubbed her eyes with the back of her hands. The prosthetic was beginning to ache. 'Of all the places he could have chosen to go, why pick here?'

'I don't think he made any decisions himself, guv. He's told what to do by his brother,' Stirling said. He leaned closer and looked around the nearby tables. Everyone was wrapped up in their own conversations. 'According to the INTERPOL report 'Ivor' is in charge and he calls the shots.'

'The Barrat woman said that she overheard that name being mentioned, didn't she?' Miranda said distractedly. She was going through the motions. Her mind was fixated on the loss of her colleague.

'Yes. I think Ivor told Andris where he would be going to work.' He stopped to read the information from the screen on his phone. 'He is Ivor Markevica, older brother to Andris. His civilian files have been lost or removed. All that remains is a birth certificate. In effect, he doesn't exist.' Stirling held up a finger and took a sip of his drink. 'However, he does have what's left of a military record. He joined the military from leaving school.' Stirling opened another email on his phone and read from it. 'Most of his file has been redacted but we know he was Specialo Uzdevumu Vieniba,' he tried his best with the pronunciation, 'Latvian Special Forces basically. He was reported as missing in action twenty years ago.' Miranda and Annie exchanged glances. Their dangerous suspects had just become considerably more dangerous. They were both well-practised killers, one highly trained and the other born to it. 'It gets worse,' Stirling grinned sourly. He'd read their concerns from their expressions. 'Ivor Markevica is reportedly the head of an organised crime family known as, Tris. Apparently, Tris is Latvian for three. They sprung up during the soviet occupation following the war. Originally started by three brothers, they were rebels who ran contraband, drugs, alcohol you name it until the Soviets left in ninety-one. Some of them wear tattoos; three skulls on a playing card or a three on a spade. Permission to wear the tattoo is not given lightly. It has to be earned.'

'Let me guess,' Miranda said, 'they have to kill three people?'

'Minimum of three,' Stirling shrugged. 'From the INTERPOL report, they say that 'Three' was also the name for the punishment for any soviet in occupation that killed a Latvian.'

'I don't follow,' Miranda said.

'If the occupiers killed a Latvian or were responsible for their death indirectly, then they were kidnapped and made to watch two members of their family die before being killed themselves. It was a way of discouraging the occupying soldiers and policemen from being cruel.'

'I can see how that would work,' Annie grimaced.

'It did. Initially they treated the Latvians like animals; thousands were murdered every year but as word of Three spread and pictures of slaughtered policemen and their families were printed in the underground press, things improved dramatically. Three became notorious. According to INTERPOL, Ivor Markevica is the latest in a long line of leaders of Three.'

'I would imagine it's a position that few retire from.' Annie sighed. 'No pension scheme in a job like that one.' She sat back and sipped her wine. 'So, they have been established for decades. Brilliant.' Annie said sarcastically. She looked at their expressions. They showed the same level of concern that she felt. 'They will have networks and contacts so far and wide across Europe that we couldn't stop them if we had an army of detectives,' Annie said morosely.

'Some crime families are simply too deeply entrenched abroad for us to make more than a dent in their operations.' Miranda turned her glass in her hand. 'We're wasting our time thinking otherwise. What goes on here is the tip of the iceberg,' she added. 'Do you know how many foreign crime families we have established in the UK now?'

'Lots,' Stirling grunted sarcastically. He had stopped counting years before.

'More than lots,' Miranda said with a sarcastic smile. 'We're fighting a losing battle.'

'We obviously can't shut them down, but we can bang up Andris if he is stupid enough to hang around. My worry is that we're standing on the sidelines watching a gang war unfold. If Three are responsible for bringing in the zombie and the mules, then they're going to be pretty pissed off that someone took it from them and that their men are dead, or as good as.'

'You're right,' Miranda agreed. 'I think that they're trying to clean-up their mess, find out who their leak is and find out who stole their drugs. We're witnessing the fallout, picking up bodies and chasing shadows.'

'I agree but there's another problem too. Where does the Karpov family come into this?' Annie raised her glass. 'We watched one of their men being brought out of the Latvian's property. They left him near the door so that he would be found and yet, we haven't stumbled across an obvious connection between the Karpovs and what's going on. The Russians are not going to let that go unpunished.'

'Are they involved in this though?' Miranda shrugged. 'That could be something unrelated. The Karpovs aren't short of enemies.'

'I hope you're right,' Annie said. 'This could get considerably worse very quickly if they step in.'

'Let's hope not,' Miranda chipped in.

'If you ask me, they're biding their time,' Stirling said. He emptied his glass and stood up. 'It's just a matter of time.'

'Wait a minute.' Annie opened her bag and searched for her purse. She handed him a twenty-pound note. 'My round. Same again?' Miranda nodded and Stirling went to the bar. A sea of people parted as he lumbered through. He stopped to exchange the latest findings with several groups of detectives and uniformed officers alike. 'Today has taken a toll on him,' Annie said quietly.

'It will take a toll on everyone, whether they knew him or not.' Miranda said bitterly. Annie could see her face darken with anger.

'Are you okay?'

'I don't want to talk about it right now.' Miranda filled up. Her eyes glazed. The muscles in her jaw twitched. She changed the subject quickly. 'I heard that Barrat gave up some photographs.'

'Yes, eventually.'

'Were they of any real use?'

'They are well connected. We ran them through facial recognition, turns out the rib pilot was an ex-sergeant in the river force.'

'Bloody hell.' Miranda was shocked but not surprised. She sipped her wine from an oversized glass. 'No wonder they know the old canal systems so well.'

'They seem to have all the bases covered.'

'They do.' Miranda nodded. She looked uncomfortable; her eyes darted everywhere as if she wanted to be somewhere else. 'We've got plenty to work on in the morning. Is that everything that you wanted to tell me?'

'It was not really anything that couldn't have waited.' Annie shrugged. Her colleague looked thinner than usual. Her face had lost its colour and she looked gaunt. 'I was gagging for a drink and thought you could probably use one too. I just thought that you might want some company.'

'That's thoughtful of you.' Miranda smiled thinly. Annie sensed a patronising tone.

'Did you speak to Dalton's family?'

'Yes.'

'How did it go? Or is that a stupid question?'

'Yes, it is a stupid question.' Miranda shook her head and looked around. She could feel her stomach tightening. Dalton Sykes had been her best detective for years. Beneath his frightening exterior beat a heart of gold; at least it had. They had become close friends with a deep mutual respect. There was a black hole in her world that was set to grow bigger as the realisation of his loss hit home. She spotted a group of her detectives at the end of the bar. They were raising shot glasses and toasting their fallen colleague. It was the third round that she had seen downed, not that she was counting. They were entitled to grieve. She wanted to grieve with them. She felt like standing with them and drinking shots until she was absolutely shitfaced. A glass of Merlot and a chat with Annie and Stirling just wasn't cutting it. In fact, it was becoming irritating. She appreciated their concern, but she needed to be with her team. 'Listen,' she stood up and made her best effort to smile. 'Thanks for the chat but I'm going to buy my team a few rounds. You understand, don't you?'

'Err…' Miranda was gone before Annie could answer her. 'No problem,' Annie mumbled to no one. She waved goodbye meekly and felt both hurt and incredibly clumsy. She had invited Miranda for two good reasons. The first was to catch-up with Stirling's news and the second was to offer a consoling shoulder to lean on. She wasn't surprised that she had declined the latter. They were hardly best friends, but she thought that they had a bond. Maybe she had assumed that because they were successful females in a predominantly male profession. In reality, the only thing that they had in common was the job and they didn't agree on that very often. She watched Stirling chatting to a group of men at the bar. He towered over most of them. The conversation looked serious; their faces were stern but full of respect for the big sergeant. She wondered as the members of the shift drifted into groups. They mostly split into groups of the people that they worked with daily. Traffic cops stood with other traffic cops. Uniformed officers stood with other uniformed officers, detectives with detectives. Birds of a feather, she thought. Some of the groups were all male, some mixed. There were no groups entirely made up of females. She couldn't decide if that was odd or not. Miranda had joined some of her team. Part of the group were leaving, making their excuses and saying their goodbyes. Throwing shots down one after another wasn't everyone's bag. The wise ones knew when to call it a day and leave. She watched Miranda lift and swallow, two shots in quick succession. There would be a painful price to pay in the morning.

Annie looked at her empty glass and decided that she needed to be away from these people. As much as she loved some of them and respected most of them, she had a sudden urge for her own company. Stirling was still engrossed at the bar as she slipped her bag over her shoulder and headed for the side entrance. The drinks were flowing, and the volume was rising. Conversations were becoming more animated and more intense. Annie was almost invisible as she opened the side door and stepped out into the rain. Almost.

CHAPTER 34

Peter Fletcher paid the driver and climbed out of the cab. The suspension bridge was illuminated against the night. From below it where he was standing, it seemed to dominate the sky. An express train thundered by along the viaduct on its way south to London and an Easy Jet flight roared overhead on its approach to John Lennon Airport. It was refreshing that after a surreal day, life in the big city trundled on regardless. He had had enough of the hospital and tried to sign himself out, but the doctors and the police were adamant that he should stay. The doctors said that medically he should remain until the morning; the police were less vague about how long they would need him, but he got the impression that they wanted to keep him indefinitely. It was only when he had asked to be discharged that he realised he wasn't being treated just as a victim. When he had asked about going home his armed guard had scoffed. He heard him mumbling abuse as he made a call to the detectives on the case, who were elsewhere in the hospital and they'd said that they needed to interview him under caution before he went anywhere.

The armed guard appeared to be incredulous and a little bit insulted that he had thought that he could leave at any time he chose to. The detectives had said that they would be down to his room within fifteen minutes, but Peter had decided that he wasn't hanging around. He changed into his clothes, opened the window, and dropped down onto some freshly dug flowerbeds below. He had called his brother Paul but couldn't get an answer. The chances were that he was in custody or if not, he had self-medicated with a bottle of rum and was crashed out on the settee at home. It was late and it had been a long hard day. Peter decided to make his own way home. After a short walk through the hospital's rear car park, he flagged down a taxi and asked to be taken home to their garage.

When the cab drove away, he felt saddened by the view in front of him. Fletcher Bros was in darkness and crime scene tape crisscrossed the service bay doors. It flapped in the breeze. The seriousness of their situation hadn't sunk in until he saw it. He wanted to go to bed and rest his aching head and then wake up in the morning and walk across the yard to work. They had the same routine every morning. Paul would go over to the garage, switch on the lights, fire up the equipment, and most importantly, switch on the kettle and the radio. Pete would fry a full packet of smoked back bacon, four rashers each on toast, red sauce for Pete, brown for Paul. He would take them over to the office where they would swig their tea and munch their breakfast while they prioritised the day's workload. That wasn't going to happen again for a while.

Pete trudged across the yard and peered into the reception area. The floor was marked with muddy footprints, dozens of them. Fingerprint powder glinted on the doorframes and flat surfaces. He sighed and walked around the conservatory towards the house. The windows were black like sightless eyes staring at him. There was no sign of Paul being at home. Pete wondered if he was tucked up in bed snoring, or if he was shivering on a rubber mattress in a police cell. He knew that the police would come looking for him soon, but it didn't matter. Being home for a few hours would be enough. He just needed to rest in his own bed. They hadn't done anything so bad that it was worth running away and leaving their lives behind. It would be better in the long run to face the consequences of their mistakes now. They had taken a gamble and lost. It wasn't a disaster that was so great that they couldn't come back from it.

As he dwelled on things, a shadow seemed to move in his peripheral vision. He looked up at his bedroom window, but it was empty, black, and uninviting. There was something foreboding about the house tonight, something menacing and sinister. As he looked at the windows the darkness behind them seemed to deepen. It gave the illusion of shadows moving behind the glass. The harder he looked the deeper the darkness became. He felt as if someone was staring back, hidden in the shadows beyond the range of his vision. He blinked and tried to focus again but the blackness just shifted, teasing him, tempting him to come in and investigate. 'Come and see, come on.'

His home had changed from a warm and comforting sight to a cold and sinister one, but he couldn't understand the shift in his perception. He stared at the windows in turn. The two bedrooms and the two downstairs windows stared back at him unflinchingly. He tried not to blink in case they moved when his eyelids closed. His brain played tricks on his mind. As his eyes moved to the next window, the previous window seemed to come to life. His eyes would snap back immediately but the shadows would become still once more. He took the door keys from his pocket and studied the house again. It had been his home for years yet here he was like a frightened child outside a haunted house. Peter cursed beneath his breath and kicked himself mentally. The bang on the head had caused his trepidation. The doctors had told him that he may have concussion. It was a perfectly reasonable explanation. He had suffered the trauma of being held up by armed men wearing masks, being bashed over the head and rendered unconscious and then being traumatised by the news that their greed had led them to being linked to a gang implicated in drug dealing, people trafficking, and murder. If he hadn't been affected by it all then he wouldn't be normal. Pete steeled himself against his fears and took a step towards the house. As he did, the darkness behind the windows deepened. The voices in his head whispered to him, 'Come in, come and see… we won't hurt you'

CHAPTER 35

Annie pulled her coat tightly closed and stepped into the night. The temperature had dropped a few degrees in the short time that she had been in the pub. She took a deep breath and savoured the salty tang. The sea air seemed to lift her spirits, filling her body full of energy. It was dark and the lights from the pub dissipated quickly as she moved away from the building. The sound of gulls crying drifted to her from somewhere further upriver. She shivered and headed towards the bright lights of the main road. As she walked up the side street behind the pub, she saw headlights sweeping around the corner up ahead. Her skin began to prickle. Something didn't feel right. She stopped and felt the urge to run in the opposite direction.

Thoughts of Dalton Sykes being mown down were fresh and raw. She was trapped in a narrow street, high walls on each side. The vehicle picked up speed as it approached; the headlights dazzled her. The driver switched to full beam, which blinded her momentarily. Stunned by the lights she froze; her tired brain was further slowed by the red wine that she had drunk. She heard the engine growing louder, water spaying from beneath the tyres. Every sound was amplified by her fear. The lights seemed to grow brighter as it approached her, filling her mind with white light. Annie held up her arm to protect her eyes. She squinted against the glare. The vehicle changed direction. It moved across the road heading directly for her. Annie closed her eyes, her breath stuck in her lungs. Fear took over and she was frozen to the spot waiting for a catastrophic impact to come.

CHAPTER 36

Peter Fletcher suppressed his irrational fears and walked cautiously towards his home. The front door was to the right of the building hidden by a brick porch. Normally a nightlight illuminated the porch and the area immediately around the doorstep, but it wasn't lit. That was odd itself. It was out of the ordinary, unusual, not normal but then it hadn't been a normal day. He ignored the voices in his head and the fear that nibbled at his mind. 'It doesn't feel right does it?'

As he neared the house, the sound of traffic crossing the bridge drifted to him. That wasn't unusual but he thought that he could hear an engine running closer to home; petrol not diesel. Most people couldn't distinguish between the two but that was what he did. Engines had been his life since leaving school. He turned and listened to the darkness. It was an engine; he was sure. It was idling though, not travelling. There was a difference and he could tell from a distance which was which. He cocked his head to gauge the direction that the sound was coming from. As he listened, an express train from London approached the Silver Jubilee Bridge that ran parallel to the suspension bridge. It carried the trains eighty feet above the Mersey; the height meant that the sound carried, especially at night. The noise drowned out everything. Peter waited until the train had gone, its sound faded to a distant rumble. He listened more closely this time. The petrol engine was running somewhere behind the main structure of the garage. They had a few smaller outhouses there, which they used to store MOT failures and restoration projects. Why there would be an engine running was beyond him. There was only one reason that made sense and that was car thieves.

Peter glanced back at the house. The blackness behind the windows seemed to drift and float, changing in density. It was his mind playing tricks on him. His eyes couldn't penetrate the inky darkness, so his brain filled in the gaps. 'Is it your imagination though? Are you sure?' He wanted to go into the house and go to bed but he couldn't ignore the fact that an engine was running on their property and he could hardly call the police. He looked at the house again and a shiver ran through him. Pete shook off the negative thoughts again and headed for the outhouses. As he navigated the rear of the garage, he could see the outlines of the engine sheds. They loomed up against the darkness of the fields beyond. Dark shadows against a darker sky. He stopped and thought for a moment. The engine seemed to be running constantly on idle and the noise was coming from the furthest building. It was a single garage with an inspection pit where there was an old Alfa Romeo stored inside. It was a runner but needed new suspension all around and three bushes replaced to get it through an inspection.

His brother Paul was an Alfa nut and had insisted that he would fix it up in his own time. That had been two years earlier and all he had done was to remove the wheels and leave it on jacks. The more he listened to the engine the more convinced he was that it was the Alfa. It crossed his mind that Paul might be in there tinkering with his project, taking his mind off their problems. 'Really… why is he tinkering in the dark?'

Peter flicked through the scenarios in his mind. Some bad people had used them and their premises to do illegal stuff. It had all gone pear shaped. Maybe some of the gang had hidden in the outhouses and they needed a getaway vehicle. Maybe they were putting the wheels back on the Alfa so that they could simply drive away under the cover of darkness. 'Or maybe the Alfa Romeo pixies were in there repairing it. Go and see… go on. You're not scared, are you?'

His imagination taunted him. He was scared. Peter headed for the nearest shed to source a makeshift weapon. He felt for his keys and fumbled through them until he found the one that opened the padlock. They used the shed for nonvaluable bits and pieces that may have a use in the future. He opened the door and stepped inside. The air was thick with the smell of paint and petroleum. He knew the layout from memory; the position of every half full tin of paint and shock absorber were mapped out in his mind. To his left was a shelf where there was a heavy torch that they used to find things in the winter months when the daylight faded early. He felt along the shelf until his fingers touched the handle. It was there. He picked it up and switched it on, aiming the beam at the floor where it wouldn't attract unwanted attention. The light was dull, the batteries weak, but it was better than nothing. Its weight was reassuring. He panned the beam around the shed and stopped when he saw a length of chain that had broken off from a towing rig the year before. He walked over to it and picked it up. The links were rusty, but it would make a decent weapon. He wrapped some of it around his left hand and let the remainder hang loose. Armed with the torch and chain, he stepped out of the shed and headed cautiously towards the sound of the engine. He had only taken a few steps when a crushing blow to side of his head dropped him like a stone.

CHAPTER 37

As the vehicle approached, Annie stepped back against the wall but there was nowhere to go. Visions of Dalton Sykes flashed through her mind. She held her breath and waited for the impact. The engine roared and then suddenly seemed to grow quieter. Instead of a catastrophic thump, the vehicle stopped next to the kerb. The driver leaned over and opened the door. Annie nearly laughed in relief as she stared into the craggy face of her Superintendent, Alec Ramsay.

'I thought you might be in there,' he said over the engine noise. 'Have you had enough to drink for one night?'

'It's been a long day, guv,' she said leaning against the roof. 'You do realise that I've just crapped myself?'

'What?' Alec frowned. His wrinkles deepened. The dimples on his chin looked like they'd been carved into his skin. 'Why?'

'You heard about what happened to Dalton Sykes from the Drug Squad?'

'I've heard but I haven't heard the details,' Alec shook his head. He checked his mirrors to make sure that he wasn't blocking the road. 'I've come straight from the airport. My mobile battery is dead. What's happened?'

'If you give me a lift home, I'll tell you all about it and you might even get a brew out of it.'

'Jump in.' Alec smiled. 'It'll be kicking out time soon and I don't want rumours of me kerb crawling outside the pub spreading through the nick.' He laughed and put the vehicle in gear. 'They'll be saying that I cruise around at night searching for young detectives.'

Annie climbed in. 'There's no young detectives out here, guv, just me. How was your trip?' Alec waited for her to belt up and then drove off.

'Interesting at best. It was a sad succession of presentations about how to treat migrants when they land on your shores. They all have similar stories, but no one has the answers yet.' He glanced at Annie, but she seemed to be distracted. 'Have you ever been to Malta?'

'No, but it's on my list.'

'You should go. It's a lovely island, not much vegetation though.' He added as an afterthought. 'It's just a big rock in the middle of the Mediterranean really, but the sun was shining, and the lager was cheap.'

'Who needs grass?'

'Sheep.'

'Fair comment.' Annie smiled weakly. She looked tired. Alec knew full well that she had been running on adrenalin all day. The intense pressure of an investigation fuelled them but when their working day was done and the adrenalin waned, exhaustion would hit. It was sudden and it was debilitating. He had been there more times than he could remember and knew that he would have to tread carefully. Alec remembered that when his wife Gail was alive, he would arrive home late, wrapped up in an investigation, his mind going around in circles processing the evidence and possible scenarios. Poor Gail, who hadn't seen him for fourteen hours, would want to talk about her day, discuss plans for their time off and talk about their families and friends and what she was going to cook on Sunday. Alec could remember clearly how she would chat tirelessly, her voice nothing more than an irritating drone, a distraction from the jigsaw that he was constructing in his mind. Nodding in the right places, the odd smile and occasional 'Yes, dear' became an art form that kept the peace. Now that her voice was silenced forever, he missed it terribly. He wished that he had made the effort to switch off work from his mind and listen to her. Had he done so she may well have been alive. Regret was a weight that he had to carry with him. He couldn't fix anything because she was dead. How he wished he could turn back the clock and have his time with her over again. He would have treated her differently, cherished his time with her. Now all he could cherish was her memory. He left a comfortable silence so that Annie could settle before he spoke.

'I haven't come to give you a hard time. I know you've had a tough day,' he said. 'I've had my ear bent at the airport. I've spent an hour on the phone talking to the ACC and an hour talking to a detective from Riga. That's why my battery is flat,' Alec glanced at Annie as he spoke, but she was looking out of the passenger window. 'The long and short of it is the Chief Constable isn't happy with the way the investigation is moving,' he said quietly.

'He's an 'acting' Chief Constable,' Annie corrected him sarcastically. 'And more importantly, he's a wanker.'

'Agreed.' Alec nodded. 'Wanker or not, he's not happy. He thinks that we've lost control of this Latvian case.' Annie remained tight lipped. She was angry and didn't want to say anything that she would regret. Alec sensed that the day had made her volatile. He left it alone for a few minutes and then prompted her. 'Have we lost control of this, Annie?'

'No is the honest answer.' Annie shrugged and raised her hands palms up. 'We haven't lost control of it because we never had bloody control of it. The entire shitty case has been a runaway juggernaut from the moment Antonia Barrat called 999.' She snorted and shook her head. 'I thought I'd seen it all, I really did. What the hell happened to the job, guv?' Annie ranted. 'We used to have a half a dozen gangs responsible for most of the drugs and prostitution in the city. We knew who they were, we knew all their names, their families, their friends, and we knew what colour underwear they were wearing and what time they went for a crap. Okay, every now and again they might give each other a good kicking or someone would disappear but now we have Russians, Turks, Albanians, Estonians, Romanians, and whoever I have left off the list, running around shooting one another willy-nilly like they don't give a fuck about the consequences.' Her eyes were wide and her expression incredulous. 'This Latvian mob is something else entirely, guv. Dalton Sykes was scraped off the pavement today.' She tapped the dashboard with her index finger. 'They mowed down a witness and a detective this afternoon in broad daylight as if they're fucking untouchable!' Annie shook her head and took a deep breath. She realised that she was ranting but she needed a good rant. 'I thought that the Russian mob was bad, but this bunch makes them look like boy scouts!' She shook her head and pointed her finger at Alec. 'You mark my words that they're the worst that we've seen, guv. I'm telling you that I've never experienced such a bunch of arrogant merciless bastards in my career.' She paused for breath again. 'I'm sorry for going on, guv but if the Acting Chief Constable isn't happy then tell him to get off his fat arse and go to the mortuary. Tell him to go and take a bloody good look at the bodies that these bastards have left behind so far and when he has, then he can sit me down and tell me exactly where I went wrong!'

'Hmm,' Alec shook his head. 'I could tell him that, but I don't think he would be too happy about the fat arse comment. Maybe we should just get an action plan together and send him that instead.' Annie ignored the joke. Alec clenched his jaw and gave her a chance to cool off. Turning the radio up a touch, he nodded slowly as he drove. Birdy was singing 'Skinny Love' in her mournful tone. Alec wondered how someone so young and pretty could produce such a world-weary voice. 'I love this track,' he said changing the subject.

'It's not a floor-filler,' Annie said looking at the Anglican cathedral. Her anger was spent, her frustration vented. She was exhausted. Alec was the last person that she wanted to shout at.

As they neared Annie's house, he turned the radio off and spoke to her softly. 'I think you should start at the beginning and tell me exactly what has happened.' He held up his finger to his lips and smiled. 'But wait until we are at your house and we have a drink in our hand. By that time, you should have calmed down.'

'Hmm.' Annie crossed her arms. 'Don't count on it,' she joked. They spent the rest of the short journey in a comfortable silence. Their mutual respect made it easy to discuss the job calmly. Annie was stressed but not with Alec. Never with Alec.

Alec parked up in the driveway and they walked to the front door, their feet crunched on the gravel. The clouds parted and Alec caught the glint of a silver orb from the upstairs windows. It would be the full moon the next day and the estuary would be full of big fish, although he didn't think that he was going to have much time to get his rods out. He could hear his late wife's voice in his mind, 'Fishing? When are you going to go fishing? I hardly see you as it is, and you're planning to spend what little time we have fishing. You don't even eat fish!' She hadn't understood that it was his way of escaping the world for a few hours. Alec hadn't understood that Gail didn't think that she should be escaped from and therein lay a problem that dogged their marriage through the later years.

'Do you want coffee?' Annie asked as they climbed the stairs to the living room. The architect had put two bedrooms and a garage on the ground floor to make the most of the views from the upper rooms of the house. 'I'm going to have something stronger to knock me out. I need to sleep tonight.' Annie added. She tried not to make it sound as if she was apologising for having a drink, but it did. The truth was that she found it much easier to switch off her brain after a couple of glasses of brandy. Sometimes she added Bailey's and ice cubes made from black coffee. That was her favourite at the moment. Remembering to make the coffee ice cubes was the key.

'Coffee would be good,' Alec called after her. He sat on an L-shaped leather settee and looked around. It was tastefully furnished with laminate flooring and IKEA shelving units. There was no sign of anyone else sharing the house. 'Did you have any luck finding a lodger?'

'Not really,' she answered from the kitchen. 'One woman asked if the house was carbon neutral and the other one wouldn't stop staring at my prosthetic. She hardly said a word and then didn't get back in touch. I think it freaked her out.' Alec could hear the kettle boiling and cups clinking. 'I'm going to put my cosies on I'm afraid; I won't be two minutes.'

'No problem.' He heard her padding down the stairs, doors opening and closing, the toilet flushed and then in less than five minutes, she was back. 'That was quick.'

'There's a trail of clothes behind me but it has to be done when I get in. Clothes off, cosies on.' Annie smiled. She had changed into grey flannel tracksuit pants and a matching top. 'I don't really need a lodger and I'm not sure that I want one. I just thought the money would come in handy and it might be nice to see the lights on when I get home after work.'

'That, I can identify with,' Alec agreed. 'I still get home and see the house in darkness and wonder where Gail is.'

Annie popped her head around the door. 'How long has it been now?'

'Three years.'

'Bloody hell.' Annie sighed. 'They say it gets easier with time.'

'They say a lot of things. Most of it is bullshit.'

Annie smiled and went back into the kitchen. She reappeared with a cup in one hand and a tumbler in the other. 'Coffee for you and brandy and Baileys' for me.'

'Cheers,' Alec said raising his cup. He sat back and sipped his brew. 'Right then, start at the beginning.'

Annie took a long gulp of her drink before she started. It took her over an hour, three glasses of brandy and Bailey's and two cups of coffee to explain the day's events. Ten minutes after Alec had left, she was already in a deep sleep.

CHAPTER 38

3 a.m.

Toni Barrat was asleep. Not a deep sleep but a fitful, nightmare filled doze. Kayla was calling to her from the window of a burning house. The flames were creeping higher and higher. The smoke was becoming darker and thicker. Her cries were becoming louder and more frantic. The heat was becoming more intense every second, but she couldn't move an inch. The flames snaked along the ground towards Toni. Kayla's face began to melt, and her arms flailed wildly. Her nightmare mingled with her memories of Bonfire Night, many years before. The stench of burning human flesh filled her senses. She looked down and watched her own skin blister and peel and then suddenly the flames were gone, and she was standing in a silent black void. Alone and frightened, she called to Kayla but there was no reply.

When she felt a gentle tap on her shoulder, she twitched violently and opened her eyes, but it took a few seconds for her to realise where she was. It was a relief to be out of her nightmares, but she knew that she would have to return to them later on. People look forward to their slumber, but for Toni sleep was the place where her demons gathered to taunt her. She always had to return to them, and she knew that she always would. The harsh light made her blink and the smell of stale sweat masked by disinfectant told her that she was still deep within the bowels of the Police Headquarters. She didn't feel rested at all. Her eyes were sore, and her head felt like it was full of cotton wool. She felt sick to the stomach with worry. She had stayed awake as long as she possibly could, but exhaustion had caught up with her. Waiting for Kayla to come out of surgery was torture. She felt guilty for sleeping when her partner was seriously injured. She wanted to be there with her, but the DI was adamant that she would take her there as soon as Kayla came out of surgery. It made sense. One waiting room was pretty much like another and if she was honest, she was very scared of the men who had hurt Kayla and then broken into their home. They had broken into their house while she was under police protection. That showed a ruthless disregard for the law. They had no fear. They could get to her if they really wanted to; they wouldn't think twice about trying to get to her in the hospital. The DI was right; it was safer to wait at the station. She felt a hand shake her gently once more.

'Wake up, Toni. We need to get you to the Royal,' Stirling's voice was vaguely familiar to her. 'I'm taking you to see Kayla.'

'Kayla?' Toni snapped awake. She could see that it was still pitch-black outside. It was the middle of the night. 'Is she okay?'

Stirling shook his head slowly, 'She's out of surgery but she's taken a turn for the worse. We're going to take you to her. Quickly, get your bag. We need to leave now.'

'Oh my God,' Toni whispered. 'She's dead, isn't she?'

'No.' Stirling touched her arm gently. 'I would tell you if she was. She's alive but she might not make it through the night, Toni. Best that we get there as fast as we can so you can spend some time with her. I need you to put this on underneath your coat,' Stirling said handing her a bulletproof vest.

'Underneath?' Toni asked. Stirling had donned one earlier. His was sitting above his other clothes. She was groggy and confused. 'Yours is on top of your clothes?'

'They won't be shooting at me because I'm not the target,' Stirling replied gruffly. 'If they see that you're wearing a vest, they'll shoot you in the head instead to make sure that you're dead. Now put it on quickly. We need to go.' Toni nodded timidly in agreement although she felt as if she had been punched in the stomach. The thought of being shot in the head had rattled her. She let Stirling guide her to the lift where they were met by two armed officers. They exchanged a few brief words that Toni heard but didn't compute. As they descended to the car park, she looked at their holstered weapons. They were officers from an elite unit highly trained in the use of firearms but for some reason, she didn't feel in the slightest bit safe.

CHAPTER 39

Late at night when the traffic has gone, Alder Hey Children's Hospital is a ten-minute drive east from the Royal Liverpool Hospital. It is a huge facility with over two thousand staff, treating hundreds of thousands of children from all over the UK every year. Because of the nature of its patients, it functions twenty-four hours a day. Parents are allowed to stay with their children around the clock and at night, when their offspring are sleeping, they can use the time to take a break from the wards. Some of the shops and restaurants stay open. Andris Markevica walked into the reception area and checked the floor plan of the hospital. He made a mental note of the layout in his head before walking into Cafe Nero and buying a large latte. The barista was young, firm, and Asian. She was attractive and had he not been in such a rush, he would have asked her out for a drink. She would have said no but then they always did. She would refuse because he was too old, then he would have bullied her into dating him regardless. No was a word that just didn't compute in his head. Andris wasn't as handsome as his brother Ivor, nor was he as intelligent. His brother had the looks and the charm. Andris both admired and envied his brother. Women found his brother irresistible, but they found Andris intimidating. He had lost the bottom half of his left ear in a bar fight and his nose had been broken badly and was crooked and bent but it wasn't his facial features that scared them, it was his demeanour. His eyes were piercing and undressed them indiscreetly, his smile was a sneer and his language was from the sewer. Women were sexual objects to be abused mentally and physically. To most females he was intimidating; to the rest he was just plain frightening. Andris had no awareness of the fact that he made women recoil, quite the opposite. In his mind women wanted him and if they said no it was because they were playing hard to get. Either that or they were lesbians.

'Large latte,' the young barista, whose badge identified her as Leah, said as she handed him his drink. She had all the enthusiasm of a teenager who had drawn the late shift for the third day on the trot. 'Anything else?'

Andris opened his leather jacket and nodded down towards his belt. Leah reluctantly looked down. She really hoped that it wasn't his penis that he was gesturing to. She didn't want to look down, but she couldn't help herself. The butt of a black pistol protruded from his waistband. She had never seen a semiautomatic before, but it looked real enough to strike fear through her. In hindsight, his penis would have been less frightening. Her face drained of colour.

'You can give me all the notes from the till,' he grinned. The girl nodded and opened the till. She snatched at the notes and handed them to him with shaking hands. 'Very good. Well done. Now go and phone the police and tell them that you have been robbed by a man with a big gun.' He leaned over the counter and stroked her chin. She froze like a statue. 'Make sure that you tell them it was a very big gun.'

She nodded timidly; her teeth chattered with fear. He picked up his coffee, turned and walked out. There were a handful of dumbstruck customers watching but none of them fitted into the hero bracket. No one made eye contact with him and no one dared to use their mobile while he was in the near vicinity. Andris smiled at them as he left the coffee shop and walked back into the foyer. They looked at each other in disbelief. To his right was the main entrance door where he had entered; to his left was the information desk that doubled as the reception. He headed towards the desk and sipped his latte as he went. The reception was manned by a female civilian employee and an aging male security guard, who eyed him suspiciously as he approached. Andris took another noisy slurp of his coffee, which left a milky moustache on his lip.

'Good evening.' Andris smiled and raised his cup in greeting.

'What can we do for you?'

'I need you to tell the police that there's a madman running around the hospital shooting at people.'

The receptionist frowned and looked at the security guard. They rolled their eyes towards the ceiling. 'Now, why would we do that?'

Andris took out his gun and showed it to them. It had barely registered as being real before Andris pointed it at the clock on the wall and fired. The clock face exploded into a dozen shards and the casing dropped onto the desk beneath it with a deafening clatter. 'Tell them that I intend to shoot as many kids as I can before they get me. Understand?'

The security guard nodded silently and picked up the phone. Andris waited for him to dial the emergency number before he walked off towards the wards.

CHAPTER 40

Letva Lapsa was at the rear of King David's School. It was a prestigious boarding school that accommodated children of the Jewish faith from all over the world. The building was built from granite in a mock castle style with turrets and crenulations topped with a dark slate roof. There were a handful of lights still burning and he could see the reflection of a television flickering on the ceiling of a room on the second floor. That was the room that he needed. It would be perfect. He sighed and checked his watch. It was time. He dialled 999 from his mobile.

'Emergency, which service?'

'Police.'

'Connecting you now.'

'Police emergency.'

'Hello, I am outside King David School, Childwall Road,' he looked at the school as he spoke.

'Okay, what is the emergency?'

'There are two men with rucksacks loitering near the rear of the school. They look very suspicious to me.'

'Where are they exactly?'

'They're in a copse of trees and bushes near to the rear entrance on Childwall Road.'

'And they're behaving suspiciously?'

'Yes, they're crouched down behind the wall.'

'Can you describe them for me please?'

'They're dark skinned, maybe Middle Eastern with long beards. I think they're Muslims. One of them has a gun,' Letva said excitedly. 'Quickly, get someone here. One of them is pointing a gun at the school!' He took the mobile from his ear and aimed his nine-millimetre at the window of the room that still had the lights on and squeezed the trigger three times.

CHAPTER 41

Ivor Markevica drove north along the dock roads. They had enjoyed a meal and a few drinks listening to a tribute band in a bar and now it was time for business. The traffic was negligible, mostly taxis, delivery vans of all sizes and Hackney cabs. Marika was sitting in the passenger seat; her beige leather miniskirt had ridden up to expose her tanned thighs. Ivor glanced over at them each time the street lights illuminated the vehicle. He allowed his hand to slip from the gearstick between her legs, stroking the soft flesh of her inner thigh with his fingertips. Her eyes filled with mischief and she allowed his fingers to linger there a second before gently moving them down to her knee.

'Enough! It tickles.' She looked out of the window, a sultry look on her face. The chemistry between them was still as strong as when they'd first met. She used his desire for her to her advantage. He was a tough man with a strong character but when she could see desire in his eyes, she could wrap him up and tie him in knots. If she wanted something particular, she waited for the right moment to ask for it. He wanted her now. That was obvious. There would be time enough for their lovemaking once they'd retrieved the zombie.

'Turn right,' she said pointing to a junction about a hundred metres further on. The GPS on her phone was guiding them to an address on the edge of the city centre. The tracker in the briefcase was still active, the signal strong. Ivor turned and then five hundred metres on, she pointed to a turning on their left. 'Down here. It's the second close on the right, third house along.'

Ivor indicated and pulled the car to the kerb. 'Give me the tracker,' he said checking around. The houses in the street were in darkness. 'I'll go on foot from here. If anyone pulls into the road, drive off and text me.' He leaned over and kissed her lips.

'Be careful,' Marika warned him.

'Always,' Ivor said as he opened the door and climbed out.

The air was cold, and the breeze had a bite to it. Stars twinkled through an occasional gap in the clouds as they raced across the night sky. He could hear the city behind him in the distance; the sound of sirens blaring drifted from all directions. Despite the size of the city, there seemed to be a lot of sirens; too many. It made him feel uneasy. He had warned Letva and his brother not to attract any more attention and he hoped that they'd listened. They had lost a lot of key men in a short space of time. It should have been a simple operation. Ivor had made plans to replace them quickly and to bolster their operation with more personnel. He could flood a European city with men in under forty-eight hours. Luckily, their businesses in

London, Brighton and the south-west were well established, and his employees were easily redeployed without affecting operations. He had made contingency plans already and would supervise the reorganisation of the hierarchy himself. Oleg had crossed the line by all accounts. Taking one of the Karpov's senior men was bad enough but to allow him to be found on property that belonged to Three was unforgivable. If he had disappeared, so be it. The Karpovs would have had their suspicions but without a body, nothing could be proved. The way things had unfolded, not only did they know that he was dead, they knew who had done it and there would be a violent price to pay. It seemed obvious that Andris wasn't capable of controlling things alone. He would have to appoint an advisor, who would report directly to Ivor. Hopefully Andris wouldn't realise that he had been demoted. Letva was a different matter altogether.

Ivor crossed the road, his hands deep in his pockets, collars turned up and shoulders hunched against the breeze. His footsteps echoed from the pavement as he reached the second close. He checked the tracker as he neared the entrance. The briefcase was moving. He frowned and checked again. It was moving east to west slowly and erratically. He listened but couldn't hear a car engine nearby. He walked further into the close and watched as the tracker showed the briefcase moving in ever decreasing circles. Ivor looked around and checked the GPS. This was the right place but the houses on his Google map were not actually there yet. The foundations had been laid and the first course of bricks had been built and then covered with Visqueen. The case moved again, stopped and then began to circle once more. Ivor cursed and reluctantly entered the street.

'What the fuck are you doing with my drugs,' he muttered under his breath. When he reached the third plot, he checked the tracker again. The red arrow was still moving. It appeared to be zigzagging five metres left and right and then it circled again but in the opposite direction. It stopped and he looked up. The tracker was pointing to a position just a few metres in front of him. Ivor contemplated his next move. Had the chip corrupted giving the impression that the case was moving, or had Gary Powell hidden his merchandise, buried it maybe, and the movement was simply refraction from the ground?

He checked around him and stepped from the pavement onto the plot. As he reached the concrete footings, he checked the tracker once more. The signal was now behind him. Ivor turned and retraced his steps. He was level with it, but it was a few metres to his right. Taking a penlight torch from his inside pocket, he scanned the ground. Perhaps there would be signs of something buried or maybe a manhole cover. He was anxious as he studied the ground. There was a scratching noise to his left. He heard breathing. As the torchlight illuminated the ground in front of him it suddenly became obvious to him. On the next plot was a Portakabin that had steps leading up to its door. Ivor guessed it was the site office through daylight hours and a security hut at night. Whatever it was, it was dark inside. At the side of the steps was a kennel. As he shone the torch, a German Shepherd trotted out of the kennel. It went to the end of its tether and then trotted in a circle before slipping back into his kennel. Ivor checked the scanner and looked around. The tracker showed the case had stopped moving and was close. Ivor scanned the ground with his torch. A metre to his left was a curly pile of dog shit that had steam still rising from it. Without checking the excrement, Ivor knew that the chip from the briefcase had been removed and then replanted into some food, probably a sausage before being fed to the dog. Now, it had a smelly new home and Ivor had been duped. Ivor shook his head and bit his bottom lip. He had underestimated Gary Powell this time, but he wouldn't underestimate him again.

CHAPTER 42

Annie yawned and stretched her aching limbs. Five minutes earlier, she had taken a call from the hospital; the situation wasn't good. Two hours sleep had left her groggy and weak, but the news woke her up quickly. Kayla Yates had crashed in surgery. She had died on the operating table. Her heart had stopped, and they couldn't restart it for over two minutes. It was touch and go. Concerned about her brain being starved of oxygen for too long, the surgeons almost gave up, but she responded at the last second. They had stabilised her and put her into an induced coma to allow her body to rest and repair itself, but they were not convinced that she would make it through the night.

Annie didn't want Antonia Barrat to go to the hospital. She simply couldn't protect her there. Despite her concerns, she had no choice. She had arranged to have her taken to see Kayla under escort. The Royal was under reconstruction and as such was a security nightmare. The new building had twelve storeys, twenty-three wards, six hundred and forty-six en suite bedrooms, a forty-bed critical care unit and nineteen operating theatres. It would take a small army to secure the building and defend their witnesses. Raitis Girts, Peter Fletcher, Kayla Yates, and an unnamed Latvian woman were all under armed guard at the hospital. They were all on different wards in separate parts of the huge building. Adding Toni into the mix would only make a fragile situation critical. She had a limited amount of armed resources to utilise and they were spread thinly.

Earlier on, after a few drinks, Stirling had gone back to the station. He had intended to sleep in one of the bunks but when the call came in from the Royal, he insisted that he would escort Toni Barrat to the hospital. It had been a stretch for Annie to acquire and deploy another two armed officers to escort them but she had pulled it off. She looked at the clock and wished for the daylight hours to come quickly. The doctors had indicated that Peter Fletcher and the Latvian woman could possibly be released by lunchtime, which would mean two less targets to protect. It would be easier to protect Toni in the daylight and she would have more men at her disposal.

Annie lay awake for a while mulling things over. Alec's return was both reassuring and disappointing. She enjoyed the support that he gave to her during an investigation, but she also liked being in charge without him around. Her mind was too busy to allow her to sleep. She threw off the quilt and pulled on her dressing gown. Her feet were cold, so she stepped into her tiger feet slippers and padded through to her kitchen. She filled up the kettle and switched it on. Coffee would take the edge off her tiredness. She avoided her reflection in the window and spooned the granules into a mug and waited for the kettle to boil. As she opened the fridge to get the milk, she heard her mobile ringing in the bedroom. It rang twice before her landline began to ring in unison. With both phones ringing at once, she didn't need to be a detective to know that something major had happened.

Annie jogged into her living room and picked up the handset. The number dialling was withheld so she knew that it was work. She walked to the window as she answered it.

'DI Jones.'

'Annie it's me,' Alec said hurriedly. 'I know that you have only just gone to sleep but we've got problems.'

'What's happened?' Annie looked past her reflection in the glass. Something in the near distance had caught her attention. The trees in her garden swayed gently in the wind illuminated by a dull yellowy orange glow from the street lights. At night, it glimmered from the bark, almost flickering. In the winter when there was snow on the ground, the bare branches would almost glow in the dark, the flakes tinged yellow with the artificial light.

'Area Command has pulled all armed officers from non-essential deployments.'

'What?' Annie asked tiredly. 'Why would they do that for God's sake?'

'Four armed incidents have been reported in the last hour. They have deployed every armed officer that they have, and all leave has been cancelled. Unless they're out of the country, they're on their way in now.'

'How many officers have they taken from us at the Royal?'

'All of them.' Alec sighed. 'They're being deemed as non-essential. I've replaced them with uniform for now.'

'All of them?' Annie moaned. 'Are you fucking kidding me?'

'What do you think?'

'Sorry, guv but this is madness. How can they possibly prioritise anything over this?'

'Simple,' Alec explained. 'Children.' He paused to allow her to catch-up. 'There's a report of a gunman on the rampage at Alder Hey Hospital. He's held up the coffee shop and shot up the reception area before threatening to kill as many kids as he can.'

'Jesus,' Annie moaned resignedly.

'Add to that someone has reported that King David's School has been attacked by Muslim extremists; three bullets were fired through a window. Another report says that shots have been fired into a residential tower block in Netherley and a geriatric nursing home has reported that several windows have been shattered and there are bullet holes in the ceiling. They're spread out across the city. The emergency lines have gone mad. You can see why they're redeploying the armed units. The emergency switchboard is inundated with firearms incidents.'

'It doesn't feel right.'

'It doesn't but what else can the ARU do?'

'Nothing, I guess. Are the same people responsible for them all?' Annie asked. 'What the bloody hell is going on?'

'I don't know, Annie. AC has no other choice but to respond to every incident as an individual episode. Especially where kids are involved.'

'Can you really see an extremist attack happening at King David?'

'Yes,' Alec said flatly. 'It is full of rich Jewish kids. Some powerful people send their offspring there and it is a soft target,' Alec said thoughtfully. 'Apparently an eyewitness reported two men with beards shooting at the school. Can you see the headlines tomorrow? A school full of Jewish children under attack is a political minefield. AC has to respond with everything that we have.'

'I have a bad feeling about this, guv.' Annie sighed. She noticed that the yellowy orange glimmer on the trees had become considerably more orange than yellow. It flickered and danced much more than it should even if there was a stiff breeze. She frowned and walked back into the kitchen. 'Four armed incidents of this gravity in one night. Bit too much of a coincidence for me to swallow.' She paused and peered out of the kitchen window. 'Fucking hell!' Annie swore loudly.

'There's no point in shouting at me. There's nothing that we can do. Area Command is trying to draft in reinforcements from neighbouring...'

'Fuck, fuck, fuck,' Annie shouted.

'Annie?'

'Call the fire brigade!'

'What is it, Annie?'

'Someone has set fire to my house!'

CHAPTER 43

Raitis Girts was semi-aware of his surroundings. He had vivid memories of the African women attacking Oleg; their anger and hatred was aimed at him initially. Raitis had watched helplessly as they rained down brutal blows with a variety of makeshift weapons. Oleg had put up a monumental struggle before he finally succumbed to the beating. He eventually curled up and tried to protect his head with his handcuffed arm. It was quickly broken and useless leaving his skull vulnerable. That was when Oleg sought respite from the attack by hiding behind his associates, which made them targets too. Raitis remembered the first blow to the top of his skull from a sledgehammer. It was enough to turn the lights out. He lost consciousness quickly, although he was aware that his body was being battered regardless. The pain still registered somewhere in his brain. The screeching of the women during their frenzied attack was like a chorus from a choir of demons from the darkest reaches of hell itself. He was aware of his bones being fractured and broken and at that point he embraced the idea of dying. Death was a far more attractive option at that point. The incredible pain and the paralysing fear of more pain to come were too much to take. He didn't want to die but he didn't want to live if it meant suffering.

The ambulance journey was more of a sensation than a memory. The sensation of intense pain and the feeling of motion flashed into the dark parts of his mind. He wasn't sure if he was alive or dead, but he had memories. *Maybe that's what we all become*, he thought, just memories. Part of him wanted to wake up but another part of his brain had embraced the morphine. It was intelligent enough to recognise that when the morphine entered his bloodstream, the pain stopped. It also knew that fighting the morphine would lessen its effects and the pain would return; dull and muffled at first but it would intensify to the point where it would be unbearable. That part of his brain wanted nothing to do with reality and waking up was not an option, his body was broken, bones cracked, muscles crushed, tendons and ligaments torn. He embraced the opiate and the tranquillity that it gave. Better to be numb and oblivious than awake and suffering.

While his mind debated with itself, he was unaware that the nurse in the room had a syringe full of insulin in her hand. She searched along his thigh, which was black and purple, his femur cracked in three places and she injected the liquid into his bruised muscle. Raitis didn't feel the jab, nor would he have cared. There was a slight moment of panic in his brain when his heart stopped beating but it wasn't prolonged and then even his memories stopped.

CHAPTER 44

There was no going back and going forward would be more of the same. She vividly remembered that bastard Oleg had fastened them to a radiator and left them for dead. She didn't know why they'd left in such a hurry and it didn't matter. Being left to burn had hurt her feelings. Feelings? Yes, she still had them although they were complicated and confused. She felt that she was the lowest of the low. Sold into slavery by an alcoholic father to be used as a whore indefinitely was bad enough, but to realise that she had no value at all was devastating. She wasn't worth taking. It was better to let her burn. Krista struggled with it. The police and doctors were horrified that someone could tie another human being to a pipe and leave them to suffocate and burn but that didn't surprise Krista. They were violent, brutal men. Her issue was that they didn't think that she was worth taking with them. She was a whore, but she was their whore and they didn't think that she was worth keeping. She had no value at all and that hurt dreadfully. It was as if the fragile walls of her shit life had tumbled down on her. Her feelings were irrational, yet she was devastated by their betrayal. The only identity she had had been snatched away. She was Krista the whore, but they had valued her once. They had invested time and money into breaking her and shaping her into what they wanted her to be and they valued her. That misplaced assumption was shattered into a million pieces. Even as a whore she was worthless. That realisation had broken her heart.

As she lay in the hospital bed and contemplated what had happened, she began to feel sorry for herself. She had never allowed herself to do so before. She was trapped from the moment she stepped on the plane. Krista toyed with the idea of freedom for a while. The policeman with the cheeky smile had made her think about being free. The reality was that there was no way of gaining it without hurting her family. One way or the other she would be found and forced back into the life of slavery servicing a succession of sweaty balding men month in and month out. There was a never-ending queue of fat middle aged men waiting to use her and others like her. She couldn't go back to that life; not for one moment. Her life was already mapped out for her and there would be no happy ending. She would never meet a good-looking man like the policeman who guarded her room. There would be no fairy-tale romance, no wedding, and no children, not for her. Fate had conspired against her and she was destined for nothing but more of the same abuse that she had suffered for five years. There was no going back and no end to her suffering going forward but there was a way out. Krista slipped out of her bed and walked to the window. She marvelled at the lights of the city as she opened the window and climbed onto the ledge. A breath of cold breeze whispered in her ear.

It made her skin tingle and she welcomed it. It made her feel clean and pure for the first time in years. There was no hesitation in her mind as she took one last mouthful of fresh air and stepped off.

CHAPTER 45

Toni Barrat felt sick to the core. The anticipation was torturous. The big sergeant hadn't told her much. She knew that he was beating around the bush. The police wouldn't be escorting her to the hospital in the dark unless the doctors had said there was a chance Kayla may not make it through the night. If there was nothing seriously wrong, they would have waited until daylight. She felt like her intestines were being crushed in a vice. Her expectation was that the worst that could happen would happen. She was setting herself up, steeling herself against the bad news. Kayla would die. Everyone she loved died, that's just how it was. This time would be worse because she was to blame. Guilt was crushing her. Toni had stepped into something that was way out of her league and then led the gangsters straight back to Kayla. Mike was already dead. That was her fault too. Thinking about what he had suffered made her feel nauseous. They must have tortured him for information, but the poor man didn't have any, nothing worthwhile at any rate. Kayla hadn't discussed the source of the information with him. They took his eyes out and put them in a bag. Who would do that? The detective at her house said they were sending a message. Toni had flipped. 'No shit Sherlock. I can see how you got out of wearing a uniform; a one-man crime busting phenomenon. They were sending a message. Do you think so?'

She wasn't the biggest fan of the police and that swung both ways. As a journalist she was aware that there were plenty of hardworking talented police officers on the force but sadly she had encountered corrupt, incompetent, and unintelligent officers too. In her opinion, the latter were in the majority.

'Are you okay?' Stirling asked from the seat next to her. He disturbed her thoughts with a stupid question.

'Would you be okay if we were going to see your wife in the ICU?' Toni tried to smile but it didn't work. 'I'm absolutely shitting myself if I'm honest.'

'Nothing wrong with that, I would be too.'

'I'm trying to think positively but it has never worked before, so I don't see why it should now do you?'

'Sometimes all we can do is hope, Toni.' Stirling nodded 'I'm sorry. It was a stupid question.'

'No worries,' Toni said. She looked out of the side window; the rain streaked the glass blurring the street lights as they raced past. The armed officers sat stoic in the front of the X5 as they weaved through the traffic. 'What will be, will be.'

'She's in good hands,' Stirling said. She saw The Royal Court Theatre across the road and remembered going to see Adam and the Ants there. They were well past their sell-by date by then, but she enjoyed the night. She felt the X5 veer sharply to the left. The vehicle slowed as a removal truck switched lanes. The driver switched on the blues and twos to shift them, but it was too late, their path was blocked. The traffic lights up ahead turned red and there was no way through. Toni felt anxious. The driver peered around the removal van but until the lights changed to green, they couldn't move. She could feel the tension rising as the X5 stopped completely. The seconds ticked by. Nobody wanted to speak. Toni watched the traffic lights changing, red and amber, then green. The vehicles at the front of the queue began pulling away but when it became the turn of the removal van it didn't move. Its reversing lights came on and it lurched backwards at speed, smashing into the front of the X5. Toni shrieked in surprise, her voice shrill in the confined space of the vehicle. Their driver slammed the vehicle into reverse and turned to look over his shoulder. Toni heard the engine roar and waited for the X5 to reverse. Every muscle in her body was taut. Stirling put his arm across her to protect her.

'Hold on!' the driver shouted. Toni thought that it was a warning that they were going to fly backwards at speed, but they didn't. Instead, there was a violent impact to the rear and the X5 was flung forward, smashing it into the removal truck again. The airbags deployed, stunning the officers in the front. Stirling reached for the door handle and put his shoulder to it, but the impact had buckled the chassis. The door was wedged closed. Toni heard the engine behind pull away and then it roared once more. A second violent impact shook the X5. She felt her head flung forward; her spine cracked like a whip. The collision knocked the wind from her chest. She heard the thud of heavy objects against glass. One, two, three, and then it shattered. The air was filled with flying shards. She felt them stinging her hands and face. The cold night air rushed in. There was frantic activity around her, both inside and outside the truck. Stirling positioned his body to protect her with his bulk. She heard him shouting something about closing her eyes, but it didn't register. Toni heard a hissing sound, then another and then a third. It was the sound of aerosol canisters being discharged. Suddenly her eyes, nose, and mouth were on fire. She heard Stirling growling like a wounded bear. Toni couldn't breathe.

Rough hands grabbed at her. She felt her hair being twisted and ripped from her scalp. She screamed for help, but it came out like a gurgle. Mucus hung from her nose like slime stalactites. Her head was snapped backwards; she felt the seat belt being cut and she was dragged upwards and outwards through the window. The remaining glass dug into her flesh. She felt a rent open in her side and the warmth of blood running down her back. Her eyes were stinging, and her vision was blurred but she saw glimpses of the armed officers writhing in agony in the front seats. The side windows had all been smashed in and men in balaclavas continued to spray mace into the vehicle. It was completely debilitating. Toni knew that armed or not, they could no longer protect her. She grabbed at the doorframe in an attempt to stop them taking her, but the men smashed her fingers with something heavy and hard. She felt her right index finger snap and the pain shot up her arm like a lightning bolt. Her body was almost completely out of the vehicle when she felt powerful hands garb her ankles. Stirling gripped her legs and tried to stop her kidnap. Toni felt a glimmer of hope. The sergeant was a beast, big, strong, and powerful. If he could hold on to her long enough for the armed officers to recover, she had a chance. 'Sometimes hope is all we have,' he had said to her not long before. He pulled with all his strength and managed to get her back into the X5 up to her waist. Toni thought he was going to win the battle when three gunshots exploded next to her head.

Boom.

Boom.

Boom.

She heard a whelp of pain and felt Stirling's grip released immediately and they ripped her from the vehicle. A bolt of electricity shot through her neck. The smell of singed hair and burning flesh drifted to her and then she was in darkness.

CHAPTER 46

Annie disconnected the call from Alec and dialled 999. Flames jumped and flickered from the front of the house. She thought about getting dressed but it was a foolish thought. The house was full of thick black smoke within minutes. The stairwell that led down to the bedrooms and the front door was filled with choking fumes. She stood and looked into the shifting black smoke and quickly made her mind up that she couldn't make it that way. Whoever had set the fire could be waiting outside the front door. Had they come to kill her, or was this a threat? Another very subtle message, maybe. Annie didn't know which and she didn't have time to debate it.

She ran into the kitchen and grabbed a tea-towel. Switching on the tap, she soaked it and placed it over her nose and mouth. She ran through the kitchen into the bathroom, slamming the door behind her to stem the smoke for a few valuable minutes. The window led out onto the garage roof. Annie twisted the handle, pushed it open and climbed over the ledge. As she looked back inside, black smoke poured under the bathroom door. She pushed the window closed and sprinted across the roof towards the back garden. Her tiger feet slippers were saturated with rainwater in seconds, the cold water squelched uncomfortably between her toes. The cold night air bit into her exposed flesh. She headed for the side of the garage at the rear of the house where her wheelie bins were lined up. She moved to the edge and lowered herself over the roof. Her feet dangled in mid-air for a second before her slippers contacted a bin. She lowered herself a few inches further until her feet found purchase on the lid. Annie sighed with relief and let go of the roof, relieved to be out of the house. She took a deep breath and relaxed for a moment. Her heart somersaulted when she heard footsteps behind her. She felt gloved hands grip her ankles. Annie cried out as her legs were snatched from beneath her. Her head clattered against the garage wall scraping the skin from her cheek. She felt one of her front teeth crack on the wall and then her face impacted with the edge of the bin. White lights exploded in her brain like a giant camera flash going off. Annie felt herself being dragged off the bin, crashing onto the path with a sickening thud. Her skull cracked on the concrete. She felt the sensation of being dragged over the wet grass before she lost consciousness.

CHAPTER 47

The Morning After

Alec watched the ruins of Annie's house smouldering. The sun had made a weak attempt to brighten and warm the world, but it had failed miserably. He trudged around the property for the fifth time, trying to fathom what had happened. The thought of Annie being trapped inside was a constant in his mind. Half the roof had collapsed exposing the trusses to the elements. Orange flames hissed and sizzled when they came into contact with the water being sprayed from high-pressure hoses. Alec guessed that the settee he had been sitting on the night before was hidden beneath a pile of slates and charcoal. Thoughts of his late wife drifted to him. She died in a fire in the arms of her lover, Alec's detective sergeant and close friend. The memories burned painfully inside him. His guts twisted every time the images returned. Looking at Annie's house brought it all flooding back.

'Superintendent,' a voice chased away the ghosts from his mind. Alec turned to see who was speaking. The fireman waved and pointed to the garage roof. 'She made it out.'

'You're sure?' Alec was physically relieved.

'Yes. The bathroom window was opened from the inside and there are no bodies inside. Good news but it begs the question as to where your DI is.' Alec didn't answer. His face was ashen. 'I heard about Big Jim Stirling. How is he?'

'Not good.' Alec shook his head. 'His vest took the brunt of it but one of the rounds ricocheted up and entered his neck beneath the ear. The initial x-rays show that the bullet has lodged at the base of the skull next to his spine.'

'Jesus.' The fireman sighed.

'Was it arson?' Alec steered the conversation back to work. He had lost his two best detectives and his two best friends overnight and he didn't have a clue if either would make it. Talking about it was difficult.

'No doubt about it. They poured accelerant through the letter box and placed two old tires soaked in petrol against the front door.'

'That's pretty conclusive,' Alec said sarcastically.

'Brazen too. They made no effort to make it look like an accident.'

'Subtlety isn't their strongest point,' Alec said quietly. 'Call me directly if you find anything else.' He walked around the path until he was next to the garage. It was too high to consider jumping without causing an injury. He saw the wheelie bins lined up to the rear. If he was in Annie's shoes, he would have lowered himself down onto the bins. He approached the bins and studied the lids. There was blood and half a tooth on the middle one. She had either fallen or been attacked there. He sucked air between his teeth and felt anger boiling inside. Annie had suffered enough. There was no sign of her which meant only one thing. She had been removed from the scene forcefully. Where she was and what was happening to her didn't bear thinking about; he shuddered as he remembered how shattered she had been when a scumbag called Tibbs had plunged a pen into her eye. She had bounced back eventually but he had seen how she glanced into mirrors or caught her reflection in glass. He couldn't bear to think of her suffering, not then, not now, not ever. Part of him had fallen in love with Annie Jones, not in a lustful way, but because of the woman she was. He would never cross the line and declare his feelings, but they were there, and he couldn't ignore them. As he ran through the scenarios of what had happened to her, he didn't think telling her how he felt would be a problem that he would ever need to face. It didn't look good at all. Alec looked around and noticed drag marks on the lawn. Two lines of flattened grass ran parallel from the path to the garden gate. Beyond the gate was the road that exited the housing estate. Alec reckoned that Annie was already a distance away and in the hands of some of the most dangerous, reckless criminals that he had encountered.

'Guv,' a familiar voice called from the front of the house. As he walked along the path from the rear, the handsome black face of Detective Maxwell appeared around the corner. 'We've just had a call from the CSI unit sent to finish up at the Fletcher Bros garage.'

'And?'

'They have found two bodies in an outbuilding behind the main service bay. It looks like suicide, guv.'

'Suicide?'

'Yes, guv. It looks like the Fletcher brothers attached a hose to the exhaust of an Alfa Romeo and topped themselves.'

'Jesus Christ, what is wrong with these people?' Alec shook his head and ran his fingers through his hair. 'Our witnesses are dropping like flies. Any news on the vehicles they used to snatch Toni Barrat?'

'Nothing of any use, stolen, dumped, and burnt out. Every man and his dog are hunting Andris Markevica, but no one is talking. Even our best snouts are coming up zip. They either know nothing about the Latvians or they're too scared to speak up.'

'Something will break,' Alec said. He didn't feel as confident as he sounded.

'Any news from the Royal, guv?'

'No. He's still in surgery,' Alec said quietly. Jim Stirling's condition was critical, but the surgeons couldn't give him a prognosis until they opened him up. 'I'm on my way over there now.' He paused for a moment. 'When CSI are finished with the Fletcher brothers, get yourself over there and have a good look around. Everyone else stays on Markevica.'

'Yes, guv.'

'Do you think the Fletcher brothers would sit next to each other and choke to death?'

'No, guv.'

'It just doesn't smell right,' Alec said to himself as he walked away. 'In fact, the whole thing fucking stinks.'

CHAPTER 48

Toni watched as a man pushed a fork into Kayla's eye socket. He turned to her and smiled as he twisted the fork and pulled. There was an audible popping sound as the eyeball was ripped free and he held it up for Toni to see more clearly. The eyeball turned on the fork, looking right and then left as if it had a life of its own. The man opened his mouth and put the fork inside. He began to chew Kayla's eye and Toni couldn't stop him. She couldn't shout and she couldn't scream. All she could do was watch. She looked down at where Kayla lay but she was gone, her body replaced by Mike's. His skin was pale, almost blue in colour. The eye sockets were black holes that crawled with maggots. Mike sat up and turned his head towards her. He pointed a finger accusingly. Maggots fell from the eyes onto his lap. He raised his hand and slapped her face hard. Toni felt the stinging slap and tried to move away from it, but she couldn't move. She shifted uncomfortably as he struck her again. The images blurred as her mind was dragged back to reality by the pain.

She opened her eyes and realised she had been dreaming. Mike was gone, replaced by a man she had never seen before. He grabbed her chin and roughly turned her head to one side. She was tied to a hardback chair, her arms behind her. Toni felt bruised and battered. Blood had congealed on her side, but she could feel glass stuck in her skin. Her fingers felt swollen and broken. Pain pulsed up her arms with every beat of her heart. Her wrists were bound painfully with zip ties. They cut into her flesh. Her ribs were aching from where the seat belt had bruised her, and her scalp was sore where her hair had been ripped out. Toni was terrified. She knew who had taken her and she knew what they were capable of. Kayla drifted into her thoughts. Would she die knowing that she never had the chance to say goodbye?

'She's okay,' the man said with a thick accent. She heard movement from behind her.

'Antonia Barrat,' a voice from behind her said rhythmically, as if it was the start of a song. 'What a terrible mess you have created, Antonia Barrat.' Toni didn't respond and she didn't attempt to look behind her. She was frozen by fear. 'I don't suppose when you set off in your little car with your little camera that things would go this far, did you?' Toni didn't move. She didn't want to answer him in case she said something wrong. There was a long pause. When he spoke again, there was venom in his tone. 'Answer me,' he snapped. 'I said you didn't think things would go this far, did you?'

Toni shook her head almost imperceptibly. 'No,' her voice was barely a whisper. 'I had no idea what would happen. I didn't see anything that could hurt you.'

'Your friend, Mike took pictures.'

'Yes.'

'They upload automatically?'

'I've deleted them.'

'You can never delete things from the Internet, Antonia. Not completely. You know that. I know that and the police know it too. They saw them?'

'Yes, but they didn't show much.'

'They showed enough.'

'I am sorry. We didn't know that you would be there.'

'What did you think?'

'I thought it would be a handover. That's what I was told.'

'It was a handover but not the type you expected, right?'

'Right.'

'I don't blame you for being there,' he said with a shrug. 'You were doing your job, yes?'

'Yes.'

'I appreciate that you have a job to do and I hope you appreciate that I have a job to do too.'

'Yes,' Toni mumbled. She didn't see any parity, but she was hardly going to raise it.

'In my job, we must have total trust in our employees, you understand this, yes?'

'Yes.'

'Then you will understand that the fact you were at the mill tells me that someone has betrayed that trust.'

'Yes.'

'I have a problem. It is all about betrayal, Antonia. I can tolerate most things but not betrayal. You must understand that, don't you?' he asked flatly as if it was an obvious answer.

'Yes.'

'My problem is now your problem too.' The voice was closer now, almost at her ear. He stepped alongside her and looked down. Toni tried hard to keep her eyes forward, but she couldn't help herself. She glanced sideways and looked into the pale grey eyes of Letva.

'You were outside my house,' she whispered.

'I was inside your house.' He smiled coldly. Toni shivered. Letva walked around her with his hands clasped behind his back. 'We have a business to run. The stakes are high, and the consequences of betrayal are devastating. It cannot be tolerated. I don't want to hurt you, Antonia. It would give me no pleasure to do so, however, some of the people that I work with would be happy to hurt you for the sake of it. Your friend, Mike discovered that the hard way, as did your partner. Are you following me?'

'Yes.'

'Good. I need you to tell me who told you about the mill?'

'His name is Richard Grainger,' Toni said without hesitation.

Letva turned on his heels quickly. He put his hands on his knees and looked at her hard. 'Richard Grainger?'

'Yes. He called me at about half past ten that night,' she said hoarsely. 'His number is in my contact list. You can check my mobile and see the call.'

Letva looked thoughtful. He tilted his head to one side. 'Rick Grainger,' he said rubbing his chin. 'I didn't expect that. Check her phone,' he ordered someone behind her. She could hear voices chattering as they scrolled through the call logs.

'She is telling the truth.'

Letva nodded knowingly. It was as if his suspicions had been confirmed. 'Thank you, Antonia. This is the name that you gave to the police?'

'Eventually, yes.'

'Naturally, I will need to verify this with the police,' he said cordially. 'It shouldn't take too long.'

'Naturally,' Toni swallowed hard. She didn't want to ask the next question, but it needed to be asked. 'What are you going to do?'

'I don't know yet.'

'I can't do you any harm.'

'Oh, you can, Miss Barrat.' He smiled coldly. 'You most certainly can.'

'I've told you what you wanted to know. What will happen to me now?'

'Sorry, it is remiss of me to leave you in limbo.' He shook his head apologetically. 'To be honest, I didn't expect you to be so forthcoming. I thought it would take us longer to persuade you to tell us who your source was.' He seemed to be debating his next move in his mind. He nodded and shrugged. 'Once the police confirm that Grainger is the name that you gave to them too, you'll be taken to Delamere Forest, shot and buried.'

Toni tried to stop the bile from rising but she couldn't, and she vomited all over herself.

CHAPTER 49

Annie was cold and wet; she woke up shivering and in pain. Her tongue found the gap where her tooth had chipped and broken, and she could taste blood in her mouth. She opened her eye and searched the blackness around her. The flesh on her face was swollen around her cheekbone. Her hands and feet were bound tightly. She looked around and quickly deduced that she was in the boot of a car. The smell of exhaust fumes was choking; it mingled with odours of petrol and sawdust. Annie didn't want to be there. She wanted to wake up safe in her bed. Why had they taken her? If they wanted her dead, then she would already be dead. She didn't want to contemplate the alternative reason. They wanted her alive in order to question her. Questioning would probably involve pain and fear and she couldn't handle much of either. She knew that what Richard Tibbs did to her hadn't just changed her life, it had fundamentally changed who she was. Annie wasn't planning on being a hero. She would tell them whatever she could and hope that whatever happened, it would be quick. She couldn't face the thought of suffering. Annie wished that she had never set eyes on Antonia Barrat. She had never felt so terrified in all her days. She curled up in the foetal position and felt hot stinging tears on her cheeks.

CHAPTER 50

Marika pushed a shopping trolley into the Tesco superstore. It was busy as she made her way to the beer and wine section. Gary Powell was waiting there as planned. His trolley had a carton of milk, some bread, and a case of beer inside and a sports holdall hanging from the back. They caught each other's eye and she headed towards him.

'Ivor sends his regards,' she said quietly. 'He apologises for not coming himself, but you know how it is.'

'Of course. He needs to be careful.' Gary cocked his head as he read the label on a bottle of red wine. 'I bet he doesn't know who is on his side and who isn't right now, eh?'

'He never does.' Marika smiled. 'That was clever what you did with the chip by the way. He was so mad. I haven't seen him that mad for a long time.'

'I was just doing what he pays me to do.' Gary shrugged. 'Tracking devices are not exclusive to whoever plants them; especially the cheap ones. Anyone with a half decent tracker could have found that chip. I don't sleep well if I think someone might be coming to my house uninvited. I'm sure you understand?' he looked around and then checked the contents of the envelope that Marika had brought in her trolley; four prepaid Visa debit cards. 'That will do nicely.' He smiled. 'You should try this wine, it's excellent.' He placed the bottle into his trolley and then stepped behind hers. He put another bottle of red into his new trolley and pushed it away. 'Give Ivor my regards.'

Marika waved and pushed his trolley in the opposite direction, the exchange completed safely. She wandered up and down the store, stopping to put a new pair of jeans for her into the trolley. As she looked at the newsstand, some of the headlines caught her eye. Ivor would be beyond angry when he saw them. She dropped the newspapers into the trolley and then headed for the checkout.

CHAPTER 51

Annie felt the vehicle stop and her heart pounded dangerously quickly. She was safe when they were travelling. They couldn't hurt her while she was in the boot. Stopping wasn't good. It suggested that they'd reached their destination and the next phase of her kidnap would begin. The next phase would be brutal. They had dislocated Kayla Yates's joints to get answers. Annie could only hope that they would accept her first answers. She tried to control the panic rising inside her. She heard muffled voices talking and gruff laughing. Maybe it was okay to laugh in that part of the vehicle. Inside the boot, there was nothing in the slightest bit amusing. She could hear three voices. They were inside the car, the backseats between them and her. It was too distorted for her to identify the language, but it wasn't English. She was certain of that. She heard the engine go quiet and the doors opened. Three doors opened and then closed almost simultaneously. Annie was so frightened she could barely breathe. She listened so hard that she could hear the blood pumping through her ears. It was nearly deafening. She heard footsteps approaching the boot. They were coming for her. The click of a cigarette lighter drifted to her. It clicked three times and then she heard the beep of a remote. The boot lid clicked open and dull daylight poured inside. The light hurt her eye. Blurred faces peered in at her, but she didn't have time to recognise them; they had close-cropped hair, greying designer stubble, and heavy leather jackets. Movie stereotypes maybe but that was how she would describe them if she escaped; when she escaped, not if. She had to think positively. *Keep control, Annie or you'll die here.*

She could smell tobacco smoke mingled with expensive aftershave. They pulled a pillowcase over her head and lifted her out roughly. She tried to stand but her legs were weak with fear. Her knees buckled and she collapsed against the car.

'Stand up,' a voice barked. She tried again but her muscles couldn't take her weight. Her legs weren't functioning, and she felt like a baby giraffe trying to stand for the first time. 'I said stand up!'

Annie swallowed hard and tried to regain her composure. Her feet were wet, and her teeth chattered with the cold. She could feel her entire body shivering, a mixture of fear and exposure to the elements. Desperation sapped her energy. She could see no way out at all. Annie listened intently to get some idea where she was. Hands grabbed her arms from either side and forced her away from the car. They half carried and half dragged her. Annie could hear birds and the rustle of the wind through tree branches. Leaves and twigs snapped and crackled beneath her feet and the faint whiff of conifers drifted to her. She was either in woods somewhere in the countryside or worse still, in one of the forests that were dotted around

Cheshire. The further they walked, the deeper into the trees they went. There was less light coming through the makeshift hood and the breeze couldn't penetrate the forest. She knew that they were going to question her and then bury her. She would never be found, and no one would ever know what they'd done to her. Annie felt a terrible sense of dread mixed with the sickening sense of resignation. She wondered what it would be like to die and she was scared, very scared. Panic gripped her and she struggled but she was helpless. Fighting against it was hopeless. There was no hope left. This was the end. This was where she would die, in the forest, killed by a bunch of strangers, evil men driven by money and power. She felt sick to her core. She wanted to beg and plead for her life, but terror had taken her voice. She didn't want to end her days in a cold wet hole in the ground but here she was approaching it rapidly.

They dragged her for at least twenty minutes. Every minute took her further away from help, accidental intervention by a passing stranger, a chance sighting maybe. The chances lessened with each step. Every second felt like an hour. She lost her slippers as her feet dragged along the ground. The cold had made her legs numb and she could no longer feel her toes. Twigs and branches cut and scratched her skin. She wanted it to stop. She wanted them to let her go and leave her alone. For the first time in her career, she didn't want to be a detective anymore. She would find a new job if they would give her another chance. If only they would let her live, she would do anything that they said.

They stopped and she heard them having a heated discussion, then they seemed to change direction. After another ten minutes or so of nightmarish progress, they stopped again. One of the men pulled the hood off her head. Annie blinked so that she could focus. She was surrounded by a thick forest of conifer trees. The ground beneath her was thick with needles and pine cones and the smell of pine was almost eye-watering.

'Kneel down,' one of the men shook her roughly. Annie collapsed down on her knees. In front of her was a shallow grave, a metre deep. Two shovels stood against a nearby tree. Her breath stuck in her chest. It had been dug recently; the soil piled up next to it was still moist.

'Oh. God please don't do this!' Seeing her own grave made her gag and choke. She wretched but nothing came up. Annie broke down. Her voice was wet with tears and phlegm. Saliva dribbled from her chin and she could hardly suck air into her chest. Her body trembled with unadulterated terror. 'Please don't kill me!'

'Get a grip of yourself. Make this easier for yourself, Inspector. Tell me what I need to know, and it will be quick and painless.' Annie nodded but she couldn't find her voice. She mewed like a wounded cat. 'You are the detective who interviewed Antonia Barrat?'

'Yes,' Annie whispered. Her shoulders were hunched against an attack from behind. She didn't want to feel anything when it came. Tears mixed with snot and made slimy rivulets down her neck. She couldn't control her breathing. Panic had stripped her of her faculties. 'I'll... tell... you... everything... that... you... want... to... know...' she gasped, a breath between each word. 'Please, don't kill me!'

'Take a deep breath!'

Annie nodded and tried to slow her breathing down. Tears streamed uncontrollably. Her body was now numb to the core with the cold. She concentrated and managed to quell the panic slightly. They waited for her to regain control before the questioning began again. Annie knew that they'd experienced prisoners losing the plot before. It had no effect on them. There was no sympathy or empathy. They were ice cold. There was no consideration for the victims or the families that they left behind. Fear was their weapon and they yielded it freely.

'Can you speak?'

'Yes,' Annie sobbed.

'You asked Antonia Barrat about her informer?'

'Yes.'

'Who was it?'

'Richard Grainger.'

'What?'

'Richard Grainger. That was the name that she gave to me.'

'You're sure?'

'Yes.'

'That is good,' the voice said happily. 'I killed him.' He stopped to think. 'You know that though, yes?' He paused and stood over Annie. Annie recognised him as Andris Markevica. Her blood ran cold.

Annie nodded. 'They have you on film driving the vehicle. You killed a detective sergeant too.'

'He wasn't the first pig we've killed, and he won't be the last,' he sneered, and his colleagues laughed raucously. He looked closely into her face and pointed his index finger. 'You won't be the last either.'

Annie bit her bottom lip and tried not to break down again. Her breath was coming in short sharp gasps. Panic was squeezing the air from her lungs.

'Hmmm,' Andris shook his head thoughtfully. 'What happened at the garage?'

'They had arranged to switch vehicles,' Annie sniffed. 'Someone hit them at the switch, took the drugs and handcuffed your men. Two of them died. One of them was your cousin, Oleg.'

'Go on.'

'They left them fastened to the van and the mules broke free and killed them.'

'That is what I heard but I didn't believe it until now.' Annie shrugged as if what he thought didn't matter. It didn't. 'Do you know who took the zombie from the garage?'

Annie shook her head.

'No ideas?'

'No.'

'We know that the pictures they took at the mill were uploaded,' 'Did you see any of them?'

'Yes.'

'And what did you see?'

'Not much. The mules being herded from a rib. Three men in balaclavas and one man that piloted the rib. That's it.'

'They were uploaded automatically?'

'Yes.'

'The man in the rib?'

'He was an ex-sergeant from the river force.'

'I'm impressed,' he cooed. 'That didn't take long.'

'He was burnt. He had a false hip. Forensics traced the hip joint.'

'Clever.' He crouched in front of her. 'What else do you know?'

'There are outstanding warrants across Europe for you and your associates.' Annie swallowed and thought about what she knew and what might keep her alive. She decided that nothing could. They were going to bury her regardless. 'We have some names at Companies House linking some of your associates to a property in Aigburth where at least three people were murdered.' She stopped and gasped for breath. Her voice was flat, monotone and uninterested. 'One was a Russian male, who we think belonged to the Karpov gang, an African female, and a Latvian female. Another woman is critical in hospital.' She paused for breath. 'There are also photographs of you leaving a pawnbroker's shop where a serious assault took place.'

'The woman in the safe?'

'Yes.'

'You know who took them, don't you?'

'A guy called Jason Greene.'

'Jason Greene?' he repeated sarcastically.

'Yes,' Annie said. 'You were driving his vehicle when you killed Rick Grainger and DS Dalton Sykes,' she said with a sniffle. 'Coincidentally,' she added.

'Coincidentally?'

'Yes.'

'I can't believe he is the same guy, can you?' Andris smiled. 'He takes pictures and then I am in your pictures driving his vehicle. You couldn't predict that could you?'

'Nope,' Annie said sarcastically.

'What an unlucky guy, yes?'

'Very.'

'Do you know where he is?'

'No. We haven't found him.'

'I'll let you into a little secret,' he leaned in and lowered his voice. 'You're about to become his next-door neighbour.' Andris grinned and nodded towards a freshly disturbed patch of ground a few metres away. 'You'll be next to an informer, cosy, yes? And now his pictures are of no value to you, are they?'

'Not really.'

'Wow, that's unfortunate, isn't it?'

'Very. There's still enough evidence to put you away for the rest of your life.' Annie looked away from him. She felt exhausted. Fear had pumped adrenalin into her system, but shock and the cold had sucked the life from her. She was beginning not to care anymore. 'They'll lock you away.'

'I don't think so. Not that it matters,' he smiled slyly. 'I'll have to leave the country for a while, won't I?'

'It would be wise.'

'You know it has been nice chatting to you but I'm getting hungry and it's time to eat.' He cocked his head and gestured to the men behind her. They picked up a shovel each and stood behind her. Andris smiled. 'Goodbye, Inspector.'

Annie heard a whistling sound. White lights erupted in her brain as the face of a shovel hit the back of her skull with a sickening thud. She felt the shovel vibrate and a boot placed between her shoulder blades. He pushed hard and she was flung forward into the grave. Annie landed face down in the damp soil. The thick odour of decaying foliage filled her senses. She heard the metallic click of a semiautomatic being readied. Suddenly her panic slipped away, and she felt almost at peace. There was no more struggling to be done. She just wished that she could have said goodbye. As the first shovel full of dirt landed onto the back of her head, Annie closed her eyes and waited for a bullet to come.

CHAPTER 52

Alec looked through the glass into the ICU. Jim Stirling looked smaller somehow as if he had shrunk into the bed. Seeing him there made Alec think about Annie. Annie and Stirling lived in each other's pockets. Wherever one was the other was never far behind. He worried about her, but he worried less when she was with Stirling. Big Jim Stirling, the indestructible detective; except he wasn't indestructible, and he couldn't stop a bullet. Alec thought about going in, but his wife and daughter were sitting on one side of the bed; other members of his family that Alec didn't recognise were sitting on the other. He didn't want to intrude on their privacy. It was police work that had put him in that bed and often grieving family members could harbour thoughts of blame aimed towards the force. It was rare but it happened. Alec had met Janice many times and she knew that Big Jim Stirling was a copper through and through. He lived to be a detective, although dying because he was a detective was a different thing completely.

'Superintendent Ramsay?'

'Yes,' Alec turned to greet the surgeon who had led the operation to save Stirling's life. 'Thanks for coming to see me, Doctor.'

'No problem,' the doctor said tapping the glass with his pen. 'Your sergeant is a strong man. If he wasn't, he would be dead already.'

'What are his chances?'

'Minimal, I'm afraid.' He took Alec by the arm and walked him away from the window. 'On the Glasgow Coma Scale, Jim scored a three, now in layman's terms anything below an eight is considered to be a coma. Jim is deeply comatose with minimal evidence of brainstem activity. There are a lot of what we call eloquent brain cells in that area of the skull. The bullet did a lot of damage on its way through. We removed it but we won't know anything for days, possibly weeks. Unless we see some brainstem activity soon, I'm almost certain that he won't make it.'

Alec sighed and shrugged. He felt like he had been punched in the guts. 'His wife?'

'It's important that they know exactly where he's at,' the doctor nodded and removed his glasses. 'He's been shot in the head for heaven's sake, she's not stupid. If there's any change, I'll let you know immediately.'

'Thanks.' Alec sighed again. 'How is Kayla Yates doing?'

'The lady in the safe?'

'Yes.'

'She's not my patient but I believe she's in a fragile condition at best,' he replaced his glasses and blinked. 'They resuscitated her in surgery and made her comfortable. She's stable but she's very poorly.'

'Thanks, Doctor.' Alec shook hands with him and walked away. He took the lift to the ground floor and wished that he had some cigarettes. His on and off affair with tobacco was in an off phase again. The lift dropped without stopping. When the lift doors opened, he stepped into the lobby and saw Maxwell standing outside of a newsagent studying the front page of a redtop. The shops and cafeterias were busy with patients and staff. Alec stepped aside to allow a porter to go by with a patient in a wheelchair. The woman in the chair looked old, almost reptilian in appearance. Her head lolled from side to side, saliva dribbled from the corner of her lips. Alec debated if it was better to grow old and become completely reliant on others to feed you and wipe your backside, or to die while all your facilities were still intact. Annie and Stirling would know what was happening to them. The old lady didn't. They would feel fear and pain. The old lady wouldn't. Which one would he be given the choice? Neither, he hoped. Thinking about them suffering could drive him insane if he allowed himself to dwell on it. He checked his watch and made his way across the reception area to where Max was standing.

'Hello, guv,' Max said holding up the newspaper. 'Have you read this?'

'Not yet.' Alec shook his head and scanned the headlines. A photograph of the mules being shepherded by men in balaclavas dominated the front page. The headlines screamed at him from the paper.

THE REAL PRICE OF HUMAN TRAFFICKING

Beneath was another photograph from the mill. Alec flushed red and walked to the newsstand. Four of the national redtops were sporting pictures taken on Antonia Barrat's camera. At first glance, they looked the same but each one was slightly different.

'Jesus Christ!' Alec snapped. 'How the fuck did they get hold of these pictures?'

'File sharing, guv,' Max suggested. 'It's fairly common practice nowadays. If the photos were uploaded, it makes sense that someone where she worked could access them.' He paused. 'Look at pages two and three.'

TRAGIC LIVERPOOL REPORTER KIDNAPPED FROM AN ARMED POLICE CONVOY

'I didn't realise that Toni Barrat had such a colourful past, guv.'

'Bloody marvellous,' Alec moaned. 'As if things weren't bad enough.' The story went into grim detail about her becoming an orphan at a young age and it also placed the blame for her kidnap squarely on the heads of the Merseyside force. He turned over again.

EVIL LATVIAN GANG, 'THREE', RESPONSIBLE FOR HUNDREDS OF MIGRANT DEATHS

'Where are they getting their information from?' Alec shrugged. He felt defeated. They hadn't mentioned Annie's disappearance, which was a relief for now, but it was probably destined for the later editions. He glanced over an abbreviated version of the history of Latvian occupation and the rise of the organisation Three. He handed Maxwell his newspaper. 'The brass will be shitting their pants about now and I know where they will apply the pressure.'

'On us, guv.'

'Correct.' Alec nodded. He changed the subject. 'How did it go at the Fletcher place?'

'Just like you said. It's a total pantomime. The Fletchers were sitting in the front seats of a classic Alfa. There was a hosepipe attached to the exhaust pipe and the engine was running. It looks like a double suicide at first glance but Kathy Brooks isn't convinced. She found an untreated injury on Peter Fletcher's skull. He was admitted to hospital with a head wound but that had been stitched earlier. The other wound was fresh. She thinks that he was knocked out and then put into the Alfa and suffocated. His brother Paul has signs of being restrained before his death. I think they silenced them, guv, but proving it is another thing.'

'I agree,' Alec nodded. 'The Latvian woman?'

'There are no signs of foul play. She just opened the window and jumped. The other bloke died in a coma. If they didn't, we have nothing to prove otherwise.'

Alec checked his watch again. 'We'd better get back to HQ and bring everyone up to speed.'

'With a bit of luck someone will have dropped on some information that will lead us to this mob, Three.'

'Fingers crossed, Sergeant,' Alec replied. Although he thought it would take considerably more than a bit of luck. 'Listen, I want you to have a word with Google.' Google was the nickname of an MIT detective, affectionately called so because of the vast amount of trivia he could store in his brain.

'What about, guv?'

'I'm stuck on the company that owned the Aigburth property,' Alec said with a sigh. 'I know that we've searched Companies House, but I think we looked in the wrong place.'

'I'm not following you.'

'We traced them to a shell company in the Caymans, right?'

'Yes, guv.'

'That's where we should be looking. Ask Google to crosscheck his searches with companies registered in tax havens. Tell him to start with Bahrain, Jersey, Switzerland, Hong

Kong, and Luxembourg. I want him to search for Latvian directors. If he finds any, tell him to run the companies against the land registry going back, say five years.' Max made a note of the havens. 'Tell him to do it today.'

'Yes, guv.'

'I'll see you back at MIT,' Alec said with a wave. He had a hunch that the Latvians owned more than just a Victorian terrace. If they did, Google would find it.'

CHAPTER 53

Ivor looked much older with his glasses on. He smoothed his faded jeans as he finished reading one newspaper and then angrily slammed it down onto his desk. Marika sat beside him and stroked his hair. Six of his men were sitting on a three-piece suite on the opposite side of the room. They listened to him ranting as he read the news and commented when he asked for an opinion. Everyone was aware that Ivor had a violent temper. He could move from irritated to psychotic in the space of minutes. Marika knew that nobody made him as angry as his brother could, but this time Andris had surpassed anything that she had seen before. He had always been careless and arrogant; complete opposites to Ivor but this time his crimes were all over the British press.

'Can you believe what they have done?' Ivor threw the question to the room. Ivor was a smart boss. He was crafty, cunning, and inventive. He employed scientists to explore new ways of transporting drugs so that they couldn't be detected. Everything was about being smart. Ivor wanted Three to be invisible, not even on the radar. In the beginning, Three was a mythical organisation. Their reputation was built on whispers, fables and the exaggerations of drunken old men. They were legends but no one was absolutely certain that they existed, bar the members themselves. Secrecy was sacrosanct. Their power was due to their obscurity. Ivor lectured Andris a thousand times, 'The other gangs fear us because they can't attack what isn't there, brother, and the police fear us because they can't capture ghosts,' but he didn't listen.

'He has ruined decades of our work,' Ivor bellowed. He stood up and slammed his fists onto the desk. He pointed to his men. 'You get it, don't you?'

'Of course, Ivor,' one of them answered and the others nodded their heads enthusiastically.

'We have always blended into the background,' he looked around at them in turn. 'That has been our strength.' They nodded in agreement. 'He doesn't get it, does he?'

'He doesn't want obscurity, Ivor,' Marika agreed. 'He wants to be known as a big man, a gangster. He wants everyone to know how much power he has, how dangerous messing with him can be; he is an idiot!'

Ivor shook his head and steepled his fingers beneath his chin. 'The police here will not stop looking for us for a century.' He slammed the table again. His black shirt was tight around his muscular shoulders. 'One detective dead, one shot in the head expected to die and a female inspector kidnapped from her home.' He held up his hands in question. 'How am I supposed to bring us back from that?' Marika shrugged in answer. She thought that the less she said the better. 'This is without mentioning the civilian deaths and…' he tapped his index finger on the desk to emphasise his point. 'And I haven't mentioned killing one of the Karpovs. They know who did it, and they will want payback. What can I do with him?'

No one answered. There was no useful answer.

'As for Letva,' he snapped. 'I trusted him to oversee things. He has as much to answer for as Andris. Where is he?' He turned to his men.

'He is at the recycling plant,' one of his men answered. 'He took the journalist there.'

'Fucking idiot. Call him and tell him to wait there. If he breathes without permission, I will rip his heart out!' Ivor growled. 'Take me there now and find out who is with Andris. Whoever is with him needs to bring him to the plant immediately, by whatever means possible. If he gives them any shit, tell them to kill him.'

CHAPTER 54

The recycling plant was on the outskirts of the city near to the river. Ivor and his men arrived in a discreet convoy of three cars. Marika turned to him and said, 'Your little brother would have us travelling around in shiny black four by fours with bodyguards running alongside.'

'And machineguns on the roof in case we get spotted.' Ivor laughed dryly. He looked at her and squeezed her knee gently. 'You know that this is the end for us, don't you? We will have to leave Europe for a long time. I can leave men in charge here and there. Some things will tick over, but others need my direct supervision. If I leave, they will be swallowed up by other organisations and once they smell weakness, they will move in and take everything.'

'You really think that it is that bad?'

'It is worse than bad. There is no way back from this. We cannot hide from this kind of exposure. The police will hunt us down. We will be target number one.'

'We have enough money to do as we please. Maybe it is time to move on.' She shrugged and touched his hand. 'As long as I'm with you, I don't care.' He leaned in and kissed her lips. 'We can go wherever you like, whenever you want to,' she whispered. 'I love you and whatever you think we should do is all right by me.'

'I want you to go back to the hotel and sort out travelling arrangements. Make sure that we can leave unnoticed at short notice.'

'I'll make sure we have a couple of options, yes?'

'Yes. None of the men must suspect we are leaving.'

'Okay,' she whispered in his ear. 'Leave it to me.'

Ivor opened the door and climbed out. He tapped the driver on the shoulder, 'Take Marika to the hotel. Stay with her until I call you.' The driver nodded and pulled off. Ivor looked around the plant. It was built when recycling was a buzzword and people's enthusiasm to save polar bears made them believe that it was financially viable to separate society's waste. The plant owners found out very quickly that it wasn't. Ivor bought the site via a broker and an untraceable umbrella company. The real estate on the land was worth fifty times what its business value was. He would have to grease the right palms to change the land use to get permission to build houses but that wouldn't be difficult, and the profit would be in the millions. In the meantime, it was useful for storing vehicles and occasionally running operations. He looked east towards the river. Bales the size of cars made from crushed aluminium cans were stacked four high and three deep. To the west, cages of corrugated cardboard covered several acres and offered an excellent sightscreen and a wood shredding machine had turned tons of waste branches into a huge hill of sand coloured sawdust.

'Letva is inside,' one of his men said. 'He's a bit upset that we've told him to remain here. He doesn't know that you're here yet, but he's pissed off.'

'Is he now?' Ivor said, his face darkening.

They walked up a concrete ramp built to give access to forklift trucks and then used a side entrance into a warehouse facility. Skips full of green bottles lined the wall on his right and a mountain of newspapers climbed almost to the ceiling six metres above them. Open girders supported a corrugated plastic roof and long fluorescent tubes bathed the building in cold harsh light. Letva was arguing with another man when he saw them coming in. Ivor spotted the hunched figure of a female tied to a chair. Vomit pooled around her feet and Ivor could smell urine. She had wet herself, either through fear or desperation. It was one of the reasons that he sent Marika back to the hotel. He didn't need her to see everything that went on. Sometimes his business required unsavoury methods to be employed. That part of the operation needed to be kept quiet. The other reason he had sent her back was the newspaper articles he had read.

'Ivor, what is going on?' Letva asked. 'You are back in the country. I thought that you would ring when you arrived. Why have you brought these new men here?'

'They are not new, Letva,' Ivor corrected him. 'They have been with us for a long time, but they usually work elsewhere.'

'Even so, there's no need. We can handle things.'

'It looks like it,' Ivor handed Letva a newspaper. Letva looked at it and blushed. Ivor noticed the woman's head snap up and focus on the headlines. 'Don't pay any attention to the press. They exaggerate everything. It is not as bad as it looks. Andris and I have done our best to clean-up. It might look messy for now, but things will settle down again soon. You'll see.'

'Clean-up?' Ivor said with a chuckle. 'It might look 'messy'?' Ivor emphasised the word. 'Do you have any idea how much damage you have done?'

Letva could see how annoyed Ivor was. He was holding back but his experience told him that it wouldn't last long.

'I have to be honest with you.' Letva softened his tone. 'I know he is your brother, but he is a liability. I warned Andris what he was doing was madness. I told him a hundred times that we shouldn't attract attention to ourselves. He is out of control, Ivor.' He paused while his words sank in. 'As for Oleg and Raitis, they encouraged him to be reckless. Oleg especially. You know how crazy he can be,' Letva pleaded with Ivor. It was time to employ plan B, which was blame everyone else. 'Andris is responsible for all of this shit,' he continued with the wave of an arm. 'When the handover went wrong, he panicked. He doesn't think things through.'

'You stepped back and thought things through, did you?'

'I was trying to identify the leak. You said it was the priority.'

'I also explained that the UK is not a warzone.'

'Things got out of control.'

'That is an understatement.'

'Andris is the source of your leak, Ivor.' Letva dropped a bombshell.

Ivor appeared to be genuinely shocked. He opened his mouth to speak but no sound came out at first. Long seconds ticked by as he mulled over the situation.

'You had better be able to substantiate an accusation like that.' Ivor looked at his men and they stared in silence. All eyes were on Letva. To accuse one of their own of being an informer was one thing, but to accuse their leader's kin was unheard of. 'Explain yourself.'

'How long have I worked for you?' Letva asked. Ivor shrugged and his face flushed with anger. 'Do you think that I would speak of such a thing unless I was sure?' Ivor put his hands into his pockets and waited for him to continue. He was in no mood to waltz around the facts. 'She is my proof, Ivor. Ask her where the information came from yourself,' Letva pointed at Toni. 'Go on, ask her.'

'Are you telling me that my brother is talking to a journalist?' Ivor frowned and looked confused. Anyone found leaking information to the mainstream press was dead. Three had manipulated underground publications many times but the nationals were their enemy. 'Have you lost your mind?'

'Ask her who called her with the information about the mill,' Letva stabbed his index finger towards her, his face twisted in anger. 'Ask her.'

Ivor looked at Toni and lowered his voice to speak to her. 'Did my brother call you with information?' Toni shook her head. His eyes went to meet Letva's.

'Ask her who called her,' Letva insisted.

'Who did call you?'

'Richard Grainger,' Toni said hoarsely. Ivor's eyes flickered with recognition. He didn't look pleased to hear the name.

'You have checked this information?'

'Of course,' Letva answered. 'The call is logged on her phone. We checked his number.'

'Richard Grainger?' Ivor looked at Toni again. He seemed to be struggling with the information. 'You are sure?'

'Yes.'

'Did he tell you where he heard the information?'

'No. I wouldn't have asked, and he wouldn't have told me anyway.'

'Did you pay him?'

'One hundred for a tip and another hundred when the story was substantiated. You can check my PayPal account if you like.'

'All this for a few hundred pounds?'

'I told you,' Letva said smugly. 'This is down to Andris.'

Ivor looked at his watch and the put his hands onto his hips. He blew air from his cheeks. 'And this Grainger character is dead?'

'Andris flattened him with a Range Rover.'

'And a detective too I believe,' Ivor added. 'What was he thinking?'

'The copper was collateral damage.'

'Killing a police officer is never collateral damage to them, you idiot. It is an act of war to them!'

'Either way, he silenced him.' Letva shrugged. 'You're missing the point.'

'What is the point?' Ivor frowned. 'Enlighten me.'

'He took Grainger out because he didn't want him spilling his guts. The police had arrested Grainger and he would have used any leverage he had to make a deal.'

'What do you mean?' Ivor asked quietly. He noticed some of his men shuffling uncomfortably as if they didn't want to hear the conversation any longer. 'What leverage did he have?'

Letva thought about his next words carefully. 'You know that Andris and Grainger socialised, didn't you?' Letva nodded and held out his hand palm up in question. 'You knew his name when she said it didn't you?' Ivor gave a gentle nod. 'They were more than just friends, Ivor. The information about the mill was pillow talk.'

'I think you should shut up.' Ivor held up his hand.

'It is the truth.' Letva sighed. 'Andris killed him so that he couldn't go blabbing about their relationship. He didn't want everyone to know that he swung both ways. When he realised that Grainger had betrayed him by selling the information, he decided to shut him up permanently. The detective was in the wrong place at the wrong time.'

Ivor shook his head in disbelief. He turned and walked away. Shooting Letva dead would be very simple now but there was something in what he said. Part of it rang true. He looked into the eyes of some of his men and they didn't look surprised. Some of them couldn't make eye contact with him. They had obviously suspected that Andris was a bit too close to

Grainger. He turned back to Letva. 'You're making a lot of assumptions.' He pointed his finger as he spoke. 'You wouldn't be trying to deflect the blame, would you?'

'It is true.' Letva shrugged. 'Ask her how she knows Grainger.'

'How do you know him?'

'I met him at a club a few years back. We got talking.'

Ivor raised his eyebrows, 'A gay club?'

'Yes. I was there with my partner and we got talking. He was bisexual.'

'I told you,' Letva clapped his hands together. 'I can't prove it yet, but I bet Grainger took the drugs from the switch.' Ivor was still shell-shocked. His mind wandered. Andris had always been awkward around women; awkward and aggressive. Ivor had seen him with hundreds of women, but it didn't mean he wasn't bisexual. It was not like he would share such information with his older brother, who was also his hero and his boss. Letva coughed and repeated himself. 'I said, I think he took the drugs from the switch too.'

Ivor ignored his comments. 'Too many people have been killed in public, Letva,' Ivor changed the subject. He needed to compose himself. 'You should have stopped him from making such a shambles.'

'It will die down.'

'It will die down! Are you fucking blind, or stupid?'

'The press will move onto something else next week.'

'No, they won't, Letva.'

'We have been here before.'

'No, no, no.' Ivor wagged his finger. 'We have not been here before, not here, not like this.' He glared at Letva. 'This is way beyond anything we have experienced before. Every rag across Europe will be digging up anything that they can connect to Three. We're going to be front-page news for a long time, and you know what happens when the Press get excited about something like this?'

'They make shit up…'

'No, Letva!' Ivor cut him dead. 'Every fucking empty head on the planet calls them up with their true stories about the 'Three gangsters'' Ivor reddened and picked up a newspaper. 'Can you see the headlines?' he said angrily. 'My father was killed by Three. My mother was killed by Three. Three robbed my bank. Three killed my dog. Three fathered my ten children.' He threw the paper onto the floor. 'Can you see it, Letva?'

'Yes,' he agreed reluctantly.

'You and Andris have put us into the spotlight and every grass from here to Hong Kong will be pointing their fingers at us for cash.'

'I don't see what else we could have done.' Letva shrugged sulkily. 'We had to find out where the information came from, didn't we?'

'Who took her from police protection?'

'I did.'

'You hijacked an armed unit?'

'I did it with three other men. It was clean and simple. We were in and out in a few minutes.'

'You shot a detective and you think it was a clean operation?'

'He hampered the snatch. I had to neutralise him.'

'Subtle, Letva. Very subtle.' Ivor shook his head. 'Who killed Karpov?'

'That was Oleg. We didn't know anything about it until he had him at the house and by then it was too late. Oleg hated the Russians; you know how much he hated them. He was a lunatic.'

Ivor thought about it for a moment. Oleg did hate the Russians, but he was too shrewd to snatch one of the Karpovs and dispose of the corpse in plain sight. He had been around the block with the soviet gangs a dozen times or more and he knew what would happen if he kidnapped, tortured, and killed one of them for sport. Something wasn't right. There was a lot that wasn't right. He changed tack while he mulled things over.

'Have you seen the headlines about her?' Ivor pointed to the block print.

'Not all of them. Why should that matter?'

'Tragic Liverpool reporter?' Ivor read it out. 'Every bleeding heart in the country will be waiting for news about her. She's a poor orphan snatched from the protection of the police on the way to see her dying girlfriend. Do you know how much focus that will bring?'

'Well, it will be bad for a while, but they'll forget her when another story comes along.'

'Wrong!' Ivor shouted. He pointed to Toni. 'They will never stop looking for her, not in our lifetime, you idiot!' Toni watched them arguing. Ivor looked at her curiously. Letva followed his gaze. 'Have you seen these headlines?' Ivor held the paper closer to her and turned the pages as she scanned them. She shook her head, the colour draining from her face. 'You didn't help to write this before this idiot kidnapped you, did you?'

'No,' Toni answered with a tremor in her voice. She shook her head vehemently. 'I deleted those pictures. They must have recovered them. I certainly wouldn't have written that about my family history, not ever.'

'Who could have recovered them?' Ivor asked politely. 'I'm sure that you think it doesn't matter now that they're out in the public domain, but it does matter to me.'

'Why would it matter now?' Toni was baffled. She was going to die anyway, why not ask the question? She had nothing left to lose. 'I don't understand.'

'Untie her hands and give her some water,' Ivor ordered.

'Are you mad, Ivor?' Letva complained. 'This bitch started all this. If it wasn't for her, none of this would have happened…'

'Shut up,' Ivor said bitterly. His eyes drilled into Letva challenging him to defy him. Letva didn't dare. 'Do it now!'

One of the men moved and cut the ties and another handed her a bottle of water. Antonia rubbed her wrists and frowned. She wiped at the vomit on her jeans, embarrassed. 'Thank you.'

'It is important to me. I am interested in whoever authored the article about us.'

'Doesn't it say a name next to the article?' Toni asked. She gulped at the water thirstily.

'No,' Ivor looked again. 'The name Julia Fox is next to the main article but not the one about us.'

'Good old Julia. When that happens, the article has been written by a team of journalists, but Julia is claiming credit for it all,' Toni said bitterly. She was nervous and rambling. 'She had access to my deleted files. It is to stop sour grapes when an employee leaves just in case they try to delete all the photographs they uploaded.'

'I see.' Ivor nodded. 'So, she works for the locals?'

'She is the editor of *The Echo* and *The Daily Post*.'

'And she sold your pictures to the nationals? That is criminal,' he shook his head not realising the irony. Toni looked at him as he spoke. His eyes moved left to right reading the words again. 'Here,' Ivor handed her the newspaper. 'There's something to read. I have some business to attend to. Maybe we can talk later.' Toni took the newspaper and nodded. She heard Letva calling him Ivor. The men at the handover had used the same name. It was obvious that he was in charge. 'Letva, come with me. We need to sort our problems away from the press. No offence,' he said smiling thinly at Toni. He turned and walked across the warehouse. Letva followed him flanked by six others. 'You two stay with Miss Barrat,' he called as they left. Two men hovered behind her. Toni didn't know how to feel. Letva said that she would be taken to the forest and shot but now she had a newspaper and water. Relief, fear and confusion battled for a place in her mind. She took a sip of the water and read the newspaper. Tears filled her eyes and blurred her vision and her mind drifted to Kayla.

CHAPTER 55

Ivor looked out of the window and watched Andris being marched into the building at gunpoint. He thought it was typical. The man wouldn't do anything that he was asked without causing a fuss. It always had to go to the wire before he would capitulate. It was as if he constantly had a point to prove. Whatever Ivor asked him to do, Andris had an alternative method that was quicker and easier. He had to butt heads with him over the smallest issue and challenge his authority. It was this attitude that had forced Ivor to move him to the UK. He had burnt his bridges in Latvia. Every judge and bent detective that they had on the payroll had refused to help any more if Andris was involved. He had become a liability not only to himself but to Ivor and more importantly to Three. Enough was enough. He had sent him to London first but when things didn't improve, he sent him north to Liverpool. He didn't think that he could create too many problems there. How wrong he had been. There was a knock on the door and then it opened before he could speak.

'What the fuck are you playing at?' Andris burst in. His face was deep red with embarrassment and anger. He pointed to the two men behind him. They each held a Glock 17 on his back. 'These fucking monkeys had the nerve to tell me that I was being summoned immediately by the great Ivor Markevica,' Andris pointed to himself dramatically. 'Me, summoned by you!' He looked at everyone incredulously. 'Who are you again?' he waved his arms theatrically. 'Oh yes. You're my fucking brother!'

'Sit down and stop being so dramatic,' Ivor pointed to a chair. Andris made to argue but Ivor gestured to one of the men behind him. He hit him on the side of the head with his gun. Andris dropped to his knees. 'Do you have to make everything such a drama, Andris?'

'Fuck you,' Andris moaned. He rubbed the fast-rising lump on his head. 'I'm going to slit his throat,' he said looking at the man that hit him. 'The minute he steps back onto an airplane, you're fucking dead meat.' The man didn't flinch. He didn't look frightened at all.

'You will be leaving here for good, Andris,' Ivor said flatly.

'What are you talking about?'

'You are going from Hull to Rotterdam in the back of a lorry, today,' Ivor paused and stared at him. 'Your face is all over the news. You are a liability now.'

'Fuck you. I'm going nowhere.'

'Drama, drama, drama, Andris.' Ivor shrugged. 'You will go willingly, or you will go bound and gagged like a hog. It is your choice.'

'Come on, Ivor!'

'You just do not understand how things work, do you?'

'I understand that you're a fucking arsehole,' he snapped. 'You turn up here like Dynamo the magician and start poking your nose into my business. You have the audacity to order my men to bring me here at gunpoint and tell me that I am being shipped out. Who the fuck do you think you are?'

Ivor sat down and sighed. He put his head in hands and sighed. His temper was beginning to fray. He counted to ten before looking around the room. 'Your men brought you here at gunpoint?' He shrugged. 'Your men put a gun to your head? That would tell any intelligent person that they are not your men.'

'I was busy sorting business out…'

'You were busy fucking things up for the next thirty years, you idiot!' Ivor snapped. Andris paled visibly. 'You and your big mouth caused all this.'

'What are you talking about?'

'Richard Grainger.' Ivor glared at him.

'He's not a problem anymore.'

'Just because he is dead doesn't mean he isn't a problem.' Ivor laughed gruffly. 'You see that this is your problem all the time. You think that by killing him he has gone away but he hasn't, has he?' Ivor asked the room. Most of the men shook their heads. 'They all know that you were fucking Richard Grainger, killing him doesn't change that. Is that your problem, Andris?' Andris changed colour. 'Were you repressed all these years?' Ivor snorted. 'Was hiding in the closet too much for you so you feel that you have to walk around like Johnny Concrete, so that we all think you're a big macho man?' Andris glared at his brother. Ivor pushed him. 'Is that it?'

'Fuck you!'

'Letva guessed it was you.' Ivor gestured to the seated figure on his left. 'You can thank him for that.' Andris looked across at him and scowled. 'You can put your differences aside for now. I don't want to hear you blaming each other. You have destroyed our anonymity here and across Europe. It will take years for us to recover from this, if we can at all.'

'I told him he had gone too far.' Letva sighed, 'I cannot trust him again. Not now I know he is a fairy.'

Andris launched himself across the room. He covered the three metres between himself and Letva in a flash but Letva was quicker. He stood and stepped to the side, tripping Andris. Andris clattered to the floor and Letva was on him. He wrapped his arm around his neck, tucking his forearm under his jaw and squeezed. Andris struggled violently but the chokehold became tighter. When a gun was pressed against Letva's temple, he released him. They stood up, three men between them.

'You and your fag boyfriend stole the shipment too, didn't you?' Letva turned to face Ivor. 'He must have taken the zombie from the switch,' Letva shouted. 'Don't trust him!'

'I didn't take the drugs, you prick,' Andris replied angrily. 'He is a liar!'

'Who else knew about it?' Letva pointed his finger. 'Only you and your boyfriend. You make me sick!'

'I will kill you!'

'You can try, you queer.'

Andris launched himself again, but the men held him firm.

'Shut up both of you!' Ivor ordered. An uneasy silence fell across the room. 'I arranged for the drugs to be taken,' he growled.

'What?' Letva asked confused.

'You fucked up a simple handover and I didn't know who was responsible for the leak. I brought in an independent to make sure the shipment was safe.' All eyes fell on Ivor. His men exchanged uneasy glances. Letva and Andris relaxed a little and stared at Ivor with contempt.

'You arranged the snatch?' Letva said rolling his eyes.

'Who did you use?' Andris asked incredulous.

'It doesn't matter,' Ivor snapped. 'He did what he was paid to do, and the zombie is at the press being converted into tablets. I finished what you should have done in the first place!'

'Who did you use?' Andris repeated.

'It doesn't matter.'

'Tell me you didn't use that snake, Gary Powell.'

'What?' Ivor felt prickles of uncertainty touching him. 'Why not? He has been a reliable asset.'

'He is a mercenary and he can't be trusted…'

'Enough!' Ivor shouted. 'He is good at his job.'

'Andris is right,' Letva said softly. 'We haven't used him for nearly a year. We found out that he has been working for the Karpovs too.'

'What?'

'We heard whispers and they turned out to be true.'

'The word is that he has been working directly for Victor Karpov,' Andris sneered. 'You see you don't know everything that goes on here. This city is full of snakes and he works for anyone who pays him. Did you use him to take the shipment?'

'Yes.'

'And then you arranged for him to hand it back?'

'Of course.'

'But none of our men knew that you were back in the country.' Andris frowned. 'Did you do the handover with him?'

'No.'

Andris shook his head in disbelief. 'Did you send Marika?'

Ivor realised what Andris was saying. If Powell had followed Marika back to the hotel, then the Karpovs would know where they were staying. He was in deep trouble. He reached for his mobile phone and dialled Marika. There was a feeling of dread in his guts.

CHAPTER 56

Marika put her iPod into a docking port and selected a Rihanna album. She opened her suitcase and emptied the contents onto the bed, then unzipped the liner and slipped out a panel from the base. Inside were two passports that identified them as Estonian newlyweds. A second pair said they were a Lithuanian couple, who dived a lot in the Red Sea and on the reefs off Australia. Living with Ivor was like being a character in a Bond movie. They were always changing identities, nationalities, and appearance. It was part of the excitement for her. During the last twelve months her hair had been long, ridiculously long, short, auburn, blond, and black and she loved every one of the styles. Ivor loved it too. It kept her fresh and attractive for him, not that it was hard to keep Ivor interested. He was fascinated with her from the first time he had set eyes on her. The animal magnetism and sexual chemistry between them never waned. As if reading her thoughts Rihanna and Eminem began to sing her favourite track. Marika smiled and sang along with them.

You ever love somebody so much you can barely breathe when you're with 'em? You meet and neither one of you even know what hit 'em…

That was how it had been and still was. She never tired of him physically and never bored of his conversation. When they were together, there was no one else in the room. She had been a pole dancer and more when she couldn't pay the rent, but Ivor didn't care about her past. His was hardly full of rainbows and unicorns. She had no idea if they would feel the same in five years time and she didn't care. They loved each other dearly now and now was all that mattered. Her only regret was not having a family. She wanted a child, but Ivor wouldn't think about it. He said that his life was too violent to bring children into it. He said that children would be deemed as a weakness by his enemies. 'If we can't kill Ivor Markevica, then kill his children.' The thought terrified her, and she had never talked about it again but now they had to disappear for a few years things could be different. Maybe fate was taking a hand in things. Maybe he would consider having a child now… maybe.

She took out her tablet and swiped the screen to bring it life. Searching for flights that would leave Manchester in the next twenty-four hours, she booked flights for each imaginary couple using different debit cards each time so as not to spark a security alert with the airlines. One flight was to Bangkok and the other to Singapore; they could decide which to take when Ivor returned. If they needed more time, they could change the flights to a later date. Then she booked taxi transfers to the airport, four in total all from different hotels in the vicinity. No one could discover their getaway strategy; they didn't know which one they would use themselves yet.

She spent half an hour transferring American dollars into prepaid cash passport accounts and bought thirty-day visas that meant they could stay in Thailand for a month before they had to leave. She checked out flights to Indonesia and the Philippines. They could disappear among the islands for years if necessary. She was almost excited about the prospect. It was a part of the world that she had always wanted to visit. Every cloud has a silver lining etc. She repacked the case and cleared her search history to prevent prying eyes from seeing their travel plans.

There was a knock on the door. Marika jumped and turned down the music. She walked to the door and looked through the security glass. Her driver was standing in the hallway. She guessed that Ivor had sent for her. Her heart fluttered a little at the thought of months in the sunshine with him all to herself. She opened the door.

'I'll just grab my coat,' she said smiling. Her smile vanished when the driver fell through the doorway. He fell facedown, arms and legs splayed like a flying angel. 'What the fuck…' Marika began to say. Her voice was nothing more than a whisper.

'Victor Karpov sends his regards,' a man said as he stepped into the room. He closed the door behind him and aimed a silenced Tokarev at the driver's head. The pistol hissed three times and then he turned it towards Marika. She stood open-mouthed, frozen to the spot; she couldn't even scream. The gun bucked in his hands six times before he stopped firing. The white bed linen was soaked in blood, the walls splattered from floor to ceiling. He ejected the empty magazine, clicked in a fresh one and then emptied the entire clip into her already dead body.

CHAPTER 57

Alec climbed into a white paper suit and ducked beneath the crime scene tape. He pulled on latex gloves and walked down the corridor to room 808. Detective Maxwell walked alongside him. They had been quiet all the way to the scene. Neither man felt like making small talk while Stirling was critical and Annie was missing. As they approached, the familiar smells of death met them, subtle at first but quickly becoming stomach churning. The metallic odour of blood mingled with the victims' bodily fluids; a mix of vomit, urine and excrement drifted in the air. It was a thick cloying mixture that clung to back of their throats, made their eyes water and their stomachs churn regardless of how many times they experienced it. Crime scenes were always gloomy sad places but this one had something else attached to it. It felt oppressive. Alec had a terrible sense of foreboding. This wasn't the end. There was definitely more violence to come. The angst was suffocating.

It was difficult to concentrate on this violent crime wave when Annie was intrinsically wrapped up in it. Instead of leading the investigation, she had become a victim of it. She was in dire trouble, suffering, or already dead. He couldn't bring himself to focus on anything else. He had come a long way down the road to recovery since Gail's death. Losing Gail and Will simultaneously had been a hammer blow to his emotions, despite their betrayal. He was obviously still fragile, but he hadn't realised how fragile until he saw the smouldering ruins of Annie's house. Nothing else seemed to matter. The hopeless search for Annie was chipping away at his soul. Where do you start looking? He didn't know the answer and he was in charge so what hope was there? Wherever she was, she would know that too. She would be only too aware of how helpless she was. There was no way of knowing where they'd taken her, no way of rescuing her from the jaws of death like in the movies and no way to take away her pain before they finally killed her. Alec wished that he could swap places with her but such wishes fall on deaf ears. No one was listening; no one could help. Barring a miracle, Annie Jones was gone from his life too and he didn't know how he would cope with that. In fact, he didn't know if he could. 'I wish I could have told you, in the living years…' He didn't tell Gail how he felt when she was alive. Some people never learn. He had done the same thing with Annie, always waiting for the right time. Now it was too late.

A uniformed officer nodded a greeting as he reached the room. The CSI photographer was leaving. He half smiled a hello, but Alec could sense that he couldn't get away quickly enough. He took a breath before he stepped into the room. Kathy Brooks was knelt over a man's body, her auburn hair tied tightly at the back of her head.

'Alec,' she said in greeting. 'Max.'

'Hello, Kathy,' Alec mumbled. His mind was already analysing the carnage. 'First impressions?'

'We have a male, mid to late thirties with three gunshot wounds to the back of the head and over there is a female. By the look of her body I am guessing mid-twenties to early forties. If you take a look at her face, you will understand why I can't be more specific.' Alec moved closer and looked at the body, which was wedged down the side of the bed against the wall. The face was a bloody mess with no distinguishing features. 'I think our shooter emptied an entire clip into her face.'

'Gangland revenge shooting?' Alec mused. 'Do as much damage to the face as possible to degrade the victim. They certainly achieved that.'

'I would say so,' Kathy agreed. 'She has expensive clothes, breast implants, and her teeth have veneers. This fellah is scruffy and unkempt. His nails are dirty, his teeth are stained and badly decayed and his clothes are cheap; they're not a couple.'

'Minder?' Alec guessed.

'Not a good one,' Max added. He looked around and saw the fake passports, one Estonian and one Lithuanian. Both countries bordered Latvia. He handed them to Alec. 'Any other ID on them?'

'On the dressing table there's a driving licence but it's fake.'

'What about their mobile phones?' Max asked.

'I haven't found any, which is odd.'

'The killer took them,' Alec said. 'There will be others on his hit list and their details might be in those phones.' He studied the passports. The man's photograph was familiar. There was a distinct likeness to the pictures he had seen of Andris Markevica driving the Range Rover that killed Dalton Sykes. 'Are you Ivor Markevica?' Alec asked no one in particular. He thought that he probably was. 'In which case you must be Mrs Markevica.' He looked at the congealing mass that used to be a woman's face. 'I wonder if he knows that you're dead yet,' Alec muttered.

'There will be hell to pay when he does,' Max mumbled.

'What are you thinking?' Kathy asked.

'I think the Karpovs have come to settle a few old scores.'

'That isn't good, is it?'

'Ask her.' Alec gestured to the dead woman. 'She knows just how 'not' good it is.'

CHAPTER 58

Ivor Markevica looked at the Holiday Inn through binoculars. There were police cars parked on the pavements and uniformed officers were buzzing around outside. He had called the reception and pretended to be a concerned guest. They said that there had been a suspicious death in the building, but the hotel was operating as normal apart from the fourth floor. Marika was dead. He knew she was. Neither Marika nor her driver, were answering their phones. There was no sign of an ambulance, which was a bad sign. An ambulance is no good to dead people. He knew that the police or the Karpovs would now be in possession of the mobile phones that Marika and the driver had used. That compromised all the phones that had had contact with them. He ordered that everyone should destroy their existing phones. The numbers logged in the captured mobiles could be tracked and he didn't want that.

However, there was a way that he could use the stolen phones to his advantage. He was counting on the fact that whoever had the mobiles, hadn't switched them off. If they were still searching the logs for information, they would be on. If they were on, he could find them. He scanned the surrounding area again. The hotel was situated at the south corner of the Albert Docks. It was busy with tourists and the car parks nearby were full. He focused on the multistorey to his right and scanned it with the binoculars. The chances were that the Karpovs would be waiting for him to return to the hotel and if they were, the multi-storey offered the best vantage point. He took out his phone and dialled.

'Letva,' Ivor said. 'Check the spyware for Marika's phone. If it is still on, we can trace it using the SIM cards. I want to know where it is.'

'I'll do it right away. Anything else?'

'Yes. Send four men into that multi-storey car park opposite the Holiday Inn,' Ivor added. 'Tell them to look for someone watching the hotel. If the Karpovs are still here, that is where they will be.'

'Got it.'

'If you find anyone, bring them to me alive. I will be at the plant.'

'No problem.'

'One more thing and this is very important, Letva. Find Gary Powell and bring him to me.'

'Yes, Ivor,' Letva agreed enthusiastically. 'He has a number of properties around town. We'll have them watched. He'll turn up.'

'Good. Make it the priority.'

'I won't let you down this time.'

'You had better not.' Ivor hung up and leaned his head back against the seat. Marika was dead. The only woman that he had truly felt a connection with was gone, ripped from him by an enemy. He was angrier than he had ever been before. His heart was racing, and he was certain that he was going to vomit. He was desperate to go into the hotel and see Marika for himself. How did they kill her? Did she suffer? Was she raped before they killed her? His head was spinning around with terrible scenarios of what had happened. The more he thought, the more his guts twisted. Marika was dead. The obvious kept jumping to the forefront of his mind. She was dead. He had loved her. She knew that he loved her even though he didn't tell her enough. Every time she walked in the room, he wanted her. Every time she smiled at him, he wanted her. When she laughed, his heart skipped a beat. She was truly beautiful in a way that no one had been before. He felt empty inside. The thought of laying low without her was unbearable. He would end up drinking himself into a stupor, crying into his beer about the love he had lost. She couldn't be replaced. He had been with a thousand women and not one had come close to Marika. He had heard the saying that you meet the love of your life once if you're lucky. He had and she had been stolen from him. Marika was dead. She was dead. Someone would pay dearly for it. They would pay a terrible price and they would wish that they'd never set eyes on his Marika. If it was that last thing that he ever did, they would pay.

CHAPTER 59

24 Hours Later

Gary Powell woke up with a throbbing head. His eyes were sticky, and he couldn't open them at first. He felt dizzy and his brain felt as if it was about to explode. He couldn't remember much. The last thing he could recall was putting the key into the front door and then everything was black. It was a blank. He could hear someone moaning nearby and then he felt someone knocking his arms, legs and back. It was as if he was being slapped. He tried to sit up but couldn't and his body jerked violently. There was a gurgling sound like a man trying to talk with a mouthful of custard. His limbs were knocked, and he moved jerkily again. The movement was completely involuntarily, and he couldn't fathom what was happening. His legs and ankles were in agony. The blood supply had been cut off and the numbness was crippling. As consciousness beckoned, he opened his eyes. The world began to spin and the nauseous feeling intensified. He tried to move his head and right himself, but he could do neither. His blood was running to his head and the pressure behind his eyes was excruciating. He felt that they might pop out of his skull.

Suddenly, his brain clicked, and he realised where he was. He was hanging upside down, his legs and ankles bound tightly. The blows to his limbs were from another man, who was in a similar position. He was a metre or so away from him, suspended from something. Gary writhed in pain and tried to look behind him but all he could see was the man's dark hair and an ear. As his vision cleared, he could see skips full of bottles, newspapers stacked to the ceiling and blurred faces. Some faces were staring at him. Some were standing and some seated like an audience. Beneath him was a concrete floor. The dust was heavily stained with a dark liquid that looked like blood. He felt himself being lifted higher. A diesel engine chugged away, and he could smell the exhaust fumes. As he was lifted, he turned on the rope. His ankles ached as the fibres cut into his flesh. He saw a yellow machine and realised that he was dangling from a forklift truck. The forks were extended as far as they could go. Gary was upside down, four metres from the ground. The man behind him was moaning in pain, his body twitched and writhed. Each movement sent bolts of pain through Gary.

'I'm glad you're with us, Gary.' Ivor's voice registered in his brain. 'We have all been waiting for you join us.'

'Ivor.' Gary recognised his voice immediately and fear shot through him like a white-hot knife. Ivor Markevica had him trussed beneath a forklift truck. That was bad, very bad indeed. He tried his best to think of a way to escape his situation. 'Whatever this is about, we can sort it out,' Gary said in a panic. He realised there probably wasn't any way of sorting it out, but self-preservation had taken over. Ivor Markevica was pissed off about something, very pissed off. Gary had a good idea what it might be. He prayed that it wasn't what he suspected it was. 'Please, Ivor. Let me down. We can sort this out.'

'Sort it out.' Ivor repeated slowly. 'Sort it out, hmm.' Ivor looked thoughtful. 'I don't think that we can sort it out, as you say. Where is Victor Karpov?'

'Let me down from here and I'll tell you anything that you want to know.' Gary tried to negotiate. His head was spinning. 'We can't talk like this.'

Ivor walked towards the forklift and kicked at a pinkish lump on the floor. It tumbled across the concrete and landed beneath Gary. One end was a bloody lump of vein filled muscle. The other was tapered and pale.

'That is what your friend said. He asked to be let down so that we could talk,' Ivor gestured towards the man behind Gary. 'He lost his tongue. We ripped it out with pliers.'

'Please, Ivor.'

'Have you ever seen a man having his tongue ripped out?'

'Ivor, whatever I have done, we can sort it out. Please talk to me… let me down, please!'

'Your friend screamed for a long time. It must be incredibly painful don't you think?'

'He is not my friend. I have never seen him before in my life.' Gary closed his eyes and began to sob. He was in dreadful pain and the realisation of how dire his dilemma was, was sinking in quickly. 'I never let you down. I thought we worked well together.'

'You didn't let me down?' Ivor repeated. 'Oh, you let me down all right.'

'What did I do?'

'You followed Marika from the handover, and you told the Karpovs where she was staying. They sent the man behind you and he shot her.' Ivor paused and cocked his head slightly. Gary closed his eyes in despair. The news made him sick to the core. 'That pig shot my wife.'

'I'm so sorry, Ivor. I didn't know they would do that.'

Ivor ignored him. 'Before we cut his tongue out, we showed him a video of his wife and daughter back at home in Moscow.' Ivor held up a tablet and clicked the start tab on a video. The mother and daughter were tied to chairs. A man walked behind them and poured petrol over them. Gary cringed at their faces. The expression of sheer terror was etched into them as they were set alight and left to burn. 'I take no pleasure from killing a mother and her child like this but then they have no one to blame but that piece of shit there, do they?' Ivor pointed at the other man. He grabbed the Russian's hair and punched him in the face. The man gurgled and spat blood onto the floor. Tears streamed from his eyes. Gary had never seen a human being that colour. His face was totally purple, almost blue. 'We showed the video to your parents too,' Ivor gestured with his head to a place behind Gary. 'They were very upset by it, especially your mother.'

'What are you talking about?' Gary wriggled and tried to turn around. As the rope twisted, he focused on the blurred faces that he had noticed before, the faces of the people who were seated. He had to look hard. His parents were sitting next to each other, bound and gagged. His father had dried blood beneath his nostrils and his eyes were black and swollen as if he had put up a fight. His mother was staring at him, eyes pouring with tears, pleading him, begging him to help them. 'No, no, no, no, no!' Gary bellowed. Panic gripped him. 'Ivor please let them go. They have nothing to do with this. Let them go, Ivor. I'm begging you, please.'

'Oh, they were involved the moment you chose to tell Karpov where Marika was,' Ivor said flatly. 'As for begging, do you think my Marika begged for her life?'

'Ivor, please! I didn't know. Let them go, please, Ivor.'

'Did anyone offer my Marika mercy?'

'Please let them go, Ivor. This is my fault. They haven't hurt you, Ivor, please!'

'Nobody gave my Marika mercy, did they?'

'I didn't know what he was going to do, Ivor. Please let them go. They're old. They can't handle this at their age. Please, Ivor.' Gary turned slowly on the rope. His breath was becoming shorter. He wriggled to try to keep his eyes on his parents. They looked vulnerable and frail. As he watched them sobbing, frightened, and in pain, his heart was being ripped to shreds. 'Ivor, I'll do anything you ask just let them go. I didn't know, honestly. Please…'

'Please don't insult my intelligence by denying that you didn't know what Karpov would do, or I'll have them dissected piece by piece for the next month.'

'I'm not denying it, Ivor. I fucked up by trusting Victor. I didn't know what he was going to do,' Gary was blubbering now. His eyes were screwed up and his chin trembled as he talked. 'Victor said he wanted to know where you were. He wanted to set up a meeting,' Gary garbled. 'Please Ivor, I didn't know he would kill her. Please let them go.' He realised how weak his explanation sounded but he couldn't bear to see his parents trussed up and he didn't want to die. 'I'm begging you, Ivor. I didn't know anything about this…'

'One more time. Where is Victor Karpov?' Ivor ignored his pleas.

'I'll tell you anything that you want just let them go.' Ivor gestured towards the parents. One of his men stepped behind Gary's father and struck him hard across the back of his head. Gary writhed on the rope, terror, anger, and helplessness coursed through his brain.

'Okay, okay! He flew to Europe this morning,' Gary gasped. Ivor waited for specifics. 'Bratislava, I think. He has business there. Now let them go.'

'I don't think so, Gary,' Ivor said shaking his head. He clapped his hands together and his men picked up two green canisters of petrol. They poured the stinging liquid over Gary's elderly parents. Their eyes streamed and they began to choke on their gags as the fluid soaked into them and the fumes filled their airways. 'This is on your own head,' Ivor said.

'Ivor, Ivor, Ivor! No, no, no, no,' Gary shouted at an increasing volume. 'Stop it now, you bastard. Stop it. Stop it. Stop it. Please stop it!' He heard the whoosh as his parents were set ablaze and his heart broke into a million pieces. He watched in abstract horror as they twitched and jerked. Their grey hair flamed brightly, and their mouths twisted into blackened holes as their gags burned away. They seemed to twitch and tremble for hours, all the time Gary couldn't catch his breath. 'You fucking bastard,' he whispered as he watched them turn black, their flesh turned to carbon in front of his eyes. 'You fucking animal. I'll kill you…'

'Your killing days are long behind you. Remember whose fault this is. Have a good hard think about it.' Ivor waved to the forklift driver. Gary felt the truck reverse and then it turned ninety degrees. The forks held them over the feed tray of an industrial wood chipping machine. A man started up the shredder's diesel engine and the grinding wheels began to spin so fast that the jagged teeth became a silver blur. The driver dangled them over the spinning blades as it roared. They bucked and twisted and screamed and begged and pleaded, their words were nothing more than a collection of gurgling and sobs. They had plenty of time to think about what was about to happen. Ivor ignored Gary's desperate pleas for forgiveness. He gave the signal and as the truck driver lowered them towards the whirring grinding wheels, Gary screamed louder than anyone that he had heard before.

Toni Barrat watched the nightmare unfold before her eyes. She couldn't turn away. Fear and morbid fascination forced her to endure the horrific scene. As she watched the almost comedy moment when two pairs of kicking legs protruded from the feed tray and a stream of pink goo sprayed from the exit port, she wondered if she would be next.

CHAPTER 60

Alec walked through the MIT operations room. The feeling of gloom was oppressive. The usual chatter of voices was there but it was hushed. There was no laughter and the usual dark humoured banter was gone. Stirling's empty desk was a stark reminder of the seriousness of the case. Annie's office was in darkness, the blinds drawn, and the door closed. The effect of their absence was profound. Alec looked around. The teams were hard at work despite working blind. Until the forensics came back, they were fishing for a break. Alec stared at the case review board; each picture linked to another with a thin red line. The man at the top was Ivor Markevica but his brother Andris was Alec's prey. Alec wanted to bring him in and smash his head against the walls of a cell. There wasn't a copper in the building that didn't. Obviously, he couldn't do that but there was no harm in feeling that way. He wasn't bad, he was just human.

'Guv,' the familiar voice of Google called from across the room. 'I was just about to call you.'

'What's up?' Alec approached his desk. The other detectives at his workstation were frantically making calls and tapping at their keyboards like demented typists.

'We crosschecked all the well-known tax havens like you suggested and came up with a few Latvian directors with property registered here, guv,' Google said pushing his thick glasses up his nose. He blinked. 'I discarded the smaller properties and we found one company that owns a recycling plant on the outskirts of town. The place went bankrupt when the recession hit. It hasn't traded for five years yet when I checked with the local uniforms, they said that there has been activity there recently.'

'How recently?'

'All week, guv.' Google pulled up an aerial shot of the site. 'See these bales of tin stacked here and here,' Alec nodded yes, 'There are hundreds of them. They were valueless when the place was sold but they're worth a small fortune now, yet the new owners haven't sold them on. It makes me think that they act as a good sightscreen and they like them where they are.'

'You have a suspicious mind, Google,' Alec said sarcastically.

'Don't you agree?'

'Of course, I do.'

'Oh! Good!' Google said without smiling. 'I have taken a liberty and alerted uniform to place marked vehicles on the motorway here and here. That way we can observe comings and goings and seal the exit and entry slip roads if we need to.'

'That is good work, Google.'

'What do you think?'

'I think that you could be on to something. They have to have a hole to retreat to and that place is perfect.'

'What do you want me to do?'

'I'll speak to Area Command and commandeer a chopper to take a silent fly over and see what is going on there now. If we like the look of it, we need to surround the property. If they're in there we can't just knock and the door and ask them to come out. We need armed units here, here and here, and more on the gates here and we'll need boats on the river. It's time to call the cavalry in.'

'What about us, guv?'

'I want every man and his dog vested up and ready to go in an hour.'

'Yes, guv,' Google looked genuinely excited, which was rare. 'Do you think the DI is in there, guv?'

'I hope so, Google. I really do.' His stomach tightened as he spoke. He looked at Annie's abandoned office and felt drained.

CHAPTER 61

Toni was sitting in awe of the clean-up process that was going on around her. She was in complete shock. The Latvians had cremated an elderly couple alive in front of their son, ripped out a man's tongue with pliers and then fed two men through an industrial shredding machine. It was more than anyone could bear to watch and remain sane. Now they were cleaning the place as if the Environmental Health Office were on their way to do an audit. The shredder and the floor of the recycling warehouse were hosed and steamed and bleached for what seemed like hours although in reality it was less than half an hour. They used a JCB to cover the pinkish remains of the men with wood chippings. It took a few passes, but they were soon buried.

Everything went like clockwork until it was time for Andris to leave. He kicked up a fuss and began screaming and shouting abuse at Ivor. Eventually, he was overpowered by five men and bound and gagged. Ivor had him thrown into the back of a van where he was left while they finished their clean-up. She listened intently to what they were saying. From the bits and pieces she could hear in English, Andris was destined to go to a lorry park in the North-East where he would be transferred into a heavy goods vehicle and taken by ferry across the North Sea to Holland. None of the men had much sympathy for him. She didn't know what would happen to him from Rotterdam onwards and she didn't care. They were getting ready to leave and she knew that she was a loose end. It wouldn't be long now. Toni thought about her children. She would miss them terribly, but they would be safe with their father. That thought gave her a little comfort. She wondered if Kayla was still alive and decided that she would find out soon enough when she crossed to the other side.

Ivor walked towards her; his hands shoved deep into his pockets. He looked almost apologetic as he approached. His face was dark, deep lines were etched around the corners of his eyes. He had aged dramatically in the space of one day. Maybe the strain of losing his partner was too much for him or maybe orchestrating the horrific deaths of other human beings had taken its toll. Toni was beyond caring. She was anaesthetised to it all. Her brain could only process so much horror and then it stopped functioning at the same level. After that, reality became fiction. What was happening took on a surreal quality. Ivor Markevica was the most dangerous individual that she had ever encountered, and he was approaching her, yet she felt nothing. Nothing could surpass the horror that she had witnessed, not even her own demise. Waiting around knowing that she was going to be murdered had become tedious. Her mind just wanted the anxious wait over. 'Kill me and let me rest!' her mind screamed. Ivor grabbed a chair and sat down opposite her.

'I'm sorry that you had to witness that, Antonia,' he sounded genuine. 'They murdered my partner and so I had to claim justice on her behalf. It was brutal I know, but some things have to be balanced. Life is all about balance.' Toni didn't speak. She didn't nod, she didn't even blink. There was no response to what the psychopath in front of her was saying, no matter how emotionally disturbed he was. She stared blankly at him. 'You know all about loss, don't you?' Ivor leaned forward and picked up the newspaper. He opened it at the headlines about her. 'You know how it feels to lose your loved ones, don't you?' This time his expression demanded an answer.

'Yes,' Toni said quietly. Her loss wasn't like his. Anger bubbled away in her guts but she daren't tell him that his loss was his own fault. Marika was murdered because he was a killer. 'I know how it feels to lose someone.'

Ivor leaned closer to her. He grimaced and touched her knee gently with his fingertips. His touch felt strangely reassuring. 'I have debated telling you this but somehow I feel as if I owe you.'

'Tell me what?' Toni asked with a sigh. What on earth could he tell her that she would want to hear?

'I knew your father, Antonia.'

'What?'

'Yes. I realised when I read the article about you and your family.' He nodded, and half smiled. 'I knew him.'

'How did you know him?'

'He drove a lorry on the continent many years ago, didn't he?'

'Yes,' Toni replied, suspicion in her eyes.

'He used to pick up some of our products and take them back to the UK. We became friends over the years.'

'What products?' Toni gasped. In her mind the scenarios ran riot. Had her father been mixed up with Three? Is that why he was murdered? Was he a drug runner? She felt stunned by the fact that it was even a possibility that he was an associate of Ivor. 'What are you talking about, products?'

'All kinds of stuff.' Ivor shrugged.

'Illegal stuff?'

'Sometimes, but he didn't realise what was in the trailer,' he brushed off the question. 'I met you when you were a little girl once.'

'What?'

'We were in Austria. The snow was very deep that year. Do you remember being there?'

'Yes,' Toni frowned. She did remember the trip, but she didn't want her memories hijacked by Ivor. 'I don't remember you.'

'It was a long time ago, Antonia,' he smiled sadly. 'I liked your father. He loved you very much. You were the apple of his eye, you say?' he frowned. 'Is that the saying?'

'Yes.'

'I gave you a stuffed toy. A reindeer.'

'Oh my God!' Toni put her hands to her mouth. 'You gave me Rudolph?'

'Yes. You loved it. I remember you hugged it and didn't let it go, even when it was time to go. Your father had to lift you into the cab.'

'I still have him,' she said in a whisper.

'Wow.' Ivor shook his head. 'You still have him?'

'Yes.'

'What a pleasure to meet you again, Antonia, although the circumstances are somewhat unusual.'

'It all makes sense now,' Toni said quietly. Everything clicked into place. All the whispering and interest from the police was because her father was working for Ivor Markevica. It all added up and the wheel had turned full circle. They had killed her father and her mother and now by a strange twist of fate she had stumbled into their clutches. 'It all fits into place now.'

'What does?' Ivor frowned.

'My father.'

'I don't understand.'

'I didn't until now. You killed him. You burned him like you did to those people today, didn't you?'

'No, Antonia,' Ivor said softly. 'I liked your father. I didn't have him killed.'

'What?' Toni was gobsmacked. 'You said he carried your products in his lorry.'

'He did but he didn't know that he was carrying them. Your father was an honest man. He wouldn't have had anything to do with drugs. He thought he was carrying electrical goods.'

'You didn't kill him?'

'No.'

'If you didn't kill him, what happened?'

215

'There was a period of time where his lorry was never searched. Not once in months,' Ivor smiled. 'Your father was a clever man. The odds of never being searched were too great. He grew suspicious and approached his employer with his suspicions and that was the last that I heard of him,' he paused. 'Until we heard that he had burned to death in a fire.'

'His employers killed him?'

'Yes.'

'But I thought he worked for…' Toni was lost in deep thought, her face a mask of confusion.

'He worked for your aunt and uncle,' Ivor filled in the gaps. 'Your aunt was quite a lady. She had your father killed because he realised that someone was bribing customs officers to allow her shipments into the country without challenge. The more trucks she got through, the bigger the shipments became. Your father thought someone in the company was using her lorries to smuggle drugs. He never thought for one minute that it was her. Other drivers had the same concerns but when your father was killed, nobody dared step forward.'

'My aunt did all that?' Toni was stunned.

'Yes. She arranged the importation of our products via her haulage company and she laundered the money through her accountancy firm where your mother worked.'

'I don't believe you.'

'Think about it,' Ivor said calmly. 'Why would I make it up?'

'But my mother…'

'Your mother disappeared when she became suspicious. After your father died, she started digging and found that several million pounds had been redirected from the haulage company's account.'

'What? Are you saying…?'

'Your aunt had your mother killed. She was never sure how much your father had said to her.' Ivor nodded. Toni was stunned. 'She embezzled a lot of money and went into hiding. The money belonged to my company. She stole my money. Every time that we got close to her, she packed up and moved again. It was much harder to find people back then, no Internet, no mobiles, no easy access to credit card records. She vanished for years and years but was still in the city right under our noses. Of course, we caught up with her eventually, but she wouldn't divulge where the money was hidden. She was a tough woman, your aunt.'

Toni looked deep into his eyes. He wasn't lying. Why would he? 'My aunt's car crash?'

'That I'm responsible for. She didn't die in the crash, she was already dead,' he explained calmly. 'You shouldn't shed any tears for her. She was a murdering conniving bitch.

She murdered your father and your mother and then came home and gave you a hug. How cold can you be?'

Toni opened her mouth to answer but decided not to. She had no idea what had just happened. Was he fucking with her head, or had he just answered all the questions that she had had for decades?

'Why are you telling me this?' she asked hoarsely. 'Are you going to kill me anyway?'

'I feel like I owe you,' Ivor said. 'I liked your father and I remember that beautiful little girl that I gave a stuffed toy to. You were such an innocent little girl. All your family were killed at some point and then by coincidence, I discover that my men may have killed your partner too. Enough is enough. I am not going to kill you, Antonia.'

'You're going to let me go?' Toni thought it was a trick. How could he let her go?

'Yes, but we have a deal.'

'What deal?'

'If you breathe a word of what you have seen and heard here, you will be silenced.'

'Okay.' Toni shrugged meekly. She didn't care what he wanted. She wanted to live. She wanted to see her children again. She wanted to see Kayla again whatever it took.

'Believe me when I tell you this'—he sat forward and raised his index finger—'if you ever speak of this again, I will send someone to silence you and you will watch your children die before you do, understand?'

'Yes,' she answered glancing at where the old couple had burned to death. She had no doubt in her mind what he was capable of. 'I won't say anything.'

'Good. What I have told you about your family is for you and you only. When the police question you about being here, you cannot remember a single detail, understand?'

'Yes.' Toni nodded. She didn't care about telling anyone. She didn't want to tell anyone. She didn't want to think about one second of her time with Three. She wanted to live and if that meant lying and losing her memory then so be it.

'I have your word?'

'Yes.'

'Good,' Ivor said standing up. 'We will be leaving soon. When we do, wait one hour and then call for help, understand?'

'Yes.'

'Be warned that this is up to you. Break our pact and the next time you see one of us you will be dead soon after. Go and live your life, Antonia Barrat and never step into ours again.'

Toni just nodded her head in agreement. 'Thank you,' she said looking him in the eyes. There was nothing else to say.

CHAPTER 62

Alec listened to the radio chatter as the force copter described the layout of the plant. It hadn't changed much since the aerial photo that they'd seen was uploaded onto the net. There were three vehicles and a van parked outside a warehouse that seemed to be the centre of the plant. The Acting Chief Constable had given Alec everything that he had asked for on the proviso that there was no siege. He had insisted that Alec surrounded the site without the occupants knowing and play a waiting game. Alec was fine with the request. The area was filled with armed units, sharpshooters, and unmarked traffic interceptors. The motorway access roads were blocked, and the river was covered with police launches and coast guard boats. If Ivor Markevica was inside, he was caught like a rat in a trap. Within an hour, they had sound equipment listening to what was going on. It wasn't long before two men left the warehouse, climbed into the van, and headed for the plant gates.

'Let them leave,' Alec said into the comms. 'We'll take them when they're well clear of the plant.'

The van stopped while the driver hopped out and opened the gates. He climbed back in and drove through them before stopping and closing them again. They drove towards the motorway unaware that they were being monitored every metre that they travelled. As they reached a roundabout that linked the industrial area to the normal roads, the driver unexpectedly stopped the van in the middle of the road. Alec watched him through binoculars.

'Something has spooked him,' a voice came over the comms.

'There's nothing else on the road,' Alec replied. 'That roundabout is usually backed up to the motorway with traffic. Move in now!'

Two interceptors roared onto the roundabout blocking the exits. Armed officers dressed in full body armour sprung from the vehicles and others ran from the bushes and trees at the side of the road. The driver hesitated and raised his hands. The passenger opened his door and jumped down onto the road. He reached into his jacket and pulled out a nine-millimetre. Shots rang out from all directions and the man dropped to the floor, a pool of blood spreading from beneath him. The driver panicked and put the vehicle into gear. He reversed the van at speed and smashed it into one of the interceptors. Shots hit the windscreen, shattering it. Shards of glass exploded into the vehicle, but the driver wasn't ready to surrender. He floored the accelerator and the van lurched forwards and mounted the kerb onto the roundabout. The tyres ripped up the grass and hurled dirt high into the air behind it. Bullets peppered the van on both sides but didn't halt its progress. It picked up speed, knocking over one of the armed officers. He was catapulted onto the bonnet and then tossed over the roof before crashing to the ground as the van accelerated across the roundabout. It bounced over the kerb as it screeched back onto the road; sparks flew from beneath the wheel arches. Another hail of bullets hit the vehicle. The driver was hit in the forehead, snapping his head backwards and spraying the interior with bone fragments and grey matter. The driver's foot wedged down on the accelerator pedal and the van sped uncontrollably towards a crash barrier. Armed officers scattered in all directions as the vehicle careered onwards. It hit the barrier at speed with catastrophic force flipping it over the railings. The vehicle fell into a concrete storm drain, landing on its roof. The engine roared at full revs and grey smoke began to pour from the bonnet. A fuel line ruptured and the escaping petrol hit the exhaust pipe. The vehicle burst into flames which crept their way down the fuel line to the tank. Seconds after the flames ignited, the petrol tank exploded.

'The other vehicles are leaving the plant,' the helicopter pilot said excitedly. 'Three cars in convoy, four occupants in each.'

'Take them as soon as they pass the gates,' Alec ordered. 'If any of them want to be heroes, drop them where they stand.'

Ivor was in the middle vehicle when the police swooped. Unmarked interceptors surrounded them blocking their progress and their escape to the rear. His men tried their best to manoeuvre the vehicles away but there wasn't a chance. Each car was swamped by armed officers pointing Heckler and Koch MP5 submachine guns. Two of his men opened their doors and made a gallant if not stupid bid to run but they were tackled to the ground before they took more than a step. None of his men drew their weapons. To do so would have been suicide. The police were too fast for them to react. One by one, they were dragged from the vehicles, forced face down onto the floor and handcuffed. As Ivor was pulled up from the floor, he noticed one of the men in charge staring at him. He thought that he resembled a television chef whose name he couldn't remember.

'Take your unit and comb the warehouse for stragglers,' Alec ordered. He didn't want any of the gang sloping off. 'Make sure all these vehicles are searched for weapons before they go to the lab. The more we've got to charge them with at booking, the better.'

'Guv.'

'Take him separately,' Alec said. He singled out Ivor Markevica. 'Make sure he's processed separately from the others.' Ivor smirked as he was led away. Alec couldn't see Andris Markevica among the other men and that bothered him immensely, 'Wait a minute,' Alec called after him. The arresting officers turned Ivor to face Alec. 'Where is your brother?'

Ivor smiled and shrugged. He wasn't going to answer Alec; that was obvious. A thought occurred to Alec.

'He wasn't in the van that left earlier, was he?' Ivor's eyes flickered. Alec knew the answer immediately. 'Oh dear,' Alec said. 'I'm afraid he's probably not going to be stood in the dock next to you. Not unless we put him in an ashtray anyway.' Ivor tried to break free from the officers, but they held him firm. 'Take him away,' it was Alec's turn to smile as they dragged Ivor Markevica away.

CHAPTER 63

Kayla Yates looked grey. Her limbs were plastered and bandaged, and she was attached to monitors. A tube was taped inside her nose and both hands had drip feeds inserted into them. Toni was sitting in a chair next to her bed holding her right hand in both of hers. She had stopped crying now. There were no tears left for a while. She was emotionally drained. What she had witnessed earlier had sapped her strength and made her feel numb. The euphoria of being allowed to live was swept away with the agony of seeing Kayla broken and beaten in a hospital bed. She was still alive, which the doctor said was incredible. They hadn't expected her to survive the night, but against the odds she had. Toni leaned in and kissed her on the forehead and said a prayer to herself. She didn't believe in God. If there was one, he had abandoned her decades ago when he let her father burn to death in front of her eyes. She had seen evil up close. What type of God would allow an animal like Ivor Markevica to live while innocents died every second of every day? Jewish, Buddhist, Hindu, Christian, or Muslim, none of the above were getting a good deal from their God. Toni had given up caring. Whoever they claimed made the earth did a reasonable job but then they fucked it up by putting humans on it. A sympathetic entity wouldn't allow all the suffering to go on. A tear ran down Kayla's face. Toni wiped it away and kissed her cheek.

'I love you,' she whispered into her ear. 'Don't you leave me, you hear? Don't you dare.'

Alec appeared in the doorway and she smiled tiredly at him. 'Come in,' she said.

'Sorry to interrupt.' Alec felt a little embarrassed. 'How is she?'

'As well as she looks.' Toni touched her face. 'They didn't expect her make it this far.'

'No,' Alec said. 'She is strong.' They both looked at Kayla, no words came to mind. Alec needed to talk to Toni about her ordeal, but it would wait, for a few days at least. She wasn't exactly busting at the seams to tell him what had happened to her and she didn't look injured physically. 'I just wanted to say that you have my number and if you need anything, call me.'

'Thank you,' Toni said without averting her eyes from Kayla. 'Detective Ramsay,' she said as an afterthought.

'Yes.'

'We don't need that armed guard outside.'

'I hope that you don't.' Alec frowned, and his face filled with deep creases. He thought it was an odd thing to say especially after what they'd been through. 'At this point, it's better to be safe than sorry, okay.'

'Okay…' she seemed to be thinking about her words '…they won't come after me again. He promised me.'

'Ivor Markevica promised you?'

'Yes.'

'And you believe him?'

'He could have killed me there and then, but he chose not to.'

'Toni,' Alec rubbed his chin. 'If Markevica left you alive then it's because he has a reason. Men like him don't have empathy. He has plans for the future. Let's hope they don't include you or Kayla. Don't believe a word that man said to you.' Alec raised one finger. 'Not a single word, you hear me?'

Toni nodded and looked away. She did believe Ivor. Nobody would understand that, but they didn't need to. He was a monster, but he had shed light into the darkest reaches of her past and for that she was grateful.

Alec slipped out of the room quietly. He walked to the lift in deep thought. They had all hoped that they might find Annie during the raid but there was still no sign of her or her body. The plant had revealed little information on first inspection. The forensic results could be weeks away. Ivor Markevica was saying nothing, and his men were playing the same game. Alec knew that some, if not most of them would walk away. It was difficult to make charges stick by association alone. They had recovered a body from the rear of the van. It had been bound and gagged and everyone feared that it might be Annie until a CSI confirmed that it was definitely a male. Alec hoped it was Andris. He had a suspicion that it was, just because of how Ivor had reacted. The lift doors were opening as he neared it. He allowed people to step out before he stepped in and pressed the button.

When the lift stopped at the third floor, Alec followed two nurses onto the ICU. They nodded hello. He had been to see Jim Stirling several times daily and the nurses recognised his face.

'Are you here again?'

'For my sins.' Alec nodded. 'How is he?'

'No change, I'm afraid. His wife is with him.'

'Isn't she always?'

'The poor woman doesn't know what day it is. Go through and I'll bring you both a drink.'

'Thanks,' Alec said. Just as he did an alarm went off. The nurses nearby headed in the same direction. A doctor came out of the room to Alec's right and ran by him. He stepped back against the corridor wall. More staff hurtled down the corridor and Alec had to admire their urgency though he couldn't swap places with them, not for a second. The responsibility of life and death was too much for Alec. They were handicapped from the beginning of every individual case. No one walked into hospital fit and strong. They were all weakened by some form of injury or illness. He felt as if he was intruding in a world that he didn't belong in. When he saw Janice stepping into the corridor her face white and drawn, he realised that it was Stirling's room where the emergency was taking place. A nurse bundled her out and closed the door in her face. Janice pushed her face against the glass, her palms flat against it like a child looking through a window.

'Janice?' Alec said as he approached her. She looked at him with tear filled eyes; dark shadows had formed beneath them. The spark in them had gone out. He stood next to her and held her around the shoulders. They watched as the doctors tried CPR. Nurses took turns doing compressions and fed adrenalin into him. The defibrillator whined and hit Stirling with electric shocks. Time and time again. Alec was aware that he was holding his breath. Hot tears ran down his cheeks before he knew that he was crying. Janice squeezed his arm painfully tight and as they watched, her legs failed her, and she fell to the floor. The monitor displayed three flat lines as Big Jim Stirling lost his battle for life.

CHAPTER 64

When Alec returned to the station the news had arrived before him. The MIT section was in shock. They all knew that Stirling was critical, but no one wanted to believe that he had lost his fight. Alec was lost for words. The time to address the troops would come but it wasn't now. They had a ruthless gang of criminals to process, interview, and charge. The job had to be done despite their grief. Max approached him and handed him a stack of notes

'Tragic news, guv.'

'Yes, it is.'

'No one seems to know what to say.'

'Better to say nothing for now. Where are we up to?'

'The phones have been going, guv,' he said. 'Kathy Brooks has been on. She needs to talk to you urgently and the Area Commander wants you to call him as soon as possible.'

'Thanks,' Alec mumbled. He didn't want to make that call just yet. Whatever he had to say, it could wait. Kathy on the other hand could have something solid that they could use to bury Markevica and his cohorts.

'Guv!' a voice called from the next desk. 'There's a Chief Inspector on the line for you, says he's from the Frodsham nick.'

'Frodsham?' Alec said with a shaky voice. It was the nearest station to the expansive forests of Cheshire. This was the call that he had been dreading. He couldn't take it in front of the troops. All eyes were on him. Every detective in the department knew where Frodsham was in relation to the forests. A Chief Inspector calling from there could only mean bad news. An ominous silence descended across the MIT office. Alec gestured that he would take the call in Annie's office. The detectives exchanged worried glances. No one dare speak. Now was not the time for speculation. It was the news that every member of the team was dreading.

Alec walked into Annie's office and flicked the lights on. He could smell her perfume and it brought a tear to his eyes. He put his hand on the phone but couldn't pick it up. Never had he felt so traumatised by a phone call. He just didn't want to answer it. Time seemed to warp into a treacle filled void where everything moved slowly. He gripped the handset and picked it up with trembling fingers. Placing it to his ear, he connected the call.

'Ramsay,' he answered nervously.

'Alec,' the voice sounded grim. 'Bill Kingsley here.'

'Hi, Bill.' Alec said.

'I heard about Jim Stirling. I'm very sorry; he was one of the best.'

'He was,' Alec agreed. 'Look, things are a bit chaotic here.' Alec tried to be as civil as possible. As much as he appreciated the sentiment, he didn't have time for condolences.

'Of course, they are, sorry.' He cleared his throat nervously and Alec braced himself for the news. 'I'll get straight to the point. We had a report from a dog walker up in the forest at Delamere.'

'Oh.' Alec's stomach flipped. He was filled with dread. His eyes closed, tears escaped them and rolled down his cheeks. He pinched his nose between his finger and thumb and waited for the hammer blow.

'His dog was running off the lead and found something in the trees, a shallow grave, partially filled in.'

'Partially?'

'Yes. There were a couple of shovels discarded nearby. It looks like someone left in a hurry and didn't finish the job. Maybe they were disturbed by walkers. Anyway, she wasn't buried completely.'

'Oh Jesus,' Alec sucked in his breath. He said 'she'. It had to be Annie.

'We have found a female dressed in her nightgown. She's got a very bad wound to the back of her skull and she's suffering from hypothermia but she's alive. They've taken her to the head trauma unit at Walton Hospital by air ambulance. I think we've found your DI.'

'She's alive?'

'Yes.'

'Fucking hell,' Alec whispered. He couldn't process the information. 'Thank you for the call,' Alec felt his knees weaken. He fist pumped the air and slammed the handset down. When he opened the office door, a sea of silent faces stared at him. He looked around them with tear filled eyes. 'They found Annie,' he said. 'She's in a bad way but she's alive.' The office erupted with cheers, some excited, some incoherent, and some were downright abusive.

EPILOGUE

One Month Later

Annie was sitting up in bed, waiting patiently as her consultant and a gaggle of student doctors studied her notes. Their discussion was short and to the point. Her skull fractures were healing nicely and the bruising on her brain was shrinking. That was the good news. The bad news was that she was being plagued by dizzy spells and they didn't know why. The consultant had told her that they may pass and then again, they may not. A brain injury as serious as hers could always leave permanent damage. He had explained that the brain was a complicated organ that surgeons knew too little about. Time would tell. She spotted Alec through the window, waiting in the corridor and her spirits lifted. She was never one to be still and being confined to a hospital bed was mind numbingly boring. The doctors said their goodbyes and Alec waited patiently for them to leave before coming in.

'Hello, you,' he said brightly.

'Oh, thank God you're here,' Annie said. He kissed her on the cheek, and it felt right. 'I am climbing the walls in here.'

'I've brought you some magazines and another couple of books.'

'You're a lifesaver.' Alec put the reading material on her locker and sat down next to the bed. 'Tell me what is going on in the real world. What is new?'

'Well the CPS is happy to proceed against Markevica and his men. They'll throw away the key.'

'How many of them?' Annie asked abruptly.

'Ivor and five others,' Alec said proudly.

'For fuck's sake.' Annie sighed. 'That is a joke!'

'It cuts the head off the snake and his key men will go down with him.' Alec felt a little bit miffed by her response. 'It is a good result.'

'Meanwhile, he'll run everything from behind bars and nothing has changed.' Annie sighed. She could tell that she had upset Alec with her comments but that was how she felt and that was that. She had a lot of time to think about things; to put things into perspective. 'Change the subject. Is there any good news?'

'Kayla Yates was released from hospital yesterday,' he said smiling. Annie's expression changed slightly. 'She'll need to use a wheelchair for a while, but they think she'll make a full recovery.' Annie didn't respond. 'That's good news, isn't it?'

'Yes,' Annie forced a smile.

'What's wrong?' Alec touched her hand with his fingers. Annie adjusted her hand and squeezed his tightly. Alec liked the feeling and reciprocated. They had been growing closer during her recovery period. The professional barriers seemed to be breaking down. 'Are you okay, Annie?'

'No, Alec,' Annie said with a shake of her head. 'I'm not okay. Every time I think of what happened, I feel sick.' She paused. 'Of course, I'm glad Kayla is on the mend but talking about it makes me feel... scared.'

Alec held her hand tighter. 'That is only natural. It will pass. You bounced back last time and you will again. You'll see.'

Annie shook her head. 'Not this time, Alec. I have made my mind up.'

'About what?'

'Coning back to work,' she said. Alec knew what was coming. 'I can't do it anymore. I'm sick and tired of feeling sick and tired. Do you never get weary of it, Alec?'

'What you're going through is a natural reaction, Annie. You don't need to make any decisions right now. Who knows how you will feel in six months time?' He smiled and leaned closer. 'You love your job.'

'Not any more, Alec. I don't love it anymore.' She touched the faded scar on her face. It had started to ache recently. 'In fact, I hate it.'

'Annie...'

'No, Alec. Don't patronise me, please. I know how I feel.'

'I wouldn't patronise you, Annie. All I'm saying is that you know how you feel right now. That could change.'

'It won't change,' she said with a smile. Her lips were quivering a little as she spoke. 'Do you know when I changed my mind about it?' Alec shook his head and listened. 'They made me kneel down and look into my grave,' she said slowly. She stopped as if taken away by thought. Alec felt sick. He couldn't bear to think of her there alone. Deep in the forest thinking that she was going to die. 'When I looked into that hole in the ground, I thought, is this it? Is this what all the sixteen-hour days were for? Have I sacrificed becoming a wife and a mother, a grandmother even, just for this? What the fuck have I achieved? In the grand scheme of things, absolutely nothing,' Annie said. She looked at Alec and he could see that she meant it. Her expression told him that she wasn't for turning this time. 'When I was kneeling there, I didn't want to be a police officer anymore, Alec. I wanted to be a civilian. I wanted to be safe at home with my husband and my kids and my dog with nothing more to worry about than what to make for tea. Do you get that?'

'Of course, but...'

'But what?' she interrupted him curtly. 'But fucking what?'

'I get it, Annie honestly I do. I guess I just don't want to lose you,' he said touching her face with his fingertips. She placed her face against his hand. 'When I thought that we had lost you, I didn't think that I would cope without you. I don't want to lose you from the job, and I don't want to lose you from my life.'

'That is the thing, Alec.'

'What is?'

'It is the same thing.'

'I don't follow.'

'The job and your life are the same thing. Your job is your life. My job nearly cost me my life twice. I am not going to give it the opportunity to do it again.'

'What are you saying?'

'I'm not going back to work. I'm not going home, Alec. The insurance company will rebuild my house, but I won't go back there.'

'What are you going to do?'

'I'm going to sell it.' She nodded adamantly. 'I'm going to retire, take my pension, sell my house, and travel the world. I've given enough of life to the job. No more. Seeing my own grave made me realise how much I want to live my life.' She kissed his hand. 'We don't live in that job, Alec. We exist. We spend years chasing the dregs of society, weeks of sleepless nights to lock them up so the system can spit them straight back out again and for what? I could earn more in a mid-management job in retail. I have given enough of my life to this impossible cause, Alec. We can't win. We will never win, and I don't even care anymore. It is time to live a little before I die. Look what happened to Jim for God's sake. Is that not enough to convince you that it's time to get out?'

Alec sighed. He felt defeated. It was a powerful argument. He couldn't challenge a single point. 'What the hell would I do at my age?' he said with a shrug.

'Travel the world, Alec.'

'Is that an invite?'

'I could do with the company. I'm fragile at the moment.'

'Never thought of myself as a bodyguard.'

'Neither have I,' Annie said. She pulled him towards her, their lips touched, gently at first but it soon became more urgent. Alec knew right then that wherever Annie Jones wanted to be, he would be right next to her.

****

Across the city, Julia Fox was holding court at the cocktail bar. Panoramic 34 was packed with diners and drinkers. Below them, the city lights twinkled into the infinity of the night. She was lording her success at selling another exclusive to the nationals and a number of follow up articles had already been sold. This story had attracted global interest for the best part of a month. Channel 4 had approached her with the idea of a drama documentary about the Latvian gang Three and she was only too happy to sign up for it if the price was right. European law enforcement agencies were queuing up to charge Ivor Markevica and his cohorts, but they would be tried in the UK first. Media interest in the gang had gone off the scale and Julia had suddenly become the recognised source of information about them. What she didn't know, she made up. Despite the tremendous amount of legwork done by her team, she was basking in the praise and using the word I far more than we. It had been an expensive project. They had bought and bribed more informants than on any other story. The interest from the nationals was unprecedented as were the amounts they'd paid. She looked around. Her staff were as drunk as monkeys. The volume was increasing with every round of cocktails and at nearly two hundred pounds a round, it was going to be an expensive night.

She excused herself and made her way through the throng of employees to use the toilets. The crowd thinned as she reached the corridor that led up some stairs to the restrooms. The ladies were spacious and brightly lit. The porcelain gleamed and the woodwork was polished and waxed. The mirrors were spotless and offered users a view from floor to ceiling. Julia used the toilet and flushed the chain. She opened the cubicle door and looked at the magnificent view through the window. Thirty-four floors up from the city streets she was celebrating a month of success that would surely see her going to London to further her career. She believed that it was her destiny to be a well-known name among the capital's journalists. She washed her hands and reapplied her lipstick before heading back to the bar. As she walked down the corridor, a door opened behind her. She paid no attention until she was yanked violently by the hair. Her attacker lifted her off her feet and dragged her backwards. Her feet danced in thin air. The pain was excruciating, and she could feel her hair being ripped from the scalp. She tried to scream but a hand clamped over her mouth and all she could manage was a muffled squeak. Her attacker dragged her through a utility room and slammed her against the wall. Julia was convinced that she was going to be raped.

The man produced a hammer and she closed her eyes. He raised it and brought it down in a wicked arc against the window. The glass shattered. A second blow punched a huge hole in it. Julia felt the wind blowing through it. It was icy cold. Her attacker lifted her up.

'Ivor Markevica doesn't like what you have written about him. He wants you to think about that on your way down.'

Julia was hoisted up further and then launched from the window. The diners and drinkers on the floor below were horrified as Julia whizzed by the restaurant on her way down to the pavement below.

A NOTE FROM THE AUTHOR

I hope you enjoyed *Thr3e*... If you want to continue following the MIT, read the Inspector Braddick books here;

https://www.amazon.co.uk/gp/product/B07X11C27N

Could you do me a massive favour and take two minutes of your precious time to post a review via the link below. They really help an author much more than you think... thanks again for reading my novels.

http://www.amazon.co.uk/Three-Detective-Alec-Ramsay-Series-ebook/dp/B018CXQVZ4

Printed in Great Britain
by Amazon

79621971R00133